SHADOWS

ON THE

GOLDFIELD TRACK

Sequel to "Shadow of the *Northern Orchid*"

Genre: Historical/Adventure/Romance/Fiction

Cover design created by Cat Petersen

SHADOWS

ON THE

GOLDFIELD TRACK

Sequel to "Shadow of the *Northern Orchid*"

Written by Elizabeth Rimmington.

Shadows on the Goldfield Track

Published at Ingram Spark
by Elizabeth Rimmington. 2020.
Queensland
Australia

 A catalogue record for this
book is available from the
National Library of Australia

ISBN
978-0-6485257-3-8 (Print)
978-0-6485257-4-5 (Epub)

Disclaimer

This novel is entirely a work of fiction. While some of the names, characters and business places mentioned may have existed, their interaction with the story characters is pure fiction. The granite mountain with its hidden oasis is a fictional site. All incidents are either the products of the author's imagination or have been used in a fictitious manner. The opinions expressed or beliefs held are those of the characters and should not be assumed to be the opinions or beliefs of the author.

APPRECIATION

To Caroline, Margaret and Natalie for sharing their wisdom.

To Tricia who once more tamed the formatting dragon.

To Anne who assisted with the research material.

To the fellowship and support of good friends within the local writing groups.

To the staff at the Gympie Library for their support.

To the Cooktown History Centre, the Cooktown museum and the Cooktown Library from where I gleaned considerable background and enormous inspiration.

PART ONE

THE GOLDFINCH ENTOURAGE

CHAPTER ONE

LONDON 1867

ABIGAIL

Abigail's eyes remained downcast. Papa's voice washed over her in waves. She peeped out of the corner of her eye. As expected, her mother sat perched on the edge of her Queen Anne chair beside her father's desk; her back rigid. The grey hair was pulled back in a knot at the nape of her neck. Mama nodded at everything her husband said; she always did. Abigail never expected any support from her. Mama always agreed with every utterance her father spewed from his mouth. As she did on many occasions, Abigail wondered if Mama truly agreed with Papa or whether, in secret, she despised the position of subservience he inflicted upon her.

"Now daughter, it is time to look for a replacement husband for you." A pale hand smoothed his thinning grey hair then returned to twiddle with the pens in the silver holder.

Abigail's eyes shot up to meet the steely blue eyes of her father.

"But Papa, don't you think that might appear a little hasty? After all, it is only three months since Edward was killed."

"Yes, it is. Why the fool of a man had to go out racing horses in the middle of the night, I cannot fathom."

The slim fingers folding pleats in the brown skirt began to tremble. Abigail clasped her hands together and concentrated on her slow breathing. Visions of the night flashed within her head. As usual, rough, cruel Edward had taken his marital pleasures without any thought to her needs. It was certainly never lovemaking. His ravishments were more like blatant rape. Bruises decorated her body and her lips were chewed almost to tatters after he had his fill of her. That night had been no different. She still felt like spitting each time she recalled the smell of his breath thick with the foul odour of his cigars. The cadavers in the morgue smelt better. Her eyes sparkled for a moment. Her memories took her back to the day several of George's friends smuggled her, dressed in her brother's clothes, into their dissection class. The glint in the green eyes faded. She never wept one tear at her husband's passing. Her lips pressed in a straight line as she silently vowed never to let her father choose another suitor for her. In fact, she planned never to take another suitor if she lived to be one hundred. Now, she just needed the courage to outwit him.

"Surely one should not speak ill of the dead, Papa." A faint tremor betrayed her. She cleared her throat.

"Don't forget your place, young lady. I am still your father, remember. Don't go telling me what I should or should not say. Edward was a fool and now he has left the estate in such a muddle, one does not know if you will be able to maintain yourself in a suitable manner."

Pausing to gather her thoughts, Abigail cast her eyes around her father's study. Every morning, the pretentious dark timbered walls, bookcases, cabinets and floors were polished to within an inch of their lives by the young lass, Mary, the housekeeper's assistant. Woe betide her if one smudge was to be seen anywhere.

"Papa, the estate is owned by the Baldwin family company. I have been allocated a generous annuity. There will be more …"

"Don't interrupt me, daughter. I do not know what the world is coming to. My daughter contradicts me. My son defies me and talks of leaving London for an uncivilized country full of convicts and natives. He has the chance of a practice in Harley Street but against my wishes, he chooses a tent somewhere in the jungles. Now, your mother tells me, you have more than yourself to consider as well. Edward has left you with child. Who is going to be responsible for this, I ask? No, you have no choice. You must take another husband as soon as possible."

Her eyes fell again to her lap. Ah yes, the baby; a small complication. She must remain strong.

"It is all organized. I have spoken to Mr. Jamieson and he has agreed to take you as his wife on his return from Paris next month."

Abigail jumped to her feet. All patience forgotten. Desperate eyes glanced from left to right in a vain hope of finding a reprieve. Her mouth opened and closed twice before she was able to speak.

"But Papa; are you talking of the old widower, Mr. Jamieson, with seven obnoxious children who run wild at every public outing?" Her head swirled as she scrambled through her brain searching for an excuse her father might find acceptable. "To be married, widowed and remarried all within twelve months might test the tolerance of the most liberal of gossips, father; particularly with the birth of a child in the midst of it all."

"Enough," Mr. Goldfinch roared. "Mr. Jamieson is a respectable man with a healthy bank balance. His children just need a firm hand and kindness."

"A drowning more like," she whispered to herself. Aloud she spoke again praying her voice remained strong. "Papa, won't he be suspicious if we appear too desperate. Perhaps we should think on his offer and give him an answer in one month. Tempt him, so to speak."

"Semantics Abigail, but if that is what it takes to make you less contentious, so be it. Then you can marry Mr. Jamieson, in one month, as I planned."

Mr. Goldfinch brushed his hat as he lifted it from the hat stand in the corner. He swung his cane into the air and picked up his gloves off the desk.

"I am away to the office. This household business is too tiring by far."

Abigail sat still. Her head spun. Once again, she remembered her vow; never, ever. Her mother rose and walked to her side. A soft hand fell upon her shoulder.

"Don't judge your Papa too harshly, dear. He only wants what is best for you."

"For himself, I think," she answered quietly.

"A headstrong woman is most unattractive, dear. Try to be accepting and compliant. A man will appreciate you more."

"Yes, Mama." Abigail only just managed to force the words between her teeth as she rushed out of the door.

Jane Stanley dropped the baby bonnet she was crocheting as Abigail stormed into the apartment. She gasped.

"Oh, Abigail you've been fighting with your father again, haven't you? You promised not to lose your temper, remember."

Abigail clasped handfuls of the unruly auburn curls on either side of her head. She tightened her fists with the locks entwined.

"Jane, that man is the most infuriating I have ever met; no, the second most infuriating. Edward wins the title by a whisker."

Jane's smile was strained as she watched and listened to the anger of her employer and her friend.

"I can hear your teeth grinding, Abigail. You'll soon wear a track in the oriental rug if you keep pacing back and forth. Please sit down, you are making me dizzy."

Abigail stamped her foot. Her green eyes flashed.

"I don't want to sit. He tells me I am to marry the dreadful Mr. Jamieson with those abominable children; in one month. Never, never, never."

Jane stood up and walked over to hold her friend.

"It is too horrible to contemplate but what else can you do? I wish you wouldn't get upset like this. It can't be good for you, in your condition. You know, in the end, your father will have his own way."

"We'll see about that. Come, get your things, we are going for a walk."

As Jane flustered about gathering their bonnets, gloves, and parasols, she reminded Abigail of another of Mr. Goldfinch's instructions.

"Your father says it is unseemly to be walking in the streets. He has told you to take his carriage if you wish to go anywhere."

"Pooh to him. Whose side are you on anyway, Jane? My father is only worried about what people will think of him. It will not do if his daughter is seen to be walking and not riding. Besides he wants to keep me under surveillance. His coachman, old Blather-mouth, can't wait to dutifully report back everything he sees." She dragged the door of the apartment open then swung her head back inside to call someone in the other room.

"Eve, we are off to my brother's. I am not sure when we will return."

A young girl with her brown plaits secured in circles over her ears poked her head out of the kitchen.

"Very well, Miss Abigail." Unheard, the reply bounced off the closed door.

Abigail led the way from her apartment to the rear entrance of her father's property along a circuitous path shaded by the thick foliage within his gardens.

Jane whispered as they walked.

"Please don't tell me you are going ahead with your madcap scheme to emigrate to the antipodes with George."

"Yes, I am. You are welcome to come with me; if you wish. I will not force you."

"Of course, I will go with you, Abigail; you know that. I do not want to be around when you tell your father. Australia; it is such a long way across the world."

"Yes, it is, isn't it?" A large grin split Abigail's face. "I don't remember saying anything about telling father."

"You mean … oh, I don't want to know."

"It is about time my father realized this is 1867. A woman can be intelligent. We can think for ourselves. I don't need a man to make all my decisions for me. I am a respectable widow and I intend to remain that way." Abigail's voice began to rise.

"Hush, Abigail, do you want everyone to hear you?"

Jane held her head down as she peeked under her bonnet at the passing carriages. The shod hooves of the horses' feet clattered on the cobbles in accompaniment to the jingle of the harness. The sun struggled to make an appearance through the grey clouds. Jane was almost running as she endeavoured to keep up with Abigail who strode along swinging her parasol above a head held high.

"Slow down, Abigail. This is most unbecoming." She attempted to tuck stray blond curls back under her bonnet.

As they turned into the street where her brother rented rooms in which to live and carry on his medical practice, Abigail's eyes lit up. The sign on the front door indicated the doctor was in. Without waiting for a reply to her brief knock, she entered the outer hall.

"Wait for me in the kitchen please, Jane. Maybe some refreshment will not go astray," she instructed with a smile as she tapped lightly on the door of her brother's office.

DOCTOR GEORGE

Books covered a large wooden table. It took up almost the width of the room. Two modest armchairs faced this desk. A deep muffled voice floated up from behind the tomes.

"Please sit down. I'll be with you in a moment."

"What, no kiss for your sister, George?"

A crash followed. Books tumbled. A young man, with untidy ginger hair and green eyes, replicas of those of his twin, jumped up to look over the pile. His hands shot out in all directions in an attempt to prevent a total disruption of his filing system.

"Abby, it is so good to see you. You could not have come at a better time. I need to decide what medical books I should take with me to Australia and those which I can do without. Letters need to be written to the Medical Board and ..." His hands gave up rescuing books and flew into the air. "There are a million and one things to do and less than three weeks to do it all. You are a better organizer than me. You know more of what is in these medical books than I do if the truth be known. Will you help?"

"Of course, I'll help, George; on one condition." Her smile stirred a mischievous emerald glint in her eyes.

As George restored order to his desk he glanced warily at his sister.

"What exactly is the condition?"

"I need you to escort myself, Jane and Eve on the ship to Australia. You know my companion, Jane and my maid, Eve. I have already booked our passage on the *Young Australia*, the same ship on which you are travelling."

George flopped back into his chair, disappearing once more behind the desk of books.

A strangled voice asked, "Are you mad? Papa will hit the roof. Mother will have a fit of the vapours. This will be worse than the day you told him you wanted to study medicine with me."

"Yes, well I wish I had defied him at the time and done just that. I could have passed the exam with flying colours. I knew the answers to all the questions."

George shifted three books and spoke to his sister through the gap. "That may be, but Australia? Papa will never allow it."

"If I plan carefully, Papa will not know of my departure until the ship has left the docks."

"You wouldn't." He looked closer at his sister. "You would too. I give it to you, Abby, you are definitely the braver twin."

George jumped up and came running around the table to hug his sister and dance her around the room. His face became serious.

"Does this mean you will help me organize my things to pack?"

"Yes, of course, George. I could not let you go over there on your own. Who would you have to discuss a patient's diagnosis with? You will need someone who can make a bandage stay on for more than five minutes. Who would help you look after the patients? Who would ensure you stopped to eat, bathe and dress occasionally?"

The pair waltzed around the room again until gasping for air. George tried to speak. "Let's go and see if Thomas has returned. He will make us a pot of tea."

Abigail led the way into the kitchen where they found Thomas, George's man-servant, filling the teapot from the steaming kettle on the woodstove. Jane looked up as she spread small sandwiches on a plate. Jane's smile lit up her face and her eyes melted at the sight of her friend's brother.

"Hello, Doctor George. I hope you do not think I am being presumptuous but I thought a mid-day snack may do us all good. Did Abigail give you the news?"

Abigail stepped forward. "Er, well no, not all of it actually."

George's eyes opened wide as he turned to his sister.

"What, there is more news; good or bad this time?" He saw an expression of annoyance, or was it a warning, flash towards Jane. George thought it best to intervene.

"Come, let's go and sit down. You can confess all. Thomas, will you carry the tray in for us?"

Thomas picked up the large wooden tray as if it was no heavier than a newspaper. Only by turning sideways did he fit his shoulders through the doorway leading back to the surgery office. He bent his head at the lintels. Thomas placed the tray on a corner of the desk where Jane had cleared a space.

George smiled his thanks before asking, "Thomas, will you call me at two, please? We have to visit the acute abdomen. We'll take the carriage just in case the boy needs to go to the hospital."

The deep voice replied. "Yes, Doctor George."

George settled his guests in the clients' chairs while he dragged his own seat to the front of the desk. Abigail poured the beverages. When the three were re-settled, George asked the question uppermost in his mind.

"So, my dear sister, you had better tell all."

Abigail concentrated on selecting her sandwich and drinking her tea. It was some time before she felt able to contain her emotions. It surprised her at how close to tears she felt. Eventually, she took a deep breath before repeating her father's instruction regarding Mr. Jamieson.

George coughed and spluttered. His face turned beetroot red. Jane jumped up and ran to his side. She patted his back.

"Are you all right?" she asked.

The door opened without a sound. Thomas looked in. When George managed to choke out, "Don't fuss, Jane, I'm fine." Thomas's head disappeared and the door closed with a small click.

"Tell me you are not talking about THE Mr. Jamieson and those dozen noisy monsters of his?"

"The very same; and there are only seven children." Abigail smiled.

"Well, they make enough noise for a dozen, at least. The man has been searching for a wife for years. What on earth is father thinking of, to lumber you with him? So, this is the reason for the sudden exodus to Australia? You were not coming to save me from myself at all. You cunning little fox."

"That is so unfair. Actually, I had booked our passage before this was dumped upon me today. So there, it was you I was thinking of. And, by the way, Papa is not too pleased with you leaving all this," Abigail glanced around the room with its walls needing a coat of paint before going on, "... for the antipodes. He really wanted a son in Harley Street."

"He'll have to be satisfied with our older siblings, who can do no wrong, won't he?"

After Jane promised not to repeat a word, all three became engrossed in their plans for the subterfuge.

ABIGAIL, JANE & EVE

Goldfinch House was in sight when Abigail clasped Jane's upper arm and dragged her into the shrubbery in the park.

"What, what on earth are you doing, Abigail? My hair; you have pulled it all out from under my bonnet."

"Shush; look." The eldest Goldfinch daughter, Abigail's least favourite sibling, was visible as she climbed into the carriage at the front of the house. "There goes one person who would be delighted to see me get into trouble with Papa. She definitely must not see or know what we are doing."

They huddled near the bushes for ten minutes trying not to look conspicuous. Farewells seemed to be going on forever, through the carriage window. Abigail was grateful when the pair of fractious horses stomped their feet, snorted and worried the traces or they may have been waiting there longer.

The days passed in a whirl of surreptitious preparations. Abigail could scarcely move in her bedroom which now contained an extra three sea trunks and three large suitcases along with many smaller bags. This was the only bedroom in the apartment which had a lock on the door. Abigail was determined not to take any chances.

With only four days to go until they were to set off on their journey, Abigail's worst fears seemed to become a reality. Mother sat near the bay window talking knitting patterns with Jane. Abigail had been only too happy to desert them to assist Eve prepare morning tea.

13

She stood in the kitchen placing small cakes on one of the few china plates not packed when her mother's voice drifted in. Abigail froze.

"Abigail, I am just going into your bedroom to get your old wedding gown. I will have the seamstress take a look at it. She may be able to revitalize it for you."

Eve and Abigail stared at each other, in horror. Fear lent wings to Abigail's feet.

"It's not here, Mama." The call sounded loud in her ears. She moderated her tone when she came into the sitting room where her mother was preparing to move towards the main bedroom.

"The wedding gown is not here," Abigail repeated.

"Nonsense, it is not two months since we were looking at it," Mrs. Goldfinch made three determined steps towards the bedroom again.

Abigail swallowed. "Sorry Mama, but I took it back to my cottage at the Baldwin estate. I needed more space in the wardrobe here." She glanced back to the kitchen choking on a sigh of relief when she saw Eve emerging carrying the tea tray. "Look, here is Eve with our tea. Please sit and make yourself comfortable, Mama."

While the women were otherwise occupied, Eve slipped unnoticed into the hallway. Her nimble fingers searched the tall cupboards there until she held four rugs. Using her key, she slipped into Abigail's bedroom and covered their luggage as best she could. At least the trunks and bags did not look quite so obvious when she had finished.

Abigail's gaze was never long off the clock. She thought her mother was never going to leave. Mama's final goodbye included a reminder to ensure Abigail brought the dress back to London when next she was going to the cottage. After a final wave to her mother, she wiped the perspiration from her forehead then closed the apartment door. She leaned against the warm timber with her eyes shut. Her heart pounded in her chest. After some moments, her eyes shot open. A dreadful thought washed over her. Her parents must have spare keys to this apartment; after all, it was an extension to their own home. Would her mother come in uninvited to snoop around? Yes, such a thing was quite possible.

"Eve," was almost a screech.

The young maid came running out of the kitchen, a tea towel hung from her fingers.

"Yes, Miss Abigail, whatever is the matter?"

"I want you to run over to see my brother. Ask him if we can borrow Thomas and the carriage this afternoon at three-thirty. We need to transfer the bulk of our luggage to his rooms. Blather-mouth, sorry Mr. Blattermut, leaves about then to collect Papa from his office in the city. They never return before five. We will have an hour and a half to hide the evidence. Have you got that, Eve? Do you understand?"

Eve nodded her head. "Yes, Miss Abigail; as clear as a bell. Can we have Thomas and the carriage at three-thirty this afternoon until five to transfer our luggage to his place."

"Wonderful. I could write him a note but I am reluctant to commit anything to paper unnecessarily."

For the remainder of the day, Jane hopped up and down from her chair. She picked her knitting up then placed it back down again on the table beside her. She paced back and forth near the windows. She went to the kitchen to offer help to Eve but was politely sent away. Abigail sat reading in a corner. Only the tapping of her fingers on the arm of the chair gave away any internal unrest she felt.

"Abigail, how can you sit so calmly? What if this doesn't work? What if Thomas cannot come? What if your father discovers our plans?"

"Jane, will you stop worrying. Eve has given the message to George. He has assured us he will do as I asked. What more do you want? Now sit still, please."

The clock on the mantelpiece chimed two. Jane jumped up again.

"Are you sure the clock isn't slow, Abigail? It seems slow. Will I go and ask Eve if she remembered to wind it on Monday?"

"Just leave Eve alone, she has enough to be getting on with. She does not need us to be interrupting her."

When the clock did strike three, Jane had sunk deep within her chair. Her eyes were closed and her hair in disarray. A hint of a snore burbled from her mouth. Abigail was hard-pressed not to burst out laughing. She sighed, grateful the time for action was nearly upon them.

DOCTOR GEORGE and THOMAS

Three faces peered out of the kitchen window which provided the best view of where Thomas should soon appear. As soon as they heard the sound of the horses' jingling harness and the creak of the carriage wheels, the three moved swiftly into action. Eve unlocked the bedroom door, Jane joined her in collecting the smaller of the items. Once Abigail was sure it was Thomas and not Blather-mouth, returning for some unfathomable reason, she unlocked the door and let her brother and his man-servant in.

Abigail whispered. "George, what are you doing here, too? You don't want to get into trouble, along with us, if we are discovered."

"Don't fuss, Abby. The job will get accomplished quicker with two men. Besides, which of you women can help Thomas lift the large trunks? He may be strong but it will still take two men."

Abigail stood guard outside the door. Jane and Eve delivered the smaller articles placing them on the carriage seats while the men manhandled the trunks one at a time.

"What on earth have you women put in here, rocks?" George complained at every step. "Thomas, are you sure you are lifting your end?" He questioned his off-sider.

"Doctor George, Sir, I was just going to ask you the same question." Giggling like schoolboys they cautiously moved out to the coach.

It was not a task to be completed at speed. Abigail's sitting room clock pinged the half-hour after four when the trunks along with the

17

smaller articles were finally packed inside the carriage. Everything was safely concealed when Thomas pulled the curtains across the windows.

"Hurry, hurry," Jane said in hushed tones. "Mr. Goldfinch will be coming home at any moment."

Thomas flew up into the driver's seat. George was not so graceful making the climb on the other side of the vehicle. The rear-end of his trousers barely touched the wooden seat when his mother's voice fell on all their ears.

"Oh, George, is that you? I thought I heard your voice."

Five pairs of guilty eyes turned to stare at Mrs. Goldfinch as she stood near the back wheel of the coach. In her gloved hands, she held her flower basket and a small sharp pruning knife.

"George, your Papa will be home shortly. He will be wanting to talk with you if you have a moment."

"Er … Mama, er … look, I have to fly. I have two house calls to make before dark. I really must go. I just popped in to confirm arrangements with Abigail. We are going for a spin in the country on Thursday." He nudged Thomas in the side.

"George, that will be the last day, before you sail. You will be here for the family dinner in the evening, as you promised, won't you? We will all want to say goodbye. Particularly as you made it quite clear we are not to go to see you off at the docks."

"Yes, yes, Mama. I'll be here for my last good meal."

Abigail stepped forward from where she had been standing in the shade of the bushes.

"Mama, I am sorry but I will not be able to come to dinner on Thursday. George is dropping me at the cottage for a few days. I will say my goodbyes then." She looked down and began brushing an imaginary speck of dirt from her skirt.

"What a disappointment, Abigail. You could have arranged things differently seeing as it will be your brother's farewell dinner." A frown walked across Mrs. Goldfinch's face before disappearing. "At least there will be no arguments between you and your father to upset everyone."

George leant forward and released the brake as he gave Thomas another nudge in the thigh.

"Let's get out of here," he whispered. "I can hear Papa's landau at the front entrance."

Thomas clicked his tongue. The horses moved off. They had only rolled out onto the street, through the rear entrance, when the wheels crunching on the gravel at the front of the house could not be ignored by the ladies waving farewell.

"That will be your Papa now. I'd best hurry." Mrs. Goldfinch moved swiftly past the gardens beside the building.

ABIGAIL

"Quick! Inside!" Abigail hustled her accomplices to the door. Before entering herself, she paused to ensure they had not dropped any evidence for Mr. Blather-mouth to discover.

The trio moved through to the kitchen where they collapsed into the wooden oak chairs. Not a word was spoken as they digested their close call. Eventually, Eve rose and began to stir the coals at the fire.

"Do you think she saw anything?" Jane asked.

"I am sure, if Mama saw us stashing heavy sea trunks into George's coach, she would be bound to say something. No, I think we are in the clear."

"Only two days to go until we will be at the River Docks Hotel. I am sure I will be a nervous wreck before we make it out onto the ship." Jane chewed at her bottom lip.

Pots rattled as Eve commenced preparations for their evening meal. A wide grin split her face.

"I think it's all a grand adventure. Who would have thought I was once an unwanted unfed orphan and now I'm going to Australia; unless it was as a convict."

"Eve, you are not an orphan anymore. You are part of our family now. Jane and I could not manage without you."

Abigail stood at the hotel window with her russet bonnet dangling from the ribbons in her hands. Her dress of a similar shade brushed the floor. Only the tips of her shiny leather shoes peeped out under the hem. The highlights of her hair gleamed in the glow of the lamp on the table. The winter cold hung on. Light snow drifted down from a dreary sky and floated in on the intermittent breeze which stirred the heavy blue curtains. Several of their smaller bags still remained beside the door. George and Thomas had delivered the heavy trunks to the docks when they had gone to the shipping company to confirm final preparations, earlier in the day. Was she actually going to get away safely? She could not deny the pain in her heart at leaving her home behind; especially as Easter was not too far away. Light fingers stroked her abdomen. Awe and a touch of fear sent a shiver down her spine. What challenges awaited her and this infant to be born in Australia? Droplets of moisture dampened her eyelids. When the thought of being Mrs. Jamieson, mother of seven horrors, flashed through her mind she looked forward to exploring a new life and new country, even if it was so far away. Anyway, she would not really be alone; not with her brother, Jane, Eve and Thomas; a whole crowd really.

MR. & MRS. GOLDFINCH

"Well, he has made his bed; now he must lie in it." Mr. Goldfinch took one last sip from his wine goblet.

The parlour maid had taken away the evening meal dishes from which little had been eaten. Friday night and the *Young Australia* had left on the afternoon tide. The previous evening after the family dinner, George and his father had shaken hands amicably. George had placed a warm kiss on his mother's cheek.

Now Mrs. Goldfinch stood, a forlorn figure.

"I feel rather under the weather; what with all these good-byes. I think I will turn in early." She bent to receive her husband's kiss before leaving the room without waiting for a reply. Not that it was worth waiting for; just a grunt.

Lizzy, her maid, rushed forward to help her mistress undress when Mrs. Goldfinch arrived in the bedroom chambers.

"Just release the hooks and laces, dear, I will manage the rest. I wish to be on my own tonight."

With her modest white cotton nightdress sweeping the floor she stood up from the dressing table where she had brushed her hair one hundred times. Some habits cannot be stopped. She knelt by the bedside and prayed. Her whispers went on for five minutes before she spoke out loud.

"Please God, keep them all safe; and if you're talking to the youngest daughter of mine you can tell her she never fooled me for one minute; not for one single moment. Lord God, please be with them."

Her head fell onto the feather-down quilt. Deep wrenching sobs tore from her throat. Her heart felt like a heavy weight in her chest.

CHAPTER TWO

Brisbane Australia 1867

THE ARRIVAL

The *Young Australia* tugged at the anchor chain. The at-rest paddles clattered with each wave passing under the vessel. It had been stationary off a place called Lytton in the Brisbane River since early this morning. Abigail took hold of her brother's elbow. Her other hand held onto the wide-brimmed hat employed to control the unruly auburn curls in the fresh sea breeze.

"George, how much longer do we have to wait for the boat to take us to the mainland?"

"Patience, sister." Doctor George Goldfinch pointed to a much smaller boat steaming towards them. "That will be *The Platypus* now."

"I do hope Jane and Eve have organized to have our luggage ready for loading." Abigail stumbled as the deck heaved over a rogue wave. "No doubt, your man-servant will have everyone doing his bidding."

George grinned. "Thomas is truly an asset. People listen to his requests. I guess it is what happens when others are in awe of your size." He flicked a large white handkerchief out of his pocket then wiped the perspiration from his face. "Phew, it's hot. I thought this was the beginning of the colder season in this country. What will summer be like? We'll need to wear large hats, I think."

Standing on the upper deck, George and his sister watched the activity as *The Platypus* was secured. Men from both vessels shouted instructions and curses as lines were thrown and tied. They both turned at the sound of Thomas's voice.

"All is set, Doctor George. Miss Jane and Eve are on their way up, Mrs. Baldwin."

"When they get here, we'll make our way down to disembark," George added.

The purser of the *Young Australia* endeavoured to make sense of the hustle and bustle around the disembarkation point. George and his group were first to be assisted across the connecting plank and taken on board *The Platypus*. When the smaller boat began to pull away, there were only a few inches of freeboard left. *The Platypus* appeared to struggle against the outgoing tide. Excitement and anxiety stirred within the hearts of the newcomers. What exactly were the conditions going to be like in this country called Australia? As they moved up the river nearing the township, there were things going on all around them: ships on the river, building construction on the land, industry noise, traffic of horses pulling carriages or drays, pedestrians on the nearby streets. Wide-eyed, the group stared turning this way and that trying not to miss a thing. Eve laughed out loud. Jane's eyes followed Doctor George's every move, which Thomas did not miss.

"This is not the uncivilized camps Papa warned me about," George laughed. "It appears to be quite a progressive little town." He was having trouble taking it all in at once. Buildings and houses spread out from both sides of the river. Admittedly many of the houses were only one step up from huts but there were some stately homes lining the river's edge. Handsome structures could be seen as they approached the Botanic Gardens. He assumed the large building in the gardens must be the new Parliament house the purser had told him they were building.

"Papa will be disappointed. I have not been consigned a tent to live in." Abigail grimaced. Her head swung left and right. "Look, Jane, this river is quite busy. When we have a day free, we must take a river jaunt. We can explore further upstream. As you can see, there is no need to feel isolated now."

"Look, Miss Abigail," Eve pointed to a strangely shaped building on the rise behind the town. "If that had sails, it would look like the windmills in the book you got from Holland."

"Very similar, I should imagine. Maybe they grind their grain there too."

It took a moment to attune their balance to dry land when they stepped off the boat. A stranger approached. He addressed George.

"Excuse me, Sir. Would you be Doctor Goldfinch and group heading for Millie's Mariner's Rest: Hotel and Lodging?"

Abigail had to crane her neck back to look up at the solidly built man. A sprinkling of grey dusted the black hair curling at his collar as well as the dark moustache and short beard on a sun-hardened face. His hands were covered with thick calluses interlaced with a pattern of scars.

George reached out to shake the man's hand.

"Yes, we are and yes, we are. And what may we call you?"

"My name is Jacko Benson, Sir. Miss Millie has asked for you to come with me. I will see you sorted out at Customs then deliver you back to The Rest. Our housekeeper, Miss Sarah, has a roast dinner awaiting your arrival."

"Oh, George, how marvellous; I am so hungry." Abigail smiled as she fanned her flushed face.

The group followed Jacko to where a well-polished carriage with two equally well-groomed chestnut horses waited patiently. Jacko slipped a hand into the pocket of his trousers. The two horses snickered briefly before snaffling up the treat. He then turned to help the guests into the carriage.

"Our handyman, Ned, has the dray here today and will collect all your luggage."

As soon as they entered the foyer of the Customs House an officer stepped out to guide George and his group into a room.

"I'll be waiting here," Jacko informed George. "Just you call me if you have any problems."

Abigail bent to whisper in her brother's ear. "Do you think we are getting preferential treatment because we are with Jacko or do you think Papa's influence may be at work here?"

"There have been many incidents on this trip to make me suspect our Papa's reputation may be travelling with us. How anyone knows we are related, I've not the foggiest idea."

"Well brother, don't look a gift horse in the mouth. I'm looking forward to a roast dinner and a cup of tea and to be able to settle into a room not moving in all directions at once."

MILLIE'S MARINER'S REST HOTEL

Sarah waited at the foyer steps after having cleaned up and changed her dress. Her dark hair had been brushed into submission with a white ribbon adding security to any wayward tendrils. As the guests climbed down from the carriage, she curtsied and marvelled at the difference in the colour of their pale skins compared to her tanned lower arms not concealed by the sleeves of her dress. Not the foreign-looking gentleman though; his skin was like golden honey. She learnt later he was called Thomas.

Sarah tried not to stare at the similarity between the doctor and Mrs. Baldwin. It was easily seen they were siblings. She curbed her curiosity to wonder where Mr. Baldwin might be. Sarah gathered her wandering wits.

"Welcome to Miss Millie's Mariners Rest; Hotel and Lodging. My name is Sarah Dougall. I am the housekeeper. Miss Millie sends her apologies. She is unable to be here to greet you today. We do hope you enjoy your stay. Would you like me to take you to your rooms and allow you time to freshen up? Dinner will be served in the private dining room."

Abigail introduced her group. She turned to her brother for his opinion. He lifted his shoulders in acquiescence with her needs. She raised her eyebrow in question to Jane and Eve who were also happy to let Abigail make the decision.

"That sounds very nice; thank you, Sarah."

Abigail cast a glance over what was to be their home until a suitable residence became available. The two-storied timber building with its central hub and wide verandahs looked well cared for; albeit a coat of paint would not go astray. She turned and joined the group as they followed the housekeeper.

Sarah led them up the steps from the foyer to the private wing. She opened the doors into the front rooms, A-1 and A-2.

"These rooms have been reserved for Doctor Goldfinch and Mrs. Baldwin," she addressed the doctor.

"The agent was not sure where you might wish to have your staff accommodated. We have the three back rooms here, almost opposite you and Mrs. Baldwin, and we have one front room spare. If you prefer, we have the second-class rooms at the other end of the hotel."

George scratched his head. Abigail stepped forward.

"Thank you, Sarah. The rooms opposite ours will be most suitable and easily accessible to us. Miss Stanley, Eve and Thomas will be most comfortable there I am sure."

SETTLING IN

Doctor George Goldfinch threw himself into the laid-back canvas chair on the front verandah of Millie's Mariner's Rest. He dragged a large white handkerchief from his jacket pocket and began to wipe the rivulets of perspiration on the side of his face.

"It's time we gave your hair a trim, Doctor George. If your mane was brought under some control, you may not feel the heat quite so much," commented the man-servant as he joined George.

"Thanks, Thomas, you don't need to remind me it is like a mop-head. You can do your worst with the scissors later today. Good grief, it's hotter than a summer day."

"We may get a thunderstorm this evening."

"Something has to give, that is for certain."

Both men stood to attention when Abigail joined them. Since their arrival several months previously, she waddled rather than walked over to the balustrade rail where her fine hands held firmly while she stretched her upper body. She savoured the cool river breezes blowing in along the front of the hotel.

As George watched his sister, a frown slid over his face.

"I hope you are not doing too much, Abigail. It is not long now until the birth, remember."

"George, don't fuss. Next thing you'll have me in tight corsets and resting twenty-four hours a day." Her smile softened the snappy voice.

"Heaven preserve me from the modern woman."

"Good afternoon, Miss Abigail. Can I get you a cool drink?" Thomas asked.

"No, thanks, Thomas. I spoke to Sarah on my way up here. She is bringing us a large jug of freshly made lemon water."

Thomas retreated into Doctor George's room. At this point, Sarah arrived leading a procession of Eve and Jane. Between them, they carried two jugs of water with slices of lemon floating on the surface and a tray on which stood half a dozen glasses. These were placed on the small table near the railing.

As she turned around, Sarah spoke. "Doctor George, Miss Jane tells me the house-hunting did not go well again today."

"No, Sarah, it was another hot and unproductive day. At this rate, I will be treating patients in my bedroom here until I am old and grey. I do appreciate Miss Millie allowing me to see these people here at the hotel." There were only a few at the moment but he expected this to change. The town was not oversupplied with medical practitioners. "If I don't find something soon, we will be delivering my sister's baby in these rooms too."

It was Jane who blushed, not Abigail.

Sarah poured the drinks.

"Sir, I'm sure something will turn up soon. 'Good things come to those who wait', my mother always said."

"I do hope she is right, Sarah." George smiled.

The young housekeeper had become a firm favourite with the Londoners. The stiff London attitudes to the classes mellowed under the warm sun of the southern hemisphere.

"Oh well, I guess tomorrow is another day," Sarah commented as she disappeared down the staircase.

Sitting on the small wooden chair against the rail in the corner of the verandah, Eve rubbed her ankles as she drank thirstily.

"My feet are ever so sore. Sometimes I think I was better off running bare-foot around the streets of London."

Jane smiled. "Your feet might not have hurt then but can you remember the pain of hunger in your belly?"

"Oh, yes, Miss Jane. I will never forget the hunger; and the cold," Eve replied fervently.

Abigail placed her glass on the table.

"I think I will have one more glass and then I must lie down."

Eve jumped up slipping her feet into her shoes.

"I'll just go in and turn down your bed Miss Abigail."

George watched his sister for a moment before commenting.

"Sarah may be right. Tomorrow is another day and with any luck, we may very well be ensconced in our own house before the little one arrives."

Abigail walked over and patted her brother's hand.

"We'll be fine whichever way things go, George. You must not worry."

"Not worry, you say. How do you think I'd face Mama and Papa if I let anything happen to you?"

"Nothing bad is going to happen. Anyway, the way Papa is feeling about me these days, he has most likely disowned me."

George turned his attention to Jane who was sitting quietly sipping her lemon water.

"I suppose you'll be assisting Abigail and me at the birth, Jane?"

Jane's mouth dropped open. She paled. Her eyes widened. A flush crawled up from beneath her bodice returning colour to her face.

"Oh, Doctor George, please don't ask that of me. I could never do it. I cannot stand the sight of blood. I would do almost anything you ask of me, but not that." A tear welled in each eye before overflowing down the sides of her narrow nose. She stood up blindly and stumbled past Abigail on her way to the room.

32

"What did I say wrong?" George threw his hands into the air.

His sister grinned and rolled her eyes. "Men! Anyway, it will be Eve who'll hold our hands when the time comes. She fetched and carried for an accoucheur in London for two years. She has seen it all; mind you, this was before the girl was twelve years old. Now I'd best go in and wipe the tears, then rest."

LETTER FROM LONDON

Thomas arrived to tidy the glasses and the empty jugs. He deposited a letter on the table.

"This has just been delivered by the letter carrier." The glasses clinked against each other on the tray. "I'll take this back to the kitchen for Sarah." As he passed by George's chair, he noticed the puzzled frown on his face. "Are you alright Doctor George, you look flummoxed."

Scratching his head, George answered. "You know, Thomas, if I live to be one hundred, I will never understand women."

"Aha, one of the most important lessons in life. A man should not waste his time trying to understand women. Women don't understand women so what chance has a man got?"

George burst out laughing. "I bet you've never told a woman that then, eh?" He picked the mail up from the table and turned it over. "I don't believe it." It was addressed to Abigail written in their mother's spidery scrawl.

He jumped up and called through Abigail's doorway.

"You decent, Abby?"

"Yes, George, you can come in."

He pulled aside the privacy curtain and poked his head into the room. In his hand, he waved the letter. Abigail was stretched out on the bed with her feet elevated on a pillow.

"An epistle from Mama; for you."

"From Mama? Oh, George, do you think everything is alright at home? What if something bad has happened?"

"There is only one way to find out."

A frown marred her forehead as she took the proffered letter.

"I'll let you read it in private," George said as he returned to his seat on the verandah.

The continuous tapping of her brother's fingers on the arm of his chair reached through to Abigail. Even though she knew her brother must be dying of curiosity, she was not going to be rushed. She dropped the envelope on the bed beside her and stared at it for some time. Tears trickled down her cheeks. She swiped at her face with the lace-edged handkerchief drawn out from under her pillow.

"Just my condition, I guess."

Abigail shook her head before picking up the envelope again and began tearing at the seal. She shook out the five pages and began to read.

My darling daughter,

By the time you get this letter, it will be approaching your time to have the baby and I want you to know my thoughts are with you. I am not sure how I will be able to get this out past your father but I will pray for some of your courage to enable me to do so.

Again, Abigail wiped at her eyes. Had she been too hasty in her assessment of her mother?

"Oh, Mama, I wish you were here with me now." She began to read on.

Make sure George engages the best of medical assistance for you at this time. Is there a suitable hospital where you can have your child or do you plan on delivering in your home? You do have a home, don't you? It is not as bad as your father said, is it? Please tell me you are not living in tents.

I do worry about Jane too. She is not as strong-minded as you and may find the difficulties of living in rough conditions rather distressing. On the other hand, I know Eve will be able to cope under the most difficult of times. You will most likely find her a tower of strength.

"Mama; how very true." Abigail sniffed then blew her nose. She turned the page and read further.

Your father keeps up his tough façade. I am sure you remember the haughty look he does so well. But I overheard an interesting comment he made at Harvison's dinner party yesterday evening. He was talking to Samuel Harvison, himself. I heard your father say, 'It is George, the younger son, the doctor, he is the one in my family with all the adventure and courage. He has taken his medicine and some culture out to the colonies.' Abigail, I want you to tell your brother just how proud his father is. Your Papa will eventually forgive you too, Abigail, but it will take time. You were always his favourite. 'The only one who stands up and gives me a bit back' is what he often said. I want to tell you both how proud I am too, and I miss you both.

The remainder of the letter was full of news of her older siblings and finally ended with a notice of best wishes and love for herself and George. Abigail was about to fold up the pages when a small piece of paper slipped out onto the bed beside her. Her mother had scribbled a further note.

Abigail dear, if you feel you want to reply, please forward your letter to Agnes Hetherington. You do remember her; my friend from my school days. They still live in the same house. I yearn to hear your news. May God look after you at your accouchement. With all the love of a mother.

"George, are you still out there?" The tapping on the chair had stopped.

"Yes, Abby, I am still here, waiting patiently."

"George, you need to read this letter."

George sat looking out over the river. His mind churned. Several pages of paper lay on his lap. He found it hard to imagine his father being proud of him. Always, it had been the achievements of his older brothers that were waved in his face. He was pleased Mama had reached out to Abigail, particularly at a time like this. Later, Thomas found him here still deep in thought.

"Bad news, Doctor George?"

"Not really, Thomas. It's a letter to Abigail from my mother. It seems we are not the unmentionables we once were. We are still a long way from being forgiven but at least communication has been re-established."

"That has to be good news. Rifts within families are not good. No one knows it better than me."

"You're right, Thomas. I still feel only a shade above a remittance man, though."

Thomas shook his head impatiently. "You are a lucky man to have a family who cares. Now come, let us cut your hair. You will have something else to worry about."

An expanding carpet of ginger hair circled the chair placed in the shade outside the back door of the hotel. George sighed and twitched impatiently in the seat.

"You'll lose an ear if you don't sit still, Doctor George. These scissors are quite sharp." Thomas spoke quietly.

Both men looked up as the two Dougall boys, Josh and Gus, rushed out of the door. They were headed towards the cottage in the back yard in which they lived with their sister, the housekeeper, Sarah. Josh, the older boy, skidded to a stop. It had surprised George to learn the well-built lad with dark hair and piercing blue eyes was only fifteen years of age. The brother, Gus, nearly two years younger, could have been a twin. Josh came back and spoke quietly to the doctor. George's impatience dissolved like a teaspoon of salt in a cup of water. Haircutting was suspended for a moment while the doctor relayed this news to Thomas. He turned back to where Josh hopped from one foot to the other.

"Are you sure it's for sale, lad?"

"I think so. I heard about it today at work. It is either for sale or for lease and it is only up the road a little from the hotel."

"Sounds wonderful. If I remember, it is quite a large place and well kept." George turned back to Thomas. "Come on, Thomas, haven't you finished yet? If we get a move on, we can duck up and have a look at this house before it gets dark."

The pair stood for a moment at the wooden gate. Both bent double gasping for air after the uphill run.

"I don't think it's too late to call. There's at least an hour of daylight left," George said as he put his hand through the gap in the gate to reach and lift the latch.

The shade of the two fig trees spread over them like a warm welcome, cooling their sticky bodies. They followed a well-maintained path winding its way towards the house.

From the shadows, a harridan, with stringy grey hair brushing bony shoulders, screeched at them.

"Get out, get out and take that blackfella with you. If you come an inch closer, I'll shoot you myself." Gaps in her gums were given an airing as she yelled her abuse. Those narrow shoulders failed to adequately hold up a flimsy undergarment of some sort. Thick uncut toenails of her bare feet stuck out from under the long hem of the slip.

"But … but … Thomas is Egyptian; he is not a blackfella." George was unsure whether to be afraid or to laugh.

He did have to make a decision because right then a tall man with a thick white rim of hair around the base of his otherwise bald head, came shuffling around the corner. This man wrapped what appeared to be a carriage rug, around the woman's body and held her close to his side. The old lady hid her head within his arms.

"My apologies, for my wife. She has been frail. Do I know you, gentlemen? Can I help you?"

George stepped forward with his hand outstretched.

"Good evening, Sir. Doctor George Goldfinch and my manservant, Thomas." George stepped aside to allow the man to see his companion.

"Doctor James MacDonald." The two men shook hands.

"Sorry to barge in on you unannounced like this. I realize it is getting late. I was hoping for confirmation of something I heard today."

"You are not selling anything; I hope?" James MacDonald scrutinized the strangers in front of him.

"Rest assured on that score, sir. In fact, I am hoping to buy or lease this house; if the story is true."

"If you are asking, is this house for lease, the answer is yes. I may consider a sale but would prefer to lease for five years. With my wife poorly, things are a bit up in the air at the moment. We will go back to the family, in the old country, and make a decision there."

"What a good idea. Is it possible to arrange a viewing tomorrow morning, say about ten?"

"Ten o'clock will be most suitable. By then the nurse will be in to keep an eye on Elizabeth for me."

The two medical professionals shook hands again, offering their farewells. The old doctor slowly led his wife back to the house while George and Thomas found their own way out through the wooden gate. Once on the street, George jumped into the air clicking his heels together.

"Most dignified. You look like an Irish dancer." Thomas raised his black-trimmed eyebrows.

"Don't be a stick-in-the-mud now, Thomas. What do you think?"

"What is it the English say? 'Don't count your chickens until they hatch.' Let's wait and see what tomorrow brings."

"Well, I thought you'd be delirious. You're forever grumbling the girls are always underfoot."

"Doctor George, I just think we should not build up the ladies' hopes too high. Not until we are sure of the outcome. Miss Abigail does not need to be disappointed at a time like this." Thomas patted his groomed and oiled dark hair. "Do you think I look like a blackfella?"

George slapped Thomas lightly on the shoulder. "You a blackfella? More like one of the many ancient Gods the Egyptians spent half their life praying to. As for my sister, you are right, as usual, Thomas. I'll keep stum until we view the property tomorrow."

George slipped into the private bar at the Mariner's Rest for an ale before his meal. Neither Spud Murphy, Ned Turner nor Jacko Benson was behind the bar. This evening, Miss Millie herself, held court over the clientele present. The rings on her fingers flashed in the lantern's light as she smoothed her hennaed hair. Hazel eyes sparkled in competition. The woman's full skirt swished as she moved behind the bar. Two men in business suits had their heads together in the corner near the window. Their voices were a soft undecipherable rumble. Outside, the dusk fell silently. The noises of the town echoing across the river began to fade. An occasional clatter of cutlery and plates reached them from the kitchen.

"So, you've been looking at old Doc MacDonald's place. Now there's a sad story, Doctor George."

George pricked up his ears. "Oh ...?"

"The pair of them came out here just after Brisbane opened its doors to the free settlers. It must have been about eighteen thirty-eight or nine. The town was very lucky to have him. The doctor built a large house thinking their two sons would join them after they finished their university studies. The boys had other ideas and chose the softer life of civilized London. Obviously, they did not have the adventurous spirit of their parents. Over the past few years, poor old Mrs. MacDonald has been losing her mind. The doctor does the best he can but he is not too strong himself these days. He has a lady comes in daily to cook, clean and keep an eye on Mrs. MacDonald. He also employs a gardener, two or three days a week. It is a struggle, though. I understand they are leaving at the end of this week; sailing back to the family in Britain."

George felt his spirits lifting even further. He made his way into the private dining room walking on air. He joined Abigail and Jane at their usual table. Thomas and Eve always ate at a separate table near the kitchen door.

"Good evening, ladies. How are you this evening, Abigail?"

Jane smiled in return. Abigail rolled her eyes.

"George, you really do not want to know. This child is never still and I am quite fed up with carrying this extra ton weight around everywhere."

Jane blushed and hushed her friend.

"Abigail, really. This is a dining room remember."

George just laughed.

"Nothing to complain about then, have we? What's to eat tonight? I'm famished."

41

"Mrs. Hamilton is cook tonight. Sarah said we are having crab and shrimp for what she calls, 'tea'. Apparently the black-fellow they call Billy Toe-bite catches them in the river and sells them to the hotels and to the people in the town." Jane spoke softly. "I did not ask how he got the name Billy Toe-bite. I'm not sure I want to know." She took a sip of water from her glass.

"Some things are best left unknown." Abigail turned to her brother. "What have you been up to all afternoon? I see Thomas has cut your hair at last. That is an improvement."

George did not look his sister in the eye. He scratched his forehead.

"Er .., we er .., Thomas and I went for a bit of a walk."

Abigail knew her twin well. She raised an eyebrow.

"Oh, yes?" She did not pursue the question further. For the moment, he would keep.

The morning sun penetrated deep into the room when Thomas pulled the curtains aside.

"Are you awake, Doctor George?"

"I am now."

"You know what you have to do today. The ladies have been up and had their breakfast already. I have yours here, on the tray."

"Spare me from early risers. What's the time?"

"Eight-thirty, Master," Thomas said with a grin.

George threw back the covers and dived out of bed.

"Goodness, I must dash. I have to be at the MacDonald's at ten."

"I shall draw a bath for you while you eat," Thomas said as he eased out of the door.

CHAPTER THREE

THE BIRTH

The hotel was in an uproar when George and Thomas returned after one o'clock. Sarah ran to greet them as they came in through the side door.

"Doctor George, Doctor George, it's Miss Abigail."

"Oh, my God. What's happened?" George grabbed Sarah by her two upper arms. "Where is she?"

"She's fine. Her time is starting, that's all. Eve is settling her in upstairs. I'm just on my way to ensure we have lots of warm towels and hot water."

George took the stairs two at a time calling to Sarah as he did so. "Thanks, Sarah, thank you."

Thomas followed Sarah into the kitchen. "May I give you a hand in here? I don't think I will be of much use upstairs."

The pencil, held in fingers the colour of rich honey, danced back and forth across the paper. Thomas sat at the end of the verandah, furthest from all the drama going on in Miss Abigail's room. With the sketch pad held on his lap, he concentrated on the golden blooms covering the vine as it twisted and twined its way up the drainpipe running down from the roof.

"Very good, Thomas, may I sit and watch?" Miss Millie, the friendly woman who owned the hotel, slipped into the rattan chair beside him. "How is it going, down the other end?"

Thomas looked up in surprise. He had not heard Miss Millie's arrival from the lounge room.

"I don't know and I don't really wish to know; until it's all over. They'll send for me if I'm wanted, I'm sure. Eve and Doctor George are in with Miss Abigail. Miss Jane is busy organizing and reorganizing the baby things in her room."

Millie smiled. "Some people cannot cope with sickness, pain or blood. I had such a friend once. She was as tough as nails in everything else, though."

"Everyone is different, I guess," Thomas mumbled around the pencil held crossways in his lips.

"Where did you learn to sketch like that?"

Thomas removed the pencil from his mouth.

"In Paris, some years ago. An old master took me under his wing."

"Hmm. I would like to see more of your work. Not that I know much about art, mind you. My husband, Christopher, did. He knew all the great artists and their work. My life has been too busy chasing other occupations, I guess." Millie smiled ruefully before going on. "But I know what I like. What were you doing in Paris; if I am not being too nosey?"

"My people are of the royal blood in Egypt and I had been sent to Paris to study. After family misfortunes and other issues, I could not return. I met Doctor George. I have worked for him ever since."

The fingers holding the pencil continued drifting across the paper with feather-light strokes. "What about you, Miss Millie, when did you come to the colonies?"

"Thomas, I was born here, in Australia; in Sydney. Mister Carson brought me to this place in 1849. Jacko, our foster-son, was about twelve then. We had a wonderful seven years and then my husband died."

"I'm sorry to hear that, Miss Millie. You and Jacko have managed on your own since then, have you?"

Just then, Eve's head appeared through the doorway at the other end of the verandah.

"Oh, Miss Millie, would you mind very much sitting with Miss Abigail for a bit. It's getting very close now and Doctor needs me to help him."

The chair creaked when Miss Millie stood.

"Of course, dear, I'd love to help." The blue skirt swished around her legs and her fingers scrambled to tidy her hair roll as she made her way to the room.

After coming from the bright afternoon sun outside it took a moment for her eyes to adjust when she entered through the curtains. Doctor George and Eve were at the far end of the bed sorting through several instruments lying upon a cloth covering a small table. The doctor looked up to greet her.

"Thanks, Miss Millie."

Millie smiled as she turned to Abigail who was lying back on the pillows weakly fanning her perspiring face. Millie immediately sat on the vacant chair near her.

"Let me do it, dear." Millie took the fan from the pale hands and picked up a damp cloth from where it hung on the bedpost. She began wiping Abigail's flushed skin before resuming with the fan.

"Thank you for being here, Miss Millie." Abigail gave a wan smile. "This little one is being rather obstinate."

Millie took her hand and squeezed. "I feel honoured to be asked."

Abigail's eyes closed. Millie looked around the room. The bed had been pulled out from the wall. A table near the opposite doorway held a jug and bowl. Also, on the table was a kettle with steam rising from its spout and a large saucepan from the kitchen. Millie knew this held warm towels. She had seen Thomas collect it from the stove earlier. A groan from Abigail and the increased pressure on her hand drew Millie's attention back to the young woman on the bed.

Doctor George spoke. "Right Abigail, we're nearly there. Now don't rush it, let the baby dictate its arrival."

"Don't you be telling me, brother. I was the one who practically wrote the paper for your degree on this very subject."

"Glad to see you still fiery as ever, Abby. Now, the head is showing; just a little push." George mumbled something to Eve which the women at the top of the bed could not hear.

Abigail strained and groaned. She gritted her teeth.

"You know; you can yell if you want to." Millie squeezed her hand.

"Thanks... Millie... but... I really... would prefer... not to." Abigail gave another deep groan and strained hard.

"Yes, beautiful. Head's out. Oh, bother." Doctor George bit down on the curse that threatened.

"What's wrong George, what is it?" Abigail's voice rose.

"Nothing, Abigail. Just breathe slowly for a moment. The cord is around the baby's neck. I'll just release it."

Abigail lay gasping. Perspiration ran in rivulets down her face in spite of Millie's continually mopping up with the cloth. Her eyes never left those of her brother who stared in concentration over her sheet-covered legs.

With one hand supporting the head, the fingers of his other hand, by touch alone, gently slipped in under the cord and slowly eased it out and over the slippery skull. Beads of perspiration stood out on his forehead too. Eve wiped them away. Her hands hovered over the instruments while awaiting instructions.

"All right; done. It's fine now." He relaxed.

At the other end of the bed, Millie's and Abigail's eyes met. They both smiled. Millie gave Abigail's hand another squeeze as the younger woman gave a low growl and strained once more.

"The first shoulder's out and … there… is… the… other."

Abigail's body gathered itself before the final push. She groaned a long, low moan.

"Well done, the baby is delivered. It's a boy by the way." Supporting the baby's back George held the slippery little mite by the legs and gave its posterior a sharp smack. The child roared its protest.

"Quick Eve, pass the two clamps then the scissors. After that, we'll want the towels to wrap him up."

"A boy, I could have guessed. Only a boy could cause all this trouble."

"Well, that's a nice way to say thanks," George grumbled as he helped Eve wrap the greasy bundle into the warm towels.

Abigail held her arms out and drew her child to her chest. "Only the one then, George? Were we right; there is no sign of a twin?"

"Yes, Abigail, we were right, no twins." Doctor George took out his fob watch to check the time. As he massaged the abdomen above the slack uterus firmly to encourage contraction, he spoke to his twin sister. "Sorry, this hurts a bit. For the record, this baby boy came into the world at eight minutes past five on the afternoon of the last day of August 1867."

Abigail ran her finger lightly across the baby's forehead. Tears welled in her eyes. She looked up at Millie who had tears pouring down her face. They both laughed. Eve came to stand beside them.

"Miss Abigail, can I take the baby to Miss Jane now? She'll clean him up and wrap him in fresh dry towels."

"Tell her to be careful and bring him back as soon as you can."

"Yes, Miss Abigail."

Reluctantly Abigail watched Eve leave the room with her son; HER son.

George continued rubbing Abigail's abdomen.

"Once this placenta is delivered, we'll get you tidied up. You're not too cold, are you?"

Abigail shivered. Millie straightened the bed clothing pulling a shawl about Abigail's shoulders.

"Thanks, Miss Millie. I hope I have not made a mess on your bed."

"Eve covered the mattress with a large mackintosh this morning. It will be no trouble at all to remove it and the sheets and give them a wash. You are not to worry yourself. Have you decided what you are going to call the little one?"

Abigail rubbed her forehead. "I am not sure what to do. Of course, his second name will be George after my brother." She chewed her lower lip. "I suppose I should call him after his deceased father but to be honest I don't want him to grow up anything like Edward. Sorry, I should not burden you with my problems."

"Abigail, sometimes it's good to share one's troubles. It does help you know. You can rest assured whatever you say to me remains with me. In my position, over the years, I know the importance of confidences. I recently came into contact with a fellow calling himself Edward. He was not a pleasant chap either. I'm sure there are some very nice Edwards around though. The name does not make the man remember." She smiled gently and wiped Abigail's face once again.

"Thanks, Millie. Edward's family was very nice but Edward was not what I would have chosen in a husband. My father organized that. Perhaps I could name it after the paternal grandfather; he was a lovely man. What do you think, George?"

"I think this afterbirth is about to deliver. Yes, old Henry Baldwin was a good old stick. Or you could call him Red. Take a look at the pair of you up there. One with flaming red hair and the other an auburn top."

Abigail sniffed. "Men! That's it then. His name will be Henry George Carson Baldwin."

George looked up. "Where does the Carson come from?"

"It's Millie's surname, silly. I couldn't call the boy Millie, could I."

As he lay in bed trying to encourage his body and mind to relax, George remembered. The house; he had forgotten to tell Abigail about the house. What was it, Sarah said yesterday? Something about tomorrow's another day. His eyes closed; his mouth slackened. Soft snores drifted into the night air.

CHAPTER FOUR

THE NEW HOME

The morning sun had yet to warm up. Abigail was already sitting out on the verandah enjoying the fresh air. On the table in front of her lay a tablet of paper, a bottle of ink, a square of blotting paper and her pen with a shiny new nib in place. She still had not put pen to paper when George, still wrapped in his dressing-gown, stepped out of his room.

"Good morning, George. Did you sleep well?"

"Abigail, are you alright. You should be resting. Is the baby doing well?"

"Stop fussing, dear brother. I am well. The baby has had his early feed and I could not return to sleep. I want to reply to Mama's letter but am not sure what to say. You can help if you wish."

"Gosh, leave me out of it, Abby. I'm in enough hot water as it is." George turned around as Thomas arrived with a pot of tea and two cups.

"Oh, Thomas, thank you." Abigail took her cup and drank.

Thomas then handed the other cup to the doctor.

"Have you told Miss Abigail, yet?"

Abigail nearly choked on the mouthful of her drink. She cleared her throat.

"Told me what?" But Thomas had retreated into the room and pretended not to hear. Abigail turned back to her brother. "George; told me what?"

"Mmm, yes. If you remember, you and young Henry stole my thunder yesterday afternoon. When Thomas and I returned to the hotel, I was full of good news but I walked into bedlam here. You had taken centre stage. The news I had to tell you went clean out of my mind."

"So, how long am I to wait to hear this news, George? Has this got anything to do with your guilty behaviour at tea-time the night before last?"

"Eer… well, yes, it has really. I think we have found our new home. It's not too far from here. It's a large house owned by a retired physician. He is returning to England." George went on to tell of his excitement at the property. He took her pen and drew sketches of the layout. Abigail became as excited as her brother when each detail was shown and explained. This is where Jane found them on her way to the dining room for breakfast.

"Abigail, I have requested a tray be sent up to you. You may like to take it easy today. Those steps are rather steep. Henry is still sound asleep in the baby-crib, so you need not worry at the moment."

It was not until late morning when Abigail, once again, made another attempt on the letter to her mother.

Dear Mama,

I cannot tell you how pleased and relieved I was to receive your loving and very welcome letter. Firstly, I must apologize for leaving home and England in the manner I did. I am sorry but I just could not face another disastrous marriage to a man I could never love. I understand Papa was only doing what he thought best but, as I see it, matters of the heart can never be planned like a board meeting's agenda.

You timed the letter perfectly. It arrived the day prior to my delivering a wonderful baby boy into this world. His name is Henry George Carson Baldwin. I felt much more relieved going into my confinement knowing your thoughts were with me.

Abigail rested her pen on the blotter and sat for a long while watching the boats moving up and down the river below. She struggled with what to mention and what not to mention in this letter. There was no point worrying her mother, so far away. Perhaps it might not be the wisest thing to let Mama know Henry was delivered in a hotel room. Perhaps she need not mention George delivered the child with only her maid, Eve, to assist. Mama would expect at least one specialist to have been present. On the other hand, she could mention the house on which George was, even now, finalizing the paperwork. Mama need not know they were not actually living in it just yet. Of course, it would please Mama to know Brisbane town boasted a museum. Perhaps she need not mention it was set up in an old mill where convicts, for punishment, had been forced to manually grind the grain for the new settlement, years before. She picked up her pen and began writing rapidly.

A week later, Abigail sat rocking in the chair while the baby snuffled at her breast. This was one of her favourite moments; feed time. From where she sat, just inside the back door of her room, she could watch the bright green and red plumage of the birds as they squabbled and drank from the coloured flowers on the trees. This doorway was becoming her favourite place in their new home. The pinks and apricots of the early spring morning tinted the native bushes in the large garden. At that moment, the sound of her brother's horse and sulky rumbling into the driveway caught her attention. She drew a sharp breath when he stumbled on the step as he climbed to the ground. Even Thomas, who led the horse to the stable was seen to be dragging his feet. It must have been a long night for them both. She drew the baby rug up over her bared breast as her brother approached.

"Good morning, Abby. How's the champion doing today?"

"Hello, George. Henry is fine. As long as he is eating, he is happy; a bit like most males."

"Sounds a bit harsh." A tired grin spread across his face.

"You look like you need a bath, a feed and a sleep. What kept you up?"

George sat on the verandah floor with his shoulders against the post. He rested his head back. "Mrs. Bayley had her baby during the night; all night actually. It did not survive."

"Oh, George, I am so sorry." Abigail knew how her brother took every life lost, to heart. "This is her twelfth child, or is it her thirteenth? She may be relieved there is not another mouth to feed. They are struggling, I think."

Thomas waved as he made his way to the far wing of the house where George and he had set up residence. The ladies lived in this wing and between the two was the kitchen, common rooms and the doctor's surgery. Abigail waved back before turning her attention to her brother again.

"I'll let Eve know to prepare your breakfast so you may get an hour or two of rest before the morning calls begin."

"That will be nice." An involuntary groan escaped his lips as he struggled to his feet.

George entered his office and placed the medical bag in the corner before he noticed Jane sitting at the desk. Candlelight flickered over the paper on which she was writing.

"Sorry, you startled me," he said. "What on earth are you doing here at this hour? The cocks have barely crowed."

"Good morning, Doctor George. There is no sleeping in with young Henry in charge now. I thought I could prepare the patient-cards for today's surgery before I help Eve with the breakfasts." A flush crept up her neck and face. She lowered her eyes. "I'll go now."

Only a quick eye would notice the trembling hands as Jane tidied the desk before she made her way to the kitchen.

The rippling muscles on Thomas's brown arms dripped with sweat. The jerkin he wore was dark with moisture. Without stopping, the rhythm continued. Select a block of wood from the pile. Stand it on the chopping block. Lift the axe overhead then bring it down with a force to split each block of wood with one sweep. Chips of wood flew from the sharp edge of the axe. The sound reverberated off the iron sheeting walls of the washhouse.

George arrived with a jug of lemon water and two glasses. He sat in the shade of the wattle tree watching his friend.

"You know, an anatomist would like to analyse your muscle structure under a microscope."

The ringing of the axe continued unchanged.

"Something up your nose, Thomas? If you keep that up, we'll have enough stove wood chopped to last the next five years. Want to talk about it? There is plenty here for you too." He held up a glass of the liquid.

The tempo of the axe continued for a few more minutes. The axe rang out one last time as it was embedded into the chopping block. Thomas grunted with the effort before walking over to the water pump where he took the handle and pumped energetically up and down. Water gushed out into the bucket under the outlet. Taking hold of the full bucket he upended it over his head. As he swung his head back and forth blowing through his loose lips, the noise sounded like a snorting horse.

Thomas took the offered drink and drained the glass without stopping. He passed it back for a refill before sitting in the shade.

"So, let's have it," George said, with a grin.

Thomas sat with his head resting back on a post. He looked about him left and right before speaking.

"It's not easy, George, living with the women, I mean. I enjoyed cooking for ourselves in the kitchen when we lived in England. I'm terrified to walk into the kitchen, here. Eve hands out one of her frowns if I touch anything. It's like running into a wall of fire."

George tried hard not to laugh at the thought of his big muscly friend being afraid of little Eve. Thomas would not take kindly to being thought of as a joke.

"With the women doing all the cooking, it leaves you free to assist me at any time of the day or night. I would have thought you'd be glad to get out of the kitchen."

"One can become sick of cooking when constantly having to do so but I do enjoy creating new dishes. Sometimes I just wish we had a kitchen of our own. What you said is right though. It is good I'm available to help prepare the horse and sulky when you have call-outs."

"How about I talk to Abigail. Maybe she can work out a roster so you have charge of the kitchen and the cooking for two days of the week and Eve can do the other five days in each week."

"Sounds a good compromise; certainly, worth giving it a go." Thomas drained the glass. "And, when you're talking to Miss Abigail, tell her the gardener, Thumbnail, has a sister with wash-house experience. She mentioned the other day Mrs. Beazley needed help occasionally."

CHAPTER FIVE

WORK BEGINS

"Eve!" The call rang out along the hallway.

In the kitchen, Eve dropped the silver spoons she had been polishing and ran towards the doctor's surgery. When she arrived in the hallway where the patients awaited treatment, Jane stumbled out of the doctor's rooms with her hand clenched over her mouth. Blue eyes opened wide in her stark white face as she collapsed onto one of the patient chairs lined up against the wall.

"Put your head between your knees, Miss Jane," Eve instructed as she dashed in to see what was happening.

Lying on the examination table was a large man with his hairy chest, arms and legs all covered with mud, sweat and blood. Two other men stood in the corner in a similar state.

"It's alright, Miss. This's 'is blood. He fell on the adze blade when we were out getting timber. We wrapped 'is leg in some 'essian bagging we 'ad with us and tied it wif 'is leather belt." One of the men announced before Eve could ask.

The man on the table was losing further blood as it pumped out of a wound in his right thigh. With bare hands, Doctor George probed within the depths of a large gaping laceration.

"Got you," he muttered. "Eve, pass the suture instruments. I need you to clamp this artery."

"Can we wait outside, too?" The men asked as their tanned faces began to pale. At George's nod, they retreated through the doorway into the hall.

Doctor George and Eve found the sliced arteries, clamped them with the forceps and tied them with catgut suture. The haemorrhaging eased. Eve used clean rags to swab up the blood. Once satisfied they had done all they could, George began to sew the inner layers of the wound. He then followed with the skin closure. The grey-faced patient lay limp and silent; his eyes closed. The barrel chest barely moved with each shallow breath.

"Eve, before you begin to clean up, will you find Thomas. I want this man taken across the river to the hospital for observation for a few days. Ask Thomas to organize transport. He can come with me to help if needed." Doctor George issued his orders as he washed his hands in the basin provided.

The sound of crying children and the high-pitched inhalation of a baby with croup greeted Abigail and Eve as they walked along the unkempt path to where the front door sagged on its frame. Abigail knocked firmly. She knocked again; louder this time. The door groaned in protest as it was pulled open. Abigail's eyes were set at her own height but there was no one to be seen. Her eyes dropped to rest upon the serious face of a girl who appeared to be about ten years of age.

"Hello, dear. I'm Mrs. Baldwin, the doctor's sister. Is your mother in?"

The small child did not have a small voice. Abigail's eyes and mouth opened in surprise at the volume achieved. Eve held her hands over her ears.

"Ma! It's the lady from the doctor."

A tired voice struggled to reach the visitors.

"Bring them in, Maureen. What are you thinking? Don't leave them standing at the door."

The pixie face haloed by light brown hair tied with string, looked up at Abigail. "Come in, Missus. Ma's busy with the baby."

Single file through a narrow hallway, Abigail followed Maureen with Eve close behind. The unpainted walls pressed in upon them. They entered an equally dingy kitchen, where a thin woman sat on a wooden chair by the stove, nursing an ashen-faced baby whose chesty stridor had been heard from outside. The mother's dull blue eyes peered out from within the black circles of fatigue. Steam from a boiling kettle wafted over the woman and infant.

"'E's no better, Missus. I give 'im the medicine just like the doctor said, but 'e's no better. 'E's got the croup real bad this time. Sometimes 'e just stops breathing altogether. Then 'e starts again. 'E's a fighter, I'll give 'im that."

Abigail pushed aside some of the clutter on the bench near the sink to make room for her large brown bag. She delved around in the contents until her hand emerged with a small metal spatula. With one hand, she gentled the child. With the other, she reached over to feel the damp forehead. Her fingers moved with the lightest touch down the left side of the straining chest to where the baby's feeble heartbeat raced.

"Eve, will you pull aside the curtain and open the window?" Abigail then turned to Mrs. Ryan. "Can you bring the child around to face into the light? I'd like to have a quick look down his throat; if he'll let me."

At the child's next breath, Abigail slipped the spatula over the small tongue and peered into the depths; briefly. The child attempted to cough and appeared to choke. The pallor of the face turned to a blue sheen. Tears rolled down the sunken cheeks but no air could be wasted on wailing.

Abigail watched as the woman, her face grey with exhaustion, petted the child and hummed a soft melody.

"You have had little sleep, Mrs. Ryan. This child should be in the hospital, I think. We have the new hospital in town now which is a big improvement on the old one, I believe."

Mrs. Ryan's head swung slowly left and right.

"Missus, thanks for coming and everything but people who go into 'ospital don't often come out. If my baby's to die, 'e'll do so 'ere, with 'is family, not in a 'ospital full of strangers."

Abigail bit her lip. Her heart was heavy with anguish for the mother and the baby.

"Can I leave Eve to help out here for a couple of hours? You may get a rest, at least?"

Tears rolled down Mrs. Ryan's lined face. It took her several attempts before she was able to speak.

"It's good of you Missus, but the baby will only settle with either me or Maureen 'olding 'im."

Abigail patted the woman's arm.

"If Maureen will hold the child, Eve can be here to help with the other children while you take a sleep. This illness may go on for some time. You cannot continue like this for too long."

Abigail turned to Eve who was helping Maureen feed her siblings their porridge. One girl looked about eight-year-old; another girl may have been six. A boy who looked no more than three scraped at his dish feeding the empty spoon into his mouth unnoticed as he watched everything going on around him. Abigail was pleasantly surprised to see all the children looked clean, even though their clothes were threadbare.

"Eve, would you mind spending the day here helping Maureen with the children and allowing Mrs. Ryan to rest?"

"Yes, Miss Abigail. It'll be no trouble at all."

As she walked back home alone, Abigail pondered the frailty of children and the high death rates in the very young. She worried about her own son. As the front door clicked shut behind her, Abigail went straight into the quiet surgery. Water splashed over the bowl and onto the wooden bench as she washed her hands with the lye soap.

"You'll wash your hands away, if you keep that up, Abby. How's the Ryan child?"

Abigail looked up in surprise.

"I did not hear you arrive." She gave her brother a rueful smile as he strode in and dropped his black bag on the table.

"I cannot see the little one lasting another day, George. It is difficult to get a decent look down the child's throat but I'm sure I saw a white film there. I think you are right, he has more than just the croup."

"I'm sure the child has diphtheria. There will be little chance for him if it is."

"The older child, Maureen, cannot be more than ten, at the most. She seems to be carrying the whole family. Anyway, I have sent the mother to bed for a rest and left Eve there for the day to give the lass some help."

"The baby needs to be in the hospital."

"The mother will not hear of it. Her belief is people only go to hospital to die."

George wiped his hair from his forehead and sighed.

"She may very well be right there."

"So, how did you go with the new patient? It should be nice to have a patient who can pay for services rendered."

George laughed.

"Rubbing shoulders with the elite in town you mean? I nearly forgot to leave the bill." George opened his bag and took out items for cleaning. "The man has bad gout. From what I can gather he has refused to listen to the advice given to him by two other physicians. It is why he asked, or should I say, demanded, I go to see him. You know, the new doctor in town."

Abigail smiled. "Yes, his note was rather abrupt. Will he listen to you, do you think?"

"Most likely not; he was drinking his rum and eating all the wrong foods when I was shown into the man's rooms." George shrugged his shoulders and grimaced. "He made a rather snide remark on the fact I have been looking after many of the poorer people of the district. In his opinion, I shouldn't be visiting the lower classes and then walk into the home of an upper-class family."

"Oh, he sounds just like Papa. Don't listen to him, George. You are a wonderful and good person. Now, I must go and feed young Henry. Jane must have everything under control as he cannot be heard exercising his lungs."

Abigail was halfway through the doorway when George called, "By the way, I saw Millie at The Rest this morning. She wants us over for dinner on Sunday morning after church. I accepted on our behalf. I do hope it suits you."

"I look forward to seeing Millie and Sarah again. They are good people. I have not seen them since Sarah's brothers went to sea with Millie's friend. What was the name of his ship? The *Northern Orchid*, I think; or was it, *Flower*?"

CHAPTER SIX

FANTASY

Jane sat at his desk. A shiver ran down her spine. How she loved these mornings; particularly when they were here together; alone. Eve was busy in the kitchen. Saturday was baking day. It was most unlikely Eve would emerge before lunchtime. Abigail had taken Henry, in the pram, for a walk to visit Millie and Sarah at The Mariner's Rest Hotel. Thomas was away sketching at the river.

She pressed her back into the polished wooden slats of his chair. She wiggled herself into the well-padded cushion she had made for Doctor George with her own hands. Only the best of the hens' feathers was chosen to fill the bag. Her finest work was incorporated in the complicated crochet design of its cover.

Jane leant forward to ensure the account book was opened at the correct page, the ink well was full, the pen held a new nib and a thick wad of blotter was on hand. Her heart beat faster when his footsteps approached down the hallway.

"Good morning. Sorry to keep you waiting, Jane. I'll be with you in a moment. I need to get my daily-record book."

"Good morning, Doctor George. No rush, I was just catching up on a few other things."

George dragged the patient's footstool closer to the desk and sat near Jane. Her heart stopped beating for a brief moment. The panting of her breath sounded loud in her ears. Beside her, George opened his small notebook. From the corner of her eye, she watched as his slim finger traced down the pages looking for the beginning of the current week. He sat up straight when he found what he was looking for.

"I'll just go through these entries with you, Jane, to ensure you understand my writing and the abbreviations or medical terms I have used."

She did not know why he insisted on this routine each Saturday morning. She knew every stroke of his writing no matter how abbreviated. And there was always the dictionary available to help with medical terms he may have used. She had no intention of reminding him of these facts. Why should she deny herself these delicious moments?

His dulcet baritone voice washed over her while, surreptitiously, her eyes explored every facet of his profile. The pale freckled skin of his face which reddened on a summer day despite his always wearing a hat. Ginger curls twisted over his collar. It was nearly time for a haircut again. No doubt, Thomas would see to it, soon. Why didn't he ask her to cut his hair? She cared for her own hair, as well as Eve's and Abigail's hair quite splendidly; even if she did say so herself. Dark circles rimmed his deep green eyes. This worried her. Too much work and too many late nights reading the medical literature, when he was not out on a call.

His soft lips laughed so readily. The same lips tightened in anger when an injustice was done. Those very lips struggled to contain emotion at a heartbreaking event. With her pale fingertips, she outlined her own lips. What would George's soft lips feel like upon her own? She felt a fire smouldering in the hollow of her neck.

He turned briefly to smile as he made a comment on a patient. The dimple in his left cheek twinkled like a star; popping in and out of sight. Her heart raced. Her breathing came in short, sharp gasps. A flush crawled up her neck, engulfing her face before disappearing within the blond waves at the hairline.

"…I've put this arrow here to show where I called into the apothecary for medication for the man…" George turned his face toward Jane to see she understood.

Jane descended into the ocean depths of his eyes. A small squeak escaped her parted pink lips. Silken whips of fire flicked through her chest stirring her heart to greater speed. This searing heat stole the breath from her body. Strands of fire churned and tumbled within her stomach before a ball of flame drifted down to her very core. The internal heat throbbed with sweet pain.

"Jane, are you feeling alright? You are quite flushed. You look like you may have a fever." His hand reached up and touched her forehead. "Hmm, warm but not overly hot. Maybe you are just sickening for something."

Those long fingers slipped around her wrist. Her heart thudded within her chest. The colour faded from her face. Speech was impossible. She sighed.

Black silence enveloped her like night engulfs all. She gave herself up to the warm softness. With a groan, dredged up from the ball of fire within, her head sank onto the desk. Her arm collapsed upon the inkwell.

"Creeping cadavers; Jane, what's wrong?" George jumped up.

The stool skated across the floor. With fumbling fingers, he took up the blotter and attempted to confine the flood of ink. His other hand reapplied itself to Jane's wrist. A small frown sat upon his forehead as he concentrated on the rate and quality of her pulse. Once satisfied Jane was in no imminent danger, he ran to the door and called down the hallway.

"Eve! Eve! Drop what you are doing. Come quickly."

With gentle arms, he gathered Jane up from the chair. He was pleased to hear Eve's footsteps running through the hallway.

"Oh," she cried as she swung into the room. "What's happened. What can I do to help?"

"Thanks, Eve, Jane's fainted. Can you support her arms for me so they don't get hurt? We'll rest her on the couch."

Jane's body lay limp and unmoving on the medical couch in the surgery room. Her flushed face of earlier, now ashen grey. Her pulse still thready.

"Eve, get a wet cloth and wipe her face, will you? I'll get the smelling salts." George reached for his bag and tossed things out onto the bench before he turned with a small clear vial in his hand. He released the stopper and placed the bottle under Jane's nose.

Almost immediately, Jane began coughing vigorously before drawing in long screeching breaths. Her face developed a bluish tinge. After some moments, she lay quietly, breathing normally, her eyes shut. As full consciousness returned, so did the memory of the events prior to her fit of the vapours. Again, her face flamed red before fading to a dull pink.

"Eve, will you sit with Jane? Don't let her get up. I presume Thomas is not back, yet."

"No, he wasn't back when I took the biscuits out of the oven."

"I'm going to harness the horse and buggy and go down to The Rest. I'll bring Abigail and Henry back."

Abigail nestled Henry on her lap as the horse trotted back to the surgery. The perambulator bounced precariously across the buggy beside her. She had been most shocked to think Jane was unwell.

"Tell me again what happened, George."

George repeated the story of Jane's collapse before he passed his opinion.

"I think she may be in the early stages of a fever. She had a flush but her temperature was only raised a little."

Later, Abigail spoke with Jane who now lay in her darkened room. Once Abigail was assured there was no serious medical issue to contend with, a faint sparkle stirred in her eyes. She may have done her practical medical classes vicariously through feedback from George but she had studied every textbook available. She was convinced Jane's ailment was not of the physical kind. A worm of suspicion weaved throughout the convolutions of her brain. Was Jane enamoured with her brother? Abigail knew if so, her friend, Jane, was never going to have her love requited. How sad for her.

CHAPTER SEVEN

THE STORM

George and Thomas halted the horse and sulky at the entrance gate to the tallow factory.

George rubbed his nose. "Whew, what a stink? Have pity on the poor wretches who have to live near this stench day in and day out, Thomas."

A man in dark trousers and a white shirt rolled up to the elbows ran out from the front door of the office.

"Are you the doctor? I've been told to take you straight down to the boiler room."

George heaved his bag out of the sulky and trotted along beside their guide.

"Come on, Thomas. I may need your help." He turned his attention back to the office worker. "Do you know what happened?"

"Not really, Doctor. I work in the office only. They just told me a bloke had fallen into the boiler. You'd think he should be dead."

As they entered the long building, with its rusted corrugated cladding, they ran into a wall of thick pungent heat which nearly knocked them over. The next things to overwhelm them were the smoke and the noise. Huge vats were lined up along both sides of the building. At the base of each vat, a fire roared pouring out wood smoke. Foul-smelling clouds of steam emanated from the vats. Everything was coated in a layer of fat. George did not have time to take in anything else.

Beside one of the vats, lay a rotund man lying in a foetal position. He was obviously in serious trouble. His whole body twitched repeatedly. Short sharp breaths puffed his cheeks but his eyes were sealed with burning-hot fat. His face was swollen to three times its normal size. The scalding mixture had pasted the man's tattered shirt and trousers to his skin. Occasional groans were generated from deep within his chest. George's face remained passive but inside himself, he was horrified at the scene.

George selected a small glass syringe, a sharpened needle and a glass vial marked MORPHINE from his bag and began to draw up a dose of the pain killer.

"I need several buckets of cool water." He turned his head and spoke to the office worker. Men began to bustle about to address the doctor's request. George looked up from his position on his knees beside the victim to where Thomas was standing quietly. "We'll need to remove what we can of this fat and then cool the little bit of skin he has left." George once more turned back to the office employer.

"Can you lay your hands on a clean sheet or some large clean cloth to wrap the poor fellow in?"

Men rushed in with the water buckets. These they lined up in a row. George opened his bag and poured some iodine into the first bucket. With cotton cloths, he began to swab the eyes. Thomas knelt on the other side of the recumbent form and washed down the remainder of the body. When the clothing broke away with tissue attached, he ceased sponging and poured the liquid over the area.

"We'll take him to the hospital in the sulky, Thomas. By the time the hospital sends their yardman, with the horse and dray, all the way from the north side of the river to here, we'll have him delivered to the hospital and in a clean bed." George turned to speak to the circle of onlookers. "I need something on which to carry the man to my sulky; something like a door, perhaps." The men looked vaguely at each other for a few minutes then one man grabbed his mate's arm.

"I've got just the thing, come on Sam." They turned and raced away.

The wild wind drove the rain against the front window near which Abigail sat in the gloom finishing Henry's midday feed. She rubbed his back as she held him against her shoulder. George did say he'd be back for his dinner but the clock on the mantelpiece was fast approaching one o'clock. Hopefully, he had not run afoul of this dreadful storm. A loud crack, like that of a cannon firing, made her jump. The baby roared his protest with renewed energy. She watched as a branch of the gum tree near the front fence snapped off and crashed to the ground.

"There, there pet. There's nothing to get upset about. Hush little one."

Gradually the baby quietened. Jane came running into the room. The swish of her petticoats made more noise than her light feet. She pulled up suddenly as soon as she noticed the child settling to sleep.

"Abigail, are you all right? What was the terrible noise outside? Eve has gone out to investigate," she whispered.

"It's alright, Jane. It was a branch from the gum tree near the front fence. I saw it snap and fall, from here."

Jane watched with fondness as Henry was placed gently in his perambulator. Abigail moved the wheels ever so slowly backwards and forwards.

"Abigail, I do wish the men were back. Do you think they will be safe out in the raging storm?"

Abigail pulled the mosquito-proof muslin over the perambulator frame and walked out into the hallway.

"I don't think there is too much cause for worry, Jane. Both George and Thomas are resourceful men. I'm sure they have stopped off somewhere to ride out the storm, under cover."

The sound of voices drew Jane and Abigail towards the kitchen.

"There you are, that will be them now," said Abigail as she opened the door to allow Jane to enter first. Both ladies were surprised to find Eve's company was not the menfolk but young Maureen Ryan.

"There you are, Miss Abigail. Young Maureen here, was on her way home from The Mariner's Rest when she was almost struck by the falling branch out the front." Eve rummaged through a draw in the wall cupboard searching for a suitable towel to dry the girl off.

"What on earth was Miss Millie thinking, sending you off in this storm?" Jane led the girl to a chair at the kitchen table. The chair scraped on the floor when Maureen pulled it under her body.

As the young girl took the proffered towel, she said, "Oh, the rain 'ad not started when I left the 'otel. Miss Millie did say I could stay but I wanted to get 'ome. The rain just came down in buckets as I turned into this street. When the tree nearly 'it me I ran inside 'ere. I hope you don't mind. I can go now. It was just a bit of a fright I got."

Abigail took the towel and began to rub the child down briskly.

"You will stay right here until this storm passes." She turned to Eve. "We have plenty of food to share, have we not, Eve?"

A watery late afternoon sun struggled through the receding clouds as Abigail sent Maureen on her way. The girl balanced a pot of soup and an apple pie in her hands.

"Thanks, Miss. I'll bring the pot and plate back to you first thing in the morning; all washed clean too."

Abigail waved to the girl and turned to go back into the house when she heard the crunching of the sulky wheels approaching on the gravel road outside. She ran to greet the men. A sparkling grin lit up her face as Thomas jumped down to open the gate wider and allow George to steer the horse into the yard.

Abigail leapt up onto the seat beside her brother.

"Very ladylike behaviour, Abs." The carbon copy of her grin flashed.

"I am pleased to see you back safe. We were worried about you and Thomas, out in the storm." Abigail reached out her slim hands and took the reins from her brother. She guided the horse to the stable at the back of the building.

George eased back against the seat and rubbed his weary face.

"We had to go to the hospital to deliver a fellow who had fallen into the boiler at the tallow works. It was extremely rough when crossing the river on the ferry to the north side. I thought we were all going to be taking a swim. Anyway, we had not long arrived at the hospital when the sky opened and the rain poured down. We sheltered inside. They even fed us. Mind you the meal left much to be desired."

"How did the patient get on, George?"

"Aah, that was the bad news. The poor devil gasped his last breath just as the wardsmen placed him onto a bed. He had nasty burns around his head and chest and down the left side of his body."

Abigail's face screwed up in horror. "Oh, the poor man, George. He must have been in excruciating pain."

"To be honest, Abby, I think he was past feeling anything when we arrived at the workplace. Now, let's leave the sulky here for Thomas to attend to. We'll go inside. I haven't seen young Henry all day."

"You spoil baby Henry too much. Oh, by the way, a large parcel came for you from Uncle John today. It looks like more medical journals. He is such a dear."

CHAPTER EIGHT

HOSPITAL AUXILIARY

Abigail relaxed back against the padded seat of the sulky. Thomas clicked his tongue at the horse; the signal to walk up. Abigail adjusted her bonnet and held her parasol firmly. Barely ten o'clock and already the day was warming up. Horses snorted and stamped their feet as the passengers and vehicles loaded onto the ferry at Kangaroo Point. With a sharp bump, Abigail, Thomas and their sulky bounced on board where they were instructed to move nearer the coach in front. Thomas stood at the horse's head speaking kind words in a strange language. Abigail listened, letting the calming intonations flow over her also.

This was to be her first meeting with the Brisbane Hospital's Ladies Auxiliary. These volunteer women assisted in raising funds to provide additional necessities for the medical fraternity as well as for the treatment and comfort of the patients. The reputation of Mrs. Granville, the chairwoman, had already reached Abigail's ears, compliments of their washer-woman, Mrs. Beazley. Eve relayed the information onto Abigail who now quailed at the challenge ahead of her. Could she remain cool and calm when in the presence of the one they called the Dragon Lady?

"Whoa," Thomas spoke quietly to the horse as he pulled it to a stop at the front entrance of the hospital. He turned his head to his passenger. "Miss Abigail, remember these people need to be grateful to have such an educated woman as yourself offer them assistance."

"Thanks, Thomas. I'm not too sure they'll see things that way; especially when I propose we work towards funds to purchase the equipment George recommended for the emergency department."

"Well, fingers crossed. One thing is for sure, you will have a better chance than George would have if he were in your shoes. You know how impatient he can be when others can't see what he can see."

"Ah, you must be Mrs. Baldwin."

Abigail looked up to see a tall well-dressed lady bearing down upon her. The woman's narrow face with its prominent nose and long dark eyelashes reminded her of a horse she rode as a girl. It had the alarming habit of taking the bit in its teeth and charging forth.

"Er ... yes, I am Abigail Baldwin."

"Mrs. Granville; how do you do? It would be preferable if you drove your vehicle around to the side of the building to alight, in future. We do not want to block up the emergency entrance in any way."

"So sorry; of course." Abigail made a mental note for future reference.

"I believe you are the sister of Doctor Goldfinch." Mrs. Granville favoured Abigail with a penetrating green-eyed stare.

"Doctor Goldfinch is my brother, yes." Abigail tried to return the unwavering gaze.

"It has been reported you accompany your brother on his rounds and even offer opinions on the patient's treatment." The woman almost sniffed down her nose at Abigail.

"I do think the rumour mill has rather over-exaggerated, Mrs. Granville." Abigail bit her tongue on what she felt like adding to the statement. "I merely offer a woman's perspective particularly when dealing with female patients. The doctor makes all diagnoses."

"I am sure my husband will be relieved when I tell him. We, in Australia, are working towards registering our medical profession. Melbourne University has already begun a degree for doctors and Sydney is not far behind. We do not want uneducated people thinking they have the knowledge of a doctor. There is enough of such goings-on, out in less civilized areas. As a newcomer to this country, you should understand that right away." The woman paused for breath.

Abigail took several deep slow breaths herself as she struggled to remember what her goal here was today. She spoke quietly.

"Of course, Mrs. Granville. Your husband is the Visiting Surgeon, I understand."

"Yes, that is correct. Mr. Granville has a responsible position and he takes his responsibility very seriously. My father is the President of the Hospital Committee."

Inwardly Abigail sighed. This was going to be worse than she thought.

"Of course."

"Come." Mrs. Granville swung around to lead off through the nether regions of the building.

Meekly, Abigail followed behind. A smile twitched at her mouth as she imagined an invisible bow wave preceding her guide. Without knocking, the leader opened a heavy polished timber door and entered. Abigail discovered an airy room with a large polished table in the centre.

"This is the hospital board room." Mrs. Granville motioned Abigail forward to meet the four ladies sitting in the chairs grouped at one end. The chairwoman made the introductions as she took her seat at the head of the table. She produced a hard-bound book from her basket and placed it open in front of her. Abigail seated herself at the edge of the group.

As the meeting proceeded, Abigail said little and listened a lot. It soon became obvious the only opinion going to be heeded was Mrs. Granville's. Abigail kept her eyes open but her thoughts, like butterflies, fluttered over the heads of the women present. Mrs. Markham, with a face not unlike that of a lap dog, surrounded by a cloud of blonde curls, sat on the right of Mrs. Granville. A lead pencil was used to write in a book, similar to the one owned by Mrs. Granville, lying on the table in front of her. At every pause in Mrs. Granville's spiel, Mrs. Markham nodded and commented on what a good idea it all was. To the left of Mrs. Granville sat Mrs. Bullock. Hers was a squarer face; possibly likened to a bulldog. She certainly dug her heels in at everything Mrs. Granville said and had a differing opinion on every issue. Mrs. Olsen and Mrs. McLean were sitting beside Mrs. Markham and Mrs. Bullock respectively and appeared to follow the lead of the woman beside them. How could anything be achieved with this sort of dynamic? Had Abigail been invited to join the committee to break the deadlock or was it to allow Mrs. Granville to keep an eye on her activities?

When it looked like Mrs. Granville might be running out of steam, Abigail made a suggestion of her own. The only individual suggestion, besides Mrs. Granville's, made during the morning's session.

"Mrs. Granville, you were talking earlier of the work being done to improve the professionalism in the medical fraternity in Australia. This is admirable. You, no doubt, will be an advocate of Doctor Joseph Lister. You asked for ideas on ways to distribute the funds raised from this year's fete. Perhaps we might be able to take a leaf out of Doctor Lister's book and provide more accessible hand-washing facilities in the building. This will benefit the doctors and nurses tremendously but will also go a long way to improving the hygiene for the patients. Doctor Lister has written several papers on the reduction in the incidence of puerperal fever in women after childbirth using simple hand-washing. He has already discovered a reduction in wound infections by using antiseptic carbolic acid spray within his operating theatre."

Silence hung on the air. All eyes turned towards Abigail. Mrs. Granville's mouth opened and closed. The lapdog beside her pursed her lips to make a silent "Oooh". The bulldog hid a triumphant smile behind her hand-held fan. Mrs. McLean and Mrs. Olsen kept their eyes glued on the hands in their laps. Abigail felt her heart begin to beat faster. Had she spoken too soon? Should she have waited until a later meeting? Did this mean she was going to be kicked out of the group before she was even in it?

With a noisy inhalation, Mrs. Granville prepared to speak. She pinned Abigail to the chair with piercing eyes.

"Mrs. Baldwin, it is unusual for newcomers to offer advice at these meetings. Given you have obviously read of this Doctor Lister's work, the subject may be worthy of further investigation. I will consult with my husband and my father on this issue." She shut her book with a slam. "I now declare this meeting closed."

Abigail walked out into the sunlight lifting her parasol over her head. She took a slow deep breath before mumbling.

"What a waste of a good morning, I think."

"Aah!" Eve grumbled. The surgery doorbell rang at the same time as she singed her finger on the edge of the biscuit tray while lifting it out of the oven.

"I'll get it," called Jane, on her way past the kitchen door. Saturday again; Doctor George would want to go over the accounts with her. A flush infused her face at the recollection of when last she worked on the accounts with Doctor George. She cringed at the thought. In silence, she vowed never to let her body betray her again.

The doorbell rang for the second time.

"I'm coming." As Jane drew the door open, the sun burst into the waiting area along with a short man with sun-hardened skin and long unkempt hair. Rope cord held up his trousers and his right hand held a stained felt hat by his side. He wiped his worn boots on the mat at the doorway. When he spoke, his Irish brogue brightened the room even further.

"Good day to you, Miss. Would the doctor be in at all now?"

"Good morning, Sir, may I ask your name and what you wish to see the doctor about?"

"Yes, Miss, I'm Bert Ryan. I believe Doctor George cared for me family recently. I's away fossicking. I owe 'im some money, I'm thinking. I'll fix the account and thank 'im for 'is care of the baby who 'ad the croup bad."

"Yes, Mr. Ryan. I'll just call the doctor for you."

Almost immediately, Doctor George poked his head out of the office doorway.

"Mr. Ryan, please, come on in."

Not wanting to miss a word of this conversation, Jane followed Mr. Ryan through the open doorway. She made herself inconspicuous at the bench where her nimble fingers began rolling bandages from a considerable pile just back from the wash-house. A shiver ran down her spine as the doctor's deep voice offered his sympathies for the loss of the baby.

"There was little I could do, really. Mrs. Ryan did not want to have the child die in the hospital."

A calloused hand ran across the shorter man's wrinkled forehead.

"Neither of us 'old much store by the 'ospitals; no offence meant. I understand your good sister and a young lady, Eve, visited. They 'elped out when things were really bad."

"Yes, Bert; my sister, Mrs. Baldwin and her maid, Eve, helped your wife cope through some hard days."

"And I understand they were kind to me eldest lass, Maureen, when she was caught in a storm too. Can yer pass on me thanks to them both and I'd like to fix yer up for what I owe? It's not been too bad a year. I've been working the gold around the Rockhampton area."

Doctor George looked up at Jane who quickly dropped her eyes back to the work at hand.

"Jane, will you look up Mr. Ryan's account, please?" While Jane proceeded to open the ledger on the office desk, George's attention returned to his visitor. "So, are you away working the gold often, Bert?"

"Aye, Doc. I try to get 'ome at least once a year. It all depends 'ow lucky I've been. Mostly I just fossick around with a few mates. I like to get in on a new strike early and stay only while the gold is making a useful showing. Then it's time to move on to the next promising area."

"How long are you planning on being in town this time?"

"Not too much longer, I shouldn't think. Next trip, I'll be 'eading up to Maryborough. Me mate drove some cattle through the backcountry there a few year ago and 'e reckons there's some 'ills south of there that's worth a look."

Bert Ryan handed over the several coins Jane requested before shaking the doctor's hand.

"I may be a wanderer Doc but I always pay me bills as soon as I 'ave the wherewithal."

"Thanks, Bert. Best of luck with your next venture." George led the way to the front door and let Mr. Ryan out. The doctor stood for some time watching as the man walked down the path and out through the garden gate.

He sighed and shook his head as he re-entered the office.

"You know, Jane, people can really surprise you at times. At first glance of Mr. Ryan, one might be tempted to pass him off as a hopeless case, yet he obviously works hard and he has principles."

Jane smiled; trust her Doctor George to find the best in people.

CHAPTER NINE

REALITIES

"You're not trying to do too much are you, Abigail?" Doctor George asked his sister as she lay the baby in the cot after feeding. "You have dark circles under your eyes this morning."

"Are you asking as my doctor or as my brother?"

"Both, I guess."

"As my brother, you should know it is not the gentlemanly thing to do to make disparaging remarks about a lady's looks. As my doctor, it is only allowed; within reason."

"Sorry, I'm just worried."

"Thanks, George, but how can I be doing too much? All I am is the milch cow for Henry. Jane and Eve hover over the child just waiting to entertain him when he so much as blinks. My meals await me, whether I'm hungry or not. Our washing is collected and returned clean and folded each day. This baby is the luckiest one in the whole world with three mothers and a doting uncle. I might add, even Thomas likes to take any opportunity to placate the little fellow. All I have to do is laze about, read books and poke my nose into your business. Talking of which, I don't suppose you've heard from the hospital board regarding your suggestions for the washbasins required to meet Doctor Lister's recommendations."

George ran his fingers through his hair and sighed. The ginger curls sprung back immediately.

"Ah, yes, the esteemed chairman collared me last night while I was up at the hospital visiting a patient. His daughter is the one you spoke of; Mrs. Granville. He explained that, while they agree there is merit in what the Doctors Lister, Holmes and Semmelweis advocate, they have the Prince's planned visit happening next year. The visit must take top priority and any monies collected by the Ladies Auxiliary will be put towards improving the gardens for the Prince's enjoyment."

Abigail threw her hands up into the air.

George smiled.

"Abigail, did you know currently, the water is brought into the hospital in barrels. The Board is, at the moment, in the process of seeking funds to lay water pipes. Patience, Abby. What is it Mother is always saying; 'make haste slowly'? Apparently, things are much better now than they were before the new hospital was built here last year."

"I shudder at the thought." Abigail stood up and took her brother's elbow. "Come, we'll go and have breakfast before it's time for you to open the surgery."

George had barely swallowed two spoons full of porridge when a pounding on the surgery door had the house trembling.

"Doctor! Doctor! Are you there?"

George looked up from his bowl. His eyes met those of his sister.

"Another gentle start to the day, I see." He jumped up, collecting his coat from the back of his chair as he did so and headed to the front door.

A well-dressed man almost fell through the door as George pulled it open. The doctor reached out to steady him.

"I'm Doctor Goldfinch. Can I help you?"

"Please, come quick; to the top of the street. Some poor fellow is under his overturned dray and the horse is going berserk. There is blood everywhere. I have my sulky here. I'll take you."

George called down the hallway. "Abigail!"

Her head popped out through the dining room doorway.

"Call Thomas and have him bring the horse and sulky. I'll be at an accident at the top of the street. By the sound of it, I'll be needing his muscles. I'm going ahead with this gentleman." He ran into the surgery from where he collected his black bag and hat.

The squeal of a horse in pain caught Doctor George's attention at about the same time he noticed a crowd gathered on the street. When his companion pulled the vehicle to a stop, George jumped out, taking his medical bag with him. He pushed his way through the onlookers. As the scene opened up to him, he stood stunned for a short moment.

A bay horse lay on its side tangled in the harness and shafts of a dray in disarray at the animal's back legs. The large head, with the whites of its eyes staring out on the world, beat a rhythm on the roadway each time the horse lifted its neck to scream out its fear and pain. The broken bone, sticking out through the skin of the horse's upper back leg, pointed to the sky. The ends of the bone twitched in rhythm with the muscle spasms of the controlling hip. The thud, thud of the hoof of the other back leg belting into the front board of the dray resonated through the ground. The front two legs of the animal had been caught up in a broken horse collar and harness which restricted their movement to a few short inches. This was fortuitous for the man lying unconscious on the ground. His head rested against the horse's belly. His body lay stretched out. His right leg was held under the edge of the dray. Every time the horse moved the dray grated on the wound exacerbating the damage. The horse's broken back leg held no threat. The hoof striking the dray did not have the reach to harm the man either, caught up in harness leather, as it was.

One could see at a glance, the man's leg under the dray was fractured. Blood ran profusely into the soil while the man's foot lay at a right angle to his leg. A distinct dark mark of a hoof print could be seen on the man's pale forehead.

A bellow drew George's attention to the head of the horse where a large man wielded the biggest sledge-hammer George had ever seen. It came down with a horrendous crunch which was destined to echo in George's head for a long time to come. Blood, bone and brain sprayed out in all directions. Quick reflexes had him drop his head. Only a small amount of the debris was taken on his face. On the other hand, his hat looked like it had been lifted off the floor of an abattoir. The horse shuddered and lay still.

"Had to put the poor thing out of its misery. I couldn't listen to its suffering any longer." The man set the hammer-head on the road and rested on its handle with his face bowed.

A curse in the Egyptian language lifted George's spirits. He was glad to hear the whisper of Thomas in his ear.

"What can I do?"

George breathed deeply, putting the scene out of his mind. He concentrated on the medical situation in front of him.

"Can you and the big man with the hammer lift this dray up off the fellow's broken leg. Prop it up securely, I don't want it falling on us while we try to get him out of there." George ran his fingers over the man's body looking for further injuries.

Splintered wood slabs fell to the ground and the timbers creaked as the dray was lifted and shifted with the assistance of several willing men.

"Thomas, ask the man to break off some timber for me to use as a narrow support for this broken leg. While he is at it, have him take the backboard off the dray. We'll use it to carry the fellow on when we transport him to the hospital."

Long gentle fingers dressed the leg wound compressing the torn capillaries. With Thomas's help, George placed the short narrow board under the right leg and used strips of cloth to hold the limb in place.

"It will be a blessing for the man if he remains unconscious until we can deliver him to the hospital. He will be in excruciating pain when he wakes up."

George and Thomas were hunched over their patient when Ned, the yardman from The Mariner's Rest, squatted down beside them.

"Is there anything I can do to help?"

"Ned, you may be an angel in disguise. Do you think Miss Millie will let us have a loan of her dray to take this man to the hospital? He might travel more comfortably in the dray instead of my sulky."

"It'll be no trouble. I'm heading over the river myself. I only stopped off to see what's going on. I'll give youse a hand to put him on board."

It was well after midday when George walked back into his surgery. Abigail was in the middle of re-dressing a patient's leg ulcer. She finished the job smartly and asked Jane to take care of the account before rushing into the room next door.

"Well, what happened? You've been gone for ages. Billy Toe-bite was here a while ago. He said there was a terrible accident up the road. You look exhausted. I'll tell Eve to bring in a cup of tea."

"Thanks, Abby, and something to eat; I'm famished."

Two days later, when Eve rose from her haunches in front of the oven, she sighed. The scones were in cooking at last. Miss Abigail always said her scones were the best she'd ever tasted. Nothing could go wrong now. Everything was under control for the morning tea. Miss Abigail and Miss Jane were having Miss Millie, from The

Mariner's Rest Hotel to visit. Eve turned to collect the bowl and wooden spoon off the table and placed them into the tub to soak. Once more she peeped under the tented-muslin covering her tea-cake. Even old Mrs. Goldfinch would have to say it was good.

Miss Jane's soft footsteps were not heard until she entered the kitchen.

"Oh, Eve. How did the tea-cake turn out? Are the scones in the oven yet? Miss Millie will be here at any moment." Jane moved to lift the muslin cloth protecting the cake when her hand froze. She gave a strangled squeak.

Eve looked up from the bench to see what had happened. She watched mystified as the gentle face of Miss Jane transformed into a picture of horror. Eve followed the gaze of the staring eyes. She caught her own breath. A large brown snake undulated along the skirting board of the kitchen cupboard; less than a yard distance from her own feet.

A soft tap at the door went unnoticed.

"Hello, I did knock outside but no one answered and the door was open. I came right in; I hope you don't mind." Miss Millie stood at the doorway with a wide smile which disappeared in an instant. "Oh, I see you already have a visitor." Without another word, she snatched up the wooden broom leaning on the wall near the door. With two light steps, which belied her years, she moved towards the reptile and slammed the broom-head down firmly, on the snake's neck. She pressed down hard on her weapon. The body of the snake twisted and twined around the broom handle appearing to tie itself into a large knot. "Eve, go and get a shovel, be as quick as you can. This broom is not going to hold the snake for too long. It's already trying to wriggle its way to freedom."

Eve bolted through the back doorway and over to the shed where the tools were kept. She returned carrying a shovel with its long handle towering over her head.

"Eve, slip the blade in behind the broom and press down as hard as you can," Miss Millie continued her instructions.

While the shovel was held in place by a strength born of fright, the snake's writhing body wound itself around the shovel handle also.

"It won't reach me, Miss Millie, will it?" Eve's usually steady voice shook.

"No, dear, as long as you keep a tight hold on its neck it cannot bite you." While she was talking, Miss Millie walked to the wood box near the stove and selected a stout stick. She used this to whack at the head of the snake with frenzied strokes. "I do hate these things; they give me the creeps." As the reptile's head disintegrated under the barrage, Miss Millie told Eve she could release her hold and take the thing outside where the men could dispose of it.

"But, Miss Millie, it's still alive; it's still wiggling."

"No, Eve, it's like a chook when you cut its head off; it flaps about for a bit. Same thing happens with a snake."

Determined not to touch the reptile with her hands, Eve used Miss Millie's bloodied stick to drape the slippery carcass over the shovel. Holding it out well in front of her body, Eve carried the remains outside. She came back in a rush.

"Oh no, the scones; we forgot the scones." Eve grabbed the towel and bent to open the oven. She coughed as black smoke billowed out into her face.

"Not to worry, Eve, you have a lovely tea-cake right here. We can have scones next time. Now, can I help you make the tea?" Miss Millie offered.

CHAPTER TEN

PLAN TO EXPAND

Abigail dug out the last of the poultice from the warm bowl with her metal spatula. The cough rattled in the man's chest as she painted the foul mixture in a thick layer across his thorax. Eve entered the room bringing another bowl. Squares of torn cotton material soaked in the hot water within.

"Thanks, Eve." Abigail took up the second bowl and squeezed out each individual cloth before laying it over the poultice.

Holding her breath and screwing up her nose, Eve picked up the first bowl and retreated back to the kitchen.

"The smell of this alone would chase away any cough, you'd think."

The two ladies smiled together. The patient struggled to breathe as he suffered another spasm of coughing. The colours in his face flowed from a red flush to a mottled blue before returning to a flushed red.

"Thanks, Missy," he whispered.

"You try and rest while the poultice does its work, Mr. Gordon. I'll just be close by if you want anything."

As Abigail fed baby Henry at the doorway of her dark room, she enjoyed the restfulness of the shadowy moonlight dancing through the trees accompanied by the soft music of the soughing branches in the light sea breeze.

"Hi, Abs, Can I sit down here on the verandah?" Her brother appeared out of the darkness on silent feet.

Abigail lifted the privacy cover over her chest and the baby. She smiled at her brother; not that George would have noticed in the scant light.

"George, is everything alright?"

George settled his back against the verandah post. He slapped at the few mosquitoes searching any exposed flesh, hungry for blood.

"Yes, yes, Abby; well, better than alright, I think. If you agree, that is."

"You are in a dither, dear brother. What news? I'd like to hear."

"I've been given the nod. There will be no objections if we apply to set up a two-room hospital here for non-serious patients. Old Doctor MacDonald used to have a similar set-up here in his day, I understand. It will be very convenient for the people living on the south side at those times when the river rises and there's no way across to the Brisbane Hospital. I was hoping you'd see your way clear to agree to such an arrangement. You know, there are the two spare rooms in my wing of the house. Thomas and I can get rid of our belongings in there. What do you think?" George stopped to take a breath giving Abigail a chance to answer.

"In principle, I think it is a wonderful plan. Take today, for instance. I had poor Mr. Gordon lying for hours on our uncomfortable patient-couch while his chest poultice set. A more comfortable bed is really what the poor man needed. We could bring in birthing mothers whom we anticipate may have difficulties, too? But what of you and Thomas? Will you have enough space with only the two rooms?"

"I thought Thomas might build an annexe off the end of our wing. When we come back at night, after late calls, we can make supper there, without disturbing the whole house. How do you think Jane and Eve will take this arrangement?"

Henry finished his feed. Abigail rose to settle him in his cot while she thought about her friends and about what she had been told, before answering.

"Jane will not be disturbed at all. Her room is at the far end of this wing. She has little to do, physically, with the patients anyway." Abigail stood with her back against the doorframe enjoying the evening air while considering their plans. "Eve enjoys helping with the patients when needed. The girl seems to have a natural nursing instinct. If her workload becomes too much, we can bring in young Maureen Ryan more often. Her family will be glad of any extra money. George, I'm sure your idea will be received with goodwill."

"Great, I'll set the paperwork into motion tomorrow morning. Thomas can start scrubbing the rooms. When you have a day free, we'll go over to town to look for furniture?"

"Sounds exciting. Henry doesn't think so, though. Listen, he is snoring." Abigail fussed at the muslin netting over the cot. "I'm about to make a warm milk drink for myself. Do you want to join me, we can discuss this further?"

They could have done with their patient beds late the same night when three shirtless young men, all unsteady on their feet, half carried, half dragged a fourth lad into the surgery. A small river of blood drizzled onto the floor from a leg wrapped in the torn-up shirts of the assistants. The wounded boy's face was grey, his eyes were closed, cold sweat stood out on his forehead. Under his touch, George found a thready pulse.

On the office couch, George, with Thomas's help, removed the temporary bandages and exposed a horrific wound. It ran from the boy's left groin, down the side of his knee and into his calf. With delicate pliers, designed for the purpose, George caught the larger lacerated arteries and proceeded to tie catgut knots around the pumping vessels. With the danger of the lad bleeding-out removed, clean rags were used to dislodge the blood and mud from the wound, allowing closer inspection. He found it almost impossible to believe there appeared to be no obvious major damage to the many nerves in the area. Several muscles were going to need repair before he could close the external wound.

"How on earth did this happen?" But George was talking to himself and Thomas only. The patient's three friends were out in the garden nourishing the plants. It was no good asking the patient who slipped in and out of consciousness. George turned to Thomas and sighed. "I'll give him a dose of morphine and then let's get this repaired while the boy is unable to feel what we have in store for him."

With her dressing gown thrown loosely about her shoulders and her bed cap sitting askew on her head, Abigail made an appearance.

"Goodness me, what have you two been up to here?"

George put the final touches to the last of the skin stitches. The lad groaned while Thomas held him as still as he could.

"Not too sure yet." George's focus never left his work. "Abigail, can you put your hand on the bottle of carbolic acid which arrived last week? Will you mix up a suitable strength for a wound dressing? You'll find the *Lancet* with Lister's article in the desk drawer. It has his recommendations for the mixtures, in it."

George looked up to where Thomas sat lightly holding the semi-conscious patient.

"Thomas, poke your head out of the front door and see if the three young men are still waiting. If so, bring them inside. I need to know what has happened here."

George finished his work with a flourish. He watched as Abigail painted the carbolic mixture onto several linen dressings. He took each one and placed them along the length of the wound before padding it with more clean linen and cotton bandages.

As Abigail turned to go, George called after her. "Any chance of a pot of tea?"

"Yes, of course, George." She looked into the waiting area on her return to the kitchen. "Would you gentlemen like a cup of tea?"

In unison, they replied with a grateful thank you.

"You too, Thomas?"

"Please, Miss Abigail."

Abigail helped the now-awake but weak patient to drink a strong cup of black tea as he lay awkwardly on the couch.

"So, boys, how did this happen?" George noted the colour had returned to their faces. They seemed to have recovered from the shock.

An uneasy look, maybe even a guilty look, passed from one to the other. At last, it was the one who appeared to be the oldest, who began to talk.

"Alf; his name's Alfred Archer. He had some debts; women, gambling and opium. He did not want his parents to know but he could not repay on his own. Satan, from the House of Thrills, had warned him; more than once, which is generous for him. Tonight, Satan sent his thugs to show Alf he wanted payment and he wasn't joking. When we arrived at the club, we found him laying out on the road like this."

George shook his head.

"He's lucky to be alive. Five more minutes may have been the end for him. It's too late to send him to the hospital tonight. We'll keep him here until morning. You are to go and tell his parents, immediately. They may wish to come and reassure themselves he is safe. We can decide what to do with him in the daylight."

Abigail commenced cleaning up as the group shuffled out of the front doorway, George turned to Thomas.

"Bring in the spare stretcher for the boy, Thomas, please. It'll be more comfortable than the couch. I'll camp on the couch. It's going to be a long night."

Dark circles framed her green eyes. Henry suckled contentedly on the breast. Early dawn seeped into the garden, encouraging the coloured parrots' morning squabble and the busy willy wagtail's scolding. A magpie sat high in the gum tree serenading her with the pure notes of its song. When Henry had had his fill, Abigail lay him at her shoulder, patting his back lightly. She noticed the gardener, Thumbnail, arrive for work. Tidying herself up, as best she could with one hand, Abigail went out to talk with him about her plans for the day.

Once Thumbnail was out through the gate on his way to the Ryan's residence, Abigail made her way to the wash-house where Mrs. Beazley was in the process of filling the copper with water. A fire was already smoking below the tub.

"Good morning, Mrs. Beazley."

"Oh, Mrs. Baldwin, you've brought the little man to show me. He is lovely." She oohed and aahed and ran a rough finger lightly across the forehead as soft as a horse's muzzle.

Abigail waited for a moment before explaining the previous night's drama to Mrs. Beazley and the extra bloody wash coming her way. She then discussed their plans for two patient rooms at the surgery and the extra workload they may entail.

"If things become too much, we'll employ the additional services of Thumbnail's sister, Sunny, who has washer-woman experience."

Jane stood at the treatment-room door. Her soft blue eyes roamed over George's body asleep on the patient couch. Her finger curled idly around a lock of blond hair at her forehead. The noises from the next room were little more than an unheard whisper. She did not notice the man lying on the stretcher until he moaned. George snorted and sat up with his eyes still shut. With a sudden intake of breath, Jane slipped through into the office before moving on into the spare room. Here she found Thomas removing the curtains while Eve gathered them up with the bedspread for delivery to the wash-house.

"Oh, Miss Jane, good morning. Did you sleep well?" Eve asked with a smile.

"Yes, thanks, Eve. What's happening here?"

Eve went on to tell of the night's adventures and the plans to open, at least, this one room for short term patients today.

"Miss Jane, do you think this pillow has enough stuffing? I have more hen feathers in the store. Do you think I should add more?" Eve nodded her head in the direction of the pillow upon a striped horsehair mattress on the bed. "We'll need the sewing repair kit and a patch for the mattress too."

Jane took up the pillow and punched it with her hand. She held it against her head.

"Eve, I think this will be sufficient. I'll collect the sewing kit from the parlour. Can I do anything about breakfast for everyone?"

Eve turned to make her way out of the door.

"I have the oatmeal on cooking, thanks, Miss Jane. As soon as I deliver these to Mrs. Beazley, I'll prepare breakfast for all of us. Miss Abigail is setting the table at the moment."

CHAPTER ELEVEN

WORKING TOGETHER

Eve held the spoon of clear soup to Alfred Archer's mouth. She watched as his blue-tinged lips moved to slurp in the sustenance. The remainder of his face was as white as Mrs. Beazley's cleaned linen upon which he rested. Morning light filtered through the partially drawn curtain. Maureen Ryan tiptoed into the room; her wide-eyed gaze fixed upon the man with his heavily-bandaged left leg resting up on a pillow. He wore a pair of night trousers belonging to someone a whole lot larger than himself. A flannelette singlet was all he wore to cover his narrow chest. She bent towards Eve's ear.

"I've pulled the oatmeal to the side of the stove like you said. Will I make the pot of tea yet?"

Eve smiled at her willing helper.

"Thanks, Maureen. You should have called me to help. I don't want you getting burnt when trying to lift the heavy pot."

"It's no bother, Miss Eve. I manage to lift the pots around the stove at 'ome."

"You had best make a pot of tea. Miss Abigail likes a cup first thing."

"Will 'e be alright?" Maureen nodded her head towards the patient as she whispered to Eve.

"Of course, Doctor George is the best doctor in town."

George entered the room in a rush. He nearly knocked Maureen over as she left to make her way to the kitchen. He caught her small body with a firm hand.

"Sorry, sorry, child. Did I hurt you?"

"Not at all, Sir. I'm as tough as old leather, me Dad says." Maureen skittered off on her way to fix the breakfast for everyone.

Dark circles ringed George's eyes but his smile was wide as he greeted his first in-house patient. "Good morning, Alf, and how are you this fine morning?"

"Bit sore, Sir; and I'm so tired."

"Yes, well it is to be expected when you get your leg slit from groin to toe. Once you finish Eve's soup, we'll give you something for the pain. In the meantime, we'll leave the wound covered for a few days before we go poking about in it anymore. By the way, I spoke to your parents last night. You'll stay here for a few days. They'll be in to see you later this morning."

Abigail joined Thomas after having been to the wash-house to see if Mrs. Beazley was managing with the extra work-load. They entered the back door of the kitchen together.

"Are you ready to eat, Thomas? I suppose you are hungry after the busy night."

"Starving, Miss Abigail."

Eve was just leaving the dining room having delivered the large tray.

"Thanks, Eve. How did Mr. Archer go with his soup?"

"Good thanks, Miss Abigail. He ate nearly all of it."

George had barely swallowed his last mouthful of tea when a pounding on the front door heralded another call on his services.

Almost ten minutes passed before he returned to the dining room with his medical bag in his hand.

"That was Ned. Miss Millie, from the Mariner's Rest, wants me to call on Jacko as soon as I can. He is very ill with his chest," George informed his sister and Jane. "I'd better not waste any time. Miss Millie does not strike me as someone who would fuss over nothing. I'll just ride the horse and leave Thomas here for the moment; until I see how serious things are."

"Oh dear, poor Millie; Jacko is like a son to her. She must be beside herself. Is there anything further you want to be done about Mr. Archer just yet?"

"No, let him rest. I've just given him a dose of laudanum."

George had been called out three times during the night. It was Abigail who went to follow up on Jacko's condition the next morning. Jane and Henry accompanied her to enjoy a visit with Miss Millie and Sarah. George greeted Abigail and Jane when they returned from The Mariner's Rest at midday.

"How's Jacko this morning?" he asked.

"You would not believe the constitution of the man. He is sitting on his bed impatient to be up and about. I listened to his chest which has improved greatly. I told him he may get up for short periods and not to do any work."

"Fat chance of that I should think." George laughed.

"What have you been doing, George? Did you manage to get a little sleep?" Abigail questioned her brother.

"The policeman was here looking into the attack on Alf Archer. I've just seen him off, along with Alf's parents."

George led the horse and sulky to the stable. Inside the house, they found Eve and young Maureen industriously scrubbing the second patient room.

A banging started up at the north end of the house.

"What is all the noise?" Abigail asked.

"Thomas has made a start on our new room," George replied with a smile. "The timber arrived this morning. Now, do you want to witness the removal of the wound dressing on Alf's leg?"

Abigail followed her brother to the man's bedside.

The following morning's dawn sparkled with the remnants of an overnight shower of rain. Jane stood at the back door breathing in the crisp freshness of the air. The dishes in the kitchen behind her clattered as Eve prepared the breakfast. The sound of a saw slicing through timber tempted her to investigate but she did not wish to intrude in the men's domain. Maybe if she walked over to talk to Mrs. Beazley in the washhouse, she might catch a glimpse of Doctor George at work. Her strategy was unneeded as Abigail came rushing out of the house full of energy.

"Come on, Jane, let's go and see what the men have been up to. Someone has to call them for breakfast; what better excuse for a stickybeak."

Jane did not need a second calling. Arm in arm, the ladies walked through the garden to where the sounds of a hammer on wood filled the air. On turning the corner of the house, they both stopped and stared. The frame of the new room stood like a timber skeleton about six feet from the end door of the house. George bounced over, pleased to have a new audience. Thomas was in close consultation with the carpenter who had volunteered to help out in return for recent services rendered by the doctor.

George explained to the ladies. Within the walls, large push-out wooden windows were to be built. In summer, they'd catch breezes from all directions. In winter, they'd close in tightly for warmth.

Between the back door of the house and the door to this room, they planned to build an arbour for protection, whatever the weather.

"I had no idea Thomas was so talented. It just goes to show you. You can knock about with someone for years and never learn all there is to know about them," he commented.

"Doctor George, you have done a magnificent job here. We've come to call you in for breakfast. Do you think the carpenter would like something too?" Jane's face flushed as she delivered her speech.

"Thanks, Jane. I for one, am starving. The carpenter is on his way to another job so I doubt if he has time to stop."

It was late in the afternoon when Jane returned to the building site with a tea tray for the two men. She caught sight of something which was to bother her thoughts for a long time to come.

The acacia bushes hid her from the view of the men. She in return could see George and Thomas sitting on a window frame leaning in close to each other whispering. They seemed ever so intimate. She did not understand why her heart pounded and her stomach felt like lead or why the tears burnt her eyelids. Her hands began to shake until the teacups rattled. She backed up against the house wall. Her repeated cough was loud. She did not know why she coughed or what troubled her so. Two friends were just talking quietly together, after all; weren't they? When she approached the building site once more, the men were at different ends of their structure working apart in silence.

CHAPTER TWELVE

THE ATTACK

Abigail and Jane stood at the front gate waving as the coach carrying Mr. Archer and young Alf headed off to the Archer home. Abigail's heart warmed as she thought how lucky the young man had been. If they had not used the antiseptic treatment the outcome could have been so much worse. It had been a monstrous wound.

The two women turned to make their way back into the house when the sound of galloping hooves caught their attention.

"It's Ned, the handyman from the hotel." Jane held her hand to her face to reduce the sun's glare.

"Yes, you're right. He seems in a dreadful hurry. I think he's coming here. I do hope there is nothing wrong at the hotel."

Ned leaned into his horse as he rode through the gateway. With the reins held taut in the one hand and the other hand threaded within the mane, he drew the animal to a stop in a cloud of dust. He slid to the ground with an ease many younger men could not have achieved. Prince's heaving sides were wet with sweat. He snorted and stamped his feet.

"Miss Abigail, is Doctor George or Thomas in?" Ned dragged in deep breaths.

Abigail shook her head. "I'm sorry, Ned. They are both out on a call. What's wrong? May I help?"

"Can I just settle Prince inside your stable? I have a message from Miss Millie."

"Of course, Ned. Come on in to the house when you are ready."

Ned sat up to the kitchen table; a pannikin of tea and two buttered scones with jam before him. Miss Abigail and Jane sat on the opposite side of the table while Eve leant against the kitchen bench. Everybody had eyes only for Ned and his news.

Ned took a deep breath and began. "Miss Millie's worried about a stranger in the bar who's asking too many questions. He looks Egyptian, she thinks; a bit like Thomas. And she said he's searching for a man named Thomas travelling with a doctor's family. Miss Millie does not trust the fellow one bit and she's a canny lady that one. Jacko and Spud will keep him occupied for as long as they can. She sent me to let Thomas know, just in case he wanted to see the man or to warn him if he did not.

"Why does Miss Millie think this stranger may mean harm to Thomas or to the doctor? What exactly did he look like?" Abigail asked when Millie's warning had been delivered.

Ned shrugged his shoulders and chomped at his scone. He took another swallow of the sweet black tea before making an attempt to answer.

"I didn't see the man myself. He was in at the bar. She just told me to come and warn the doctor and Thomas and if they weren't home, I'm to stay with you until the men return."

"Good heavens, does she really think we might be in danger? I wonder what this is all about? We'll certainly appreciate having you here, Ned, as the gardener is not in today and the washer-woman left at midday. We are on our own."

"Do you mind if I go poke about the garden to see how someone might sneak up on the place? Then we can plan how best to keep an eye on things."

Abigail looked at Ned in a new light. During their stay at The Rest, she had little to do with Ned. He was usually digging in the garden or grooming the horses. She had not seen this side of the man.

"Ned, you might like to look in at the new patient room. The window there has a first-class view of the front gate and garden."

"Yes, Miss, I will but I think I'll also prowl the gardens, front and back, regularly. I'd hate to miss anything. Miss Millie would never forgive me if anything happened to you."

Eve interrupted. "Miss Abigail, I can watch out the back from here while I'm working in the kitchen. There is very little goes on outside I don't get to see."

"Wonderful, Eve, but if anyone at all enters the yard, you are to shut and bolt the back door. Do you understand?"

"Yes, of course, Miss Abigail."

The colour of Jane's face matched the white lace collar of her dark grey dress. Her heartbeat could be counted at the base of her neck where the arteries under the skin pounded. Her voice broke as she whispered.

"What can I do to help, Abigail?"

Abigail touched her friend's trembling hands. "Jane, I want you to bolt all the doors and windows at our end of the house. Bring Henry and whatever he may need for the afternoon and evening into the sitting room. You and I can watch the front yard from there. Meanwhile, I'll go and secure the men's end of the house."

The sun was low in the sky. Doctor George and Thomas had still not returned from their callout. Standing at the window of the patient's room, Ned froze. He gently eased the curtain back a little further. Did he see a movement in the small grove of paperbark trees and banksias near the front gate? Maybe it was only a lost wallaby. The curtain dropped slowly into place before he made his way out of the room, striving not to make a noise. He flinched as the front door creaked to his touch. Through a narrow space, he searched the area where he thought he had seen the movement. He pricked his ears at the sound of a horse approaching from down the street. Laughter rang out; Doctor George's and Thomas's voices if he wasn't mistaken. Ned never took his eyes from the spot that had caught his attention. The horse and buggy rumbled in through the front gateway. Thomas, sitting in the driver's seat pulled the animal up in a flurry of dust. Doctor George made to stand up in preparation for climbing out.

Ned was already moving forward when a man in a dark suit rose from within the bushes. The stranger's right arm was raised. It was the glint of the fading sunlight reflected on the knife blade which caused Ned to snatch up a rock from the edge of the garden path. It felt good in his hand. As a child and the oldest of ten children, he was adept at knocking pigeons out of the sky to supplement their diet. Would his old eyes remain true? He stretched his loaded hand backwards.

George laughed as he stood struggling to balance on the bouncing vehicle. A movement in the grove of trees caught his eye. He swung his head to the right. A stranger was standing in the shrubbery. It took a fraction of a second to realize the man was in the process of throwing something directly at them. George threw himself forward with a yell.

"Look out, Thomas!" He crashed into his friend's back laying the both of them out onto the rump of the horse, with Thomas underneath. George felt something burn across his side. The horse began short, sharp pig-roots. This sent the vehicle hopping along behind. The men slid to the ground. Pain ripped through George's side as he attempted to scramble out of the way of the dancing horse. Strong hands reached under his armpits pulling him away from the danger.

"Are you alright, George?" Thomas asked.

"Yes, Thomas. Just a scratch I think." George groaned; his side was on fire.

"What on earth just happened?"

George's pointing fingers shook as he waved in the direction of the garden trees. "A man threw something; a knife maybe. He's probably hightailed it by now. Better shift the horse before we both get trampled to death."

As Thomas soothed the terrified horse his mind attempted to make sense of what had just happened. One minute he had been hauling on the reins and the next he had felt himself shoved forward until he lay spreadeagled across the rump of the horse. He remembered feeling the rippling muscles of the startled animal under his chest. George lay across his back. Automatically he had reached back to hold his friend who was beginning to fall but from his awkward position, he could get no leverage. George dropped to the ground. Thomas recalled his fear at the sight of the warm red blood on his hand. As he slid from the horse when it pig-rooted, the smack of his elbow against the shaft of the buggy sent pain streaking up his arm. He immediately dropped to the ground on all fours. George lay close by him struggling to evade the dancing hooves of the horse and the wheels of the vehicle. Ignoring the screaming pain in his arm he hauled George out of harm's way.

At George's direction, Thomas's glance took in the grove of trees. Ned, from the hotel, knelt on the ground beside a man lying on the path. Thomas turned again to help George. The sight of the red tide flowing across George's white shirt frightened him. He held his friend's hand.

"George, this is the second time you have saved my life, it seems."

In a flurry of skirts, Abigail dropped her bag on the ground and knelt by her brother.

"Miss Abigail, I am so glad to see you." Thomas stepped back to let the woman do her work.

Once more he looked to where Ned still knelt by the stranger's head. He blinked his eyes, then blinked again and rubbed his face. Was his mind playing tricks on him? Was he still just confused at the suddenness of the attack? Did he really see what he thought he saw? Surely it was only a trick of the light. Did Ned actually lift the chap's head and beat it down on the rock? Thomas walked over to the path and put a hand on Ned's shoulder.

"It's obvious, Ned. The man tried to escape after throwing his knife but he slipped and bounced on the rocks at the path edge."

Both men stood watching the body now lying with its head in a pool of blood.

At a closer look, surprise filled Thomas's face. He bit down on an exclamation as it threatened to burst from his mouth. A deep breath rasped down his throat before he spoke.

"Ned, shut the front gate to keep any curious passers-by away. Then will you unharness the poor horse?"

"Yes, of course." Ned nodded his head. "He's dead, you know. He won't threaten you or the doctor again."

"Yes, Ned, so it seems." Again, Thomas patted Ned's shoulder.

Abigail's no-nonsense voice drifted over to them.

"George, what on earth are you doing? Now lie still and let me have a look at the wound."

A subdued George stopped fiddling with his shirt and coat. "It's nothing, Abby. As I told Thomas, it's only a scratch."

Abigail's heart quailed when she had the chance to see the size of the wound. It spread from close to the right kidney at the back around to just above the liver. She probed with her finger and was grateful to find it appeared to be only within the upper layers of tissue. She breathed deeply and took control of her racing heart before she spoke again.

"I'll be the judge of that, brother. Today you are the patient."

"Thomas, save me." George tried to laugh but began to cough. "Oh, it hurts something fierce."

Abigail ignored his teasing and began to clear away the clothing to examine the wound more closely. The dancing light of the hurricane lamp heralded Eve's arrival.

"I brought the lamp, Miss Abigail. Is there anything I can do?"

Gratitude widened Abigail's smile. She moved Eve's hand until the light hung into a more advantageous position.

"Just keep the light there, thanks, Eve. That is really good. Once we have a better idea of what we are dealing with we'll get George inside the house to make the repairs."

After Ned left to do his bidding, Thomas stared through the fast fading light into the almost unrecognizable bearded face of his half-brother. Once assured everyone was otherwise occupied, he knelt to search through the man's pockets. A wallet from the inner pocket of the coat held a few currency notes. Beside it, he extracted travel papers in a name, not that of his brother. The pockets of his brother's trousers held several coins of different countries and two keys; one large and one small. From what Thomas could see, the larger key looked like a standard hotel room key. The smaller one was a mystery. Thomas slipped them into his shirt pocket. Probing fingers discovered his half-brother carried considerable currency in a money belt. Thomas then opened the clip and felt through the contents but he could only discern the notes. He was just about to withdraw his hand when he stopped. The sensitive pads of his fingertips ran, once more, over the odd stitching in the back of the leather container. Thomas released the buckle and loosened the belt enabling his fingers to search more intimately. A hidden slot behind the money held several folded pages. They looked like they might be business papers. He pulled them out and glanced through the first, as best he could. He would have liked to borrow the lantern but this was something no-one but he should know about; for their own safety. This identified the body in its rightful Egyptian name. He did recognize a broken seal of the head of the family on one of the papers. Thomas slipped them all into his own pockets and replaced the money and belt as he had found them. Let this body be buried in the name he chose to use in this country.

Barely had he straightened the man's clothing and smoothed the gravel which he had scuffed at the side of the body when Abigail called.

"Thomas, can you and Ned carry George inside? This is more complicated than I'd hoped. I'll need to suture and dress this wound where it is cleaner and we will have more light."

Smooth as a cat, Thomas rose and went to assist. Ned appeared from around the corner near the new building.

As Ned walked the four streets to the nearest police office, he still felt the weight of the doctor as they'd carried him into the house. The events that occurred, after he had thrown the stone at the stranger, played over and over in his head. A startled cry had burst from the man's open mouth. After the stranger released his weapon, the same hand rushed to the man's right temple. The man had spun around then tripped, landing on the edge of the path. Satisfaction still lay warm in Ned's belly. Again, he felt the surprise when he saw the man making feeble attempts to rise. Ned's hands shook and his stomach clenched in fear as he recalled how, without a second thought, he'd lifted the head by its beard and thumped it back against the rock. He could still see the blood oozing out around the dark hair. It was hard to recall what happened after that until Thomas's hand steadied him.

Jane stood in the doorway looking into the patient room lit by the lowered wick of the lantern in the corner. Doctor George lay asleep, his pale face matched the colour of the pillow slip. Thomas stretched out in the chair by the bedside. One hand lay on the covers near the doctor's leg. The other draped by his side. In the face resting on his chest, his partially open eyes glistened in the lamplight. The house was at rest. The heavy-booted police had taken the body and statements and left; and not before time. If they had asked for another pot of tea, she might have thrown it at them. Surely, they should have known better than disturb a wounded man.

She tiptoed into the room and eased into the chair on the opposite side of the bed. Thomas stirred.

"It's only me, Thomas. Abigail has left to feed Henry before she goes to bed. I promised her I'd keep you company here and call her if anything untoward occurs."

They both jumped as George slurred from the bed.

"That sister of mine has given me a dose of laudanum, hasn't she? I told her I did not need any of the stuff."

Thomas grinned.

"Well, you obviously can't be too bad. You're awake and whinging already." His words had no effect on the doctor who had already drifted back into sleep. Thomas retreated into his somnolent state.

Jane's eyes roamed about the room for several minutes until, like a thirsty animal tracking to the water trough, they returned to the frame of ginger curls around the pale face. She gazed at the regular pulsation above his carotid artery. Her heart raced and her fingers ached to enfold the hand resting above the sheet. In her mind's eye, her soft fingers traced the bare flesh of his chest. She chewed at lips which yearned to nibble the musty pink flesh of the exposed nipples. Thomas stirred in his chair as a bleat burst through those lips. Heat filled her very core. Quiet breaths panted between her parted lips. Exasperated at herself, she snatched the craft bag up from beside her feet. Without really looking at what she was doing, she thrust the knitting needles through their paces at a rate to match her heart.

Without moving his head, Thomas's partly closed eyes rolled sideways to watch the soft clicking of the needles.

CHAPTER THIRTEEN

SOLVING RIDDLES

George's eyes flew open. He stared up into Thomas's concerned gaze. A hand, the colour of golden honey, clasped his pale wrist. Early morning crept through the partially parted curtains. He looked to the foot of the bed where the weight of Jane's head asleep on the bed-coverings limited the movement of his lower legs.

"How are you, George?" Thomas's deep voice was barely a whisper.

George nodded his head and spoke softly in return.

"Been better, Thomas; been better. I'd kill for a cup of your special tea."

"I'll bring one right back. Then I'm off to find out what I can about our attacker."

A ripple of disquiet disturbed George's wan features.

"Do be careful. Should you be doing this on your own? Couldn't we just leave it to the police?"

"They have no idea of the complexities involved, George. This is something I must do alone. You'll have all the ladies fussing over you today. I'll only be in the way." He patted the doctor's hand. "I'll see you this evening."

Elizabeth Rimmington

The tea sat cooling on the bedside table as George retreated into the darkness of sleep once again.

His knock on the door was not enough to awaken a sleeping man. He heard the shuffle of Jacko's feet inside the room. A soft cough preceded the scratchy voice from within.

"Who's there?"

"It's Thomas, Jacko. Can I come in?"

The door swung wide.

"Whatever's the matter? Is everything alright? Come on in." Jacko's eyebrows lifted when he noticed the formal dark trousers and coat Thomas wore. "I hardly recognized you in those fancy duds."

Thomas slipped into the room and stood back as Jacko closed the door behind him. He sat on the chair against the wall. Jacko dropped onto the rumpled bed. As Thomas told of the events of the previous evening, Jacko sat up with interest.

"So, that's why Ned didn't return last night. I thought he was skiving off. How is the doctor this morning?"

"Sore and sorry for himself but Miss Abigail will soon sort him out. If it had not been for her quick treatment, he may not have seen another dawn." Thomas cleared his throat before going on. "Jacko, I need to find out more about the man who attacked us. I need to know why he did what he did. Were you speaking to him when he was here, yesterday? Did he say where he was staying in town?"

Jacko shook his head.

"It was Miss Millie who talked to him for the longest. She became worried when all the man wanted to do was to ask questions about you. She said he sounded very much like the way you speak." Jacko grinned before going on with an offer of help. "I can ask around the local places. Someone may know where the bloke was staying. There's no doubt he was a pretty distinctive sort of cove. I'm inclined to think he'd most likely have stayed in one of the bigger hotels on the other side of the river. The smaller boarding houses here usually only cater to the working class. The bloke didn't look as if he'd done a day's hard work in his life. Ned and I can ask around today." Jacko stopped talking and rubbed his chin, deep in thought.

Thomas stood up. He fingered the keys deep in his pocket and patted the papers secure in his jacket.

"Thanks, Jacko, I'll catch the ferry across the river and start asking around the town hotels this morning. Pass on our thanks to Miss Millie for the warning."

Jacko nodded his head, thought for a moment, then asked.

"Thomas, do you want me to come with you? Who knows what trouble may be out there waiting for you?"

"Thanks, Jacko, but no. I must do this alone."

"Can I offer you one piece of advice?"

"Yes, of course."

"Remember, the police always question the desk clerks and forget the lower-class workers in the hotels. It's the chambermaids and footmen who know most about the hotel guests. For a few pennies, they are more likely to talk."

Thomas smiled and shook Jacko's hand. "Thanks."

George woke the second time to the sound of the wood being added to the kitchen stove and the clunk of the firebox door. He was in the room alone. Jane must have slipped away without him noticing. Vaguely, he recollected Thomas saying goodbye at some early hour. Gradually his memory of the morning cleared. Thomas had said he'd find information on their attacker. What sort of crazy scheme was that? He would get himself killed, going off on his own. What if there was more than one killer out there? Pain ripped through his side as he struggled to arise. A firm hand clamped down on his shoulder.

"For goodness sake, George. I did not spend half the night sewing you up to have you now try to undo all my good work. Lie back down, like a good chap." Abigail came around from where she had been fixing the mosquito net, to stand at the side of the bed.

"Abigail, I have to find Thomas, he may be in danger." George took his sister's hands in his own. "The foolish man has gone in search of information on the attacker."

"And that will make two foolish men out looking. What good are you going to be to him, I ask? Thomas now knows of the danger. He is a grown man and quite able to take care of himself. You, in the meantime, have yet to heal. You'll only be a hindrance to him. Now settle back on the bed and I'll bring you something to eat. For the next couple of days, you will be the patient and I will get to play doctor."

Doctor George groaned loudly as he lay back on the pillows. He spoke very softly.

"That girl is getting more like her mother every day."

"I heard that, my darling brother."

For George, the day passed ever so slowly. Abigail fussed over him with her offers of opiates. Jane seemed to be forever standing with a bowl of chicken soup and a spoon in her hand. The hushed footsteps of Eve and young Maureen Ryan made uncountable trips to the door to ensure he did not want for anything. Even baby Henry seemed to be silent out of respect for his uncle's malady. He'd feel a whole lot better if Thomas walked through the door. When Miss Millie and Jacko came a calling, he was tempted to throw his hands up in the air. His spirits lifted a little when Jacko slipped over to his side and bent close to his ear.

"Thomas came to see me this morning. He's looking for where the fellow who attacked you had been staying. He's over in town searching the hotels there. Ned and I have been checking out the boarding houses here on the south side."

Just knowing Thomas was not totally on his own sent a warm feeling of appreciation through George's body.

All during the day, Thomas searched. He'd lost count of the number of people he had talked to. He searched staff out at their breaks and even followed some to their local alehouse where they were partaking of well-earned refreshment. It was becoming difficult to retain an optimistic outlook until he offered assistance to one of the chambermaids in the lane behind a hotel. She struggled to offload her overflowing basket of rubbish into an already overloaded rubbish bin which awaited in the lane in the hope of a not too distant garbage collection.

"Oh, you mean Mr. Pasha; at least I think that's 'is name. That's what it sounds like when 'e speaks. 'E went out yesterday morning but 'as not come back yet."

Thomas offered his best smile and a florin coin. Within a few short moments, he stood at the door of Room 72. His eyes scanned the corridor to the left and right as he slipped the larger key from his pocket. The keyhole received its moulded end without complaint. He twisted the handle and eased the door open. His step inside was quick and silent. The door whispered shut without a sound.

Thomas stood for some seconds looking about him. A large bed centred the room with a polished timber wardrobe to one side of it. A matching timbered small cupboard tucked in against the other side of the bed. He strode across to the wardrobe and opened the doors. A clean white shirt and dark suit hung to the left and a shelf held neatly folded underwear to the right. A pair of dark soft shoes sat on the floor of the cupboard beside a nondescript portmanteau.

Thomas removed the bag and sat it on the bed in the fading sunlight leaking through the muslin curtains. Using the smaller key, he took only a moment to open it. The first things he noticed were several items of clothes in need of a wash. They sprayed out onto the bedspread when he turned the bag upside-down. His fine fingers followed the inside lining before paying particular attention to the base plate of the bag. As he expected a secret chamber had been built within the base. Several moments were lost as his fingers searched for the opening mechanism, but find it he did. A large sum of money was discovered sequestered in the small space. His fingers were attracted to a strange texture in the lining of one wall of the bag. It was different from that of the other side of the bag. His heart pounded with excitement at the potential find but also at the raised voices coming from the corridor beyond the door. His racing fingers found the access at the bottom seam of the lining. He slid the papers down and out. They joined the other papers he carried in his jacket. The money was removed and joined the papers. Soiled clothes were shoved back inside the portmanteau, the catch secured and the bag returned to its allotted place in the wardrobe.

Thomas stood still with his ear to the door. Two male voices were heard talking in the corridor. It sounded like they were coming from either side of this room.

"Alfred, it was good to run into you again. I'll see you down in the dining room later."

"Yes, of course. Assuming those coppers in the lobby don't turn the hotel upside-down." A bray of laughter filled the air.

"I wouldn't worry too much about them. They didn't look particularly interested in whatever it was they were looking for."

Thomas's heart rolled over. He looked towards the window. Would it offer a means of escape if the police were on their way up here? The slamming of two nearby doors lifted his spirits. He gently turned the knob and opened the door a fraction before peering out into the corridor in both directions. As smooth and as silent as a raiding fox he eased the door shut before turning the lock. His feet barely touched the carpet runner as he scampered to the steps leading to the back entrance.

"Thomas, I am so glad to see you. George has been an absolutely rotten patient all day. I almost had to tie him to his bed. He was determined to go out looking for you despite the fact he can hardly sit up. Did you find what you were looking for?"

"Sorry to have taken so long, Miss Abigail. Yes, I think I have everything. I've not had the opportunity to have a proper look, just yet." Thomas laughed briefly. "George never was any good at taking his own advice. I'll go to him right away."

Abigail patted Thomas's hand.

"Thanks, Thomas. I'll bring you something to eat."

Later with the dirty dishes on the side table, Thomas emptied his pockets onto the bed covers. They spread the official documents across the bed and began to analyse them. George read the couple written in English and Thomas read the remainder written in Arabic. Eve cleared away the dishes, replenished their teacups and added oatmeal biscuits to the tray before lighting the lamps on either side of the table. Even though grateful for her care, the men barely lifted their eyes from the papers.

"This is it, George. Look here." Thomas held up several pages.

"It's no good me looking. I may as well be trying to read Chinese as that."

"Ammon, my half-brother, was in the employ of my Uncle Ishmael; a sly and devious man. He has always been involved in the seedier side of politics in my country. This is a contract signed by

Ishmael. It charges Ammon with finding and removing me from the family equation of royals to the throne; so, to speak."

"What will you do now?"

"Nothing, really. I doubt the local police will ever work it all out without these papers and I'm not going to be volunteering any information. I will have to keep more alert in the future though. Why they should want to go to all this trouble to wipe me out is beyond understanding. Surely after all this time, they must realize I'm not interested in their dirty politics. George, you do know this may put your family at risk. Perhaps I should move on."

"You will do no such thing. You belong here. You are family. I'm sure your uncle won't be so keen to send someone else after you. Remind me, how many years is it since you first fled your homeland?"

"Two years before I met you in Paris; nearly seven years, I guess."

"They're not in a great rush then, are they?"

Thomas picked up the wad of notes and waved them in front of George's eyes.

George blinked.

"Good heavens, that looks a tidy sum. Have you counted it?"

"No, George, not yet. This must have been Ammon's working capital. I suggest we use it in the running of this surgery. What do you say?"

"I have to admit this surgery does become a bottomless pit at times." George laughed briefly, which set him coughing. "Especially when we get paid in vegetables and chickens more than we do in banknotes. Maybe you might like to give it to a charity for those in need. Whatever you do, Thomas, it's your choice. After all, in a kind of way it is your money."

It was the same policeman who had taken their statements nearly a week ago. He now sat opposite Doctor George and Thomas at the desk in the surgery room. The man reached over and took his third slice of cake from the tray.

Thomas rolled his eyes at George who found it difficult not to laugh. He knew just what Thomas was thinking. Would this man ever leave? It was Abigail who saved the day; as she was wont to do on many occasions, George would willingly admit. She sailed into the room like tumbleweed before a dry wind.

"Officer, I really must insist you arrest this brother of mine …" George's and Thomas's guilty glances passed across the room. The man in uniform only noticed the elegant woman smiling gently in front of him. "… and tie him up to his bed. He insists on sitting up for far too long and I worry for his health. It is only a week since he was wounded."

"Of course, Mrs. Baldwin. I've taken up far too much of your time. I'm sorry there's nothing substantial to report. It seems this foreigner fellow 'as attacked our doctor for no good reason; mistaken identity, I'd assume. I'm sure you've nothing further to worry about. Now, I'll be on my way."

Abigail guided the policeman out through the front door and waved to him as he floated down the front path to the gate. When she returned to the room, George and Thomas were in silent fits of laughter. Abigail glared.

"I mean it, George, you really must not do too much at once. Now please lie down for a rest before the midday meal then, if you are feeling well enough, I want you to give Henry the once over. He is six weeks old."

"Already? I can hardly believe it. So much has happened in such a short time."

George was grateful for Thomas's strong arm under his elbow as he returned to his bed.

CHAPTER FOURTEEN

FRIENDS OR ENEMIES

Eve answered the knock on the front door to greet the doctor from the Brisbane Hospital. She curtsied and led the man into the surgery room. Her feet flew through to where George and Thomas were playing a game of cribbage. The two men ceased their game. Doctor George limped through to the surgery. Eve disappeared into the kitchen. Her quick hands kneaded the dough for a dozen scones. The tea tray sat on the table. She heard Doctor George greet his visitor.

"Aah, Doctor Granville, this is a nice surprise. What brings you here, today?" George tried not to appear astounded at the appearance of the Visiting Surgeon from the hospital. What on earth was this man doing here at his humble abode?

"Doctor Goldfinch, it is a pleasure to see you up and about. I heard of the attack on your person last week and have been looking for an opportunity to call on you to wish you a speedy recovery." They shook hands, albeit gently as George's side complained at any muscle work of his right arm. "I understand you sustained quite a nasty wound. Full marks to your doctor, I hear. May I ask who your doctor was?"

George felt his face cloud over. Was this man trying to belittle Abigail's abilities and practices? To his relief the door opened. Abigail walked into the room relieving George of the responsibility of answering the question.

"Doctor Granville, may I present my sister, Mrs. Baldwin."

The visitor bowed his head and mumbled. "Mrs. Baldwin, pleased to meet you at last. My wife has mentioned your name. I understand you have joined the Women's Hospital Auxiliary. My wife is grateful to have a new member to assist with the work they do, and splendid work it is too."

Abigail never flinched.

"Pleased to meet you too, Doctor Granville. I only hope I can be of some assistance in your admirable wife's endeavours."

A flush filled the visiting doctor's face. "I was passing, having seen a patient in the area and hoped you would not mind if I called unannounced."

"Not at all, Doctor Granville. It is a pleasure to see you here."

"I am pleased to find your brother looking so well. As I understand, he received a rather horrific wound."

Abigail never paused. "Yes, it was. The knife sliced the skin layers and muscle from the right loin around to the liver region. He was extremely lucky the peritoneal cavity and major arteries were not touched."

A look of surprise crossed the surgeon's face.

"But that is indeed a severe injury. It must have taken considerable skill to repair such damage and here George is up and about within a week." His gaze turned to George. "It is a miracle you have not developed an infection."

Abigail touched the surgeon's hand as she guided him to the chair by George's desk.

"It was not too difficult seeing as, other than the muscles, there were no major structures damaged. Please sit yourself down, Sir; and you too, George. We have Professor Lister and his carbolic acid treatment to thank for a clean wound. Now, I'll bring the tea tray in."

Neither man saw the smile twitching at her lips as she made her way into the kitchen.

George was hard put not to laugh outright at the look of shock as it played back and forth over Doctor Granville's face when Abigail retreated from the room having dropped her not so subtle remarks. The man could hardly speak.

"You let her treat your wound, Doctor Goldfinch; your sister, a woman?"

Doctor George then went on to tell how he'd trust Abigail to care for him in any medical emergency. He told of his twin's desire to have studied medicine with him and how she would have done so but for the refusal of their father to allow such a thing. He explained how Abigail had completed every medical course along with him even though not in the University. Her advice, when consulting with him, had proved worthy of note, without fail.

The visitor's face was a picture of consternation and confusion. "I have heard there have been one or two women accepted into the university to study medicine. I have to admit it has not been my privilege to meet a woman with the brain-set or the stamina to complete such an arduous course." He shook his head faintly. "Mrs. Baldwin has not lost any of her femininity at all, having studied this subject. She even has a small child, I understand."

"Yes, her husband was killed in a horse-riding accident in England not long before we left. Baby Henry was born here in Brisbane." George almost crossed his fingers as he looked Surgeon Granville directly in the eyes and told a rather large fib.

"Abigail is the perfect lady at all times, Doctor."

"Yes, I've noticed, Doctor Goldfinch. Your family is blessed."

Only a week passed before Abigail had the dubious pleasure of meeting Doctor Granville again, at the church fete. It had been Eve who first noticed Sarah, Miss Millie and Jacko in the crowd of people. Abigail led her small group over to meet their friends. While they had been talking, Abigail did not miss the glances of admiration passed between Jacko and Sarah. She smiled.

Barely had Abigail, Jane and Eve said their farewells and waved as Jacko led his ladies off, when they were greeted by Doctor Granville and his wife.

Abigail's heart sank. Oh dear, this was not the way to enjoy an afternoon. She held her head up high and smiled.

"Doctor Granville and Mrs. Granville; it is lovely to meet you again. What a perfect day for a church fete, isn't it?"

"Mrs. Baldwin, good afternoon. You and my wife have met, I believe?"

Abigail nodded and smiled at Mrs. Granville.

"Yes, of course. I hope you are enjoying yourself. Let me introduce you to my companion, Jane Stanley, and my maid, Eve Jones." Abigail stepped back to introduce her friends.

Both the Granvilles nodded their heads in acknowledgment. Abigail could not deny her sigh of relief when several official-looking gentlemen approached the couple and begged their attention. Doctor Granville turned to Abigail and apologized for his rudeness. He explained he was the official guest for the day and must make an announcement shortly. Smiles were interchanged and the couple moved off towards the front lawn. Abigail did not miss the comment Mrs. Granville made when the woman thought she was out of hearing.

"Really, the cheek of Mrs. Baldwin introducing me to a common maid; a companion maybe but a maid. Has she no sense of decorum?"

Abigail hooked her arms through those of Jane and Eve. "What do you think ladies, have we had enough?"

Abigail may have liked to have been a fly on the wall in the Granville house the same evening. Herbert Granville and Eleanor Granville hosted Doctor Granville's brother, Orville, who had only recently arrived from London. The afternoon fete held a prime spot in the conversation around the dinner table.

Mrs. Granville's lip turned up as if she had tasted a particular salty piece in the pot-roast.

"Mrs. Baldwin should know better, I think. Fancy expecting to introduce us to her servants. It is really too much. She takes egalitarianism too far. How can one hope to maintain a sense of civilization stuck out here on the outskirts of the colonies when we have someone like her, who should know better, flouting all rules of proper behaviour?"

The doctor patted his wife's hand.

"Now dear, don't let it upset you. Things are changing in this new world. Maybe not always for the better, I agree. But I do not want you making yourself sick worrying about it all." Herbert Granville turned to his brother. "Mrs. Baldwin is the sister of our Doctor George Goldfinch. He, his sister and friends arrived in town some months ago. Doctor Goldfinch has set up a medical practice on the other side of the river."

Orville Granville frowned. He sat silent, deep in thought.

"Did you say, George Goldfinch? His sister is named Abigail if I remember. They both have reddish hair. They're twins and look like peas in a pod."

Doctor Granville looked up from his plate.

"Sounds like them. Do you know them, Orville?"

"Know of them, more like. Their family owns the Goldfinch fortune. As far as I'm aware, the father dotes on the last of his children; the twins. Gossip had it in London before I left, the twins departed for Australia against their father's wishes. It did not stop the father depositing a considerable sum into the New South Wales Bank for their use."

"Pity he did not send the money to the Bank of Queensland. As a board member of our bank, I am very much aware of the shortage of funds therein." Doctor Granville sipped at his glass of water.

Mrs. Granville's curiosity was aroused.

"Why did they leave England, do you know, Orville?"

"Eleanor, I cannot confirm any of this. It is all pure gossip, remember. The Goldfinch twins were never conformists. It is rumoured the girl studied medicine with her brother in an unofficial capacity. When her brother was too busy, it is said she wrote his assignments for him. Some wags at Oxford said her work always got the top marks."

"Well, I don't care how clever she is. It's about time Mrs. Baldwin realized her attitude will not win her too many friends out here."

CHAPTER FIFTEEN

FRUSTRATION

A grey sky greeted the congregation as they slowly made their way out of the church. Reverend Braithwaite pumped the hand of each member with enthusiasm as they wound their way from the vestibule into the garden. Groups gathered about chatting with friends and acquaintances.

Doctor George and Abigail were the last to exit with Henry peacefully asleep in the pram.

"This chappy is not the only one who slept soundly this past hour." The Reverend grinned ruefully as he winked at George. "I do hope you are feeling better since the dreadful attack, Doctor."

George managed to look guilty as he smiled in return. "Slowly improving, Reverend. I can't complain."

Abigail looked up as a tall, well-groomed stranger approached. Her glance was captured by the glistening brown of the man's eyes under a head of neat sandy hair. She felt a quickening in her chest. The man's slow smile seemed vaguely familiar.

"Oh, Orville, please join us. Have you met Doctor Goldfinch and his sister, Mrs. Baldwin?" The Reverend beckoned the man to the group. "Doctor George Goldfinch, Mrs. Baldwin, may I introduce

Doctor Orville Granville, recently arrived from London and brother of our hospital's Visiting Surgeon."

Abigail's heart paused its beating altogether for a short moment when that name dropped from the minister's lips. Surprise filled her eyes but her smile remained fixed. One thought filled her head. "Oh, no, not another Granville, what a shame." She almost grinned at her audacity.

While the men talked of their experiences, Abigail struggled to understand her response to this stranger. Her heart had resumed its beat, at a racing pace. Her stomach was all aflutter. She felt as if her mouth covered her face with an imbecilic grin. Hands clasped the pram tightly to hide their tremor. A man was not in her future plans at all; not after her past experience with her own, thankfully, short-lived marriage. Besides, with a name like Granville, Orville automatically joined Mr. Jamieson of London on the no-go-list. Widowhood and her beautiful son suited her very well. Unconsciously she smiled at the sleeping baby. At the mention of the recently established Woogaroo Asylum, her ears pricked up. When she learned Orville was a member of the Board, her brain changed track.

"I've been reading with interest of the recent improvements to Woogaroo, Mr. Granville, and of the new approach to the treatment and care of those confined there. I am seeking opportunities to raise funds for Woogaroo and for the Dunwich Asylum also."

"Mrs. Baldwin, your efforts will be gratefully received, I can assure you. There is much work to be done yet at Woogaroo. Funding has been short as buildings have needed to be replaced or re-sited higher up the river bank when floods encroach again and again on the asylum. In my short time here, I have learnt so much about their plight. Of Dunwich, I am not so familiar. I believe they obtain most of their funding from the churches."

Again, the conversation returned to the men. Abigail analysed what she had been told. When the groups began to break away heading to their homes, she turned to Orville.

"Mr. Granville, I really would like to discuss the subject of the asylum funding in more depth. Would it be too forward of me to invite you to dine with us one evening this week to confer on the subject?"

"I would be delighted." He cast an appraising gaze over the attractive woman's figure as defined by her bodice when Abigail reached up to save her hat loosened by a sudden gust of wind.

"May I send you a note to arrange a suitable time?"

"I will look forward to hearing from you, Mrs. Baldwin."

"You're very quiet, Abby. Would the good-looking Orville Granville have something to do with that?" George turned the horse and buggy in through the gate and on to the gravel path. The baby carriage rattled where it was secured at the back of the vehicle. Henry's eyes opened wide. He stirred in his mother's arms.

Abigail gentled her child as she pondered her answer. "He was rather handsome, wasn't he? I guess it is no surprise, look at his brother. There must be quite a few years between them though. I wonder why that is, do you suppose."

"Pity about the sister-in-law, Abigail, but you are still a young woman with a whole life ahead of you, remember. Don't dwell on the past. Not all husbands and marriages are such a disaster as Edward Baldwin was."

"At the moment, I am content with just Henry and my family here, thanks, George. Mind you, Orville might be able to assist me with my pet hobby of seeking charity funding for the asylums." Abigail bit her lip acknowledging, at least to herself, this may not be the only reason why she wished to know more of Mr. Orville Granville, despite his surname.

"I thought you were going to bring the subject up at the next Ladies Auxiliary meeting this week at the hospital."

"I don't hold out much hope her ladyship will acquiesce to my requests."

With a brief thought of her mother's disappointed look at such unladylike behaviour, Abigail slammed the front door behind her. She barely noticed Eve's curious face peer from the sitting room doorway. The echo of her feet sounded loud in her ears but she was past worrying. As she stormed into the surgery room, she was tempted to slam that door too but her brother's laughing face made her pause.

"So, the Ladies Auxiliary meeting went well then?"

"Grrr," was all she could manage.

George stood and took her basket from her arm and placed it on his desk. He gently turned her around.

"Let's go and have the tea and cake Eve has served in the sitting room."

"That ... that ... woman. All she's interested in is putting on a flash show for the Prince's visit next year. When I suggested some money could be spent on the outlying facilities like the lunatic asylum at Woogaroo or the Benevolent Asylum at Dunwich, she barely gave me the time of day." Abigail allowed her brother to lead her down the hall while she released her built-up tension. She turned and faced George directly as they arrived at the sitting-room door. "She says, and I quote, 'Those facilities are of no concern to the hospital. They will not be included in the Prince's itinerary and therefore will not be requiring any extra funding.'"

At a great cost to his own restraint, George's face remained blank. He so much wanted to burst out laughing but knew his own health might be at risk if he did so.

Jane glanced up from her sewing with a curious look.

"Whatever is the matter? Abigail, you are quite flushed. Can I get you a glass of water?"

Abigail walked over to the pram where Henry examined the hands and fingers on the ends of his arms. When he noticed his mother, his legs kicked wildly and he grasped his feet. Her anger dissipated like the air from a pricked balloon.

George sighed. The storm had passed. He sat and took up his cup and cake and began the important part of the afternoon. Between mouthfuls, he asked his sister for more details of the meeting.

Abigail sat. In a more controlled voice, she related the events of her morning's meeting and the encounter with Mrs. Granville and her lap dog, Mrs. Markham.

"I know, theoretically, Mrs. Granville is correct. Currently, the two asylums are separate entities to the hospital but surely, we can expand our purview to include offering some small comforts to these patients."

Jane poured Abigail's tea and placed a piece of cake on her plate. Abigail picked at the cake and sipped at her hot refreshment. The glazed look in her eye told those in the room her thoughts were still at the meeting.

"You know, I have a good mind to start a ladies auxiliary group raising money especially for those two facilities."

George's attention returned to the conversation.

"Whoa, Abigail. That is very noble of you but you do realize we are the new arrivals in the town. Doctor Granville can make or break our medical practice. He has only recently approved of my right to attend my patients at the hospital. It would be a shame to have him change his mind now. Our future might hinge on your association with Mrs. Granville's group."

Abigail almost spat out her reply.

"Bah, hospital politics; has it followed us halfway around the world? How far does one have to go to escape it?"

"I'm afraid so, Sis. In fact, it has always seemed to me, the further from London one gets, the pettier the politics."

Abigail returned her cup and plate to the small table and stood up brushing any crumbs on her dress to the floor.

"So, I must continue to choke on my conversations with Mrs. Granville but I am still going to consider looking into an auxiliary fund for the asylums at Woogaroo and Dunwich." She moved over to the pram and cooed at her son as she steered him out to her room. "Anyway, I have more important things to worry about right now. This young fellow must be starving."

George sat in the shade of the fig tree watching Thomas putting the finishing touches to their new sitting room. He grinned.

"I bet it was an interesting journey back from the hospital earlier. Abigail looked ready to explode when she walked into the house."

Thomas finished banging the last nail into the window frame before walking over to sit by his friend.

"Your sister was upset even before she entered the hospital. When we arrived, she had me park at the side of the building and not take the buggy past the front door. All part of Mrs. Granville's instructions from the previous meeting, apparently." Thomas shook his head. "The woman sounds most unpleasant."

George grinned.

"I've been lucky not to have met the woman; touch wood I never do. Poor Abigail is only suffering her for the good of the practice. I'd like to see the pair of them go head to head without that limitation. It might be an interesting contest."

"Abigail never spoke a word all the way home. I was worried her face looked like it was on fire. I figured you'd look after her once I got her back here. When she jumped out of the buggy at the front door with the ease of a young filly, I realized she was filled with steam, not an illness."

The pair chuckled at the thought.

Orville drained his teacup and replaced it on his brother's desk at the hospital. "Herbert, Eleanor does not like Mrs. Baldwin, does she?"

"Not one bit. Eleanor likes to get her own way. She has done so all of her life. Her own father acknowledges this. He admits it was all his own fault. After her mother died, when she was only a youngster, he could not deny her anything. On the odd occasion he did, she made his life a misery. He quickly learnt it was easier to just accede to her wishes in the first place. I cannot deny I generally follow the same principle."

"Obviously, Eleanor and Mrs. Baldwin have clashed along the way, somewhere then. I remember she waxed long and loud on the subject of Mrs. Baldwin's character when I was last a guest at your place."

Herbert grinned. "They certainly have clashed. It was at the Ladies Auxiliary meeting, the first time they met. Mrs. Baldwin's medical knowledge was far superior to Eleanor's and that did not go down too well, I can tell you." Herbert Granville sucked on his pipe before warning his brother. "I will deny I ever told you all this, even under oath, if I am called to do so, Orville; not a word now."

"As I live and breathe." The matching grins crossed the desk.

"Anyway, what is this interest in Abigail Baldwin? Mind you, if I was single and a bit younger, I might be interested in the woman myself. She is a very handsome woman even if she is the mother of a small child."

"I met her after church on Sunday. She is all above reproach. The baby is her husband's. Pregnant when he died, I understand. The gossip in London was definite about that."

Herbert put his pipe in the ash-tray and leant forward to speak quietly to his brother. "Taking on someone else's child cannot be such a burden when the woman has the Goldfinch money behind her, remember. You might be surprised to find out just how pragmatic Eleanor can be when money is involved and you are her favourite in-law, remember." Herbert laughed softly. "Taming the woman's nonconforming behaviour may be a more difficult task, I fear."

"Even the wildest animal can be tamed if handled correctly." Orville rubbed his chin thoughtfully.

"Well, I'll not be placing any bets on it, I can tell you. You'll have not only Abigail but her brother to contend with. He is very protective of his twin, you know." Herbert stood up and went to stand by the window. "There is one thing you would be needing to do straight upfront; put your foot down on her friendship with the proprietor of Millie's Mariner's Rest Hotel. The hotel is only a front for a brothel when all is said and done. I would suggest if you are looking to relieve yourself you do not use that establishment because word would quickly filter back to Mrs. Baldwin."

"Good grief, how did you find all this out?"

"Easy; servants will gossip. I have learnt it is wise to keep friendly with our servants. We have a part-time cleaner, Mrs. Waterman who also works occasionally at the hotel. The Goldfinch group were guests at a Sunday lunch at the hotel recently."

When the letter did arrive at the surgery, addressed to Abigail in a bold hand, she slipped it into her pocket to be read in the privacy of her own room.

"Anything there for me?" George asked as he entered the surgery.

Abigail started guiltily. "No, George." She made a hasty retreat to her room.

As Henry suckled contentedly, Abigail held up the envelope. "He has a strong hand, Henry," she told the uninterested party. She spread out the notepaper and read.

Wednesday 3rd.

Dear Mrs. Baldwin,

I am in receipt of your and Doctor Goldfinch's welcome invitation, dated the first of this instant, to a luncheon on Saturday next. I have taken up your suggestion to invite a guest knowledgeable on the subject for discussion. Doctor Whitby has been involved with the Woogaroo Asylum since its construction and worked previously with some of the inmates when they were housed at the Brisbane Gaol. He has also been involved with the management of the Dunwich Asylum. I am sure he will have information which will be of value to yourself.

Yours with similar interests

Orville Granville.

Later, as Abigail bathed Henry in the tin tub she laughed when he kicked his legs and flailed his arms. The water swished and swirled around him.

"My mind is swirling around just like your bath water, Henry." Abigail pondered on the confusion produced by her thoughts. Her body yearned for the touch of a gentle man. But the man's brother was such a pompous ass, or so he had seemed on his visit to the surgery some time ago. On the other hand, the sins of one brother need not necessarily be repeated in the other. Just look at her own family. Her oldest brother displayed the same type of arrogance as Herbert Granville but George exhibited none of those characteristics. Doctor Orville Granville did have exemplary manners and dress sense. Or was he just a pedantic bore? Backwards and forwards her thoughts raced.

"Abigail, what are you thinking? The bathwater has lost all its warmth. Henry will catch his death of cold." Jane brought her mind back to the present moment.

CHAPTER SIXTEEN

UNREQUITED LOVE

As soon as she heard the horse and buggy pull up at the back of the kitchen, Abigail jumped up from the chair in the sitting room where she had been crocheting by the light of the lantern. She rushed to the back door holding the lantern up in front of her. Even in the dull light she could not help but notice the dark shadows around her brother's eyes. She reached out and took the bag from his hand.

"George, I was becoming worried about you. Where have you been? I thought you were only going to the hospital to see one patient."

George ran his hands down his face. Before answering his sister, he turned to call Thomas who was settling the horse in the stable.

"Do you need a hand there, Thomas?"

Thomas's voice drifted out from the direction of the faint light within the shed.

"Won't take a moment. I'll catch up with you, shortly."

Abigail put her brother's medical bag on the kitchen table and took his arm.

"Come on in. We have kept meals hot for you both. How long since you've eaten?"

Eve walked into the kitchen and across to the stove. She pulled the kettle over the heat and prepared the teapot.

"Doctor George, do you want me to serve your meal immediately or are you going to wash up first?"

"I think Thomas and I are both in need of a clean-up before we eat. Can we have ten minutes?"

"I'll have your meals ready by then."

As the doctor and Abigail walked to the surgery office, George related the events of their exhausting afternoon.

"The hospital was busy admitting people with chest infections. Doctor Granville asked if I could pop in and visit the child of a friend of his with a nasty cough. It turned out to be whooping cough; I'm sure. While there, we ended up visiting several children in the street who all seemed to have the same symptoms. We thought we were ready to turn for home at sunset. A young boy caught us and delivered a message asking us to call on a lady in labour two streets away. Her midwife was having difficulty with a breech birth. After what seemed like forever, it all finished satisfactorily. Now, I must have a wash and eat."

Later, as the men ate with relish in the kitchen, George and Abigail discussed the implications of the whooping cough and young Henry.

"Abigail, I think, while whooping cough is amongst the local children, I will restrict my handling of young Henry. He is rather young to cope with such an illness just yet."

Once Eve had served the meals, Abigail sent her off to bed. "You've had a long day, Eve. I'll clear these things away before I turn in myself."

George and Thomas were just rising from the table when Abigail remembered her own exciting news of the day.

"You'd never guess, George."

"Not tonight; I most probably won't be able to guess anything."

"Sarah and Jacko, at The Rest, have become betrothed. Millie could not wait to call around to tell me this morning. She'll put on a party sometime soon. We are invited."

The smile chased some of the shadows from the doctor's face. "Good on Jacko. Sarah's a lovely girl."

Thomas had a smile as wide as his face too. "Ah, there you go. Another good man fallen into the arms of a wily woman."

Abigail laughed as she flicked the napkin at his back when he exited the room. "Get off with the pair of you."

Abigail gave the appearance of serenity but Jane felt the excitement emanating from her friend at every breath.

"Abigail, what is this Orville Granville like and what do you know of his colleague Doctor Whitby?"

Abigail caught the grin before it burst across her face. "Er … Jane, I cannot really say. I only met Orville the once at the church. He appeared the perfect gentleman. I am sure he won't pick his teeth at the table." This time Abigail did grin. "As far as Doctor Whitby goes, I have never laid eyes on the man."

Even Jane smiled at the comment made at Doctor Orville Granville's expense.

Abigail continued, "I never thought for a moment my friend from the Hospital Auxiliary, Mrs. Eleanor Granville, would tolerate a relative who was not presentable in public."

There came a knock at the front door. Abigail almost ran down the hallway. When she opened the door, Abigail was pleased to note Orville Granville did look the perfect gentleman. The stylish suit set off his slim body perfectly. She dragged air into her lungs. How long had she been holding her breath? It took all of her self-discipline not to stare at Orville.

"Doctor Granville, it is so nice you could come." She turned to his friend; a plump man with a florid face. "And you must be Doctor Whitby. I am so pleased to meet you and welcome you both to our home."

"My pleasure, Mrs. Baldwin." Orville Granville and Doctor Whitby spoke in unison.

"Please, come inside. George is just finishing up in the surgery."

Her words were hardly spoken when George stepped out into the hallway and greeted their guests. Abigail led them to the sitting room where Jane poured the sherry.

"You have an ideal set-up here, Doctor Goldfinch." Doctor Granville relaxed back into the chair.

"Yes, Doctor. This is a lovely setting protected from the street by those large shady trees." Doctor Whitby sipped at his glass.

"Please gentlemen, call me, George." The visitors raised their glasses in acknowledgment as George continued. "Yes, we were very lucky to have found this place."

Twenty minutes later the group entered the dining room where Jane added the final touches to the table. The guests were seated on one side of the table, Jane and Abigail sat opposite while Doctor George headed the table.

As the meal progressed, the conversation flowed back and forth. Abigail had to concentrate to keep her mind on the purpose of the visit. The closeness of Orville, sitting opposite her, proved pleasantly distracting. Doctor Whitby, after many years' experience with the asylum patients, provided a wealth of knowledge on the improvements in their care. Having considerable involvement in the financial affairs at Woogaroo, he was also able to advise Abigail on the most effective way to utilize any funding she was able to acquire. Mrs. Eleanor Granville and her Hospital Auxiliary affairs were never mentioned.

It was late afternoon before the guests made their departure with an invitation to Abigail and Jane to visit the Asylum in the near future.

Abigail smiled as she watched a satisfied baby Henry settle to sleep. A hint of milk still showed on the corner of his lip. She lifted the lamp from the table and moved out into the corridor. The smile disappeared when she heard what sounded like sobbing coming from Jane's room. She paused. Would Jane think her interfering if she entered and asked to help or would she appreciate the company? She knew herself how hard it was sometimes to ask for help when feeling vulnerable. Surely it is what friends should do; offer to help.

Her soft tap on the door brought silence to the sobs from within.

"Jane, may I come in?" Abigail spoke softly. Without waiting she opened the door and poked her head inside. "Jane, I am so sorry you are unhappy. Will you talk to me about what has you so upset?" Abigail walked over to the bedside. She placed the lamp on the floor and sat on the edge of the bed. "Please tell me what I can do to help." She took Jane's hand in her own.

Jane used her already saturated handkerchief to wipe her last sniffles. "I'm sorry if I have disturbed you, Abigail. There is nothing you can do for me."

"Have the men been rude to you? Are you feeling homesick? Has looking after Henry been too much for you?"

While Jane protested none of the above was a problem, Abigail's mind went off on a tangent. In fact, she was remembering Jane's fit of the vapours several weeks earlier. At the time, she suspected Jane might be developing romantic feelings for her brother. Something told her this could be the cause for the tears tonight.

"You sound to me like someone with a broken heart. Has someone broken your heart, Jane? Has someone made you promises and not kept true?"

"No; no, I have been made no promises. I'm being foolish."

"Would my brother have anything to do with your unhappiness?"

"Abigail, George has done nothing wrong. I... I... I seem to find him in my thoughts, day and night. I do not know what I should do."

Abigail patted her friend's shoulder.

"Jane, I am so sorry. He is such a damnably good-looking man, even if I say so myself. He is a lot of fun to be around, I know. But George is a bachelor at heart. Will he ever change? Probably not. I'm convinced the only commitment he will make in life is to his medicine and patients. To those things, he gives his all. There is nothing left to give to anyone else, I think."

"I wonder if he hates me. He hardly notices me."

Abigail gave Jane's shoulder a little shake. "Now Jane, I know George does not hate you. I think he puts you in a similar category as me; like another sister. He is wrapped up in his work and does not see the world about him."

"But he laughs and talks to Thomas; never with me."

Abigail frowned and clenched her jaw. Her lips tightened. "They are friends, Jane. They have been friends for a long time. Those two have been through a lot together." Abigail sat up straight. "Jane, I think you need a change. After Millie's party, why don't you take a holiday to visit your aunt in Sydney? You always said you liked your Australian aunt and we had so little time to visit when we passed through on our arrival in this country. The weather will be warming up a little now and quite pleasant, I should think." Abigail ran her fingers over Jane's head. "Promise me you'll think about it, dear."

"I don't know if I could bear to see a happy couple becoming betrothed knowing I'll never be so lucky."

"Careful what you wish for, Jane. Look at what happened to me. Look at the brute I ended up with. What a terrible experience my marriage was. I doubt whether I'll ever be foolish enough to marry again." Abigail paused as her thoughts drifted to their recent guest, Doctor Orville. With an impatient shake of her head, she turned back to Jane and her problems. "Now, would you like something to help settle?"

"Thanks, Abigail, for stopping to talk to me. No, I think I'll be able to sleep now. Goodnight, dear, sleep tight."

With a creak, the brake handle of the buggy moved under Abigail's firm hand. She secured her bonnet strings and looked around. There seemed to be more traffic than normal in town today. The sooner they sent Jane's telegram and returned home the better as far as she was concerned.

Her heart plummeted when they entered the Telegraph Office. People, waiting to be served, were lined up to the doorway.

"Jane, this is going to take forever."

"Abigail, I'll fix this. You take a seat over there in the corner. You are lucky, it's the last seat available."

Abigail did as she had been instructed, grateful to be out of the human crush. With nothing better to do, she switched to her favourite pastime; watching people. Her fan waved back and forth across her face, shifting little of the hot air.

Eventually, Jane stood beside her.

"Are you ready to leave, Abigail? The telegram has been sent. My aunt should answer in a day or two. Hopefully, it will be suitable for me to visit her for a holiday."

"I know it's rather late but I think a cup of tea would be refreshing. How about you, Jane; will you join me at the tea-house?"

"Of course, Abigail. A cup of tea sounds excellent."

It was Jane who espied Miss Millie and Sarah. They made their way across the room.

"What a lovely surprise. Please, won't you join us?" Millie pointed to the spare chairs.

A young girl approached the table shyly and asked what they wanted. As soon as Abigail had given the order she smiled at Sarah.

"I understand you are to be congratulated, Sarah. It is lovely news." Abigail reached over and held Sarah's hand where it lay on the tablecloth.

"And my congratulations too, Sarah; to you and Jacko. I do hope you will both be so happy." Jane's smile revealed nothing of the turmoil within. Only someone looking very closely might notice the shadows of sorrow in her eyes.

A different waitress delivered the tray with a fresh teapot and cups. Millie helped her remove some of the detritus left over from their earlier refreshments. As she did so she spoke of Sarah and Jacko's betrothal party.

"We want to wait until Sarah's brothers return to Brisbane on the *Northern Orchid*. They do not know, as yet. You will all come won't you."

"I would have been bereft if I'd missed Sarah's party, Millie." Abigail smiled.

The breeze set the brim of her pale blue bonnet trembling as Abigail stood with her hands on the gunwale of the ferry. She watched Jane, who held Henry in her lap, talking to a middle-aged lady sitting beside her on a seat towards the stern. Their conversation obviously involved young Henry who did not complain at all with the attention he attracted. The day at the Woogaroo Asylum had proved a successful exercise. Jane and Henry had been left at the Whitby quarters where they were entertained by the pleasant Marigold

Whitby, Doctor Whitby's wife. Orville and Dr. Whitby took Abigail on a guided tour of the facility. Doctor Whitby spoke of updated patient treatments being introduced but the overcrowding and need of more funding for expansion were not to be ignored. Her astute questions surprised the men in attendance. Later, Orville and his friends left to attend their board meeting. Abigail joined Jane and Marigold Whitby.

Just as they had boarded *The Settler* at Woogaroo Creek, for the return journey to Brisbane, several distinguished gentlemen engaged Orville in a discussion. He excused himself with an apologetic smile to Abigail. They had travelled some miles down the Brisbane River before Orville re-joined her.

"My apologies, Mrs. Baldwin. It was imperative I took the opportunity to speak with those gentlemen today. They have considerable influence within the government and may be able to help me in some of my endeavours."

"Apology accepted, Mr. Granville. My father always said not to let an opportunity pass you by."

The pair stood in silence for some time watching the afternoon sunlight dancing on the wash of the paddlewheels.

"Mrs. Baldwin, I er … may I call you, Abigail? Only when we are by ourselves, of course."

Abigail lifted her head from her contemplation in the waters of the boat's wash. She was surprised to hear the hesitancy in Orville's voice. He always seemed such a confidant man.

"Yes, of course, but only on the condition I call you, Orville."

He smiled. Her heart smacked against her rib cage.

"Abigail, I am sure you know I have developed a strong attraction for you. I am a man of means and from a family with excellent references."

Abigail struggled to draw a breath past the pounding of her heart. Her eyes glistened. A crooked smile rested on her lips. She did not wish to interrupt Orville's train of thought.

"As you would have seen earlier, I have influential friends and a strong and notable future ahead. If you were by my side, with your family background and influence, I am sure I will accede to a prominent position. A prime minister of this country is not out of the question. Would it be acceptable for me to speak to your brother to ask for your hand in marriage?"

Disappointment flowed through Abigail's veins in a raging torrent. She forced her facial expression not to falter. Where were the words of love, she so craved? Where were the words of respect and consideration? She struggled to put her thoughts into words. In the meantime, Orville spoke again.

"Of course, in such a position, it will behove the two of us to ensure there is no call to criticize our public or private lives. For instance, you would need to curtail your ventures into the public without suitable attendance. It would be beneath your dignity, as my wife, to continue practicing medical care with your brother. The friendship you have with the hotelier, Millie Carson, would need to desist. The woman is, after all, nothing short of a brothel keeper."

Abigail gasped. She felt as if Orville had punched her in the stomach with a fist instead of words. Her mouth opened and shut several times while again Orville spoke.

"I am sure you appreciate the honour I am offering you and these changes may affect your life somewhat. Perhaps you would like some time to consider your answer."

By the time Orville finished speaking the sparks were flying in Abigail's eyes. She swallowed and breathed deeply several times to dampen the furnace inside her. For George's sake and the surgery, she knew she must filter what she would very much like to say.

"Orville, I am honoured by your proposal today. Sadly …," Abigail coughed into her lace handkerchief while she struggled to say the words she must. "I am not the person to help you fulfil your ambitions. In the short time, we have known each other, I have learnt this. It would be unforgivable of me to accept your kind proposal only to see an unsuitable relationship ruin your future. I am sure there are ambitious women out there who may be more adaptable to fitting into a life of politics. I wish you every success." At this point, she bit her tongue. She willed herself not to put forward her opinion that Miss Millie, brothel-keeper as she may or may not be, had more ethical value in her little finger than he did in his complete oh-so-handsome, but empty, body.

A wave of amusement stole up on Abigail. She was hard-pressed not to burst out laughing. The disbelief flooding Orville's face was a sight to see. His mouth hung agape. He stared unfocused. Obviously, he had never entertained the thought she might refuse. No doubt, he believed being a widow with a small child, she would jump at the chance to accept such an irresistible offer.

There was little more to say. When they arrived at the jetty, Orville's impeccable manners did not desert him. He offered his hand to assist her and Jane up into the carriage. Thomas tended the horse.

"Mr. Granville, thank you so much for escorting us on this pleasant and informative day. Once again, I am sorry if I was unable to accept your offer. Be assured, I do wish you the very best."

"Mrs. Baldwin, my pleasure." Such were their parting words.

CHAPTER SEVENTEEN

WOUNDED SEA CAPTAIN

Doctor George watched Josh Dougall as he jumped down from the back of the dray. A ship, with *Northern Orchid,* painted on her bow, lay at anchor not far from the bank on which they waited. Onboard was a new patient for George. The late sun reflected gold on the surface of the water. Jacko and Thomas laughed at the doctor who clamped his hands over his ears when Josh put two fingers into his mouth and sent a piercing whistle in the direction of the ship. A head popped out of the wheelhouse and cooeed back. An authoritative voice was heard issuing orders. Several minutes later a small boat rounded the bow of the ship from the starboard side. Two sailors pulled efficiently on the oars. It was not until they reached the shore Doctor George recognized Josh's brother, Gus. The thought passed across his mind on how the two boys had grown in the few months they had been away. They left as boys but returned as young men.

"You'd best come with me, Thomas, and Jacko too. You might all be needed if we are to shift the patient tonight."

As he climbed over the ship's rail, Doctor George was greeted by a tall grey-haired man with a scar down the side of his face and a noticeable commanding presence.

"Captain Sloan at your service, doctor." He reached out his hand which George took.

"Pleased to make your acquaintance, Captain; George Goldfinch. Josh tells me you have had great success using the carbolic acid solution my sister sent via Miss Millie. I'm looking forward to seeing the outcome. To have a compound fractured leg heal cleanly under such trying circumstances is almost unheard of. I commend your own skills also, Captain."

As he climbed on board, Josh handed the doctor's bag over to the captain. Thomas and Jacko were not too far behind but not nearly as nimble. Jacko greeted the captain, having met him on several occasions at The Mariner's Rest Hotel. He turned and introduced Thomas to Captain Sloan.

The doctor followed the captain to several small cabins at the rear of the ship. The door was opened by an anxious faced young woman. Captain Sloan introduced Mrs. Farley, the patient's daughter, to Doctor Goldfinch who bowed in his best parlour-room manner.

When he progressed into the cabin, Doctor George found a middle-aged man sitting up in his bunk with a book in his hand; reading. George was pleasantly surprised. A quick glance took in the leg with a clean well-padded dressing secured within a wooden splint. He smiled.

"Doctor George Goldfinch, Sir." He held out his hand which was taken in a firm shake.

"Captain Douglas Bruce of the *Fleur*; the late *Fleur*, I'm sorry to say."

George explained to Captain Bruce the options available. He offered to deliver him to the Brisbane Hospital where he could be treated as a public patient under the hospital doctors or as a private patient under his own care. George explained he had rooms at the surgery where he cared for some patients. There was a vacancy at the moment and he would be happy for the captain to stay there under his care if he wished.

"Doctor Goldfinch, if it had not been for your forward-thinking in using this new solution and providing it to the captain of this ship, my body would be, at this moment, feeding the fishes in the sea. If you will take me, I would like to place myself under your care at your surgery."

The two men shook hands again.

"Now, I'll talk to Captain Sloan and learn the logistics of removing you to the dray which we have waiting on the river bank."

Just as the doctor was about to leave, Captain Bruce called him back.

"Doctor Goldfinch, is there somewhere close to your surgery suitable for my daughter and her husband to stay?"

George did not hesitate with his recommendation.

"A couple of streets from the surgery is The Mariner's Rest Hotel. Basic but clean and they serve excellent food. My people and I stayed there for some time when we first arrived in Brisbane earlier in the year. In fact, it is thanks to the proprietor, Miss Millie, and my sister, that Captain Sloan acquired his supply of carbolic acid to treat the wounds of his crew."

A great sigh escaped through Captain Bruce's lips as the carry-board was removed from under him and he was made comfortable on the surgery bed. His grey face and taut skin told its own story.

"I can give you some laudanum if you wish, Captain Bruce. It may help you settle after this difficult move," Doctor George offered.

"Douglas, please. Yes, I think I would like something for the pain tonight, Doctor."

"On one condition; you call me, George." The doctor smiled.

Douglas Bruce nodded his head. Abigail stepped into the room. In her hand, she held a small glass, partly filled, with a reddish-brown coloured solution. Doctor George took the medicine from her hand.

"Thanks, Abigail."

"This, Douglas, is my sister; Abigail Baldwin," he said as he placed the medicine into the captain's trembling hand. "Abigail, meet Captain Bruce, of the late *Fleur*."

Captain Bruce tossed the fluid down the back of his throat and accepted the water offered by the lady's hand. He gasped.

"Thanks. May I say, I am very pleased to meet you, Mrs. Baldwin. I understand I have you to thank for my life."

Abigail blushed a pale pink. "Goodness me, you are overstating the situation, I'm sure. My brother and I are very excited at the outcome of this new wound treatment."

While George explained Abigail's unique position within his medical practice, she left to collect the man's dinner tray from the kitchen.

CHAPTER EIGHTEEN

MIXED EMOTIONS

Both Abigail and George were busy re-dressing Captain Bruce's leg when the knock on the front door sounded. Jane knew Thomas was out in the garden somewhere and Eve could be heard rattling amongst the pans in the kitchen. With care, she placed her crocheting on the sitting-room table. She looked again at Henry asleep in his pram before making her way to answer the call.

The door was barely open when a slim youth held out an envelope. "Telegram for Miss J. Stanley."

"I am Miss Stanley. I will take it, thank you."

"Will there be an answer, Miss?"

"Wait here, please." Jane turned and shut the door behind her. Her nervous fingers tore at the paper and released the message contained within.

Looking forward to your visit. House renovations in progress. Ready to receive you in two weeks.

Jane once more opened the door and told the lad, "Yes, I have a reply to send."

He handed over a well-thumbed booklet and a pencil for her to enter the message. It did not take her long to print a succinct answer. The book disappeared into the leather satchel hanging at the side of the boy's bicycle. Jane drew a small change purse from the pocket of her skirt and extracted the shillings required to pay for the message.

Saturday arrived; the day of Sarah and Jacko's betrothal party. Doctor George and Thomas along with Abigail, Jane and Eve were to attend. Maureen Ryan had arrived to look after the patient, Captain Bruce. Eve, fussed in the kitchen where she put final touches to several plates of scones, biscuits and cakes. All the while her instructions to Maureen on caring for Captain Bruce flowed from her lips like an unending symphony. At various intervals, the younger girl nodded her head and confirmed she had heard and understood what she was to do. Maureen did well to hide her grin when Miss Jane put her head in the doorway and delivered a litany of instructions herself. Miss Abigail arrived with Henry in the pram.

"Thank you, Maureen, for helping out today. Now, all you have to remember is to run down to The Mariner's Rest if Captain Bruce becomes unwell. We'll all be back here before dark. Are you sure you are not frightened on your own, Maureen?"

"No, Miss Abigail. I'm used to managing on me ... on my, own." Miss Millie's ad hoc classes, on those days when Maureen worked at the Mariner's Rest, were having an effect, it seemed.

The sound of Thomas leading the horse and buggy out of the stables was heard by those in the kitchen.

Abigail called down the hallway. "Are we ready, Eve? George, are you ready?"

His voice preceded him out of the patient room where he had left Captain Bruce with several books to read. A chess set, with a game in progress, sat on the table out of the way.

"Coming, Abigail. Did you bring our gift for Jacko and Sarah?"

"Of course."

Thomas pulled the buggy to a stop and secured the brake. From the jump seat beside him, George alighted and prepared to assist the three ladies to the ground. The vehicle wobbled and skirts swirled as they each stepped down with care. Thomas unhooked the perambulator and wheeled it to where Abigail stood with Henry in her arms. A small basket hung from Jane's elbow in which lay the gift for Sarah and Jacko as well as the selected music sheets which Miss Millie had asked her to bring. Eve held a larger and heavier basket holding their contribution to the feast.

Millie greeted the group as they approached the other guests sitting at tables shaded by the large trees near the hotel. A light breeze lifted the coloured decorations hanging from the branches brightening the afternoon. George and Thomas were whisked away by young Josh Dougall to join the group of men talking together beside the stable doors.

After necessary introductions were completed it was Captain Sloan who asked after the progress of Captain Bruce.

"Fine, William, just fine. You did a great job caring for the man." George Goldfinch smiled. He turned to thank Ned who handed him a glass of ale. "Hello, Ned. How is your head? All healed, I see."

A grin of many gaps filled the old man's face. "Good thankee, Doc. You done a fine job. Doesn't hurt a bit now."

Spud Murphy had Thomas in tow as he headed to the public bar. Thomas thought he was to assist in carrying the drinks to other guests but he was waylaid by Miss Millie at the kitchen doorway.

"Thomas," she whispered, "Were you able to finish the sketches of the *Northern Orchid* this week?"

He grinned. "Yes, Miss Millie and I have commenced preparing a canvas. Painting will begin tomorrow. By the time the captain returns from his next journey it should be complete."

Millie took both his hands in a tight clasp. "Thank you, Thomas. Thank you very much. William will be thrilled to see his other love on canvas."

Thomas returned to the party where Jane's pleasant soprano voice rang out over the group as she serenaded them all with two modern selections. Next, it was Spud's turn to get everyone's toes tapping as he danced in a circle fiddling with all his heart.

A hush fell over the group as Jacko led Sarah, his bride-to-be, to the head of the table. After much humming and hawing, Jacko began to speak. He thanked everyone for attending and Miss Millie for all she had done for them both. There was a cheeky comment from one of the men, which set everybody laughing. When Sarah reached up and kissed Jacko on the cheek, Abigail felt Jane's hand slip into her own. She squeezed it hard. She had a fair idea of how devastated Jane must be feeling to be reminded of the happiness of others; happiness she deserved but would need to look for elsewhere. Hopefully, a holiday away might help her friend adjust to a new future. Abigail sighed inwardly. There was no easy escape for her own forlorn hopes of love.

Shortly after the formalities were over, everyone began to disperse. Sarah and Jacko thanked the Goldfinch group for their lovely gift. Jacko's feet twitched in his unfamiliar shoes. A finger struggled to slip in under the stiff collar which looked about to choke him. He appeared ready to bolt. Miss Millie and Sarah made a fuss of Henry as they passed him up into the arms of his mother where she sat in the buggy.

"Bye, thanks for coming." Miss Millie, Sarah and Jacko waved enthusiastically as their friends moved off along the street.

Abigail stood at the bedroom doorway watching her baby tossing around in his new cot. The house seemed so quiet since Jane had left for Sydney. Not that Jane was a noisy person; not by any stretch of the imagination. George's voice came drifting through from the kitchen.

"Where is everyone?"

"Here, George." As her brother approached, Abigail explained. "Eve has gone to visit Sarah at The Rest. Jane left a crochet pattern to be delivered to her." She stepped to the side to allow room for George to watch his nephew.

"Did Jane get away alright, then?"

"Yes, George. The coach picked her up this morning."

"I cannot understand why Jane would want to visit her aunt in Sydney. As I remember, the woman never smiled once in the whole afternoon we were there."

"Oh, George, why is it men can never understand a woman's needs?"

"Don't drag me into that conversation. I am taking Thomas's advice; don't even try to understand women."

"Speaking of Thomas, where is he? I thought he was with you in the surgery."

"No, he is working on his painting of the *Northern Orchid* which Miss Millie commissioned. We won't see him for some hours, I shouldn't think."

"What about Captain Bruce, how is he this afternoon?"

George gave a short laugh. "He is bored senseless and driving his daughter and son-in-law demented. They are playing cribbage again. They need something new to challenge them."

Suddenly, Abigail and George froze. They stared at Henry who gave an enormous swing of his arm and leg which sent him rolling over onto his stomach with a soft thud. The look of surprise on his face set the watchers laughing gently.

George observed his sister out of the corner of his eye. There was a sadness about her today. Perhaps she missed having Jane around, perhaps it was more.

"I have not heard you speak of Orville Granville for some time. I thought the pair of you were getting on very well."

"Well, you may not hear me speak of him again, either. He is a Granville after all."

George was in two minds on whether to say more or to remain silent. Her face was drawn tight. He decided to brave the possible storm.

"I am sorry to hear that, Abs. Is there anything I can do?" The sight of her unshed tears caused great concern. During their whole lives, Abigail had rarely shed a tear, no matter what the provocation. She would rather rip her eyes out first. "Has the man behaved inappropriately? Do I need to speak to him?" He reached out and took her hand.

She smiled softly at her twin. "No, George. As always, he has been an impeccable gentleman. It was almost nauseating." Red curls escaped their pins as she tossed her head. "The damn man is a replica of my father I think, and just as unemotive. He proposed to me; well, he asked if he might seek your permission to propose to me. What does he think, I cannot make a decision on my own? It all sounded more like a business proposal. I would imagine it was exactly how my father requested Mama's hand forty-something years ago. I am sure you can guess. You know, we get on fine, we are from distinguished families and most important of all, your money and my money will do well together." More curls escaped with another toss of her head. "And I forgot to add his finale. I must screen my friends and acquaintances more stringently to ensure they are suitable for a person in my new station in life." The last words were spat across the room.

"Do I take it we won't be attending a second betrothal party in our street in the near future?"

"Absolutely not." She tightened her grip on her brother's hand. "Oh, George, is it too much to want a man to love me for the person I am and not for what I can provide for his future?"

George pulled her into a friendly hug. "Oh, Abby, maybe we are destined to patter about this house, trying not to get in each other's way, for the rest of our lives. At least Henry's future will give us something to strive for."

"You are right, George. Let's start by raiding the cake tin while Eve is away. You put the kettle on."

PART TWO

SHADOWS
ON THE
GOLDFIELD TRACK

CHAPTER NINETEEN

BRISBANE 1873

THE MARINER'S REST HOTEL

Dappled shade from the tall gum tree draped the group at the graveyard. From behind the small gathering, the stamp of the horses' feet underlined the words of the preacher. On either side of the casket, held steady by tensed ropes in their hands, stood the pallbearers. The brothers, Josh and Gus Dougall on one side. Spud Murphy, the barman at the Mariner's Rest Hotel and Thomas, the assistant to Doctor Goldfinch stood at the other.

Captain Sloan, of the *Northern Orchid*, in his whites, with head bowed, stood at the foot of the casket, the officer's cap crushed in his hand. His jaw clenched. On his right, Sarah held tightly to her husband, Jacko's, hand. Tears ran unchecked down her face. The woman lying in the casket had liberated Sarah from what, at the time, appeared to be a grim future. Jacko's face was an impenetrable mask. Only those who knew him well were likely to have an inkling of the deep sorrow he felt. He was here to say goodbye to a woman who had been as a mother to him since she rescued the ten-year-old from the streets of Sydney. On the Captain's left stood Abigail Baldwin and Jane Stanley. Their long dark dresses almost touched the dirt.

Black lace shawls draped their hair. Behind the pair, Doctor Goldfinch, Abigail's brother, stood with his eyes downcast. He also had reason to mourn the loss of this woman who had proved a staunch friend to his family since their arrival in this new country, six years previously. Lizzie Randal and Peggy Lawson, the regular cleaners at the hotel, stood alongside Ned, the handyman, on one side. They mourned a tough but fair boss to whom they owed many favours. On the opposite side of the coffin, also in navy whites, the ship's mate, Ewan MacGregor, stood, with head bowed. He had come today, not only to pay his respects, but to support his long-time friend. Today they were to bury the woman William Sloan loved above all others.

A sweet fragrance rose into the air as the spring breeze ruffled the flower arrangements clinging precariously to the top of the coffin. These included several ostentatious wreaths, without the names of the senders identified. Millie had many influential friends in high places who could not be seen to support a female hotelier and, to those-in-the-know, the keeper of an exclusive brothel.

When the preacher lowered his bible and commended Millie's soul to the Lord's keeping, Jacko and Ned stepped forward to remove the wreaths, putting them aside. They were to be placed on the mound after the coffin was covered. Sarah stepped sideways and took hold of the captain's hand. In the past few months, she had come to know the captain who cared for Millie with such dedication, during her decline. An admiration, as deep as the sea upon which he sailed, developed for this strong but sensitive man. Her gratitude to Captain Sloan knew no bounds for having taken her brothers under his wing on board the *Northern Orchid* and setting them up in their careers on the sea. He turned his head to her and gave a wan smile.

Sobbing of the women accompanied the rustle of tree branches in the light breeze as the casket sank slowly into the earth. Moisture rimmed the eyelids of the men. The restless horses broke the mood.

Ned moved out of the group of people to talk to the animals. He offered them carrots to nibble on. Did these magnificent beasts understand they had just farewelled a lady who enjoyed nothing better than feeding them carrots or guiding them around the streets of Brisbane unassisted? Today Prince and Emperor pulled a buggy each while Samson took up his usual position harnessed to the hotel dray. Grey hairs speckled the muzzles of all three of these beasts.

Later, back at the hotel, the mourners gathered in the dining room where Mrs. Hamilton, her daughter, Meg and Eve, from Doctor Goldfinch's household, had prepared a wake worthy of Millie Carson.

Maureen Ryan, with her two charges in tow, entered through the kitchen doorway. Abigail Baldwin made a beeline for her son, Henry.

"Hello, young man. I do hope you have been a good boy for Miss Maureen."

At six years of age, he stood as high as her waist. Henry held his mother for a brief moment before running off to search for more interesting entertainment.

The other young child, who had entered with Maureen Ryan, barely stopped to give her mother, Sarah, a kiss before rushing off to stand with her arms raised in front of Captain Sloan.

"Grampy Cap'n, pick me up, please?"

At the captain's side, Mac struggled to contain his amusement.

"Is the child calling you Grumpy, Cap'n?"

Captain Sloan chose to ignore the remark from his ship's mate. He lifted the little one into his arms.

"Well, young Lucy, what mischief have you been up to this time?"

"Nothing, honest Grampy. Isa lady." The three-year-old snuggled into his chest with a thumb in her mouth.

"Hmmm."

"Where's Grammy gone?"

The sailors' eyes met in consternation. The captain sighed with relief when the short attention span of the girl had her wriggling to be put down. An answer to her question was not required.

"Down Grampy, down. There's Uncle Gus, he's going to show me and Henry the possum's log."

Captain Sloan, Mac, and Josh gravitated to a corner. The captain was curious to hear the news of his ship's last voyage north. While he had remained in town with Millie, Mac had captained the *Northern Orchid* with Josh as his ship's mate. Gus took the position of engineer, replacing the now-retired Guthrie Winston. Only weeks before the ship had left on that journey, both these young men had returned after six months in Sydney. The captain recalled his pride in his protegees with their eyes shining like diamonds when they held aloft their Master's Competency Certificates and their Engineer Certificates; something they had been working towards over the past six years. Mac interrupted his thoughts.

"I'd like to take the *Northern Orchid* up to the Endeavour River, William." Mac took another sip from his whiskey glass before going on. "No doubt, the papers here have been full of the news about the gold rush on the Palmer River and the explosion of the population at Cook's Town. According to your friend at the harbourmaster's office, our holds could not contain all the cargo, building material and supplies required up there. It should be a profitable venture. Hundreds of hopeful miners are desperate for a berth, too."

Captain Sloan placed his glass on a ledge and took a puff on his pipe as he thought upon Mac's words. Maybe this is what he needed; to get away from all the memories here.

"Sounds a good idea, Mac. Can you take a non-paying passenger along for a ride? The sea air is what I need." Sloan noticed the shadow flash across the face of Josh Dougall. He smiled. "Don't worry lad, I'll not relegate you to the galley or the bilge pump. I'll be along strictly for the ride only. You can carry on as the ship's mate; if Mac thinks you're satisfactory for the job."

"He'll do; a bit fussy at times, but he'll do." Mac grinned. "You and China can while the time away talking about the old days. China's workload is minimal now. His nephew, Lee, has proved very efficient."

"What about my cabin; where will you bunk, Mac?"

"Your cabin has remained empty, awaiting your return. I'm still in my own cabin. Josh and Gus set up two bunks for themselves in Guthrie's old cabin; and of course, they still use The Captain's Cupboard when they want to get away from each other."

Josh grinned as he nodded at his brother who had just joined the group. "He snores something fierce, Cap'n."

This comment brought a smile to all their faces. Since his brush with death, on his first trip north, Gus's injuries had left him with a notable snoring problem.

"I don't snore." The guilty party mumbled.

The others in the group laughed.

"Has anyone heard from Guthrie since he retired?" Mac asked.

It was Captain Sloan who replied. "Yes, Guthrie and Daffy Harris have a drink together every Friday. I was only talking to Daffy the other day. Guthrie's happy enough staying with his daughter but the grandkids overwhelm him at times." Captain Sloan turned towards Josh and Gus. "Daffy told me how you both call on him when you're back in port. He appreciates your visits."

The Dougall brothers nodded their heads.

"Captain Harris's alright. He was good to us; taught us a lot." Josh spoke up. "Even the officers in Sydney knew him and spoke highly of him."

It was Jane Stanley, Abigail's companion who broke up the group. "Sarah has put on hot soup for our tea before we have to leave. Will you join us, gentlemen?" She led them to the tables.

Mac leant close to William Sloan and spoke softly. "Who is that fine looking woman?"

The captain looked first at his friend, then over at Jane who had joined the ladies at the table by the front window.

The captain raised his eyebrows. Was this his friend Mac, talking? The fellow who was so reticent in selecting a woman to admire. "She's young enough to be your daughter, Mac. Haven't you looked in the mirror lately? You've more lines in your face than a sea chart and there's grey popping up in your hair, you may have noticed."

Mac stroked the faint scar on his forehead and through his hair. "Just a simple question."

"She's the companion of Abigail; the doctor's twin sister. I think we'd best get you back out to sea." He grinned but Mac's attention had returned to this small blond-haired lady with the shy eyes. The captain took another look at the woman himself. She must be about thirty years of age, he'd guess. Good grief, that would be twenty-three years younger than Mac. Anyway, as far as he could see, she needed a good feed; too skinny by far.

Over at the table by the window, Abigail helped Henry butter his bread. Sarah was feeding a very sleepy Lucy.

"So, Sarah, how long have you got to go now?" Abigail asked.

Sarah's eyes sparkled as she lifted her head. "Only three months, Abigail." She rubbed at her swollen abdomen. "I do wish Millie had been alive to see this one arrive. Jacko and I were only talking last night. If it's a girl, she'll be called Millie and if it's a boy, he'll be named Christopher William; after her husband and also after Captain Sloan."

A borrowed lantern swung under the sulky as the Goldfinch entourage pulled out through the back gate amidst the dancing shadows it cast. At the same time, Mac and the Dougall brothers left by the front gate to make their way to their ship.

"I'll come on down to the *Northern Orchid* in the morning," Captain Sloan called to their departing backs. They waved again.

Sarah left Jacko's side and walked over to take the Captain's hand. "You know, Captain, Millie's room will always be your home here at the Mariner's Rest. Lucy will be bereft when you return to sea again. Please come back to us here, as often as you can. You will always be her Grampy Cap'n."

The captain patted her hand. "Thanks, lass. You and Jacko are good people. Now shouldn't you be off those feet and resting." Sarah linked her other arm with Jacko as they re-entered the kitchen.

THE GOLDFINCH ENTOURAGE

Abigail followed the sound of her son's voice to where she found him kneading his own small roll of dough at the table opposite Eve.

"Eve, I do hope this young man has not been getting in your way. I was sure he'd sleep-in this morning, after the big day, yesterday."

"Miss Abigail, Henry is never in my way. It's a joy to share some time with him. If you're looking for Doctor George, he's in the surgery with Thomas. They've just returned from a birthing, out past Smith's farm. They said they'll clean up before they have their breakfast."

"Thanks, Eve. I'll eat when they do. No sign of Jane yet?"

"No, Miss Abigail."

In fact, Jane was wide awake and dressed. She sat on the window seat of her room peering out into the garden. Several coloured parrots squabbled in the trees while a black and white willy-wagtail scolded them for their idleness. She could not deny she had seen the appreciative look in the eye of Captain Sloan's friend, Ewan MacGregor yesterday. What surprised her most was she could not deny her heart had beat so much faster at the time. In fact, just the thought of the red hair and green eyes set her insides fluttering like the wings of the birds in the trees outside. Maybe she was just attracted to men with red hair. Mr. MacGregor's hair was a richer shade of red than George's hair. Actually, now she thought about it, the presence of the doctor had not set her senses jumping for such a long time. Mr. MacGregor was quite a bit older than her though. He may be at least fifty. Miss Millie always said her relationship with her husband Christopher was all the better for him having been twenty years her senior. She shook herself and stood up. Her skirts swished about her legs as she gave them a good shake. It was time to join everyone at the breakfast table.

"Will you look at this, Thomas?" George Goldfinch sprawled on the padded chair shaking the paper in an attempt to fold it. His man-servant cum assistant and friend of many years looked up from the watercolour he was painting.

"What's that, George?"

"There's rather a large write-up on the Palmer River goldfields, the site of the current gold rush. The area is about two hundred miles inland from Cook's Town on the Endeavour River. According to this article, hundreds, maybe thousands of hopeful miners, are arriving by ship into Cook's Town which was no more than a muddy riverbank only a few months ago." George glanced at Thomas. "Are you listening to me, Thomas?"

"Yes, of course, George. I don't need my hands to hear." He made another slow and careful brushstroke across the canvas.

Mollified, George continued. "As I understand it, the government has not even had an opportunity to set up a suitable port on the river. Many of these people are delayed at the village waiting for equipment and supplies before they can begin, what sounds like, a torturous journey into the hinterland to where the gold was discovered. Added to this, disillusioned miners are returning to Cook's Town in a pitiable state desperately in need of supplies and medical care. Both of which are in short supply."

"Hmmm." Thomas continued blending his colours. An Australian native parrot came to life on the canvas.

George was not going to be ignored so easily. "Don't you think it would be a worthwhile challenge?"

"What?"

"Thomas, you're not listening to me. To go up there, of course. We can set up a medical clinic; a bit like this."

"By the sounds of it, nowhere near as comfortable."

"I guess not, no; but that would be the exciting challenge part."

Thomas began cleaning his brushes. "I admit the thought of change is inviting but what about the women?" He asked. "Would they want to go to such a place?"

George sat pondering the question and the logistics of such a venture. Thomas stood back to look critically at his morning's work. George's next words caught his attention.

"Knowing Abigail, she'll jump at the chance; maybe even young Eve. Jane is such a delicate flower. I'm not sure if Abigail will go and leave her behind."

Thomas moved over to sit in the chair opposite George.

"Have you given any thought to what you'll do about your surgery here?"

George rubbed at the frown on his forehead. "Actually, I haven't had the chance to give any of it much thought. I've only just become aware of the seriousness of the situation. At the wake, last week, Mac talked a little about what he knew of the conditions." George sat quietly for several moments. Thomas looked over to see if he had fallen asleep.

"Thomas, we could advertise for a locum doctor to run this place for a year or two. The ladies could remain; living in their end of the house. This should leave us free to chase all the excitement we need. What do you think?"

It was Thomas's turn to fall into deep thought.

"I agree, in principle. Maybe Miss Abigail will take the opportunity to enjoy a return trip to the old country."

"I think we can safely assume it will be a cold day in hell before she even contemplates such a thought."

THE *NORTHERN ORCHID*

The faintest glow in the east told of the dawn to come. William Sloan stood at the bow of the ship savouring a different perspective of the river than he usually had when in the wheelhouse. Beneath his feet, he felt the throb of the engine. Like shadowy wraiths, the crew bustled about the deck preparing the vessel for the call for sails when they exited into Moreton Bay. Luck had favoured him in providing this secluded area in which to enjoy the moment. Nearby, sleeping bodies, some of whom were just now beginning to stir, smothered the forecastle area. These were the men heading towards their golden dreams. He could not recall the *Northern Orchid* ever having such a manifest of cargo and passengers. The first-class cabins near the stern and both the dormitories on the lower deck were occupied. The holds were filled to overflowing and considerable building materials such as timber and corrugated iron were secured on the top deck.

A voice at his elbow reminded him he was not the only one who knew all the nooks and crannies in which to hide on board.

"I bring you tea, Cap'n Sir."

"Thanks, China. How come you're not in the galley giving some poor sailor a hard time."

China giggled. "No, Cap'n, Sir. My nephew, Lee, wields sharp tongue and knife now. He and Basil have many cauldrons of gruel to prepare for breakfast. Mac sent Keller to help also. You remember him; rescued from the *Fleur*. I cut vegetables later in day for soup. Basil make the dampers."

171

"What, no time allocated for putting a China curse or two on the crew? Maybe you can produce a curse to keep this hoard from fouling up the top deck."

China burst into laughter. "Don't worry yourself, Cap'n. Between Evans and Funny-man they behave, good. Make these fellows clean their own slop buckets. Much entertainment then."

"When you're not busy later, come to my cabin. We'll play a game of chess. This time I'll beat you."

"Honourable Cap'n, Sir, but of course. This will be the first time, yes?" China took Sloan's pannikin and went off laughing towards the companionway leading down to the lower deck.

With the sea-pilot long since returned to the lighthouse, the ship under full sail and the engine boiler dampened down, it was at the bow Gus Dougall found Captain Sloan. He watched the man, unnoticed, for a moment. The captain's gaze penetrated the depths of the sea. With surprise, Gus noticed the thick scar running down the left side of his face and neck had faded in recent years. The scar had been acquired on the day his father, Jimmy Dougall, died while saving the lives of Captain Sloan and Mr. MacGregor. Gus stepped forward.

"Hello, Captain Sloan. It's a beautiful morning. Are you enjoying the music of the sails?"

"Yes, young Gus. I have missed the sound of the sails singing to me these past couple of months. How's the engine of yours going? Sounds like its ticking over smooth enough."

"It works a treat, Sir. Doesn't take a lot of maintenance but does a good job. Have you had breakfast yet?"

"Thanks, I'm going down to the galley now. Why don't you join me?"

CHAPTER TWENTY

THE *NORTHERN ORCHID*

This journey to the Endeavour River was interrupted only by the need to acquire water, supplies, and coal; Maryborough, Rockhampton, Bowen and Port Hinchinbrook the only ports of call. Mac and Josh spent many hours a day in the chartroom constantly reviewing their library of relevant local seagoing charts. The numerous smaller shoals and reefs contained within the Great Barrier Reef were always a threat to passing mariners. Some of these were noted and charted while some were still to be discovered. Occasionally, Captain Sloan wandered in for a brief glance but he maintained only a passing interest. He gave both the chronometer and compass, in their floating capsules, a soft tap, before greeting the helmsman and walking out.

William's deep pain eased within the comfort of the familiar vessel, the hypnotic seas and days of clear weather. Many hours were spent breathing in the medicinal salt spray as it broke off the bow. He knew though, pain awaited to erode this fleeting sense of peace when he returned to Brisbane; a Brisbane without his Millie to greet him.

Many moonlit nights found China by his side, angling for the flavoursome fish of the north to add interest to the menu. Days were spent challenging his brain against China's in the skill of the chessboard. On occasion, he bettered the aging cook at both these pastimes.

The crew on watch, during the night hours, wondered at the burning lantern in Captain Sloan's cabin; sometimes until the sun broke above the eastern horizon. Inside the retreat, his loose writing style filled the pages of a hard-backed journal. He toiled at writing a book; a memoir to his beautiful Millie and the time they had spent together.

The call from the crow's nest drew everyone to the foredeck. The entrance to the Endeavour River hove into view. Long shadows fell across the ship in the late afternoon light. A cheer rang out from the fifty-four miners anxious to disembark on the morrow. Mac sent two crew members, Rollins and Stretch, to man the lead. They reported back the depths of water under the keel as he edged the ship past Grassy Hill, across the main river entrance to drop anchor in deep waters several chains off Indian Head. Mac and Josh contemplated what appeared, in the failing light, to be a wall of shoals and reefs to their north and east.

The officers, including Captain Sloan, enjoyed a rum in the chartroom after the evening meal, they drank to a successful journey. Captain Sloan removed his pipe from his mouth and grinned.

"Glad to see you didn't run the old girl up onto a reef as Captain Cook did. I'm not too sure if I'd remember how to fother a sail around the keel. Can I presume they taught you boys that down south?" He pointed the pipe at Josh and Gus.

Josh and Gus laughed fit to burst. It took a moment for them to recover. Mac, Sloan, and Evans looked askance at each other.

"Didn't think I said anything so funny. Are you going to share the joke?"

Josh was the first of the two to recover. "It was the instructor, Cap'n." The tale was interrupted as Gus began chuckling again and Josh struggled to continue. "Bacon, one of our instructors, a bit of an uppity cove, thought he'd improve our education with a demonstration of fothering a sail. He had us, there were about six in the class on the day, mix the oakum and wool and spread it over the sail. Next, he pointed to a barrel of foul smelly fluid, said it was horse and sheep dung but it smelt more like the slop buckets from the officer's quarters, begging your pardon, Cap'n. Anyways, he tells one of the blokes, Jacobson it was, to pour the mixture over the sail and let it set. The only trouble was Jacobson picked up the ladle and went to spray the stuff about without checking the wind direction. Poor old Bacon had his mouth open to call a warning when he received the full shower of shit in the face."

Almost choking with glee, Gus took up the tale. "Not one of us moved and we definitely did not laugh. All of us stood with our gobs open. Old Bacon strode off to the shower and left us standing. Couldn't have happened to a more deserving fellow; he was a bit of a cruel cow. Poor young Jacobson sweated for a week waiting for his punishment. He was convinced he'd never get his Master's certificate. He need not have worried. His father had loads of money and paid the penance."

With tears running down his face, Mac asked the burning question. "Did you ever get the sail prepared and fothered around the keel?"

"Oh, yes. Another officer, loaded down with stripes, came and finished the class."

THE GOLDFINCH ENTOURAGE

Doctor George, Eve and Abigail were busy in the surgery checking their medical supplies. From her perch on the wooden chair, Abigail passed down large reserve containers to Eve who filled the smaller bottles, used in their everyday treatments. The doctor jotted down, in the order book, items they needed to replace. Having completed one section of the supply order, Abigail stepped down to the floor and began to move the chair along to the next cupboard where dressings and bandages were stored. It was just then Henry came running into the room sliding to a stop in front of the group.

"Henry, you've been told about running in the house. You run outside but walk in the house. And look at those dirty shoes. Miss Eve does not spend her time keeping our floors clean for you to make such a mess of them. You can get a cloth and clean your mess up before you go to class with Auntie Jane."

"But Mama, I've got the mail from the letter deliverer." He passed several envelopes and a small package into George's hands.

Abigail gasped. "Henry, look at your hands. They are filthy. What on earth have you been doing?"

"Thumbnail let me plant the little cabbage plants in the garden."

"Well, those hands will need a good scrub before your class. Auntie Jane will have conniptions. Now off you go and don't forget, this floor first."

Henry made to retreat then spun back to face his mother. "What are conniptions, Mama?"

176

George spluttered. Eve bent her head further over her work. Her shoulders shook. Abigail rolled her eyes.

"We will examine the dictionary tonight, before bedtime, Henry. Now go."

Eve and Abigail continued with the stocktake while George went through the mail. He turned one letter over several times.

"I wonder who this is from." He held the envelope up towards Abigail. "Whose handwriting is that? It looks familiar. Do you recognize it?"

"George, you do realize if you open it, you will have your answer." She glanced down as she spoke. "Isn't it cousin Richard's scrawl?"

"Richard Goldfinch, you mean?"

"Who else; the one who was a year or two below you at medical school."

"What on earth would he be writing to me for? We were never that close."

Abigail's eyebrows raised. She and Eve shared a smile.

"Open it, George, and find out."

Silence reigned for several minutes. Abigail took up the scribing in the order book while George, with a frown upon his face, read the correspondence.

Eve whispered, "Miss Abigail, can I go to the kitchen and check our tea is not spoiling?"

"Yes, of course, dear."

"Can I bring anything back for you?"

"No thanks, I'll finish up here shortly."

The door clicked shut behind Eve when George jumped up and began walking around the small room.

"I presume you'll tell me, at some point, what has you in a fluster, brother?"

He could hardly speak with excitement. George looked up at his sister and began to run his fingers through his hair.

"Er … Sis … it's like this. We've got to talk. This unexpected letter is fortuitous and fits in perfectly with something I have been considering."

Brother and sister sat until the shadows lengthened across the windows. Their hushed voices carried only within the room. When Abigail eventually stopped asking questions and making her opinions felt, she stood up to leave.

"George, this needs to be discussed with everyone in the house. After Henry has gone to bed we'll meet in the sitting room and talk it through."

Abigail poured and served the hot cocoa before speaking. As she rested back into the chair, she looked around at those she called family. Her brother, George, knew what this meeting was about, as did his friend, Thomas. The men had been considering the idea for several weeks. On the other hand, she had only been aware of it this past couple of hours. Jane and Eve knew nothing of the scheme. How would they react? The arrival of their cousin's correspondence made it possible for George to put his plan into operation.

Abigail looked, firstly at Jane and Eve, then turned to her brother. "George, I think you had best start by introducing your idea and the reason behind it."

Jane and Eve's interests were engaged. Their cups sat cooling in their laps. George wriggled about in his hard-backed seat. He would have very much preferred it if Abigail had presented his plan.

"Er … well; yes … well, the newspapers; it all began when I read the newspaper articles. You will have seen them too, no doubt. All

178

about the goldrush at a place called Palmer River, near Cook's Town."

Jane and Eve nodded their heads. Both their eyes remained fixed on George who struggled on.

"The latest reports are saying the fledgling port of Cook's Town is ill-prepared to cope with the thousands of miners making their way to the goldfields and with other disheartened miners seeking to escape. The articles I've read talk of inadequate housing, supplies, and food for these hordes. With the wet season almost upon the north, what is already difficult terrain will be awash with floodwaters. The situation will only get worse. Grave fears are held for the lives of many. Medical care is urgently required."

"It all sounds rather grim. How will these people cope?" Eve bit her bottom lip.

"Grim, it certainly is." George continued. "Most of the dwellings there are tents, I understand."

"Isn't Cook's Town on the Endeavour River; the place where Captain Cook repaired his ship?"

"That's correct, Jane. The goldfields are actually at Palmer River; over two hundred miles inland."

"Then why are there all these people in Cook's Town?" Jane tried to understand the situation and geography in a place a long way from Brisbane.

"Cook's Town is the nearest port; well, suitable river. There is no port to speak of, where ships can unload the fossickers and their supplies." George took another sip of his cocoa. "Once there, these miners are faced with a walk, over almost impassable tracks, to the goldfields at Palmer River. Few can afford packhorses so the men transport everything themselves. They struggle with loads far beyond what a human body should carry."

Silence hung over the group as the pictures floated within their heads.

George went on quietly. "Already there have been reports of many deaths due to starvation, men working beyond their capabilities, aboriginal attacks and illness. No doubt there are many more deaths not reported. Things must be ten times worse at the Palmer River area. There, they have not only the miners coming from Cook's Town but others travelling from the inland Etheridge area; all needing to be fed. Supplies can only reach the area by packhorse, along a fearsome track from Cook's Town."

George paused while he drained his cup. After a long breath, he took up his tale. "Once the wet season has really set in, those who have managed to reach the goldfields will be unable to return. They will not have access to any extra supplies. Many will starve to death beside their gold. Those who do make it back to Cook's Town will have nowhere to go and little to eat until the next ship arrives."

It was Jane who asked, "But what can we do, down here?"

Eve spoke up. "There must be something we can do."

Abigail took up the proposition. "Doctor George and Thomas have suggested they travel to Cook's Town to set up a medical practice there, for a year or so, until things have settled somewhat." She paused for a moment. "We ladies can go with them, to support them, as we do here, or we can stay in Brisbane."

Jane's mouth fell open. "Surely ladies cannot go to such a place. Who knows what sort of people are to be found there or what might happen to us? It is one thing, coming to a large town in this new country, but to venture into the uncivilized jungles is another thing altogether."

Abigail went on undeterred. "If we decide to stay here, we have a choice of sharing this dwelling with our cousin who will take on a temporary medical practice at this surgery for two years, or we can return to the Mariner's Rest, to live there until George and Thomas return."

Eve's face was thoughtful as her hands pleated the skirt material on her lap. "If we did either of those two things, we would not be doing anything to help the people in Cook's Town."

"No, Eve, we would not." Abigail sighed.

"Where would we live, and what would we eat? You did say there is little more than tents to live in and the supplies were few." Jane's frown deepened.

Abigail reached out and touched her friend's hand. "Jane, I will not force you to do what you do not wish to do." Her gaze travelled from Jane to Eve and back again. "Will you both think on it for a day or two? I, for one, would really like to go up there; to feel I am doing something useful. It will only be for a limited time." She paused and grinned at her brother. "Father did say I'd be living in a tent."

George took up the tale. "Ewan MacGregor, from the *Northern Orchid*, said the government is shipping many prefabricated buildings of timber and corrugated iron to the area. The *Northern Orchid* is carrying nearly a hundred tons of this type of cargo on its current trip. We can make sure we have our own residence on board the ship with us."

Abigail turned to George's assistant. "Thomas, you're not saying much. How do you feel about such a venture?"

"Miss Abigail, I think it will be an experience one cannot miss and we are helping others at the same time. I can understand such a place may be somewhat daunting, if not terrifying, for a woman."

Abigail looked at the group. "So, we'll think on the options and rediscuss this when the men have more information available. Are we all agreed?"

Nods and murmurs suggested all present were unanimous.

THE MARINER'S REST HOTEL

After several hours and three doses of the oil of cloves to her aching tooth, the fretful Lucy settled to sleep. She sat in Sarah's lap with her dark curls resting on her mother's shoulder. In front of the chair, the fire flickered through the stove grate. At the sound of the knock on the door of the shack, Sarah sighed. She spread her shawl around the child as she stood to open the door.

"Miss Sarah, I'm just heading home." Even in the dim light, Maureen Ryan's shoulders could be seen to sag. With the hotel's guest list full, the workload of preparing and serving tea to everyone by the two young women, Meg Hamilton and sixteen-year-old Maureen, was an exhausting job. Sarah knew. She had been about Maureen's age when she first started working full time at The Mariner's Rest. Feeding the guests was only the half of it. They then had to clean the dishes, the kitchen and the dining rooms before closing up for the night.

"Thanks, Maureen. It's quite late and a black night out tonight. Make sure Ned escorts you home."

"Yes, Miss Sarah. He's going to let me sit on Prince and hold the reins myself, this time. How's young Lucy?"

"She's nearly settled, thanks. Now, you be careful on the horse. They are such big animals. We'll see you tomorrow afternoon."

Maureen went to walk away then spun back to Sarah. "I put a message from the brewery, for Mr. Jacko, on the office desk tonight."

"I'll let him know it's there."

TWENTY-ONE

THE GOLDFINCH ENTOURAGE

With care, Eve avoided the wobbly second stair and stretched her leg up to the top step. The sound of sobbing could be heard on the other side of the door. She reached up and knocked loudly.

"Hello, anyone in? Maureen, are you there? It's Eve from Doctor Goldfinch's surgery."

The sobbing stopped abruptly. Eve strained to hear the tentative footsteps as they approached the door. The doorknob rattled; a prelude to the loud scrape on the floor as it opened. Standing with reddened eyes was the youngest child, the boy; the one they called Bob. He was nine years old now. Eve had watched him growing up on her occasional visits to the family. She found it difficult to believe it had been six years since she'd come to Australia. Today she was here to say goodbye to Maureen and the Ryan family. Her heart flipped at the thought tomorrow she and the rest of the Doctor's group were to board the *Northern Orchid*. They were heading north, to a place called Cook's Town. She looked down on the solemn face.

"Hello, young fellow, is your mam in?"

"Ma's asleep and won't wake up." The boy once again burst into tears and ran in through the hall.

Hesitantly, Eve followed the boy to where the door of the main bedroom stood open. The lad rushed through into the arms of Minnie, the younger girl in the family of three girls and the boy. Fourteen-year-old Erin, the middle girl, was sitting on the side of the bed where the body of Mrs. Ryan lay stretched out; grey and unmoving. It was Erin who looked up towards the entrance where Eve stood.

"Oh, it's you, Eve. I think Ma's gone. She's been like this since I got home from work. She's so cold." Tears began to trickle from eyes already red and swollen.

Holding her brother tightly, Minnie wiped her eyes before explaining further.

"She said she was going to lie down after we had our dinner. The one o'clock gun signal had just gone off at the Windmill. Ma said she was tired."

Eve felt her own eyes sting with unshed tears. "Where's Maureen?"

No one seemed to know where Maureen was working today nor at what time she was due to return. Eve knew Maureen wasn't at the doctor's place; she'd just come from there. She knew Maureen only worked at the hotel on Saturdays and Mondays.

Eve then asked, "Do you know if the man next door, is home?" The older girl shrugged.

"He was." The boy sniffed as he spoke. "He was out the back, fixing his hen house."

Eve went on. "Right, I'm going over to speak to him. I'll send him for the doctor. When I come back, we're going to make a pot of tea."

The voice of Doctor George telling the horse to "Whoa" as he pulled up the sulky outside the Ryan house sent a rush of relief through Eve's body. She was even more pleased to hear Miss

Abigail's voice as well. Eve left the three children sitting at the kitchen table and ran to open the front door.

"Doctor George, it's Mrs. Ryan. She's passed on, I fear."

Eve led the doctor and his sister to the bedroom. She closed the door behind them and returned to the children in the kitchen.

"What'll happen to us?" Erin asked as she struggled to control her tears.

Eve bit her lip. She had seen, far too many times, what happened to young children who were left alone in the world. She had been one of that number herself.

"I'm not sure but I think Miss Abigail'll be able to tell you."

"I wish Maureen were back." The young boy whispered.

Eve held his hand. "Is she often back late?"

It was Minnie who explained. "A few of the ladies in the houses where Maureen cleans are unkind. They make her work till it is long after sundown but they don't give her any extra money."

Eve frowned. She knew just how lucky she was to have Miss Abigail as her employer and her friend.

When Abigail entered the kitchen, her face was serious.

"Children, I'm sorry but your mother has gone to Heaven. God took her while she slept."

Once more the lad began sobbing. The girls, with their hands entwined, sat stoically and listened.

"The doctor has gone to arrange for the welfare carers to come and find you somewhere to stay until things can be sorted out." Abigail's heart quailed. If it wasn't they were sailing tomorrow, she would have taken the children home with her.

"Where's Maureen?" Abigail asked. Once more the girls explained how their sister had not returned home from work just yet.

The sun disappeared beyond the horizon. The cloak of night descended forming deep shadows around the group gathered near the vehicles. One was a coach harnessed to two grey horses and the other a dray with just one brown horse. Hooves stamped impatiently and tails whipped at the cloud of mosquitoes thickening with the falling of night. Frequent slapping at exposed flesh accompanied the subdued voices of the people who were also treated to the attentions of the biting insects.

Two men gripped the poles at either end of the stretcher as they exited the house. A black sheet covered the body. They slid their burden onto and along the floorboards of the dray. The children set up a loud wailing. Their mother had, that very morning, prepared their breakfast and now, here she was, being taken away for the last time.

No one noticed the young woman as she concealed herself in the shrubbery nearby. Her hurried approach halted sharply at the sight of the glowing lanterns, the sound of the horses and the gathering at the front door of her home. She recognized Miss Abigail and Eve from the doctor's surgery. She did not know the tall fat man in the dark suit nor the matronly figure by his side who spoke.

"Thank you for notifying us of the plight of these poor children. We'll see them admitted to the Diamantina Orphanage in Roma Street until their father can be contacted." The matronly figure ushered the sobbing siblings into the coach as she spoke. Each child carried a small bundle of their belongings. The woman turned to face Abigail. "You say there is an older girl, is that correct?"

"Maureen, yes, she has not yet returned from her work. Maureen is sixteen or thereabouts. I would like to say we will wait here for her but I'm afraid we're leaving on a ship for the north tomorrow and are still in the throes of our packing."

"Of course, you must go." The fat man spoke. He turned his attention to the portly lady. "The matron and I will return tomorrow to talk to the girl and reunite her with her siblings."

Maureen withdrew deeper into her shelter. She gritted her teeth against the urge to slap at the mosquitoes covering her skin. She watched, first the undertaker, leave with his dray and her mother. Second, to depart was the coach carrying her brother and sisters, along with the man in the suit and the matron of the orphanage. Barely had they disappeared down the street when her ears picked up the sound of the doctor's sulky arriving. Maureen recognized Thomas, the doctor's man, driving. Miss Abigail and Eve climbed aboard. The deepening night swallowed up the vehicle as the horse's hooves clip-clopped down the street.

She remained in her retreat for some time. Maureen's mind swirled as she attempted to come to terms with what she had just witnessed. Like a death knell for her mother, the neighbours' doors slammed, one by one. The gawkers retreated back into their homes. The show was over.

Eventually, hunger drove her to rise. She slipped quietly into the only home she had ever known. A candle or lamp was not needed to show her the way. In her mother's cupboard, she removed the loose floorboard. Nimble fingers removed the small bag of money her father replenished every time he returned from his gold fossicking trips. Stretching on her tiptoes she dragged down, from the top shelf, an old pair of his trousers, a long sleeve shirt and a vest. These she pulled on after her skirt and blouse were tossed into a heap on the bed. She rolled up the legs and the sleeves of her father's clothes until her feet and hands poked through. Her fingers fumbled with the cord which she threaded through the waist of the trousers before knotting it with a flourish. The money bag disappeared down into one of the deep pockets of the trousers. Shaky fingers shoved her brown hair up under an old cap now pulled down tight on her head. The young girl was instantly transformed into a younger-looking boy. In the kitchen, she tore into the remnants of a loaf of bread. What remained, she stowed inside the shirt along with an old wine bottle now filled with water. The cork squeaked when slammed in tight. She slipped back out into the night.

The lapping of the water below calmed Maureen huddled down between the crates on the wharf. The briny smell of the sea drifted in on a light breeze. A half-moon lit up the ship moored to the wharf bollards. She recognized the name, the *Northern Orchid*. Maureen knew the names of most of the regular ships coming and going at the Brisbane port. She spent long hours here waiting and hoping for the return of her father. It was not to say goodbye to him nor to await his ship's arrival that brought her here this time. Tonight, she intended to be leaving on a ship herself; this ship, the *Northern Orchid*. According to Miss Abigail, this ship would sail to the goldfields of Cook's Town. There was every chance her father could be found somewhere there.

Eyes, desperate in their need to close in sleep, watched the lamplight aglow in the wheelhouse. Occasionally she noticed a man walk past the window. A murmur of voices drifted down to her. Maureen jumped at the sound of laughter followed by a man singing which came from the lower decks. She edged closer to the gangplank keeping to the deepest shadows. When the man on watch moved out of sight, she ran, as light as the shadows themselves, up and on to the ship's deck. Her first goal led her feet to the overhang of the cabins at the stern where the darkness hugged the walls. During her sojourn on the wharf, she had seen no evidence of lights in these cabins; were they empty? A water barrel stood open to collect any rain from the cabin roof. Using it for assistance and her own agility, she swung herself up. She lay flat on the timber, her panting breath roared in her ears. Above her breathing and the pounding of her heart, she struggled to hear the watchman's footsteps as he made his rounds.

After the man passed by, Maureen peeped under a large canvas stretched over a row-boat secured on the cabin roof. Everything was black. Her nimble fingers made short work of the lanyards at the canvas edge. Soon she was able to slip under the cover and into the boat. The rigid timber hull and the horrors of the day did little to prevent exhaustion from claiming her body. She slept.

THE *NORTHERN ORCHID*

A hurricane lantern hung from a hook in the ceiling. Its orange glow fell over those around the table. The familiar smell of burning oil pervaded the room.

"You sure you don't want a hand to cut up your meat, Mr. MacGregor?" Josh asked.

An untidy and stained bandage swathed the right arm and hand of Mac who sat at the table in the chartroom with William Sloan, Noel Evans, Josh and Gus Dougall.

"I would not put it past you to slip off with a chunk of this steak. I'll have you know I have salivated for weeks waiting for a feed of decent meat. This will no doubt be my last such meal until we return."

After the success of their recent venture to Cook's Town, Captain Sloan had managed to acquire a whole beast killed, butchered and delivered to the galley earlier, on this their last day before another trip to the north. In the galley, China had spent most of the day hopping around supervising the preparation of the meat for the entire crew. A round of rum had been delivered to the sailors eating in the galley. The sound of their pleasure drifted up onto the top deck. Stretch could be heard singing one of the Irish ditties he was famous for.

Mac grinned as the melody floated by. "The men seem to be in fine form down there."

"They needed a bit of a blowout. With so many passengers on these voyages north, it makes for quick trips and long days. The crew earn their keep and then some." Captain Sloan smiled as he turned to address Mac. "Last trip it was me taking it easy and now you're getting your own back, Mac. How is the arm, by the way?"

"It's alright. Doctor George said it'll mend straight but only if I don't work it for at least a month."

While the others present discussed some nautical issues of dispute, Captain Sloan leaned in closer to his friend and whispered.

"A rather drastic way of getting to visit with the Miss Jane Stanley, Mac; putting your arm in the capstan and breaking it like that."

"Stupid, but not planned. At least Josh gets to stay as the ship's mate. He'll be pleased."

"What's the final number of steerage passengers we'll have this trip, Mac?"

"Both dormitories will be full and on the top deck, there'll be twenty; all up thirty-four, at last count. It's going to be a tight squeeze on deck this time with all them plus the pre-cut house for the doctor and his family. The holds are both full of cargo mostly for Cook's Town."

"What time are they all going to embark?"

"The miners will start arriving at five in the morning. I told Doctor George to bring his people on board at seven o'clock. They have taken the three first-class cabins." Mac took another sip of his rum.

The captain interjected into the discussion at the other end of the table. "Excuse me, Evans. Can you suggest two men as ship's stewards."

Evans did not need to think for too long. "We used Manson and Keller on the last trip north. They're the two we inherited from the shipwrecked *Fleur* back in sixty-seven. They'd done that sort of thing previously."

"Righto." Captain Sloan turned again to Mac. "Will you be able to supervise them with just the one hand?"

Mac nodded.

The captain grinned as he went on in a low voice. "And no fraternizing with the first-class ladies; especially those named Jane." He turned his attention back to Evans. "What extra hands will we have down in the galley?"

Again, Evans' response was quick. "Lee and Basil are the mainstays; with China helping occasionally. Stretch fits in there quite well too when we can spare him from up top."

Sloan turned back to Mac. "Will you need extra crew on deck?"

"Not since we took on the two from Cook's Town, last month. Bains and Daly are making out fine. One thing's for sure, they're not likely to ever run off and leave us for the goldfields. They've sworn off gold-chasing for life."

Captain Sloan pushed back his chair. "I'll be off to my cot then, I think. That niece of you Dougall lads has me bushed. How can such a little thing keep going for so long without stopping?" William had been made welcome at The Mariner's Rest but the emotional strain had been enormous. He spent too much time in Millie's room with his thoughts and shattered dreams.

Josh and Gus laughed as they began collecting up their dishes and piling them on the tray. "Only a couple of weeks now until there'll be another one calling you Grampy Cap'n" Josh quipped as he swung out of the room heading for the galley with the dishes rattling on a loaded tray.

THE MARINER'S REST HOTEL

"Struth woman, your feet are freezing," Jacko complained as Sarah slipped in beside her husband. "Don't you think it's time we paid someone to help Meg with the teas in the evenings? You're going to drop the wee bairn in the middle of the kitchen floor one day soon."

"After tonight, I'm thinking you may be right. My feet are killing me. I could talk to Mrs. Ryan and ask if Maureen or one of her other daughters may like the extra work."

Jacko rolled over to face Sarah. He took her hand and held it tight. "Sarah, I haven't had the chance to tell you yet. Word is, Maureen's mum died this afternoon. The children were taken to the orphanage; all except Maureen who has not been found yet."

"Goodness me, how terrible. The poor girl. Where on earth could she be? Should we go out looking for her?'

"Don't go getting in a bother, dear. The welfare people and the police are keeping an eye out."

"The poor lass. When she turns up, couldn't she stay here instead of being taken to the home? She'll have much less work at the surgery now the Goldfinch's are leaving tomorrow." Sarah began sobbing.

Jacko stroked her hair. He pondered on the similarities between Sarah and Millie who was forever wanting to take in all the strays. Lying here in his bed beside his wife he remembered how Christopher, Millie's husband, sometimes had to put his foot down.

"Once she turns up tomorrow, we'll talk to the welfare people and offer to take her in. She may want to stay with her brother and sisters instead, you know."

"It's just terrible. Does anyone know where Mr. Ryan is?"

"Nothing definite, as far as I know." Hoping to change the subject Jacko kissed Sarah's forehead but Sarah had other things on her mind.

"Is everything organized to collect Doctor George and Abigail and the others in the dray and sulky at five o'clock in the morning? They have to be at the ship ready to load by seven, you know."

"All done, wife of mine." Jacko gave her forehead another kiss before turning over onto his side, taking cold resignation with him to dreamland.

CHAPTER TWENTY-TWO

THE *NORTHERN ORCHID*

Shadows shrouded the wharf. Voices rumbled quietly amongst the long line of passengers waiting to climb aboard the *Northern Orchid*. They stood patiently, each like a copy of the man in front. Slung over one shoulder of every man hung a dusty sleeping roll while from the opposite shoulder dangled a quart pot, a plate, a pannikin and a fossicker's pan. Mac stood at the bottom of the gangplank ticking the names off his list as each person prepared to board. His red hair glinted in the light of the hurricane lanterns hung like stars about the ship. At the top of the gangplank, Josh received each in their turn and passed them on to Manson and Keller who led them to either the dormitory on the lower deck or to the area put aside below the awning at the forecastle of the ship. China's high piping voice, along with the clatter of cooking pots, drifted out through the porthole in the galley urging Bellyache Basil, Stretch and Lee to further efforts.

Weak daylight struggled through the thick cloud cover to lift the shadows from the wharf when Gus peered out from the porthole, nearest the engine room. The creaking of harness and the plodding horses' feet as they pulled their loads onto the wharf caught his attention. Samson, steered by Jacko with Sarah at his side, hauled the dray carrying Doctor George, Ned and the considerable baggage.

Emperor pranced under Thomas's tight rein, pulling the sulky with the ladies on board. Gus resisted the temptation to run out and say goodbye to his sister and wish her luck with her imminent birthing. His first priority was to stoke his engine boiler and maintain the pressure. At any moment, he expected the order to engage the engine.

Through all of this noise and upheaval, the soft snuffles of the sleeper under the canvas of the longboat remained undiscovered. Between all the other calls on his time, Josh Dougall, as the ship's mate on this trip, began his inspection before departure. It was his job to check all storage was secure and ensure there were no stowaways on board. He slipped down the companionway to the lower deck. The number count of passengers in the dormitories tallied. All coal bags were secured against the hull of the ship. He poked his head inside the galley.

"Everything right to go here, China?" He called.

China's voice followed him on his trot around the bulkheads of the holds. His boots thudded on the rungs of the companionway as he took them two at a time. As expected, Evans had everything ship shape at the bow. Josh made his way to the aft area. He stood below the spare boats listening. There was nothing to be heard above the hustle and bustle of a ship preparing to get underway. His fingers curled around the edge of the cabin roof. Muscles rippled along his arms as he prepared to haul himself up for a closer look when a voice hailed him. As he turned, he did not notice the rope, interlacing the canvas through the cleats at the outer edge of the longboat, were unattached at one hook on the bow.

"Hello, Josh. We made it. I'm not sure how. The women looked like they were never going to get away." Doctor George laughed when his sister pretended to hit him over the head.

"Good morning, Josh," Abigail said. "Are we ready to go?"

Captain Sloan's voice pierced the din. "Do I have a ship's mate aboard?"

"Sorry, I've got to go back to the wheelhouse. I'll catch up with you later."

Maureen's eyelids flew open. The sound of voices approached her place of concealment. She clamped a hand over her mouth to silence the gasp. Her heart thudded inside her chest. She tried to adjust her position and relieve some of the accumulated aches and pains without making any sound. Sweat ran down her forehead. Her mouth felt as dry as a summer dust storm. Her terror abated a little when she recognized Doctor George's voice.

"Come along, Abigail. These two cabins at the back will be for you and your ladies. Thomas and I will share the one here at the front next to the lounge room."

In her hiding place, Maureen smiled at the sound of young Henry's excited voice.

"Mama look they have a top bunk and a bottom bunk. Can I have the top bunk?"

Maureen heard Miss Abigail settling Eve and Miss Jane into the second ladies' cabin before she followed Henry. Thomas and George were heard talking with another man. The other voice was somehow familiar. She thought it may have been the red-haired man who had been at Miss Millie's funeral some months ago but she could not be too sure. He spoke again. This time the voice came from the back of the cabins.

"Mrs. Baldwin, you and your ladies might like to stand over near the stern of the ship to wave to your friends. We'll be getting underway very shortly."

Maureen sipped a little of her water. Her ears strained to identify what was happening outside her dark cave.

"You will let us know as soon as you hear from Maureen, won't you?" Miss Abigail's voice called loudly from the deck to the wharf. A slither of guilt ran through Maureen's body but she could not tell the good lady where she was or what she was doing.

"Jacko'll go and check the house this morning. He'll talk to the police and welfare people today. We'll make sure she's safe." Again, another slither of guilt wiggled after the first. Miss Sarah shouldn't be out in this early morning air when she's so close to birthing.

Maureen's body stiffened and her eyes darted about the darkness anxiously as the sound and vibration of an engine drifted up from somewhere below. A loud voice called to have the hawsers removed from the bollards. The order was followed almost immediately by a loud splash. Her body shuddered against the hull of the longboat as the ship's engine moved into gear. Suddenly Maureen's stomach felt hollow. Her heart ached. She only now had time to really think about the death of her mother and her own separation from her sisters and brother. Sobs threatened to explode through her lips. The squeals of the farewells from the deck and the wharf went unnoticed.

Mac excused himself and took his leave from the group still waving their farewells. He had difficulty preventing himself from skipping a short highland fling. Miss Jane Stanley's smile was enough to make any man jump for joy. Even in the early morning, she looked a fine woman. He wasn't all that old yet and the lady did not seem uninterested in his attention. He looked forward to the next few weeks. As he readjusted the bandaged arm in the sling hanging from his neck, he thought it was almost worth the inconvenience to have all this spare time on his hands on this particular voyage.

The hum of the engine lulled Maureen to sleep once again. It was impossible to tell time within the covered boat. The smell of food awoke her and set her mouth salivating. Still, the rivulets of sweat ran down her face. Her clothes were damp with it and her body smelt of it. The clatter of tin plates and the sound of heavy pots were heard not too far away. She listened to the many voices arguing over food servings. Suddenly there were voices just below her followed by a knocking sound on a door.

"Doctor Goldfinch we've your meals here. Will we serve the trays in the lounge room?" It was a voice Maureen had never heard before.

Below her, the doctor answered the knock. "Thanks. Keller, isn't it?"

"Yes, Sir."

The doctor continued. "The lounge room will be splendid. I'll call the ladies from their rooms."

The aroma of the meal tormented the hungry girl exacerbating her discomfort further. Dirty fingers dug the dry bread out from inside her shirt. She nibbled slowly and sipped from her water bottle. The problem of accessing more food filled her mind. At this stage, she was at a loss. Maybe in the dark tonight, she'd investigate. Having utilized the rainwater barrel to climb up to her position, her water supply should not be a problem. The curve of the longboat received her tired body as she lay back, in an attempt to recapture her sleep.

The threatening clouds of the early morning were overhauled by a glorious sunny day. Lunch was not long over when Gus burst from the companionway landing on the upper deck with a thud of his two feet. A sharp squeal pulled him up short.

"Sorry for startling you, Miss Eve."

Eve jumped back, then laughed.

"Oh, Gus, it's you. You came out of there like a ferret from its hole with the dogs after it. Aren't you supposed to be with your engine?"

"We have passed across the river mouth and the captain had me cut the engine while he set his sails. Captain Sloan prefers the salt breezes thrumming the canvas overhead to the engine vibrations beneath his feet or the smell of burning coal clogging up his nostrils." Both looked up admiring the billowing sails. The ship forged ahead as if impatient to be getting on with the job. Gus continued. "Mind you, he's pleased to have his engine when it reduces delays in the ports or provides back up in a storm. To him, engines are nothing but a necessary evil, I think."

Eve gazed out across the sea. She breathed in deeply while holding her head on the side to better hear the hum of the sails. "I think I agree with the captain. It's a wonderful sensation with just the sails."

"How have you all settled in? Have you everything you want?" Gus asked.

"Thank you, yes. Miss Jane is feeling a bit poorly. She has taken to her cot. I remember she suffered terribly with seasickness when we sailed over from England. Miss Abigail is taking Henry's lessons, much to his disgust. He cannot put as much over his mother as he does over Miss Jane."

They both chuckled at the thought for a moment. Then Gus clapped his hand to his forehead.

"I should have thought of this earlier. China makes a great brew for seasickness. He keeps our crew on their feet. I'll talk to him."

"China?"

"The ship's senior cook. A very interesting chap."

The two walked over to the bulwark where Gus pointed out some of the landmarks fast disappearing as the ship ate up the waves.

"Miss Eve, it may be an idea not to come so far forward on the ship, by yourself. There are many men coming up and down the companionway from the dormitories below decks. They come to mix with the other miners up at the bow. If you wish, I'll be happy to be your escort when you want to see more of the ship."

"Well, thank you, Gus. I'll look forward to it."

The food arriving on the top deck for the evening meal did not torment Maureen as it had earlier in the day. She lay curled up in the blackness of the boat sound asleep. Beads of sweat stood out upon her forehead. Smudges of dirt marked her face and stained her clothes. Every last skerrick of bread crumbs from the paper bag laying upon her chest had been devoured. The empty water bottle lay against the rib of the keel. The gloom around her disappeared into the darkest of night as the sun disappeared below the horizon.

THE MARINER'S REST HOTEL

Sarah left Jacko and Ned to unhitch the wagon and sulky while she went into the kitchen of the hotel to ensure Mrs. Hamilton had managed to prepare and serve the breakfasts with the help of Mrs. Randall, the cleaner. She was pleased to see the dishes were well on the way to being washed and dried.

"Good morning, ladies."

"Oh, Sarah, you're back. Did the Goldfinch family get away alright? Can I make you a cup of tea?" Mrs. Hamilton pulled out a chair and helped her to sit. "Look at those ankles, lass. They're swollen up like a Christmas pudding."

Sarah smiled. "I'd love a cup of tea, Mrs. Hamilton, thanks." As Mrs. Hamilton pulled the kettle over to the hottest plate on the stove, Sarah went on to ask the question uppermost in her mind. "Has there been any word of young Maureen?"

Her heart sank when Mrs. Hamilton moved her head sideways, in the negative.

"Is there any more tea in the pot?" Jacko asked as he entered the kitchen in a rush. "I'll have a slice of your cake too, Mrs. Hamilton, if I may." He nodded towards the sultana cake the cook was in the process of removing from the oven.

"Oh, Jacko, this is way too hot to eat yet. You'll burn your gizzard." She admonished her new boss.

"I'm off to see what I can find out at the Ryan house. Maybe I'll go to the orphanage and see what I can learn from the other Ryan children. Who knows, they may be able to throw some light on to Maureen's disappearance."

Sarah reached up and took his wrist. "You're a good man, Jacko Benson."

Jacko drained his teacup. When Mrs. Hamilton turned away, he slipped a knife from the dresser drawer and lopped the end off the cake.

"Ooh, ooh." He juggled the hot slice from hand to hand. Sarah shook her head but giggled softly as Jacko kissed her forehead and made a quick retreat out the back door while chewing on his contraband. His voice echoed through the kitchen. "It's lovely, Mrs. Hamilton."

Prince pulled up at the front of the Ryan house in a cloud of dust. The hand brake of the sulky creaked as Jacko pulled it up tight before wrapping the reins around the side rail of the seat. When he jumped down to the ground, he slipped a carrot out of his pocket and offered it to the horse.

His curiosity was aroused when he noticed another buggy at the side of the house. He walked over but did not recognize either the horse or the vehicle. His feet took him to the front steps which he climbed gingerly. The three stairs groaned under his weight. His knuckles rattled the front door. It swung inwards, opened by a large lady with a rather officious voice. Her face was turned behind her, towards the inside of the house. Jacko stepped back down a stair. It wobbled under his weight nearly throwing him into the weeds below.

"Don't you kids take too long getting your things, now. I haven't got all day to waste." Her head then turned to see who stood at the door. "Who are you? What do you want?"

Jacko's mouth fell open. He felt like an errant schoolboy. Rough hands brushed cake crumbs from his face while he scraped his boots on the step.

"Mrs, I am Jacko Benson. I am the proprietor of the Mariner's Rest Hotel. I have come looking for Maureen Ryan who is a friend of my wife. We heard Mrs. Ryan died yesterday. We are concerned for Maureen and the other children, being as Mr. Ryan is away at the moment."

The woman almost sniffed. "You know the family, do you? Mr. Benson, you said? I am Mrs. Fothergill; Matron of the Diamantina Orphanage in Roma Street."

"Er … Pleased to meet you, Mrs. Fothergill. Yes, my wife and I are friends with the family." Jacko crossed his fingers surreptitiously. "My wife was planning on coming to see you later today or tomorrow to ask if the children can stay with us until Bert, their father, returns." Jacko hoped he had got the name right. He tried to remember back to when the doctor had mentioned Mr. Ryan's visit to the surgery some time previously. Doctor George had been impressed with the man.

"Mr. Benson, we have to keep close control over children without families. It would never do to let them wander all over the countryside." The plump hand came up to tap on her fleshy lips. "On the other hand, money is always scarce in supporting those at the orphanage. If you and your wife were willing to sign the necessary papers to take care of these children until their father returns, it would be helping us considerably. Another three, four, if we find Maureen, mouths less to feed can make a difference to our budget."

The woman's lack of compassion nearly bowled Jacko over, in spite of his own experiences as a youngster.

"Look, Mr. Benson, can you assure me you have suitable accommodation for the children. I am not too sure a hotel might be the best environment."

"Oh, my wife and I do not live in the hotel. We have separate accommodation. The children will stay there." Jacko had no idea how they'd fit the extra bodies in the small shack but he had full faith in the organizational skills of his wife.

"In that case, I'll leave the children in your charge now. I really must get back to the orphanage to supervise the others. I'd appreciate it if your wife and yourself could come to the office there at ten tomorrow morning to complete the paperwork. You can collect the few things the children took there last night, then. Please, come on in."

The woman slid past Jacko and out the front door, down the steps and disappeared around the side of the house at a surprising speed despite her size. Jacko stood aghast. Three heads appeared at the hallway door.

"Who are you, Mister?" The boy asked.

"Hello, I'm Jacko Benson. I'm a friend of," Jacko struggled for a minute trying to think of mutual acquaintances, "Maureen and Doctor George."

"Do you know Miss Abigail and Eve?"

"Yes, I do. They are my friends too. They are friends with my wife, Sarah also."

"Do you mean Miss Sarah, at the hotel? Maureen likes Miss Sarah." The tallest of the two girls spoke.

"Yes. Now, I wanted to ask you if you would like to stay with us at the hotel until we can find Maureen or until your father returns?"

"We think Maureen has gone to find our father." The second girl almost whispered.

"Will the hotel be like the kids' home? I don't like it at the kids' home." The young boy rubbed his red swollen eyes.

"Right, well come on then we'd best get sorted here and then we'll go see Miss Sarah. We'll need to find beds for you all, what do you think?"

"Thank you, Sir." The eldest girl gave a watery smile.

"Just you call me, Mr. Jacko, now shake a leg there." Jacko hoped his Sarah really meant what she said last night about having the kids stay with them at the hotel because she was going to get one big surprise when he arrived home with this lot.

THE *NORTHERN ORCHID*

"Give me a leg up," Josh spoke softly endeavouring not to disturb the passengers in the upper-deck cabins. "And try not to sound like a herd of cattle."

Gus took little notice of his brother's comments and put out his entwined hands. Josh put his right foot into the human stirrup. With a grunt, Gus heaved upwards. Josh lifted into the air with a swoosh. Outstretched fingers gripped the edge of the roof of the cabins, as Josh hauled himself up and over. Once settled, he reached his arm down to take hold of his brother's hand. Gus swung up to settle on his haunches beside Josh.

"We're only uncovering the longboat, aren't we? The timbers of the jolly-boat had a good soaking when we were in Brisbane. Do you think the captain's right in reckoning it'll rain later today?"

"It's not often Captain Sloan makes a mistake with the weather. Anyway, we'll shift the canvas off here and get on back to the chartroom."

The two young men began loosening the interlacing rope holding the canvas cover in position.

"Who last stored the boats? This rope has missed three hooks on this side." Gus observed.

Josh and Gus stood on either side at the stern of the longboat and began to role the canvas back in folds of two feet widths. As they approached the bow of the boat, Gus looked up at his brother with a startled expression on his face.

"What the devil have we here?"

"It's a damn stowaway. How'd he get on board?" Josh silently cursed himself. His guilty conscience reminded him he had only given the ship a cursory inspection before leaving the Brisbane wharf.

"He's sleeping like a baby. Seems a shame to wake him. I wouldn't like to be in his shoes when the captain sees him." Gus reached over and gave the lad's shoulder a shake. As he did so he could not help but notice the heat coming from the sleeping body. "He sure feels hot. Do you think it's just because he's been in the covered boat or do you think he's sick?"

"He'll be a lot sicker when Captain Sloan gets a hold of him. He'll likely get the cat-of-nine-tails."

Once again, Gus shook the boy's shoulders and began to drag him upright.

Maureen was only partly aware of being rudely dragged from her semi-comatose state. She attempted to stand but her knees felt like one of her Ma's Christmas custards. She jammed her cap tightly on her head and pulled her trousers further up her trunk. With head bowed she struggled to climb out of the boat and onto the roof of the cabin. It was Josh who grabbed her arm as her legs began to give away under her.

"Stand up straight, lad. We're not going to carry you to your execution."

Her heart quailed but she bit her lip and refused to cry.

Between them, the brothers lowered the stowaway to the deck. They frogmarched him to a point below the wheelhouse. Gus climbed the ladder to report to Captain Sloan. In a short time, orders were bellowed and all available crew lined up at the mainmast.

Abigail followed the sound of raised voices. On the top deck, around the mainmast, she found the cluster of crew members. Bosun Evans held them back from the cleared space in which Josh Dougall stood. His grip was firm on the elbow of a young boy dressed in dirty shirt and trousers with their ends rolled up several times. Other than the streaks of dirt, the lad's face was whiter than the sails which billowed above him. From where they stood on the walkway at the starboard side of the wheelhouse, Captain Sloan and Ewan MacGregor looked down upon the group. Inside, Gus's hand steadied the ship's helm. Whispers drifted through the men like the rustling leaves of poison ivy.

"A stowaway. Dougall found a stowaway in the longboat. The lad'll be flogged for sure."

Abigail stretched up in an effort to peer over the heads of the crew. Henry, who had been on her tail, was not so backward. He wriggled his way between the forest of legs until he stood in the front row.

"There is only one punishment for a stowaway on this ship and that is five lashes with the cat-o-nine tails. If you survive it, you'll be chained in the galley scrubbing the dishes for the remainder of the voyage." Captain Sloan's voice rang out.

Henry's eyes threatened to pop out of his head.

Abigail's, "Excuse me, please, please excuse me, pardon me, please," went unnoticed behind him.

Henry burst from the group. He ran full pelt to throw his arms about the waist of the stowaway boy, nearly overturning the prisoner and the man he called Uncle Josh, in the rush.

Instant silence struck every one present. Even the captain, gaped in disbelief. This child, Millie's god-child, who called him Grampy Cap'n, was openly defying him, here, on his own bridge. The scar on the left side of his face stood out like a snow-covered mountain ridge

209

against the tanned plains of his face. He turned to look at Ewan MacGregor for support. He frowned to see Mac's face, even though it could not be faulted on impassivity, held green eyes sparkling with amusement.

William Sloan was about to bring young Henry to order but the mother, Miss Abigail, spoke up.

"I'm sorry, Captain Sloan, but you cannot flog this prisoner."

The audacity of the woman almost left William speechless; almost. "Mrs.Baldwin, I do not take kindly to being told what to do on my own bridge."

"But you cannot, Captain, Sir. That boy may be a stowaway BUT that boy is not a boy. She is a girl."

Josh dropped the prisoner's elbow and jumped back. He gasped. It was Henry's arms which kept the prisoner upright.

The hush of the audience deepened. Abigail walked over and gently took the baggy cap from the prisoner's head. An explosion of brown curls cascaded down Maureen's shoulders. Tears ran down the girl's cheeks for the first time since her capture. She reached her arms around Henry and gave him a squeeze. Abigail turned back to look up at the captain.

"This is Maureen Ryan. A young girl who has just lost her mother in death. I think you will find this girl is here on a venture to find her father somewhere on the goldfields. No doubt she wants him to return and rescue his other children from the orphans' home." She looked down at the girl. "Am I correct in assuming this, Maureen?"

The girl could not speak. She nodded her head. A single sob echoed off the wall of watchers.

Abigail turned her eyes to the wheelhouse walkway. "May I continue, Captain Sloan?"

The captain shrugged. "Be my guest, please, Mrs. Baldwin."

"I propose to take this young woman into my care. I will pay for her passage to Cook's Town."

The captain was not given the chance to reply as the roar of the crew's cheer rose up the mainmast like a splendid sail in a full breeze. Josh did not cheer. He had a tongue lashing from the captain to look forward to. As the ship's mate, it was his responsibility to inspect the ship thoroughly.

The captain nodded then turned back to the wheelhouse. He mumbled at Mac. "I really don't know what I'm doing here. I'm surplus to demand, I think."

When Maureen was strong enough, Miss Abigail took her to see the captain. The girl hung back wishing the deck would swallow her up. At least this time, her clothes included a respectable skirt and blouse; even if it was only on loan from Eve. She almost tripped over the long skirt as she followed her mentor.

It had been Jane, who had made the arrangements for their interview with Captain Sloan, aided by her newly acquired beau, Mister MacGregor. Miss Abigail knocked on the chartroom door; the meeting place.

The door swung inwards and a gruff voice instructed the two ladies. "Come in, please."

Miss Abigail stepped forward without hesitation but Maureen paused.

"Come, Maureen. Don't be afraid." Her friend encouraged.

It was alright for her to be so brave. Maureen's back still stung at the thought of what it might feel like to suffer the lashes this man had ordered. She stepped forward to stand just inside the doorway.

The captain smiled. The scar running down the side of his face did not look half so terrifying as it had two days ago.

"Come in, lass. I'll not bite."

Maureen stepped forward another two steps. The click of the door closing behind her sounded like a death knell in her ears.

Captain Sloan moved to pull out a chair for each of his two visitors. "Can I offer you ladies a cup of tea?"

"No, thank you, Captain. The galley cooks and stewards have been looking after us like we were royalty. We have not long had a splendid morning tea."

"I'm glad to hear it. Now, you wanted to see me, Mrs. Baldwin?"

"Yes, Captain Sloan. Maureen has come here today to apologize for all the trouble she brought upon you, Josh Dougall and the crew by stowing away on the *Northern Orchid.* She had only the thought of finding her father in her mind. She did not appreciate the consequences of her actions."

While Miss Abigail spoke on her behalf, Maureen sat with her head bowed.

The captain stood quiet for a few moments observing the pair. "I have to admit you cannot be faulted for your courage, Maureen. I'm sure the reprimand I gave Josh will not go amiss. He's not one to carry a grudge. He'll be all over it by now."

Maureen dared not look up. She thought all that most unlikely given the fact Josh Dougall ignored her at all and every opportunity.

Miss Abigail spoke again. "Captain Sloan, I wish to apologize for my own behavior. I spoke without thinking at the time. It was only later I realized the position I put you in. It must have been rather galling to have a woman telling you what you can do on your own ship. Especially one who does not know the bow from the stern of a vessel."

Maureen peeped up under her eyebrows and almost gasped when she noticed the sparkling grey eyes in the man's face.

"Ladies, thank you both for your apologies. There has been no lasting damage done. Miss Maureen, I do hope your search for your father is successful. I will be only too happy to assist where I am able." The captain bowed.

This time Maureen could not prevent the escaping gasp. Words were not to be found inside her head. She nodded her appreciation.

Miss Abigail smiled as the captain drew back their chairs and directed them from the room. "Millie always said you were a most wonderful man. I find she is quite right, Captain."

CHAPTER TWENTY-THREE

THE *NORTHERN ORCHID*

Josh and Gus stood looking across at the lights of Rockhampton. Waves lapped against the ship's hull where she lay moored in the Fitzroy River just out from the livestock wharf. Behind them the voices of the prospectors camped on the foredeck rose and fell as some men argued, others laughed and a few told tales of years gone by. From the alehouses on the foreshore, occasional catches of raucous voices drifted on the night air. The intermittent hoot of an owl lifted from the trees on the river bank.

"I see Captain Sloan's keeping the *Northern Orchid* away from the wharf again this trip," Gus muttered as he sucked on his newly acquired pipe. He coughed.

"These fellows paid the full fare to Cook's Town and he's not waiting here for them to return from some drunken spree or doxy house. He just wants to get water and coal and be on his way before tomorrow night."

It was Gus who broke the next long period of silence. "I see the stowaway girl is up and about again. Eve says she's much better now."

"Well, for my money, I'd have happily chucked her overboard," Josh growled.

The chuckles from Gus threatened to evolve into full-throated laughter until his brother punched his upper arm.

"Don't take it out on me because you were bettered by a girl," Gus complained.

"Rubbish." Josh stormed off towards their cabin. "If you're going to talk rot, I'm calling it a night."

Gus puffed at his pipe a couple of times. A fit of coughing took him again. He began to wonder if he really wanted to smoke a pipe at all. It was the thought Eve might think it made him look more mature which had him persisting.

The next day, it was Gus, Bandy, Andrews and Dave who rowed the longboat. They ferried Captain Sloan, Mac and the Goldfinch group, to the wharf. The captain was happy to escape the chatter. Like a mob of magpies, was his opinion. He wasted no time disappearing off into the direction of the harbourmaster's office.

Mac, with a clean white bandage on his hand and arm, escorted the passengers on a walk around the town. His chest threatened to burst the buttons of his shirt. The smile never left his lips when Jane Stanley rested her small hand in the crook of the elbow of his good arm. All the ladies wore their bonnets and held parasols against the searing sun. With glum faces, the four sailors sitting at the oars turned the boat back to the ship. There was coal to be loaded and water tanks to be filled as soon as the coal barge and the water hoy were available.

At the telegram office, Abigail could not believe her eyes or her ears. The small room, full of noisy customers, sounded like an amplified hornet's nest. Businessmen tapped their feet, impatient to telegraph orders to Brisbane and elsewhere. Stockbrokers sought marketing information. Bank officers strived to remain unflustered as they completed financial transactions. The clatter of the machines intermittently broke through the human rumble. The body odour in the enclosed space overwhelmed her. She stood still and concentrated on breathing, slowly, in an effort not to pass out. In all her time on the perimeter of the medical world, she had never been known to pass out. She did not plan on doing so today. Her laced-edged handkerchief became saturated with the perspiration she mopped up as it trickled down her face. She had looked forward to sending this telegram to Sarah today but this room proved disheartening. Nevertheless, Abigail persisted in her wait, if not in her patience. She knew she must persevere as Sarah needed to be informed of the discovery of Maureen on board the ship. She regretted having insisted her friends wander off to visit the School of Arts on the nearby street.

The ladies returned to the deck of the *Northern Orchid* via the bosun's chair. The men climbed aboard using the Jacob's ladder. Josh stood ready to greet them. He held a pink telegram slip in his hand which he passed over to Miss Abigail.

"This was waiting for you at the Harbourmaster's office this morning. Captain Sloan brought it back with him."

"Oh, thank you, Josh. It will be from Sarah. Come with us while I open it. You and Gus will want to know what she has to say."

The group stood gathered at the door to their lounge as Abigail tore the slip open. Green eyes scanned the brief message. A wide smile lit her face as she gazed around those in the room. She felt good about spending the eight shillings to send Sarah a telegram earlier.

"Well, read it out loud, Abigail, don't keep it all to yourself," Doctor George admonished.

Abigail spoke up.

Baby boy delivered safely last night – stop - No sign Maureen – stop - Have her siblings here with us – stop - Regards Sarah and Jacko – stop.

"Maureen, did you hear? Your brother and sisters are safe at the hotel and they'll now know you are safe." She turned her head to Josh. "How does it make you feel, Josh? You and Gus are uncles once again; and a boy. Will you tell the captain for me? Sarah said she was going to call the baby Christopher William if it was a boy."

Josh's face lit up. He laughed then leapt into the air and clicked his heels together. "I'll do that, right after I tell Gus. He'll be tickled pink with a nephew."

THE MARINER'S REST HOTEL

Jacko stood at the door of the shack for some moments watching, before he moved to enter. His soft look took in Sarah who sat, with the sleeping baby on her lap, in the rocking chair he and Ned had built for her after Lucy's birth. Four children now sat at the table. Erin, Minnie and Bob; the Ryan children alongside his own eldest daughter, Lucy. In the dull light of the lamp, the Ryan siblings wrote on their slates, the lessons they learnt earlier in the day at the new government school they attended. Lucy drew squiggles on the slate Ned had given her for her birthday. Sarah offered advice to the students when she wasn't absorbing all they told her of the classes they attended.

"Is there any room for me in here?" He grinned.

"Hello, Mr. Jacko. Come and sit near me," Bob called as he shoved his sister further up the form.

"Thanks, Bob, but I think I might just sit on the chair by my sweetheart." Jacko leant down and kissed Sarah on the forehead.

All the children started oohing and giggling, with hands over their mouths.

"Mr. Jacko kissed Miss Sarah," Bob said aloud.

Everyone laughed. Lucy climbed down and walked over to her father. She lifted her arms. He swung her up to his shoulder as he reached down to touch the baby's forehead.

"How's young Christopher, today?"

"A perfect angel; must take after his mother." Sarah teased.

"And how are you coping? To go from a mother of one to a mother of five within a few days cannot be easy." Jacko spoke softly.

"How can I complain. We all eat over at the hotel so I only have the baby's' meal to provide and that is not exactly a huge effort. Most of our washing is done by Blossom in the laundry who now has the help of our new part-time employee Miss Erin Ryan."

"Erin, are you sure you want to do this? You don't have to if you don't want to."

"Mr. Jacko, I am more than willing to help out. Minnie keeps busy here helping Sarah with the baby. We are happy to repay you both for our bed and food until our Dad returns."

"I'm sure Sarah and Blossom will be grateful for all your help. Oh … talking about your Dad reminds me of what I have in my pocket."

Everyone's eyes turned on Jacko who stood pretending to forget which pocket he was talking about. It was Lucy's little fingers drew the telegram out of his top pocket and into the open.

"Here, Da. Read it?" She unfolded the sheet of paper before handing it to her father.

Jacko read the written words from memory.

Maureen on Northern Orchid – stop – looking for father at Cooktown – stop – will care for her – stop – Regards Abigail – stop.

Later, as Sarah tucked the baby into the cot at the end of their bed, she turned to Jacko.

"Are the girls settled next door? Has Erin turned the lamp off properly?"

Jacko opened one eye as he lay stretched out on the bed. He smiled at his wife. "She's a good girl. She does it every night." He paused and grinned. "And before you ask, mother-of-many, Bob is sound asleep in his own bed in the kitchen."

Sarah smiled. "I know, I know. I'm a bit of a fusspot, I guess. It's a big responsibility, taking on an extra family."

Jacko began laughing softly.

"What's so funny, Jacko?" Sarah asked as she slipped her feet under the sheet.

Jacko could hardly stop laughing enough to answer.

"Even Miss Millie might raise her eyebrows at this lot we've got here."

They both started to giggle. It was Sarah who first became serious again.

"Jacko, it is only a few weeks until Christmas. Have the supplies for the public bar been organized? Mrs. Hamilton and I spent some time sorting the menu and orders for the guests this morning. Did I tell you we have seven extra guests booked during the Christmas week?"

"Yes, yes, Sarah. All is in hand." He reached over and touched her fingers.

"Will we be able to afford small gifts for the children this Christmas? It would be terrible if we cannot give them a little something."

"What did you have in mind?"

"I thought I might get Ned to carve a wooden horse for Bob. You know how the lad never leaves the stables unless dragged out. If you would make two of those little wooden boxes, like the one you made for me, I'll turn them into sewing cases for Erin and Minnie. They are both handy with a needle and thread. I believe their mother was quite a seamstress in her day. As you know, Ned has started to carve a doll for Lucy. The dress and bonnet are almost completed for it. And don't forget, we must do the little gifts for the workers; especially Ned, who is so good to us all. What do you think, Jacko, will we be able to do all that?"

220

When her husband did not answer Sarah pushed herself up onto her elbow. The man's eyes were closed. Soft flutters of his lips as he breathed confirmed he had drifted off to sleep. Her first instinct was to give him a nudge in the ribs but she remembered how he had been up working in the kitchen with Mrs. Hamilton before sunrise and had barely stopped for a bite to eat since. A light finger smoothed the dark curls from his forehead. Smiling with contentment, Sarah settled back on the pillow.

THE *NORTHERN ORCHID*

"Miss Stanley, is that you? Is everything alright? You do realize it's near one o'clock in the morning."

Jane drew her gaze back from the moon's reflection in the now calm waters off the coast between Bowen and Townsville.

"Yes, thank you, Mr. MacGregor. After spending the whole of Christmas Day locked in our cabins against the terrible squally weather. I just needed to catch some fresh air."

Jane barely registered she should feel somewhat worried about her situation. This was certainly not something one would even consider doing in the city. Dressed, as she was in her flimsy nightgown barely covered by her coat-frock dress, she stood talking to a gentleman all alone in the middle of the night. Her mother would be horrified if she knew. Mrs. Goldfinch would not be impressed at this example to her daughter, Abigail. Mrs. Goldfinch had made it abundantly clear it was part of Jane's employment duties to ensure Abigail conformed more to convention than she was wont to do. Jane thrilled to the feel of her heart pounding in her chest.

"May I join you, Miss Stanley?"

"Of course, Mr. MacGregor. This beautiful night has been made to be shared." Her demure eyes dropped.

The pair stood leaning against the bulwark of the ship's stern peering out on the expanse of water. Luminescence rose around the anchor cable where it disappeared into the dark sea.

Ewan MacGregor looked down at this woman by his side. He smiled.

"Miss Stanley, would it offend you if I asked you to call me, Mac; or even Ewan? We have come to know each other quite well over the past few days, I think."

Jane turned towards this older man with the kind face and sparkling eyes of mischief. It had not been difficult to deduct he felt strongly towards her. Older he might be, yet this did not bother her in the least. Mr. MacGregor seemed so much more mature and appealing than any man whom she had ever met. She reached her small hand out to cover his own resting on the rail.

"Mr. MacGregor, Mac, I will consider it an honour to address you by your abbreviated name. I rather think it suits you very well. This can only occur if you agree to call me Jane."

Her small hands disappeared in the gentle clasp of Mac's calloused fingers.

"Jane, it is. A beautiful name for a beautiful lady."

Jane almost gasped at her boldness when she spoke. "I sometimes think life is too short to be wasted on protocols, don't you; or am I being too brazen? At my age now, I think one looks at the priorities of the world differently, somehow."

Mac almost whispered. "You are correct. Life can be perilously short sometimes. Please rest assured no matter what you ever do I will never judge you to be brazen. Pragmatic maybe, but not forward."

"Very good then, Mr. MacGregor, because right at this very minute I think I am going to kiss you until the moon falls from the sky." Her soft voice trembled as did her whole body.

Her arms wound up his arms until her hands rested at the back of his neck. She reached up onto her tip-toes and lay her lips lightly against his own. Suddenly she was deaf and blind to her surroundings. Only her inner being filled her mind. She felt his heart thudding against her own. Her legs trembled and threatened to collapse but it did not matter as Mac slipped his arms around her slender waist and pulled her pliant form into his own. Jane did not recognize this strange woman who pressed closer to the body of this strong man while his lips drew all strength from her being. Her lips parted. Their tongues met. A lightning streak of molten lava flashed through her body, stirring the depths of her core to fire. Her open mouth widened. Their tongues drew on each other. Pale arms clasped around his neck and pulled his hot body closer until she felt every inch of his muscled frame. She pressed in closer still. Even the pressure of his manhood into her lower abdomen caused her no embarrassment. It only made her crave for more, she knew not what, but she knew she would not be whole without it.

Lack of breath caused their lips to separate.

Mac's choked voice whispered in her ear. "Jane, Miss Jane, I'm sorry. I cannot take advantage of you like this."

Through the raging flames within her, Jane pulled Mac close again. "Mac, we are both adults. I have never known a man but I believe now, it is because I have waited to meet you. Please, this is what I want with my very being. Please show me what to do and forgive my clumsiness in this endeavour."

"Oh, Jane, my love."

Their bodies embraced once again.

"Jane, are you sure about this?"

"Mac, I have never been surer of anything." Jane knew nothing but Mac was going to be able to dampen the fire rampant inside her.

"Will you come with me to my cabin? It is rather exposed out here on the deck."

She took his hand. "Lead and I will follow."

Mac led them through the darker shadows of the ship. He opened the door and they slipped through into his cabin.

Jane only had a vague impression of the narrow space in which they stood. Her one thought was to clasp her lover into her arms and once again relish the heat building up inside her body. When it seemed almost too much to bear, her hands took on a mind of their own. Fine fingers almost tore the clothes from Mac's willing body.

In return, she felt his stumbling fingers release the buttons down the front of her coat frock. Impatiently she tried to assist. Little attention was paid to one black button when it pinged against the pannikin on the desk beside the bunk. She tugged the cotton nightdress over her head. Her firm breasts stood out with pride after being released from their long containment. Her fumbling fingers pulled at the buttons of his trousers. He stepped out of the garment as it fell to the floor. Jane sank into his close embrace. Mac lifted her with his one good arm and lay her on the bunk. His fingers roamed over virgin territory. Jane writhed with eagerness.

"Wait, my love. Do not rush. Enjoy the wait and the climax will be enhanced tenfold."

"Your wish is my command, Master." Jane giggled.

Mac slid over her gently.

George leant back against the bulwark. He laughed. "China, I don't know how you do it? You've rubbed my nose in it again. This is the third game at which you've soundly beaten me since this voyage began."

"It would appear the signs are in my favour, Doctor George."

Both men sat quietly enjoying the peace in their secluded corner at the stern on the top deck. George closed his eyes and savoured the moment. Opposite him, sitting cross-legged, with his arms tucked into the large sleeves of his tunic, China sat watching the doctor. He did not miss the shadows which drifted back and forth across his new friend's face. After some time, he spoke.

"Sometimes a man's feet must walk the rarely-trodden-path. This will always be strewn with obstacles. If the man chooses to divert to the well-worn-path, that not meant for his feet, his soul will shrivel up and turn black. If he endures the difficulties placed along the destined path, eventually, his soul will shine brighter as the way becomes clearer."

George's eyes opened as he listened to this man who seemed to burrow into his mind. He returned the Chinaman's unwavering gaze.

Henry interrupted both men's thoughts as he came skidding to a halt.

"You've been playing chess. Can I play, Uncle George?"

The one bell into the dog watch sounded from the ship's bell.

"There's the four-thirty bell. Your mother will be looking for you shortly to clean up for your tea. Maybe, if circumstances allow, we can have a game tomorrow." George began removing his pieces from the board and packing them into their little wooden box. He secured the lid.

Sunrise of New Year's Day, eighteen hundred and seventy-four, burst upon the country as the *Northern Orchid* nosed into the Endeavour River. Everyone took advantage of the cessation of the heavy downpouring of rain to catch their first glimpse of the village of Cook's Town. Maureen stood a little apart from her friends as the *Northern Orchid* made its way through the river-mouth, past a grassy hill looking down on the entrance like a sentinel. Both river banks were thick with mangrove trees draping their leafy limbs into the salty water.

On the southern bank, the *SS Ashley* lay moored at a small makeshift wharf. Not too far from this, a large area of the mangroves had been denuded. She could see a group of workers, with axes in their hands, clearing much of the growth away from where another work team was in the process of building the beginnings of a new wharf. Loud voices drifted across the water from where two ships were unloading cargo into lightermen's skiffs.

Fear set her heart pounding in her chest. The fear of the unknown churned her stomach. The fear all this had been for nothing and she would not find her father. The fear of what she might need to do to find her father.

"Are you alright, Maureen? You've gone quite pale."

Maureen looked over at Eve who had been such a support since her discovery as a stowaway. They had shared a cabin along with young Henry for the journey while Miss Abigail and Miss Jane shared the second cabin. Maureen smiled weakly and nodded her head.

"It's this dreadful heat. It's quite claustrophobic, I think."

Maureen's gaze returned to examine the shoreline. She did not hear the shouted orders by the bosun sending his men up the yards to secure the sails. Nor did she notice the splash of the anchor entering the water. She watched as men in smaller boats loaded down to the waterline by the weight of their cargo, pulled up on the muddy banks. Curses floated across the surface of the water as they slipped and sank into the sludge while straining to bring the vessel high enough up the bank to unload. Horses stood patiently waiting on more solid ground, along with the drays they were to haul. Chains rattled in the pulleys set up in a simple tripod crane system on a timber platform.

Through the scrub, some way from the riverbank, many tents were visible. In fact, almost all Maureen could see were tents. It was only an occasional small wooden structure or a corrugated iron dwelling which broke the canvas monotony. She pondered on how Miss Abigail and Miss Jane were going to survive in such accommodation.

Most looked more primitive than her own home had been. A black man, blacker than any she had ever seen in Brisbane, stood under the shrubbery further along the riverbank. He leant against a long stick. One foot rested on the knee of his other leg. She gasped when she realized, he was wearing little if any clothing. A pink glow filled her cheeks as she swung her head away returning her gaze to the variety of vessels swinging, with the waves and tide, at their anchors.

There were at least two other three-masted vessels like the one in which she had travelled. Added to this number were at least four smaller schooners. Between all of these, the barge-like lighterman's skiffs shuffled cargos to the banks or delivered people back to the moored ships.

Dotted like exotic flowers were several Chinese boats, some with brilliant coloured sails. How on earth, within this mixture, was she ever going to find her father.

"I wonder what those boats with coloured sails, are?" She asked Eve. But it was China's piping voice who answered. Neither girl had seen or heard the cook approach.

"Boats of my country, Miss. Large boats we call junks. Smaller ones, with men using poles to propel them, are sampans."

"Thank you, Sir." Maureen continued to absorb the scene. The sun glistened in the remaining raindrops on the multiple shades of green within the foliage of the trees near the riverbank.

The Chinaman beside her spoke again. "I hope you find your father here, Miss. If I can help in any way, maybe I talk with my countryman, please do ask."

"You are very kind. Mr. China, isn't it?"

"Yes, Miss. You ask any Chinaman for China of the *Northern Orchid* and they find. Now I go prepare for special dinner today."

Maureen turned and took the old man's hand in her own. "Yes, Mr. China. It is a special day. Thank you again, Sir."

The footfalls of the Chinaman whispered off towards the companionway leading to the lower deck. Eve moved over to where Henry played with China's cat. Maureen did not notice the arrival of a heavier footstep at her side.

"Excuse me, Miss Maureen."

She gasped and jumped back a step when she discovered it was Josh Dougall looking down at her. During the voyage, she could not help but notice the man had gone out of his way to avoid her. Now, here he stood, with a face quite unfathomable. His eyes did not glare at her in the way to which she had become accustomed. In fact, she thought she may have detected a hint of compassion. The tight mouth, which had been all she had witnessed, now appeared more relaxed and certainly less frightening. What even surprised her more was the look of nervousness about his demeanour. Could she be mistaken?

The man dug his hand into his pocket and drew out something small wrapped in a stained bit of cloth.

"Er … Miss … er … Ryan, I … er …"

Maureen wanted to giggle. Suddenly this man, who had been the centre of her nightmares, seemed rather soft and vulnerable.

"Yes, Mr. Dougall, can I help you?"

He pulled open the rag. Maureen could not have been more astounded if he had drawn a snake out of the cloth. There, within his hand, lay a near-transparent orange coloured stone almost the size of the cork in Miss Abigail's perfume bottle. The perfectly smooth surface told of the touch of countless hands. Maureen's finger reached out to stroke the jewel.

"This stone is supposed to bring good fortune to the one who carries it. I don't mean in money sense but in safety and contentment. Once upon a time, it kept me out of serious trouble. Now, to keep the magic of the stone, it is time to pass it on to someone worthy who may need its protection. You have proven yourself more than worthy

229

in your determination to find your father and to reunite your family. Will you take this and keep it close to you at all times?"

Maureen opened and closed her mouth but no words came out. She tried again.

"Mr. Dougall, I thank you for the kind thought but I cannot accept anything of such value."

"This stone is of no monetary value. The value is in its ..." Josh paused searching for the word he wanted. "... spiritual value." He refolded the stone within the cloth and held it out to the young woman.

Maureen's hand trembled when she took the stone. "Thank you, Mr. Dougall. I will keep this with me at all times until I find my dad. After that, I'm to pass it on to someone else. Is this what you are saying?'

"Miss, please call me Josh. Yes, it is how the stone works."

"Thank you, Mr. Dougall; Josh."

For a long time after Josh had left, Maureen watched the steerage class passengers, weighed down with their worldly possessions, disembark. A constant procession of lighterman's skiffs ferried them from the ship to the shore. Her eyes may have watched but her brain did not see as she pondered all of her conversation with Josh Dougall.

"Jane, are you absolutely sure about this? You have known the man for such a short time." A frown marred Abigail's forehead. "There is still time to change your mind, you know."

Jane walked over and put her arms around her friend. "Abigail, I am absolutely sure. I love Mac and I know he loves me too. He is a strong and kind man with a wicked sense of humour. What else could a girl want in a man."

"I will miss you, Jane."

"Abigail, I am not going anywhere; well, next door perhaps. Mac is happy for me to stay here with you when he is away at sea. In the meantime, we plan to build a cottage for ourselves near to where you and Doctor George set up house."

Abigail smiled ruefully. "Listen to me; to us. Usually, it is me calming you down. Now, on the day when you really should be having a fit of the vapours, it is you soothing my nerves. The roles are certainly reversed. Oh Jane, I really hope this marriage of yours turns out to be everything you wish for. You deserve your happiness." Abigail wiped the tears from her eyes and took up the hairbrush. "Now, let us turn you into an irresistible bride."

William Sloan and Ewan MacGregor stood in the captain's cabin, their navy whites a stark contrast to the dark furnishings. Captain Sloan poured a small rum into each of the two pannikins sitting on the edge of his desk.

"Are you sure about this, Mac? This is the last chance you have to change your mind. It has been a rather short romance, to say the least."

Mac laughed. "I guess it has, William, but I knew, from the first moment I saw Jane at the hotel, she was the one for me. It's not logical, I know, but there you are. It's true." The two men toasted each other before Mac went on. "Now friend, will you come and marry us before we have to elope unwed."

Sloan laughed. "Yes, yes, I'll come wed the two of you. Maybe you'll stop prowling around the decks at night and sneaking strange women into your cabin."

A deep red flush, almost the colour of his hair, suffused Mac's face. "You saw us? You didn't, I don't believe it. We were very discreet."

"This ship tells me all its secrets. Now, will you come on and stop keeping me from my dinner."

A round cake with white icing blobs like diamonds sat in the middle of the table at the base of the mainmast. A canvas awning had been set up to protect the bridal party and the cake from the steaming mid-day heat of the northern tropics. Captain Sloan, with the ship's bible in his hand, stood facing the bridal party made up of Mac and his bride-to-be Jane. Standing on Jane's left were Abigail, the Matron of Honour, Eve and Maureen the brides-maids and Henry the page-boy whose only real concern was how much of the cake was going to be left for him when all this lot, including the crew, were to have a helping. On Mac's right stood Josh, as his best man and Gus the groomsman. Doctor George was to give the bride away. Thomas, Evans and China stood to attention in front of the ship's crew.

In his deep clear voice, William Sloan led the marriage service. As captain of a ship, he had only performed this ritual once before when sailing across the Atlantic Ocean many years previously. Even though he wished his friend every happiness, he could not help worry maybe the pair should have got to know each other better before taking this final step. But then, who was he to offer anyone advice on the subject; one marriage on the rocks and happily living in sin for years.

When the groom was told to kiss the bride, the crew burst out with cheers and cat-wauling. Tears ran down the faces of the bride's attendants but the bride shed no tears. In her simple travelling dress, she looked radiant. There were congratulations all around before one of the crew called out above the din.

"Are we going to get a feed around here sometime today. And what about some of that cake?"

Another voice called, "I'm ready for my drachm of rum."

Mac laughed. "Come on, wife of mine, we'd best feed our guests before they mutiny."

CHAPTER TWENTY-FOUR

COOK'S TOWN

Doctor George stood at the edge of his block of land. He admired, with some trepidation, the huge pile of timber poles, wooden planks, prefabricated walls and bundles of corrugated iron secured with lengths of chain. For the third time, he turned around to absorb the scene of this amazing adventure. Horses neighed and stomped their hooves as the mounted police prepared to make their afternoon patrol. On occasions, voices of the people milling about the government buildings rose above the din of the Landing Place. Wherever he looked, there were tents. Timber structures, like the one he planned to build, were the exception. From down the main street, voices were heard arguing. Ships on the river waited to empty their holds as soon as any wharf area became available.

The grassy river banks near the Landing Place were still strewn with cargo unloaded earlier in the day. He sniffed. The smell of rotting flesh came in on the salt air. Obviously, the donkey which drowned yesterday afternoon had not been removed. It must still be lying bloated within the mangroves. The custom's official assured him at the time, 'The crocodiles will soon clear away the mess'.

Two days ago, their feet touched the soil of Cook's Town. Since then, thanks to Captain Sloan's assistance, he had liaised with the government and police officials to secure his position in the town. The corner block of land had been procured under the guidance of the recently acquired town surveyor, James Reid. Mr. Reid was in the process of preparing official plans for the town. George grinned at the man by his side. Ewan MacGregor wore an expression of pride, excitement and apprehension. George understood exactly what the man was feeling. He found it a comfort to have Mac as his future neighbour. Were they going to meet the demands of this isolated outpost? Did they have the skills and stamina to construct a home and in his case, a surgery as well? Did he have the skills and resilience to meet the demands of his profession way out here on the edges of civilization? Along with George's long list for Captain Sloan to include in his next cargo, Mac had added a prefabricated dwelling similar to the one he and Thomas had yet to put together. George withdrew a handkerchief from his trouser pocket and wiped at the rivulets of perspiration running down his face. He looked over to where Thomas toiled at erecting one of their canvas tents, in the suffocating heat of the late afternoon. They'd been advised to sleep near their building supplies to prevent any pilfering. Tonight, he and Thomas planned to forgo the questionable comforts of the hotel and camp on their land. All at once George's anxiety subsided. With Thomas's support, they'd work their way through any problems.

Sunset's paintbrush stroked the Saunders hills on the north side of the river mouth, with pastel shades of pinks and blues as Doctor George, Thomas and Mac walked with Captain Sloan to the Landing Place. The captain planned to return to the decks of the *Northern Orchid*. At the riverbank, the familiar piping voice of China was heard approaching from the busier part of the street.

"Cap'n, you leave now?" The small man, hidden under his large conical hat, puffed as he slowed to greet them. He turned his countenance to the others. "Good day, Sirs."

The greeting was returned. Captain Sloan untied the hemp line of the tender boat from the trunk of a mangrove tree.

"I didn't think you were going to make it, China." He grinned. "I thought you'd have to swim out amongst the crocs. You know how they like to chew on the bones of a Chinaman rather than those of a tasteless white-man."

The group smiled at China's reply. "Crocodiles very smart, our Cap'n."

China's face became serious. "Cap'n, Sir, I come to tell you. I stay here until you return."

The captain looked askance at his long-time friend and cook.

"I can understand Mac remaining here for a bit. He's found a wife to keep his feet warm. What's your excuse? Have you a fine young woman hidden away up here, too? You've only been in the town for two days."

China's chortle set them all laughing.

"At my age, there are other pleasures to be had. One day soon you will discover this yourself, Cap'n."

"Heaven spare me." Captain Sloan rolled his eyes. "And what else is it you are planning, my unfathomable Chinese friend?"

"The ship will manage without me, Cap'n. My nephew, Lee, is doing a fine job on the *Northern Orchid*. I stay here and help the stowaway girl find her father."

"It's a good thing you will be doing, China. Can I also assume there's a family business here that needs attention, too?"

"Always family business to sort, Cap'n," China grinned.

Henry came running into the group. Abigail and Eve approached at a more sedate pace.

"Grampy Cap'n, are you going already?"

The captain swung the small boy up into his arms.

"Yes, lad, the *Northern Orchid* will leave on the morning tide. I must return to Brisbane and bring back some more supplies for your Uncle George and Mr. MacGregor. Don't forget, I did promise young Lucy I'd return to Brisbane to see her."

"You'll see baby Christopher too, don't forget."

"I doubt if I'll be allowed to forget it. If I remember young babies, they make a lot of noise."

The captain put the boy down and reached out to shake his small hand.

"Till we meet again, young man."

Tears trembled on the boy's eyelids.

Abigail's eyes teared up also. She walked over and kissed the seafarer on the cheek.

"Thank you, for everything, Captain Sloan. We'll have you to dinner when you next return. Make it soon and keep safe."

"You too, lass." The captain held her hand for several seconds. As he turned to go, she stepped back next to her brother.

The group watched as the captain slipped the small boat out into the river. The vessel barely rocked as William Sloan jumped on board. The oars became an extension of his arms. Farewells bounced across the ripples of the incoming tide.

They stood for some time discussing their achievements to date. Henry wandered off to watch a group of people fishing on the river bank.

Maureen lay back on the bed in the Empire Hotel room which she shared with Eve. This hotel had been recommended as one of the most comfortable in town but as she looked about her, Maureen grinned ruefully. The thin horse-hair mattress did little to conceal the outline of the wire base sagging between the iron frame of the bed. A chipped jug and bowl for washing purposes sat upon the wobbly set of drawers. The water content looked as though it had been filtered through a muddy rag. In a row along the wall, wooden pegs waited to receive items in need of hanging. There was not a wardrobe in sight. They had been lucky to obtain adjacent rooms for their group.

Eve and Miss Abigail left earlier with Henry who wished to investigate the town. Like herself, Jane had chosen to rest in her room. From one direction, the breeze carried in the noises of the busy river while from the other side of their hotel, Maureen heard the voices wafting up from the numerous alehouses and billiard rooms further along the street. She patted at the perspiration on her face and neck and moved her body closer to a welcome draft of air as it slipped in between the timber slabs of the walls. The wooden slat windows rattled in their casement as an occasional breeze billowed the faded calico curtains hanging from tacks in the timber. It brought with it the smoke from the many campfires and the aroma of cooking foods. Her nose twitched at the occasional odour of unsanitary effluent.

On their arrival at the hotel, they were given strict instructions to limit their usage of water. Apparently, the water for drinking was transported, by hand, from Hill Creek somewhere up past the Landing Place. Water carriers delivered water for other purposes, at exorbitant prices, from Two Mile Creek just south of the town. The dour lady at the hotel reception had pointed to the outside toilets; a long walk from the back of the hotel. The one on the right was for the ladies and the other for the gentlemen. Both were constructed using a frame of poles chopped from the almost denuded forest surrounding the area. A heavy-weighted calico similar to the type used for the tents and on many of the building constructions had been stretched around the frame. It had been pleasing to hear the receptionist inform her guests the ladies may ask for a gozunder to be available in their rooms at night if they wished.

"It is not advisable for the ladies to be wandering about in the dark with all these strangers camped nearby."

A smile released the worry lines upon Maureen's forehead, if only for a moment, as she remembered the vague look on the faces of Miss Abigail and Miss Jane at the term gozunder. It was left to Eve and herself to explain the name of the china pot in lieu of a commode.

As her hand was wont to do in recent days, it slipped into the pocket of the skirt she wore and retrieved the orange stone. The frown returned as her eyes gazed into its core while her fingers rubbed at the smooth surface. Did this stone really have the power to keep her safe while searching for her father? With care, she returned it to its place of concealment.

Maureen threw her feet off the bed and stood upright. It was no good moping about in this room. She must go out and explore. With her bonnet secure she stepped out onto the dirt track in front of the building. Which way should she go? The road to the right led to the Landing Place. She made to turn left but felt intimidated by the number of men ambling about between the tents and buildings. She felt so alone. Her heart beat faster. A noisy group of men gathered at the doorway of a grog shanty. One day, if she was to seek out her father, she would have to brave these groups of strange and loud men. Today she chose to take the easier option and swung right, towards the government building on the riverbank almost opposite the police station.

"Maureen!" Henry's squeal led her to where Miss Abigail, Eve, Doctor George, Thomas and Mr. MacGregor waved to the captain now climbing aboard the *Northern Orchid* anchored out in the river. Maureen did not miss the Dougall men waving in return; particularly the taller of the two.

It was Thomas who broke up the group.

"I really must finish the tent if we are to have somewhere to sleep tonight, Doctor George."

"Yes, of course, Thomas, I'll come and give you a hand." George turned to his sister. "I'll see you at dinner at the hotel, later."

"Yes, George."

Maureen, Eve, Abigail and Mac turned to make their way back to the hotel when shouting and screaming drew them towards the river bank. In the evening shadows, a group of children; some native, some white and some Chinese gathered excitedly. Mac reached out and snatched Henry by the collar just as he was ready to disappear within the midst of squeals.

"Never jump into the fire until you check the heat, lad," he admonished.

"It's a crocodile; a croc; a really big croc." One particularly raucous voice was heard.

"Stand back." A man's voice called. "Get the copper and tell him to bring his biggest gun."

More screams split the air and bodies were jumping backwards around them. Maureen took Miss Abigail's hand on one side and Eve's hand on the other. They shifted higher up the bank. Mac, with Henry in tow, followed close at their heels. Mac swung Henry up onto his shoulders.

"Can you see what is happening, Henry?"

"I can't see anything, Mr. Mac."

From her position on tip-toe, Abigail stretched her head left and right. "I can't see any crocodile, either."

"It's swimming in the water, about twelve feet out from the bank. You can only see its eyes. Look for two lumps floating symmetrically, like two bits of debris. By the distance they are apart,

I would estimate the creature being at least eighteen feet long." Mac shifted Henry into a more comfortable position. "Can you see it now, lad?"

"Yes, yes." Henry pointed excitedly. "Look, Mama. Oh no, it's gone under the water. I can't see it anymore."

A policeman came running towards the melee. Maureen's hands flew up to her ears as the gun roared.

"Did he get it?" Was the question many voices asked while others remarked in awe at the size. "Twenty feet, if it's an inch." Was the accepted approximation.

"It has disappeared," Miss Abigail spoke beside Maureen.

Mac shrugged. "I'd say it's long gone. If it has been shot it'll float to the surface later." He turned his head up towards the boy wriggling on his shoulders. "Henry, now do you understand why you must not go running off in this country like a wild animal?"

"Yes, Mr. Mac." Henry's answer was automatic. His eyes were still on the water where the crocodile disappeared.

"I don't know about anyone else, but I really need something cool to drink. Let's go back to the hotel. It will not be too long before our evening meal." Miss Abigail suggested.

Maureen stood at the side entrance of the hotel for a few moments after everyone else had gone inside. She watched, with interest, as a Chinaman, leading a goat cart loaded with vegetables, made his way along the opposite side of the street. He was in deep conversation with a smaller man at his side who looked very like Mr. China from the *Northern Orchid.* One could not be too sure, with his hat covering much of his upper body. Slim fingers lifted the edge of the conical hat as he talked. She saw it was indeed, Mr. China. She waved. The man made his way across the street. When he reached her side, he bowed.

"Miss Maureen, I glad I meet you today. My family all ask for your father. China has many relatives both here and Palmer River. Some have restaurants, some grow the vegetables and some keep cows for milk. Some carry supplies to goldfields. Others scratch in dirt for its treasure. They send word back to me when find anything to help you."

"Thank you, Mr. China."

"You're welcome, Miss. You be patient. This big country with much strangers. I stay in Cook's Town for a few months on business. You need help, ask for China at the See Foo Restaurant."

"You are too kind." Maureen smiled and turned to join the others.

THE MARINER'S REST HOTEL

Jacko burst out laughing. "Miss Abigail, giving orders on your own ship. Somehow it does not surprise me. She can be quite autocratic when she wants to be."

"Hush, Jacko." Sarah admonished her husband. "You'll wake the little ones."

Captain Sloan smiled ruefully after telling the tale of the discovery of Maureen as a stowaway and Abigail's response to his order of the lash.

"I have to admit, I'd rather face the whole French fleet in nothing but a fishing boat than Abigail Baldwin in full sail." William sipped at the whiskey Jacko had poured for him.

The group sitting around the table in the shack included Jacko and Sarah, Captain Sloan, recently returned on the *Northern Orchid* from Cook's Town, as well as Maureen Ryan's sisters, Erin and Minnie. Their brother, Bob, had fallen asleep on his bunk in the same room. Sarah's children slept in their parent's bedroom. Lucy had gone to bed reluctantly, not wanting to miss a minute of time with her Grampy Captain. Only the promise of time tomorrow with her uncles Josh and Gus, if she was a good girl, persuaded her to go to sleep.

"Would you really have lashed her, Captain?" Erin asked.

William Sloan's finger rubbed at his forehead then traced the scar down his cheek.

"Certainly not if I knew she was a girl. Mind you, she looked for all the world like a lad in her father's clothes and her hair tucked up tight in his cap. None of us knew. It was young Henry who recognized her immediately he saw her. Then Miss Abigail realized soon after."

"If it really had been a boy stowaway; would you have lashed him then?"

"Probably not. I'd have locked him away in the galley helping the cook and washing the dishes to make him pay his fare. I once had to lash a sailor, a long time ago; under orders from the captain at the time. It was a barbaric thing to do but sometimes discipline is important to maintain a fighting unit. I don't think I'd like to have to order someone to do it though." The captain's thoughts turned inwards. Everyone sat quietly watching the expressions trailing across his face. Eventually, he spoke again. "It is a very brave thing Maureen is doing. Foolish, no doubt, but her intention is good; looking out for her family."

"What will happen in Cook's Town? Will she find our dad there?" Minnie asked timidly.

Again, the captain turned his thoughts inwards while he took another sip of his drink. "Cook's Town is a raw town. At the moment, everything is at sixes and sevens. Hopeful prospectors arrive with every ship. These men spend as little time as possible in the town. They collect their essential supplies and equipment before heading off, mostly on shank's pony, into the inland where the gold is to be found. With the worst of the wet season approaching, the authorities are concerned these arrivals will be stranded in Cook's Town when the creeks and rivers flood. Basic food supplies will then be scarce. They expect the situation at the Palmer River to be worse. There are hundreds, maybe even thousands, of miners in the area and when the rivers flood no supplies will be able to get through. Many will starve."

"Do we know if Dad is out there, at Palmer River?" Erin's face filled with concern.

"No, we don't. China, my long-time friend, has remained there organizing his people to report back to him on any sightings of Mr. Ryan. Doctor George tells me Mr. Ryan has been in the prospecting game for many years. It's unlikely he will be caught out by a simple thing such as the weather."

"Tell us again about Jane's wedding. It sounded so romantic. We met Mac here … one day. He's a lovely man." Sarah had been going to say, at Millie's funeral, but did not want to bring back such a sad memory for the captain. "What did she wear? I know they had only packed a few items of clothes for travelling. The remainder was sent in sea chests with the cargo."

Captain Sloan's eyebrows rose to his hairline. He looked to Jacko for help.

"Don't look at me, mate. I have bruises all over my body because I don't notice Sarah's clothes."

Sarah laughed and slapped his wrist.

"I really don't know." The captain stumbled over his words. "I think it was a blue dress and a thing on her head. China made a fruit cake and decorated it for them. The whole crew joined in the celebration with cake and rum. We were lucky to get a lick of work out of them for the rest of the day."

"What will Jane do in Cook's Town when Mac goes back to sea?"

"Keep helping the Doctor, I guess. Mind you, it will not surprise me if Mac decides to retire and settle there for a while. Now Josh and Gus have their certificates, he can please himself. He has asked me to bring him one of the latest pre-fabricated cottages." William Sloan looked over at the Ryan girls. "Mac will be there to help in searching for your father, too. I don't think you have anything to worry about." He stood and stretched his body. "If it's all the same with everyone, old age is creeping up on me. I think I'll go up to my bed. Sarah, thank you for a lovely meal."

"You have Erin and Minnie to thank for most of the meal. They have been a wonderful help to me." Sarah stood and patted the captain's shoulder as he smiled his thanks to the younger girls. "We'll see you for an early breakfast before you have to return to the ship?"

"Thanks, Sarah. Is five o'clock too early?"

"No, we have our breakfast about then."

Moonlight streamed in upon William Sloan where he lay upon the bed which held his fondest memories. His gaze never wavered from the canvas of *The Northern Orchid* Millie had commissioned Thomas to paint back in 1867. Her joy at giving this gift replayed in his mind. Soft laughter tinkled in his ears. His mind once again recalled how her sparkling eyes outshone the jewels, she was so fond of wearing. His body relaxed under the imagined touch of her soft fingers. He drifted into a deep sleep.

COOK'S TOWN

Abigail stood on the ground-floor back-verandah placing the bloody instruments into the bowl of soapy water on a wooden table. She shook the one-time preserve tin now home to their soap supply. Tomorrow, Eve or Maureen would need to obtain some lard or tallow from the butcher and render it down to make more soap.

Once again, the first patients of the day carried wounds gained while fighting in alcohol-fuelled arguments during the night. Her nimble fingers attended most of the insertion of sutures between dosing up the numerous fever patients with a Chlorodyne mixture. George looked after the more serious wounds. She heard Jane inside the office behind her. Her friend was in the process of bringing the account books up to date. Ten minutes before, Abigail had seen Mac head down the street searching for China.

Above her head, the top floor, like the ground floor, had a front and back verandah. The remainder was divided into four rooms. A room for her and one for Henry which he shared with the empty sea trunks and other baggage. Eve and Maureen shared one room. Mac and Jane currently occupied the fourth room, until they were able to build their own home on the neighbouring block. They expected the building materials to arrive on the *Northern Orchid*, within the next few weeks.

Of the four rooms on the ground floor, one provided sleeping quarters for George and Thomas. Opposite, the doctor's office opened into the surgery room where George could examine his patients. A large lock hung from the bar across the door of the fourth room. Inside held all their medication supplies, dry food supplies and other general stores. Calico walls enclosed the back-verandah to make an area for patient beds. Two men, lying weak and pale, scarcely moved in their narrow beds as they recovered from diarrhoea and starvation acquired at the goldfields. Their condition had been exacerbated during the weeks of their return journey. Thomas cared for most of their daily needs.

Abigail looked up to watch Maureen and Eve as they worked in the separate structure of the makeshift kitchen. At a rough-hewed wooden table, Eve kneaded a large knob of dough in preparation for the day's fresh bread. The girl worked in the simple corrugated structure with the push-out windows opened as far as they would go, in an attempt to entice any fluky breeze. The uncooperative air was hot and still. It promised another rain shower before dark, no doubt. Maureen worked at the open fire near the edge of the shingled-roofed awning. Steam rose from a one-time kerosene drum standing at the edge of the fire. It now contained clothes soaked in a soapy water bath. In between preparing the coals to accept the camp oven for Eve's bread, Maureen stirred the clothes. When time permitted, she sat at the three-legged wooden stool in front of a large tin tub. With reddened hands, the girl vigorously rubbed the coloured clothes up and down over the ripples of the wooden scrub board.

Abigail's gaze panned about looking for her son. She espied him sitting in front of a rotten stump at the back of their block of land. A sudden gasp escaped her lips at the sight of a native boy sitting beside him. Who was this boy? Fear clenched her belly. Willing her feet not to run, she left her work and moved towards the industrious lads. Two pointed sticks rose and fell in unison as they dug in the soil around the old tree stump. Both were talking at once, each in his own natural tongue. Henry looked up to see his mother approaching.

"Hello, Mama. Look what Smiley is showing me."

Abigail stood mesmerized by the white teeth framed within a wide smile on a face of mud-splattered dark skin.

"Oh, what, Henry?" She was surprised by her feelings. Anxiety threatened to overwhelm her. No matter what the boy's colour, he was just a small boy, not much older than Henry. She concentrated on regulating her breathing which threatened to race away like a bolting horse. There had been some horrific tales of the doings of some of the country's black- fellow population. Should she be afraid? As she looked at the boy with his smile as open as the huge sky above, she relaxed, until she heard her son's reply.

"We're finding witchety grubs to eat." Henry held up a fat whitish grub with a sprinkling of dirt over its body. Without another word, her son threw his head back and opened his mouth. Before she could call out, the grub disappeared down his throat. He then sat with a smile no less wide than the grin on the face of his companion. Abigail bit her lip in an effort not to scream. She wanted to tip her son upside-down but knew how futile it would be. No doubt many witchety grubs had been consumed by Smiley's people without any untoward effects.

"That is interesting." Her voice wobbled. "If you're hungry, can I get both of you a piece of bread and preserve with a cordial drink?"

"Yes, please, Mama. The grubs are a bit squishy and crunchy with dirt." Henry turned to his new friend. "Come on, Smiley."

The boys jumped up enthusiastically. Abigail bit down on the gasp of shock as Smiley walked off beside her son. The boy limped awkwardly on legs thick with corded scars running down their length.

Mac ambled along the dirt track they'd named Charlotte Street. The dray-wheel ruts left after the quagmire of the last rain wound their way around the tree stumps protruding like festered sores on the roadway. Many of the men, particularly the businessmen, were dressed in white suits while most of the prospective miners wore the flannelette shirts brought back from the Crimean war. All heads were protected by a hat. Some were made of straw and some of felt. He jumped aside as a pair of the clientele came rolling out of the doorway of a grog shanty and nearly bowled him off his feet. The pair jumped up; their faces twisted in anger. They joined forces and threatened to have a go at Mac but soon backed off when he towered above them. Mac smiled as he stretched and clenched his recently damaged hand in relief. It seemed there would be no need to upset Doctor George and test the wrist once again.

He doffed his hat to a lady walking rapidly through the crowds. A small girl clung to her skirts. Swinging from the woman's arm hung a woven basket holding several parcels wrapped in newspaper. It reminded him; he must collect the papers on his return trip.

This was his second visit to the Chinese area just south of Cook's Town. Here the calico covered alleys wound lackadaisically between the tents, it reminded him so much of the Asian bazaars he'd seen on his travels while in the British Navy. The argumentative blend of cooking foods and human waste hit his nose like a heavy punch.

He felt the weight of eyes upon him. Few white men penetrated behind the outer market perimeter. Inside was a colony of human ants. He smiled and nodded in his most innocuous manner. His heart lifted at the sight of a familiar face. The one whom China called Taam approached.

"Mr. Mac from the *Northern Orchid*. You have come to see Mr. China?" Taam bent his head.

"Yes, please, Taam." Mac bowed his head in return before following where the man led. "How are you and your family?" Mac asked.

"Good, thank you, Mr. Mac. And your wife is well?"

Mac strived to note different points of interest which might help him find his way back if required, but his eyes felt like they were rolling in his head. Everything within this magical cave was a point of interest. Before too long, they came to where China sat cross-legged on a straw mat in front of a small tent. Mac turned to a disappearing back.

"Thank you, Taam," Mac called. China made as if to rise but Mac motioned him to remain seated. "It is good to see you again, old friend."

China invited Mac to join him on the mat. "Can I get you a cup of tea, Mr. Mac?"

"That would be very nice thanks, China. This heat takes a bit of getting used to."

No sooner had Mac accepted the offer than a young girl arrived through the tent flaps with a tray on her arms. She knelt carefully and began to serve the cold tea and delicacies on a plate.

As the two men enjoyed the refreshment they spoke of the *Northern Orchid*, the weather, tides and fishing. When Mac drank the last sip of tea, he placed the cup on the tray and began to talk of what he had come for.

"China, I take it your people, so far, have not had any inkling of the Mr. Bert Ryan?"

"No, Mr. Mac, no word. The girl is sad?"

"She is becoming impatient. I just hope she does nothing foolish. She is rather head-strong, as you know." Mac wiggled his posterior into a more comfortable position. "I have another question. Do any of your people wish to earn a few extra shillings setting up a vegetable garden for me on my new house-block?"

China snickered quietly. "Mr. Mac don't tell me the saltwater has drained from your veins and been replaced by the mud and dirt. I always told you, women are dangerous animals."

"I think it is all your fault, China. You taught me to enjoy fresh vegetables and now I cannot live without them."

China did indeed have a young nephew who would be able to complete such a task to great satisfaction. Fees were negotiated and jokes were told before Mac made to rise. He sat down again quickly.

"Oh, China, there is one other thing. I know you have many artisans here in Cook's Town. Have you any who can build barrels like the larger water barrels on the *Northern Orchid*? I'm planning on saving the rainwater when it falls onto the roof and disappears down the street. If I am successful, it will reduce the trips to and from Hill Creek for our drinking water."

"Of course, Mr. Mac. My people can do anything. I see to it this very day."

Mac grinned. "Do you want to negotiate a price now or will we wait and see how it turns out?"

"You not leave town in hurry, I hope. No, of course not. Not with new wife to hold you here." Both men burst out laughing and Mac stood up.

China stood beside him. They shook hands.

"You looking well, friend."

"You too, China. A break onshore is not always a bad thing, is it?"

Nodding his head, China reached for his hat before leading Mac back out through the calico maze.

The evening meal had only just been consumed when dusk arrived along with the rain which came down in torrents. George rushed to shut the two back windows of the kitchen while Thomas and Mac improved on the placement of the protective corrugated iron sheeting over the fireplace. The women began cleaning up the dishes by the light of the hurricane lamp. Satisfied with their handiwork, the men finished drinking their tea.

George held his pannikin in one hand as he leant against the corner post watching the rill running through the channel Thomas had dug the previous week to prevent their kitchen being washed away. On its slightly elevated flat rock base, the fire flickered undisturbed by the rushing waters.

"Thomas, are those men coming tomorrow to dig another dunny hole for us?"

"Yes, Doctor George. That's if this rain eases up. The police inspector has a number of miners stuck in town wanting work. The creeks are flooded and the track through to Palmer River is closed at the moment. These fellows are desperate to earn a few shillings. The longer they have to wait here the more money they need to spend on accommodation and food. Others just want to get on the next ship out of the harbour."

George turned to where Mac sat under the awning. "Mac, you said this afternoon some men were coming to dig the holes for your house-stumps?"

"Yes, George. I reckon the *Northern Orchid* should be here in a week or two. It will facilitate the building process if we have the holes dug already; that is if they don't become wells." Mac looked up ruefully at the deluge of rain thundering on the roofing.

Abigail spoke from the kitchen where she helped with drying the dishes.

"Jane, you must be getting excited. It won't be long now until you will have your own home."

Jane put down the last cup. She shook out the towel and hung it over the back of a chair. "We are. It will be only the one level, though. When completed we'll have our bedroom, a sitting room and two rooms to fill with children." Even in the dull light of the lamp, the flush on Jane's face, as she realized what she had said, could not be missed.

"Good grief, are you planning on starting your own schoolhouse." George laughed.

A sleepy voice rose from the small head lying on the table. "Is Auntie Jane going to start her own school? I don't know if I want to share her with everybody else."

"Come on, my boy, it's time I took you up to bed." Abigail turned to Maureen, Eve and Jane. "Will you girls be alright to finish up, now?"

Eve dried her hands on the cloth as she answered. "Yes, Miss Abigail, we'll be right behind you."

"George, we'll leave you to shut the kitchen up, will we?" Abigail said as she led Henry and the girls off towards the house.

Jane walked over and stood by her husband. She rested her hand upon his fiery hair.

As they approached the back steps, Eve stumbled on the uneven ground. "It will be much easier when we get to build a proper kitchen, closer to the house, don't you think, Miss Abigail?"

Feet dragged as they climbed the stairs to their sleeping quarters. Abigail posed the question which had been bothering her for hours.

"Where does your friend Smiley live, Henry?"

"Mostly, Mrs. Chapple at the Queen's Hotel feeds him and lets him stay there in the stables."

"Did he say how he hurt his legs?"

"No, but I never asked."

Abigail reached over and hugged him closely.

When she lay on her own bed thinking of the day's happenings, Abigail wondered how the little black boy had obtained such horrendous burn scars to his legs. She was sure that's what they were; burn scars.

CHAPTER TWENTY-FIVE

THE *NORTHERN ORCHID*

Sullen clouds sagged in the sky. The sails moped on the yards despite Bosun Evans' attempts to have the sailors trim them first one way and then the other. There was not a breath of air to be had. The early morning sun remained hidden from view. Since coming on watch at four in the morning, Josh railed at the sultry weather. Sweat ran from his face and body, stinging his eyes and saturating his shirt. Clammy heat pressed in upon him stealing the breath from his chest. He dreaded to think what it might be like later in the day.

He'd hoped for a brisk sailing wind. If it were so, they'd have made Cook's Town by this evening, for sure. Captain Sloan had warned them at supper last night it was going to be a miserable day. As usual, the man's weather bones were accurate. Josh groaned as he thought of the elfin-like face framed with waves of brown hair. She may have to wait for a day or so, as will his chance to swim in the limpid pools of her brown eyes. Those brown eyes which could turn into a defiant, raging whirlpool at a moment's notice. He slapped his hand on the helm in disappointment.

"What's eating you, brother. You in a hurry, are you?" Gus grinned.

Josh breathed deeply, several times, before answering. His brother was too astute by far. If Gus suspected his impatience, and why; there'd never be an end to the teasing.

"No, not really, just like to get started once I'm out of my bunk."

Gus grinned again. "Never mind; the pressure is almost up on the boiler. We'll be able to get away in half an hour." Gus paused before he went on casually, "I wouldn't worry too much. The look I saw her give you before we left Cook's Town last time, tells me she'll be waiting for you to return."

"Bah, I don't know what you're talking about. Anyway, you can't say anything. You never left Eve's side when you were onshore, up there," Josh threw back.

"Yeah, well, they're as pretty a pair of fillies as I've ever seen." Gus patted his brother's shoulders. "I'll go down below and start the old girl a throbbing." Gus turned back. "I thought the captain would be up and about."

Josh nodded his head. "No, he went off shift at four o'clock thinking he may as well catch up on some sleep as watch this gloomy sky. You can make steam as soon as you're ready."

The following day, when the last leg of their journey approaching Cook's Town was underway, the sun continued to play hide-and-seek above the grey clouds. For a brief moment, it showed itself sitting upon the western horizon when the *Northern Orchid* entered the mouth of the Endeavour River. From where he stood at the rail, while Captain Sloan called the orders to cease engines and drop anchor, Josh noticed the *S.S. Leichardt* at the wharf.

Noticeable progress could be seen in the construction of the second wharf. His eyes did not remain focused on analysing the scenery or progress of the town's development. It was those people wandering around the area near the Landing Place and in the vicinity of the riverbank who took his gaze. His heart slipped down into his boots.

His brother's hand clamped his shoulder. "Cheer up, Josh. Have you not heard, yet?"

"Heard what?" Josh's head angled to allow his gaze past Gus. A slither of worry tore at his innards. Had he missed something going on he should have been aware of?

"The ship's fine. Evans has everything under control. Captain Sloan has just told me, you and I will have tonight off. We can go ashore. Four of the other chaps will be joining us. They are unloading the jolly-boat as we speak. Come on, shake a leg."

COOK'S TOWN

Maureen's arm ached as she stirred the large pot of stew over the open fire. The sooner the *Northern Orchid* arrived with their new kitchen-building materials the better, as far as she was concerned. She wiped at the perspiration trickling down her face. It had been a hot and humid day. Weren't they all? The night promised no better. Something in the heavens must give way shortly. She stood straight and stretched her back.

"Eve, I'll go feed the hens and collect the eggs." She spoke to her friend who was busy in the kitchen shed preparing ingredients for a fruit pie.

Taking up the basket and the tin of scraps from the end of the table, Maureen followed the path to where a dozen squawking hens patrolled the wire-netting fence waiting to attack the night's offering.

"What's all the fuss. Are you girls hungry, tonight?"

Peering through the fading light, Maureen prepared to ease her way into the small covered area where the nest box sat upon an open bench. She felt the hairs on the back of her neck lift. The sensuous coils slowly wound their way up the leg of the bench. She froze. The reptile's mouth opened wider than seemed possible as it prepared to devour one of the six eggs sitting in the box. Memories of Eve's instructions on how to kill a snake, learnt from Miss Millie, swirled through her brain making little sense. Only the one word of wisdom remained paramount.

"Don't move."

Her eyes widened until it seemed as if they might fall out of her head. Her breath caught in her throat. Could the snake hear the pounding of her heart? If so, it was unperturbed as the peristaltic motions of its body sucked the egg ever so slowly in through the self-dislocated jaws. She wanted so much to scream and run but remained immobile. Gradually her heart steadied, her breath came in short gasps. One foot after another, with infinitesimal steps, she backed to where her shaking hands were able to reach the long-handled shovel, always kept at the hen-house door for this very purpose. Could she do this? At first, the tool did not move when she exerted her muscles. A soft grunt exploded through her dry lips. She lifted again. With the weapon in her clenched hand, she made the return journey of three feet, which felt like three miles at least, back inside the nesting area. The snake lay re-aligning its mouth and savouring its repast. Eve's voice once more echoed in her head.

"Use the shovel to hold the snake as hard as you can at the back of the neck; close to the head. You must hold it close to the head."

The coils moved lazily within the long nesting box but the head remained virtually free. Maureen eased the shovel-blade over the edge of the box and pounced upon the reptile's neck just at the base of the head; exactly as she had been told. The brown glistening coils sprang into action, thumping on the nest before curling tightly around the base of the shovel handle in an attempt to release the most important bit of its body. Egg yolks and shells splattered over the grassy nest in the process. She nearly dropped the shovel in shock. That part of her instructions had been forgotten.

"It will wiggle and carry on for a bit but if you have the head held tightly it cannot reach to bite you. Just hold on."

Maureen held on; then screamed.

It wasn't Eve or Thomas or the doctor who came to her rescue. The tall dark-haired, blue-eyed man, who seemed never to be too far from her thoughts, spoke from behind her.

"You alright there, Miss?"

Maureen nearly dropped the shovel again but caught it just in time before the snake made good its chance to escape.

"Please, Mr. Dougall, I cannot kill this thing."

She could not deny the rather pleasurable feelings as the strong body struggled to slip past her and take the shovel from her grasp. Confident now in his ability to solve her dilemma, she might admit maybe she did take a little longer than necessary to ease by him and out of the way.

With one swift slice, the sharp shovel-blade removed the snake's head from its body. Mesmerized she watched as the coils continued to twist and twine within the nesting box. It was when Josh turned, with the head in the shovel and the long body dangling from the fingers of his outstretched arm, she pulled herself together and backed out of the pen holding the door for him to retreat also.

Laughter rang out on the night air. Josh and Gus accepted the invitation to join the group around the long table under the kitchen awning. Two lanterns sitting on the table and the flickering flames of the fireplace held the falling darkness at bay. Insects buzzed and whined as they committed suicide against the hot glow of the light. The night air sucked up the smell of their burnt bodies. George, Thomas and Mac amused their guests with some of the funnier incidents experienced in their first attempts as house builders.

"Thank goodness for Thomas and Mac. If it had been left totally to me, I would have had to save the day with Plaster-of-Paris and linen bandages," George sighed.

"Well, the house is looking pretty good, now," Gus consoled them.

"Not bad, for a bunch of amateurs," Thomas responded.

"All I can say," Mac grinned, "Is thank goodness we got to practise on George's place. When I come to put mine together, I'll be an expert."

Thomas and George pooh-poohed this comment vigorously which sent their guests into fits of laughter. The men barely noticed the ladies rise and leave the table when the meal was eaten.

As she squeezed out the towel and hung it over a nail in the post, Abigail spoke quietly to her companions.

"I think, ladies, it is time for us to retire to the house and let the men talk in peace."

"A good idea, Abigail. I, for one, have correspondence to attend to." Jane smoothed her skirt.

Eve glanced at Maureen. The silent message was clear. As much as they'd prefer to stay near these handsome visitors, it would not be proper. The men stood up, calling their thanks and goodnight wishes as the ladies filed in behind Miss Abigail making their way to the house. At the top of the back stairs, Abigail and Jane moved on into the hallway leading to their respective rooms. The younger women looked again at each other. In one accord they pulled their long skirts in under their knees before sitting down on the top step. Hidden here in the darkness, they surveyed the night and in particular the group talking under the awning in the back yard.

The approach of galloping hooves distracted their attention. Within the shadows, a rider swung off his saddle near the lights of the kitchen.

"Doctor Goldfinch, they want you down at the billiard room. One bloke's unconscious and another has a bloody head."

"Oh dear, another fight." George sighed as he dragged his long legs from under the table and stood up. "Too much of the drink, I suppose?"

"Yeah, Doc. A couple of the miners took offence at a couple of sailors. It sort of progressed from there."

"I'll get my bag." George made his way under the house. "One of yours, do you think, Josh?"

"I'd doubt it, Doctor George. The four sailors on shore leave with us are usually pretty placid with the drink. Maybe these fellows are off *The S.S. Leichardt.* Anyway, we'll come down with you and check it out. It's about time we collected our blokes and made our way back to the ship. It must be after ten."

Eve and Maureen jumped up swiftly and tiptoed inside to their room. As they closed the door, Mr. Mac's footsteps were heard at the top of the stairs.

THE MARINER'S REST HOTEL

Sarah lay on Millie's bed. Lucy lay at one side of her and Christopher lay at her other side, the dried milk still upon his lip. Since Jacko and Ned had decided to build another room onto the shack, it was impossible to get any rest during the daytime with all the noise going on over there. Millie's room had proven a haven for her. Captain Sloan would not be needing the room for some time. He should be at Cook's Town, at the moment, so she knew he'd not be in Brisbane for near a fortnight or more.

As her gaze wandered about the room, she realized everything of Millie's had remained exactly as it was before she died. The captain had not shifted a thing. Should she talk to him about sorting through Millie's belongings? Her friend and mentor wandered through the rooms of her memories until Sarah's snuffles joined those of her daughter and son.

The call of Erin from the door woke her.

"Goodness gracious me. I must have dozed off. Sorry, Erin what time is it?"

"Mr. Jacko said it's four o'clock. He said to wake you."

Lucy began to stir. The little girl sat up and rubbed her eyes. Dark locks dangled across her face. When she noticed Erin at the door, she jumped up and slid off the bed. Sarah, meanwhile, gathered the baby up and smoothed the covers.

"Come on then, Erin, I guess we'd best start preparing the guests' suppers."

263

Erin lifted Lucy up into her arms. "Mrs. Hamilton has a shepherd's pie in the oven and a pot of soup on the stove. There is little to do." The girl held out her hand with the mail. "The letter carrier delivered these earlier."

Sarah took the envelopes and admonished Erin for lifting Lucy up each time the child demanded. "She is getting much too heavy for you, dear."

When her feet touched the floor, Lucy's hands sat on her hips and the blue eyes glared up at her mother. She stomped off down the stairs.

Sarah grinned at Erin. "We'll have to watch that one, she's becoming a right little madam." She turned and closed the door as they left. "I'll take this one downstairs and put him in a laundry basket in the kitchen until Minnie comes home."

In the kitchen, Sarah drank thirstily at her cup of tea, while she flicked through the mail. Erin sat at the other end of the table writing new words on her slate.

"Erin, this letter is for you." Sarah handed the girl the envelope, with the Cook's Town post-mark. "I guess it's from Maureen. She might have news of your father for you."

"Can I read it now, Miss Sarah?"

"Of course, dear."

Erin lifted the letter to her face and sniffed. She turned it over three times before retrieving a knife from the dresser drawer. The knife sliced through the paper neatly. Erin flattened the writing paper out on the table with her hands. Concentration ploughed a furrow across the girl's forehead as she read.

Out of the corner of her eye, Sarah watched. Erin's lips silently shaped the letters in an effort to understand the words.

"If you have any trouble reading Maureen's writing, let me know, Erin. I'll be happy to give you a hand."

Between them both they deciphered the message.

Erin Minnie Bob

I am safe here with the docters famly. Peple have been asking for me about Dad but no one has seen him yet. I think I mite go to where they dig the gold at palmer river to look for him there if he dussent turn up soon. The men who helped the docter build his house cum from the goldfields. Nun of them seen our dad. They said new peple go there every day. You all be good for Miss Sarah and Mr. Jacko. Send my best wishes to them. And don't forget to say thanks. Luv from your big sister Maureen.

Sarah's face wore a slight frown. In her mind, it did not seem a good idea for Maureen to be considering going into the goldfields on her own. She would need to talk to Jacko later. Meanwhile, Erin folded the page with great care and placed it back into the envelope. It disappeared into the pocket of her skirt.

COOK'S TOWN

The lantern on the verandah table cast a yellow light on the two young ladies sitting in the wooden chairs at the small table. Eve squinted in the poor light as she patched the tear in one of Miss Abigail's day-dresses. Maureen sewed a small material envelope, with ties attached. She planned to use this to secure the orange stone given to her by Josh Dougall.

Eve sat up straight and leant her head back against the wall. She rubbed her eyes.

"Maureen, I'm sorry there's been no news of your father yet. Something'll turn up soon, you'll see."

"Thanks, Eve. It's been such a long time. Do you realize we've been here two months now?"

"I know. Seems hard to believe."

The girls sat quietly absorbing the noises of the night.

"Listen, Maureen. If you listen carefully you can hear the recital music. I wonder how Miss Abigail, Miss Jane and Mr. Mac are enjoying their evening out."

Maureen laughed softly before answering. "I'm sure Doctor George is enjoying his medical call-out more than he would have enjoyed the recital if they'd been able to drag him along."

"It'll be hot tongue and cold shoulder for him and Thomas, if Miss Abigail learns the call-out was all a setup. Do you think it was?"

"I really don't know." Maureen sucked on her finger where the sharp needle broke the skin. "They're a pair of jokers when they put their heads together, those two."

Eve cut the thread with a small pair of silver scissors. "Mr. Mac says he and Miss Jane'll be able to move into their own house this week?"

"Yes, I heard and as soon as our new kitchen here's complete, they plan to start work on Miss Jane's kitchen-wing."

Both girls bent their heads to their work again as they listened to the wisps of music drifting on the evening breezes. Eve chuckled quietly.

"What's tickled your fancy, Eve?"

"Have you heard Doctor George dropping hints to get a horse for his call-outs?" She did not wait for Maureen to answer. "It'll be shank's pony for him if Miss Abigail finds out tonight's call-out was a hoax."

"Where will they keep it, if he does get a horse?"

"He plans to make the old kitchen into a stable. Mrs. Chapple told the doctor young Smiley is good with horses. The boy can earn a few pennies taking the animal out to feed on the grass of the commons each day."

The sound of Miss Abigail and the MacGregors returning from the recital brought Maureen to full consciousness. She lay listening to Eve's soft breathing coming from the bed against the opposite wall. Did she have the courage to do this? The faint sounds of the honky-tonk piano at the Diggers Arms Hotel came to her from half-way down the street. Like sporadic visits from an unwanted neighbour, the unpleasant mixture of cooking odours and open toilets wafted in through the window. Men's voices could be heard arguing loudly, somewhere near the waterfront. The persistent call of a bird hooted from within the mangroves. A chill ran through her body at the sound of crocodiles calling from the opposite side of the river. The captain of the *Northern Orchid* had told them the bull-like roar they heard at night was the sound of the male crocodiles.

When the house had stilled, she eased her feet onto the floor. Slowly and silently, Maureen lifted the pile of her father's clothing from the box hidden under her bed. To prevent the bed squeaking, she stood to change from her nightdress into these same clothes she'd worn to stowaway on the *Northern Orchid*. Where was the *Northern Orchid* tonight? Halfway back to Townsville by now, most likely; along with the handsome Josh Dougall. She felt the tears in the back of her throat at the thought she might never see him again. In fact, even if she did see him, he'd want nothing to do with a woman who willingly wandered alone in the night, through the public houses of the town. Using only her fingers, she straightened her hair and began making two plaits, one on each side of her head. The orange stone, in its new material envelope, fitted in tightly at the base of one plait while the long ties were woven in with the hair. Pins secured the two plaits to her scalp. The large cap fitted firmly over her head when pulled well down on her face. Trembling hands lifted her boots from the floor and tucked them firmly under her arm.

Each of the two steps to the door of the room triggered a creak from the timber floorboards which sounded, to her nervous ears, every bit like a major battle of war. Ever so slowly, she turned the door handle and opened a gap just wide enough, allowing her body to edge through into the hallway. Hugging the wall, she tiptoed its length to the door leading onto the back verandah. A sigh of relief escaped her lips when this also opened without a sound.

After closing the door behind her, she held her breath and stood perfectly still. With all senses alert, Maureen remained so until sure no-one in the house had been disturbed. Her gaze searched the back yard. In the half-moon light, every shadow appeared as a lurking threat. She breathed slowly, in and out. Each breath sounded like a wind-storm in her ears. Should she go and begin her own search for her father or should she stay in this familiar and safe house? Cowardice almost won. It was the threat of the orphanage hanging over the heads of her siblings which nudged her on. Barefooted, she made the descent down the back stairs. Each step was agony as she waited for a noise revealing her discovery. At the lower half of the stairs, she bent almost double, seeking to peer in under the house. Were the doctor and Thomas asleep? A rush of small padded feet scampered across the lower verandah, free of patients at the moment. She bit down on a squeal. Rapidly disappearing into the night, along with the intruding animal, was the last vestige of courage she had been able to summon up only seconds before. The lump in her throat almost took her breath away. She froze again until silence returned.

At the bottom step, she pulled on her shoes. Her whole body shook as if with the ague. A soft groan met the clammy night air when she pushed herself upright and moved off.

Keeping within the deeper shadows of the street, Maureen walked towards the first group of lights where menfolk were gathered. The grog shanty was built of canvas walls with a thatched roof. Dim light from several lanterns barely made the journey out onto the street where men sat around wooden tables, playing cards. Pennies clinked as they landed on the coin pile in the middle of the tables when the bets were laid. Other men stood in a circle around the tables watching. Perhaps some hoped to be invited to join a game. Others there could only afford to watch.

From her vantage point in the shadows of a wagon across the street, Maureen could see an old man inside serving behind a bar made of slab timber. Frequently the man used a cloth tied at his belt to wipe at the sweat running from his balding grey head. At other times the same cloth served to wipe the benches.

Behind her, a pair of hooded dark eyes watched the watcher with interest.

Again, fear almost overwhelmed Maureen at the thought of what she was going to do. Before her feet had the chance to betray her, she stepped out into the street. She drooped her shoulders and pulled the cap more firmly over her face and hair. While shuffling along, she breathed noisily through an open mouth. The men and their audience at the card tables took little notice of this unkempt lad who skirted past them before pausing at the entrance to the bar-room. Maureen stood there for some time, surveying the inside. Deliberately she stuck a finger up her nostril and dug out a bit a snot on which she sucked. Inside the bar, the small area was crowded. Shadows hid the features of the patrons. She chewed at her fingernail, drew in a long breath and began to move amongst the men. With her head bowed and unpleasant sounds coming from her open mouth she paused to ask anyone who would listen.

"Hey Mister, have you seen my Dad at the goldfields. His name's Bert Ryan."

Some of the drinkers were tolerant of the interruption.

"No son, sorry, don't think I've run into anyone of that name."

Others were not so tolerant.

"Piss off, boy. Get home to your mother. I dunno yer father."

As her confidence in the disguise developed, she even had the courage to stand near the lantern at the bar and ask the barman the same question.

"Don't go bothering the customers, lad. Don't need yer to interrupt their drinking. I'll tell yer what. Yer bring me a written sign tomorrow and I'll stick it out the front. There might be a couple of these punters who can read. I'll ask about for yer too. What's yer dad's name, again?"

With her head kept low, she answered. "Thanks, Mister. His name's Bert Ryan. If anyone knows where he is, they can tell Doctor Goldfinch."

Striving to maintain her slouch and the drag of her feet, Maureen moved back across the street and blended into the dark shadows. Her knees trembled and threatened to give way on her altogether. She clasped her hands to prevent their shaking. Her breath came in gasps. Sweat streamed down her body. Her mouth felt as dry as a pound of flour. Of their own volition, her feet moved off in the direction of safety and home.

When her hands caught hold of the rail, her body collapsed onto the steps. She dropped her head on to her knees. Fingertips dangled in the grass. Tears ran down her face. Each breath struggled through a throat tight with nervous spasm.

Clouds built in the sky. The moon rose through them as if controlled by the strings of a puppeteer higher up in the heavens. The pair of hooded black eyes watching from the shadows across the street melted away into the darkness at the sound of the police patrol doing their rounds. Their heavy boots crunched on the roadway. Voices mumbled between bursts of their laughter.

The ties of her shoes threatened to break as Maureen's frantic fingers tore them loose. With her shoes in one hand, she made haste up the stairs on her tiptoes careful not to stumble in the darkening night. She cowered near the door leading into the washroom sectioned off at the corner of the upper verandah. Then, with little warning, the rains thundered down on the iron roof like a herd of stampeding cattle. Water gurgled down the new drain pipes and into the water barrels of which Mac was so proud. Any noise she might make now would be overridden by the noise of the cloudburst.

When she eventually lay back on her bed in her nightdress, with her heart still pounding in her ears, her mind replayed the evening. All in all, things weren't nearly as grim as she had imagined they might be. There was still the problem of how she was to write a notice, but harder still, how was she going to get it to the barman.

The morning arrived way too quickly. Maureen's head felt thick, like one of Eve's pea and ham soups. Her body felt at least twice its weight. To raise her head from the pillow was such an effort. She knew if she stayed here, Miss Abigail would send the doctor calling with a dose of one of his foul-smelling concoctions. She dragged her feet out and onto the floor.

By the time Maureen arrived at the kitchen shed, Eve had the fire lit and the porridge on cooking.

"You look terrible, Maureen. Are you alright?"

"Thanks, Eve, I'm fine. I did not sleep at all well last night. It was so hot and clammy; until the storm hit."

"I must have slept through it all. It wasn't until I saw all the water lying about this morning, I realized we'd had any rain last night."

Maureen watched several large kangaroos nibbling the short pastures on Grassy Hill. Their heads constantly lifted as they scanned the area for threats. A Chinese man approached along the roadway, leading a grey packhorse. Hanging from both sides of the animal's body rattled two large canisters.

"Look who's here. I'll just get our quart." Maureen took up the jug and the sixpence Miss Abigail left in the kitchen each night. She went over to meet the milkman.

He was all chatter and wide smiles but as usual, Maureen did not understand a word he spoke. She struggled to smile in return as she held out her jug to be filled. The bony hand took up a beaten-metal ladle and began dipping out the fresh milk. The jug threatened to overflow before he placed the lid back onto the canister and hung the ladle from the hook on the side of the can. Maureen handed over the sixpence along with a dull smile.

Back at the fireplace, Maureen stirred the porridge. She wiped the perspiration from her forehead with the back of her hand.

"It's going to be another stinking hot day again. We won't have to cook today's eggs, Eve. I think they'll come out of the hens already cooked."

"You're right. There seems to be no let-up on the heat. The new fellow, James Dick, who has set up the soft drink factory must be doing a roaring trade. Everyone is partial to a drink on a day like today."

CHAPTER TWENTY-SIX

COOK'S TOWN

Henry sat at the table on Miss Jane's back verandah. His teeth held his tongue in place as it stuck out the side of his mouth. With head bent, he took great care to copy the names of all the towns on the Queensland map hanging from the nail on the wall. The carpentering noises, coming from next door where the doctor's kitchen was in the process of being erected, marched around the side of the house like an army searching to overwhelm the vulnerable.

The native boy, Smiley, sat with his hands squashed firmly between his knees. His attention was focused on the Alphabet Book sitting on the table in front of him. The temptation became too much for the lad. His hand edged forward to reach out and turn the front cover. He gazed in wonder. The errant hand turned to the next page, then the next and the next.

A half-smile formed on her lips, as Jane MacGregor watched surreptitiously. She took up a spare slate and a slate pencil and placed them in front of Smiley. Her slim finger pointed to the boy's chest.

"You," she said. Her smile widened.

Furtively the boy moved the slate and pencil closer to his body. He turned the book back to the first page. Over the next hour, while Henry was busy at his map drawing, Smiley copied onto the slate.

Not only the letters in the book but the pictures at the side of each letter; as many as he could fit on both sides of the slate.

Jane watched mesmerized. She opened her lessons' box and removed a number of graphite pencils and sheets of plain paper. With gentleness, she took the slate from the dark child, while telling him he had done good work. She placed the paper in front of the boy and positioned the pencil correctly in his hand. With light fingers, she turned the next page of the book. Smiley's comprehension exploded onto his face. The white teeth shone out and the eyes danced.

"Me?" he whispered.

"Yes," Jane pointed again.

The teacher did not reprimand Henry when he looked up from his work to watch his friend bring the pictures to life. It was a joy to see what the strange boy could do with a simple pencil and paper.

Doctor George, Mac, Thomas and Abigail were deep in discussions on the latest information they had received at the town council's meeting the previous night. Their concerns had been raised on issues related to the hygiene of the town's water supply and the accompanying poor sanitation. The urgent need for a hospital had been raised, as well as the groundswell of arguments by the townsfolk who wanted the name of the town changed from Cook's Town to Cooktown.

It was Eve who called from inside the kitchen-shed.

"Miss Abigail, dinner is ready. Will we serve it up now?"

Abigail stood and began clearing away some of the papers from the table under the awning.

"Yes, dear, of course."

When Jane and the boys joined the others at the midday meal, Jane held up Smiley's work. Her glowing praise shone from her blue eyes.

"Thomas, what do you think? You're the one here with the artistic talent, are you not? This is the first time Smiley has held a pencil in his hand. He copied from the textbook. This seems, to my inexperienced eye, a promising talent."

All heads turned to where Smiley sat beside Henry, at the far end of the table. The dark head bowed low into his bowl of food. He squirmed on the uncomfortable stool.

Thomas peered closely at the work. "Can I see the book?"

Jane opened the Alphabet Book to the relevant page.

"He certainly shows attention to detail. If you notice, you can see where he has added extras to accentuate the picture." Thomas pointed to several areas on the paper.

Henry piped up. "I know. Smiley can draw real good. He draws maps of the tracks around here and houses. He draws all the animals. He makes the marks on hard rock with wet red mud."

"Really good." Jane corrected automatically. "Can we see these?"

"Yes, Miss Jane. When we go for a walk on Grassy Hill you will see them."

"I'd certainly like to join you on this adventure," Thomas said. "There is potential in this work." He looked down the table at the boy. "Smiley, this is very good. Do you understand, good?"

George's eyebrows rose when Henry spoke to his friend with words definitely not English. Smiley's head nodded and a shy smile peeped out from his face.

It was Mac who changed the subject. "It can't be too long before the *Northern Orchid* arrives back in the harbour. I think William Sloan will be impressed with the work we have achieved here."

Everyone's attention focused on the almost completed kitchen.

"I don't know about anyone else but I'm going to sleep like a baby tonight. Hopefully, the town will be quieter than last night," Mac commented.

Inside the kitchen-shed, Maureen scraped the plates. She listened to Mac's comment. Her heart raced. There will be no excuses. Tonight, she must go out into the town, in her disguise, to search again for news of her father. There had been little opportunity in the past two weeks for her to do so. She had spent the time in turmoil. A part of her felt relieved knowing she had a legitimate excuse not to go but enormous guilt weighed heavily upon her, knowing her siblings' future depended on her finding their dad.

He sat on a stool in the corner of the bar-room. Maureen, with her head bowed and shoulders drooped, dragged her feet towards the man. Light brown eyes glowed almost a red colour in the lantern light. They were surrounded by an explosion of dark hair and long whiskers. She caught her breath at the sight of him. This was the last punter in the place she had yet to talk to but her feet were about to turn her around and scamper. She paused when he growled.

"You the kid looking for yer father?"

Her knees trembled. "Yes, Mister. Have you seen Bert Ryan at the goldfields?"

"An Irish fella. Yeah. He's panning down the creek a bit from me."

The fear within her disappeared like hunger after a meal. "Can you give him a message for me, Mister?" She almost lifted her head. Her grin was brought under immediate control.

"The name's Silas." The stranger growled and swallowed from the pannikin in front of him. He stared at the unkempt boy as if sizing him up.

Nervous tension infiltrated her body as she stood holding her breath waiting for the man to speak. She jerked in surprise when he did.

"It'd be best coming from you. If yer interested, I'm leaving at four o'clock in the morning. I can take you to the Palmer River."

Maureen could hardly speak. Everyone knew, even in the best of weather it took a good two or three weeks to walk the narrow track to the goldfields. With the rains hanging about, as they had over the past two months, there was no guarantee they might not be stuck at a riverbank, somewhere in the back of nowhere, for weeks, waiting for waters to recede. The pounding of her heart almost deafened her. Her powers of thought seemed to be hammered flat with the beat. She so much wanted to see her dad; so very much. A thick tongue stuck to the dry roof of her mouth as she attempted to speak. She coughed and tried to find a bit of spit. Eventually, she managed the words.

"I don't have provisions to make such a journey, Mr. Silas."

A dirty hand with broken nails scratched at the hidden chin under the unruly beard. The red eyes bored into the lad chewing on fingernails.

"If yer can handle horses, yer can earn yer keep by looking after the packhorses. Yer'll get food and a bit of canvas to sleep under."

Her mind thundered along with her heart. Occasionally watching Ned and Jacko looking after the three horses at The Mariner's Rest wasn't exactly comprehensive training in the care of packhorses. More importantly, could she maintain her disguise for such a long period?

"Think about it, boy. I'll be out the back with me four horses before the dawn. Be there if you want to travel with Silas." The voiced growled. Maureen stepped back as Silas stood and moved out of the room.

With whirling thoughts, she made her way out to the front street and into the darker shadows. Her guard was down as she returned to the house. Once again, she did not notice the dark eyes following her.

Huddled inside the almost completed kitchen room, Maureen sat contemplating her options. She heard and recognized the bell of a ship moored in the Endeavour River. It was eleven-thirty at night. Intermittent periods of light sleep were all she managed. When the ship's bell marking three o'clock sounded, she was loath to move. Grubby hands rubbed her heavy eyelids. She had to move; either to her bedroom upstairs or to the back of the hotel to join Mr. Silas and his packhorses. There was something about the man. He made her flesh crawl but he did say he knew her father and where to find him. What choice did she have? Moonlight guided her footsteps.

Four horses wearing halters and surcingles stood tied to a rail at the back yard of the hotel. Maureen jumped when the growl came from behind her.

"Don't just stand there gawping. Bring out the rest of the load from the room there and don't miss anything."

Maureen turned to where the man pointed to an open room in which a lantern glowed. She groaned at the weight of a wooden box when she first attempted to lift it. Her teeth ground together as she bent once again. This time she managed to raise it from the floor. Wobbly knees threatened to give way under her. She stumbled out into the yard and placed the box near where the man had several other boxes, bags and canisters.

"Don't drop it, boy. The shop-keeper at Palmer River won't pay for broken merchandise."

Maureen watched closely as Silas sorted, and secured the load between the animals. Horses grunted as extra weights were added to their already substantial loads. Hooves stomped in complaint.

"They're a bit fresh at the moment. They'll settle down once we get a few miles down the track."

In the dark, Maureen bit her lip. Was she going to have the stamina to see this through? It became apparent the horses were not for riding.

Silas led off. Each horse was tied to the one in front of it. A long whip snaked down the length of the procession to lightly flick the rear horse. With no more than a short snort, it moved along nudging the animal in front.

"Boy, you walk beside the last horse and watch what's going on behind my back." As an afterthought, he added, "It's called Moses."

Maureen's sluggish mind took a moment to realize he had been talking about the horse's name.

"Hello, Moses," she whispered and stroked its white blaze before resting her hand on the brown neck.

The moonlight shone from a clear sky as they moved off, heading south. The horses' feet crunched on the thin gravel of the town's quiet street.

Silas led them through another tent-city on the south side of the main town. Hundreds of miners camped here while preparing to move off to the goldfields. Others waited for passage to take them well away from this hard land. As the dawn light peeped over the horizon, it revealed, only a short distance away, another tent community where hundreds of Chinese lived.

Mud squelched over her boots. The horses snorted and breathed heavily as they laboured over a road still boggy from the rain of two days previously. Before the full sun presented itself in the sky, she felt perspiration running down her face and her body. She had to admit it was easier to bear the heat in these old clothes of her father's than the many layers of a woman's everyday clothing. She closed her mind to the discomfort and like the horses, concentrated on putting one foot in front of the other.

"Goodness me, Smiley. You gave me a start. What are you doing sleeping here?" Eve stared at the black boy laying against the still-warm rock on which the coals from the previous night's fire remained. "Where's Maureen? She's not in our room. I thought she must be out here." She watched the child sit up and rub his eyes. "I guess there's no point asking you. Even if you knew the answers to my questions, I could not understand what you say."

The boy's head snapped up. "Reen," he said.

Just then, Thomas arrived. Smiley jumped up. "Reen," he repeated. He took up a piece of cold charcoal. His one hand indicated for Thomas to come closer while his other hand drew stick pictures on the large flat rock they used as a fireplace.

A skirt identified the first as a girl. "Reen." Smiley insisted.

The second figure was dressed in trousers. "Reen." Smiley looked up wide-eyed.

"What is he saying?" Eve looked at Thomas for understanding.

"Reen is Maureen, I think." He turned his head back to the black-skinned boy. "Yes?"

The dark head nodded up and down.

"Stay here, Smiley. Stay." Thomas walked back into the house. When he returned, a short time later, he held a sketchbook in his hand along with two pencils. "Now, Smiley, Come." He sat the boy up at the table.

On the paper, a story developed. The girl Reen becomes the boy Reen who meets a dark-haired and bearded man. The two of them leave town with four horses loaded down with supplies.

Eve spun around and ran upstairs. On her return, she panted. "It's true. Her father's clothes are missing. The ones she wore when she stowed away on the ship. She kept them in a box under her bed."

Thomas patted the boy on the shoulder and spoke to Eve.

"Will you be able to do breakfast on your own? I'd best go and give Doctor George this news."

"Of course, Thomas." Eve stirred the coals and gathered some twigs. Smiley jumped down from the chair and ran to help Eve get the fire alight.

Worried frowns marred the faces of the group gathered at the breakfast table. Jane and Mac joined Abigail, George, Thomas, and Eve. Henry and Smiley sat near the fireplace communicating in language, sign and charcoal pictures on the rock.

After the events of the night were explained, as best they could be with the evidence they had, a full-blown discussion followed on what they could or should do. George looked at his friends around the table.

"So, is everyone agreed? I'll talk to the Inspector at the Police Station this morning. Mac, you see if there is anything China can do to assist. Thomas, I'll leave you here to hold the fort until we get some idea of what we should be doing. Abigail, will you keep an eye on the patients?"

Abigail nodded her head as she held her arms out to Henry who moved to wind his arms around his mother's waist.

"Will Maureen come back when she finds her father, Mama?"

"Of course, Henry." Moisture shone on her eyelids. She stood tall and shook her head. "Now, how about you help Miss Jane over to her house, for your lessons. Thomas might like to take breakfast to the patients and I will help Eve clear this mess away and start preparations for our dinner."

THE *NORTHERN ORCHID*

Stacked as high as the bulwark on the port and starboard foredecks, sawn timber strained against the chains. The fore-hold held the usual stores of food, medical supplies and general household items required by a developing town while the stern-hold was almost full of more timber and corrugated iron and two steel water tanks; all for the port of Cook's Town.

Men danced across the yardarms while other sailors on the decks below hauled on the lines trimming the sails to take full advantage of the brisk south-eastern breezes. Bosun Evan's voice roared over the drumming of the sails and skirl of the winds. Regular waves crashed over the bow cooling the day with a fine spray of saltwater.

In the chartroom, Captain Sloan and Gus studied the map laid out on the table.

"I guess Captain Cook would have given anything to have had this map with him when he passed through here a hundred or so year ago," Gus pondered.

"His survival and that of his men and ship is evidence of a magnificent seaman. If his ship and all were lost, it may not have been until Captain King, in his *Mermaid,* turned up in June 1819 before the Endeavour River became a dot on the map."

Gus knew not to doubt Captain Sloan's memory for dates. He grinned. "Cook's Town would have another name too."

"No doubt." The captain stood back from the table and peered out of the window. For some time, he idly watched China's hens as they clucked and scratched within the cages just outside the chartroom. They were a peaceful influence. With China still in Cook's Town, William Sloan admitted he did miss the company of the little man. Even though the Dougall brothers meant as much to him as if they were his own sons, they did not replace the company of men his own age with whom he had experienced many adventures. He turned and watched Gus as he studied the chart of the narrow channel following the coast of northern Queensland. The boy's concentrated focus reminded the captain so much of Jimmy Dougall. In fact, like their father, the two lads had a way of staring so hard at a map it seemed as if they were trying to absorb the knowledge through their very pores. He knew Gus preferred the engine room environment but the lad … his thoughts paused here. No, not a lad, look at him; a man. He and his brother are men now. Their father would be proud of them. The captain returned to his original thought. Despite his passion for the engine, Gus never missed an opportunity to remain familiar with the sea through which they travelled. The engineer was often to be found up here in the chartroom. Gus lifted his head when the captain spoke.

"Gus, when are you going to marry the sweet Eve at Cook's Town?"

The flush gushed out from under the young man's shirt collar and swept over his face. He stuttered, "Captain Sloan, Eve hardly even knows I'm alive. She's at least a year older than me; maybe closer to two."

"Humph. Well, for someone who hardly knows you're alive, her gaze follows you around like it was hooked on to you with a fishing line."

The flush deepened. "What good would I be as a husband, to any girl? I just like to spend most days out with the ship and the salt air."

"Many sailors have wives at home waiting for them. My wife got sick of it, I admit, but Millie always accepted me for what I was. I'm sure there are other women who can live with that. And another thing, unless you're thinking of transferring to an overseas vessel, these coastal traders return to their base every few weeks. There's no reason why you cannot set up home if you find the woman who is willing to accommodate such a lifestyle."

Gus's finger threaded its way between his collar and neck. He felt the perspiration running freely.

"I have to admit I do like the girl very much; ever since I first saw her in Brisbane."

"Well, don't waste time, boyo. I know it might be easier to face up to a crocodile or hungry shark but once you say your piece to a woman, you'll find it not nearly as terrifying as you thought."

Gus's fingers pushed through his hair.

"You're probably right, Cap'n."

"And, while you're at it, talk to your brother. He needs to ask the little pixie, Maureen, the same question, judging by the way they never take their eyes off each other."

Gus grinned. "Aye, aye, Cap'n."

The door opened further as Stretch entered with a tray in his arms. He carried the midday meal for the officers.

"Cook Lee said the stew is made on tin meat and is full of beans because that is all he could get, in Cardwell. The damper is fresh though."

Captain Sloan sighed, "There's not a trader anywhere along the coast who'd refuse China what he wanted. No doubt, Lee will learn too."

COOK'S TOWN

Doctor George called to Thomas as he made his way to the kitchen-shed. The hammering ceased. Thomas emerged brushing the sawdust from his shirt.

"How did you go at the Police Station?" Thomas asked.

"Come and get a drink and I'll tell you everything. I'll call Abigail to join us."

Eve placed the large teapot on the table as Mac arrived with China at his heels. The muscles on the arms of a second Chinaman bulged as he held a large wok out in front of his body.

Abigail walked over to greet China. The man bowed low.

"We sorry girl gone to the goldfields to find her father. A sad time for you." China turned. His slim finger pointed to the wok. "A gift to make a little easier at this time."

Abigail bowed in return as she thanked the man.

Once the wok sat in the coals at the fireplace, the second Chinaman pulled a spatula from his loose clothing like a magician pulling a scarf from his hat. With great gusto, he used the ladle to stir the contents. Appetizing aromas filled the nostrils of those gathered around the table.

The chair scraped as Mac sat down next to Jane.

"Oh, China. Those smells are enough to torture a man. It takes me right back to the *Northern Orchid.*"

Jane's eyes watched her husband with interest as he settled down to enjoy his meal, the likes of which she had never seen.

"George, you have not told us yet. What did you find out at the Police Station?" Abigail nibbled at the strange food. She turned to China. "This really is a nice flavour. You will have to show us how it is made."

George nodded in agreement before relating the outcome of his investigations earlier in the morning.

"The Inspector and his men are out on a routine patrol. They are not expected back for at least two weeks. When they do return, it may be a few days or more before they are ready to depart on another patrol. The timing will depend on the state they and their horses are in when they do arrive back."

Sighs drifted around the listeners.

"Oh, dear. Does anyone know anything about this man? Can he be trusted? What are the chances of Maureen surviving several weeks?" Abigail pondered aloud.

Tears flowed down Eve's face. She pushed her chair back and said defiantly.

"Maureen might look as frail as a butterfly but she's as strong as an ox. She'll survive. She wants to find her dad and then she will come back here. You wait and see if I'm not right."

Her voice broke up in sobs.

Abigail jumped up and led the sobbing girl away towards the house.

"You are right, Eve. Maureen is much tougher than she looks. Of course, she'll return to us. Can I take you upstairs to lie down, dear?"

"No thanks, Miss Abigail. I'm dreadfully sorry for my outburst. Can I just sit here on the verandah, for a moment longer?"

Abigail returned to the meal table where China and Mac were proposing to take a small group of China's people to follow this man with whom Maureen was travelling.

Eve's squeal distracted them.

Josh and Gus strode towards the doctor's house. They were discussing the changes made since their last call at the port. Suddenly Gus was nearly bowled over by a howling Eve who threw her arms around his neck.

"Gus, Gus. She's gone off to the goldfields with a stranger to find her father. What can we do to bring her back?"

Josh's eyebrows rose as a tentative grin touched his lips.

Gus did not miss the deep look thrown at him by his brother but he was rather otherwise occupied comforting the beauty in his arms, to let it bother him. Besides, he was enjoying the feel of her body in such a close embrace.

While Gus calmed Eve, Josh approached the group around the table under the awning of the kitchen-shed.

"Mac, are you becoming such a landlubber you didn't notice the *Northern Orchid's* arrival this morning? And what is this I smell? There is definitely China's hand somewhere in that cooking." His gaze ran over each person present then over them once again. He turned towards the house.

It was Abigail who noticed his searching eyes.

"She has gone to the goldfields to find her father, Josh; with a stranger. She did not tell anyone she was going. It is why we are all here, planning on what we should do."

"You mean it was Maureen whom Eve was talking about? What's the girl got herself into now?"

After the greetings all around, the Dougall brothers were updated fully on the morning's events.

The quiet voices flowed back and forth as they discussed their plan of action. Only Henry noticed the stranger. Work-hardened hands removed the felt hat releasing an unkempt mop of brown hair.

"Excuse me, boy." The Irish brogue was thick as the morning porridge. "Can you tell me if this is where Doctor Goldfinch lives?"

"Yes, Sir. He's up there." The small hand pointed to Maureen's friends around the table. "Uncle George," he yelled. "There's a man here to see you."

George turned his head to glance at the visitor. He froze for a second. The chair fell over backwards with a heavy thump as he jumped up. The sound sent everyone's head turning to the new arrival.

Jane squealed softly. "Mr. Ryan!"

"Bert," George called. "Where have you come from?" He rushed over and took the man's hand, shaking it vigorously. "We are ever so pleased to see you."

"I… I… er... don't understand. I just arrived on the *RMS Normanby*. A barman told me, a boy, said 'e was my son, 'ad been looking for me and I was to come 'ere. My son's a bit young to be up this way on 'is own."

"Oh dear, Mr. Ryan. There is much we have to tell you. Please, will you join us for dinner?" Abigail took the man's elbow and led him to the table.

China stood and moved aside. "There is much to do. I return later." He turned to the new arrival. "Mr. Ryan, I sorry. Also, I wish to say you have an admirable daughter."

The perplexity on Mr. Ryan's face deepened.

It was not until after three o'clock the following afternoon before the rescuers were ready to set off on their trek to the Palmer River goldfields. Their friends were there to see them off. Thomas drove the borrowed dray to their starting point on the outskirts of the Chinese tent-city. By his side sat Doctor George, Abigail, Eve and Henry. Jane retained a tight grip on her husband's hand. He may not be going on this trek but he was still to leave in two days' time. Once more he was to sail as Ship's Mate on the *Northern Orchid* with Captain Sloan.

Josh, Gus and Bert Ryan stood to the side as three Chinese men led off, each in charge of a packhorse weighed down heavily with food supplies for them all. A large wok and utensils rattled from the side of the bundle on the first animal. China led the fourth horse in the line. His friends had only agreed to him coming if he consented to ride a horse when the journey became too much for him. It had been an exercise in diplomacy to reach this arrangement without having to say outright he was too old to be attempting such a trying trek on foot. China's horse also carried his tent, a thin swag and his medical supplies. Josh and Gus each led a packhorse loaded with the remainder of the tents, swags and equipment. Everyone in the dray waved farewell.

Bert Ryan followed behind. His shoulders weighed down, not only with his swag but with sorrow at the news he received yesterday of the loss of his good woman and also with concern for his eldest daughter. He had spent most of his adult life on goldfields in one place or another and he had seen men of all types. In his opinion, some were honourable, hard-working men; quick to help another. Alongside these were many who should have been drowned at birth. Which was this man who held his daughter captive by her own desires to find her father?

The heat of the day reluctantly made a slow retreat and the clouds thickened overhead increasing the muggy atmosphere. Rain was a distinct possibility for some time later. If those clouds hid the moon, they'd be looking to make camp earlier than hoped.

CHAPTER TWENTY-SEVEN

MAUREEN RYAN

The orchestra of creaking leathers, plodding, sloshing hooves and the occasional snort of a horse, all kept in rhythm by the rattle of the cooking pots swaying with the horses' rumps, mesmerized Maureen. Her body leant in against Moses's side. The beast's load pressing on her back, kept her moving forward. Unnoticed mud splashes from the hooves of Buster, the grey horse immediately in the line ahead of Moses, mixed with the perspiration running down her face. At Two Mile Creek, they passed the acres of vegetable gardens where workers hoed and shovelled and weeded almost as thick in number as the insects which threatened to demolish the crops. Maureen barely lifted her eyes. When passing through the swamps north of Six Mile Creek, the water rose up over her ankles. It never entered her mind to consider Silas's skills in guiding his team through such terrain without having them bog down. She gradually returned to conscious thought, just in time to prepare for action when her guide stopped their progress. A growl from the front reached her ears.

"We'll take a break here for dinner. The horses have to be unloaded then we'll hobble them for a couple of hours. They'll get a bit of picking here."

It was an effort but she pushed her body forward. Silas loosened the ropes and removed the canvas from over the supplies carried by the pure black horse he called Devil. This he lay on the ground. Each bag and container from the horse's back he handed to Maureen who piled them on the canvas. Her body flinched as he passed a long gun into her hands. She lay it down carefully.

"It don't look like rain so this won't need covering." He grunted as he bent to secure the hobble straps. Next, he took a belt with a cowbell attached and buckled it around Devil's neck.

Maureen was pleased to see Silas place the hobbles below the front fetlocks of the lead horse. Until then, she had no idea what to do with them.

"Right, Devil, there you go."

After each horse had been unloaded, Maureen tied the animal to the branches of the low trees at the edge of the clearing. When all were free of their cargo, she began to attach the hobbles as she had seen Silas do to Devil. A darkening bruise on her arm provided evidence of the spiteful nature of the second horse, the piebald one, Silas called Serpent.

"Do you want a bell on these horses too, Mr. Silas."

The man hawked and spat into the grass. "Course not, Boy. We don't want a bloody band playing music while we eat." He wandered over to a tree and began undoing the front of his trousers.

Maureen turned her head away sharply. She moved back to the creek and drank deeply.

"Wake up, Boy. You could have taken the billy with you to fill. Make sure you bring back a few sticks to get the fire going." Silas now stood with his hands on his hips watching her.

Devil snuffled around the scrubby bushes searching for grass to pick. Being still not too far from the town and also on the main route between the Palmer River Goldfields and Cook's Town, the local and travelling horses had left few pickings in this area. Silas adjusted one of the hobble straps before collecting the requirements for the dinner preparation from the heap of supplies.

By this time, Maureen sat waiting to light the fire.

"Have you a steel and flint, Mr. Silas?" She jumped as the camp oven landed on the ground beside her. A small calico bag with flour, another with oats and a brown packet of salt landed inside it.

"You can make a damper now. We'll be here a couple of hours; until the heat is gone from the day. In the meantime, you can cook a bit of oatmeal to line our guts with. It's been a long time since I last ate." Silas dug his flint from his back pocket and eased his knife from the scabbard on his belt. He went to hand it to Maureen then changed his mind and bent to do the job himself.

"Can't have a lad like you messin' 'round with sharp knives, can we?" He laughed; not a pleasant sound.

Maureen felt the goosebumps rise on her arms but did not really know why. Probably just feeling overtired, were her thoughts.

Once the fire was established, Maureen began placing twigs on the heap of burning grass, one at a time. Silas stood and went down to the creek where he filled the billy. On his return, he set it in the lifting fire. The man placed two pannikins, the insides of which were thick with tannin, on the ground. In one he placed a generous shake of tea leaves. In the other, a few leaves landed in the bottom of the container. Beside these, he placed two tin bowls and two spoons.

Between stirring the oatmeal in the pot near the billy on the fire and kneading the flour, salt and water in the camp oven, Maureen watched Silas out of the corner of her eye. She pondered on why the man had two of everything. When pouring the boiling water into the pannikins, she did not miss the addition of fluid to his mug poured from a flask taken from the pocket of his trousers.

After eating, Silas moved away to rest with his back against the trunk of a tree. It was left to Maureen to clear things up, wash their dishes in the creek and await the rising of their damper.

Heat still cocooned them in its suffocating blanket when a sharp growl and the scuffle of boots scraping in the dirt penetrated her awareness. Silas jumped to his feet.

"You stupid, Boy? Can you hear the bell?"

Maureen sat cross-legged at the edge of the fireplace. Her head was bowed, almost as low as her waist. When she looked up, lines of fatigue crisscrossed her face.

"N-n-no, I can't hear the bell, Mr. Silas."

"That's exactly it, Boy. It can't be heard. So, where is the horse? Move your stumps, Useless. Go and find the sod and bring him back here."

Rubbing her eyes, Maureen moved out through the trees following the direction in which she had last seen the horses. Before her spread a creek-flat with short-cropped grasses. Not one horse was in sight. Her gaze scanned the bordering tree-line. The white blaze on Moses's brown face caught the sunlight. She tramped the two hundred yards to where the four horses rested in the shade. Using the bell strap on Devil's neck she led him back to camp. At her urging, the other horses followed behind.

The sun hung halfway across the western sky when Silas, with Maureen's help, reloaded the horses. It was time to move on. Ignoring the pain in her back and legs, Maureen took up her position.

From Maureen's point of view, the following miles to their night camp at Eight Mile Creek was just a repetition of the morning's mind-numbing heat, pain and exhaustion. The sun settled below the horizon when Silas chose a campsite. With trembling knees and nerveless arms, she once more helped the carrier unload the horses.

This time he piled all the cargo on a large oilcloth rolled out on the ground.

The horses were hobbled. Each horse now carried a bell around its neck. These clunked dully as the animals moved. The horses drank thirstily from the creek before shifting out to graze the low grasses on the flat seen, in the faint light of the dusk, through the thin line of trees.

In the meantime, Silas slung the larger canvas over a rope between two tree-trunks. He draped it across the heaped cargo. The ring of steel on steel rang out through the bush as he hammered stakes into the four lower corners, securing against the weather.

Anxiety gnawed at Maureen. Was she going to have to sleep under the tent with Silas and the supplies? As far as she could see, there seemed little enough room left for one, let alone two people. Her heartbeat settled when Silas threw a much smaller heavy-duty calico from Buster's load, her way. A narrow strip of oilcloth was tossed on top of it, along with a length of rope.

Again, Maureen was in charge of setting the fireplace and preparing the evening meal. A slab of beef landed in the pot near her side.

"Cut this into small bits. Boil it up, with water." He threw a potato her way. "Add that too. We'll have soup, damper and tea; a king's feast. You better appreciate it, Boy, for it'll be rat's stew before we get to where we're going."

In the shadows cast by the flickering light of the fire they ate. Later, Maureen did not notice the hard ground under her or the tree root digging into her hip. She collapsed into sleep.

A boot in the ribs transmitted through the wall of her tent brought Maureen to a conscious state with a grunt.

"Smarten up there, Boy. The day's half over."

Agony ripped through her side. With bleary eyes, she peered through the end of her tent to discover no sign of an imminent sunrise. In fact, it seemed pitch black outside. When she struggled to her feet, she realized clouds were thick in the sky. Silas had rekindled the fire and water boiled in the pot. She watched as he cut chunks from the left-over damper using a knife drawn from a scabbard in his belt. After spearing it with a thin stick, he held it to the fire for a few minutes while it darkened. This he dipped into his pannikin and sucked up noisily. She limped over to make a drink of tea for herself and broke off some damper to chew on. Her head cocked to the side as she listened intently. Swallowing the last of her tea and damper she headed towards the bells.

Day two on the road followed a similar pattern to day one except the track held no swamps to suck in unwary feet. The sun chased away the clouds in the sky. The litter of human discards left to decay by the side of the track held her attention. Old clothes, a rusted billy with a hole in its base, an odd broken wheelbarrow and even a rotting cart with its axle and wheel smashed were identified.

Pain became a constant companion. Only the thought of being reunited with her father at the goldfields, kept Maureen going. They left the flats and climbed a winding path on the side of a ridge. She noticed where some work had been started to widen the track to allow drays access. Maureen felt her feet slipping on the gravel. Fear kept her awake as she endeavoured not to fall over the edges on some of the narrower paths along this uneven ground. She tried to walk on the off-side of the horse but the blades of the long-handled shovel and the spade nipped at her back like a dog nipping at the heels of an errant beast. She sighed with relief when Silas called a short halt at a high point of the terrain. If she dared to sit down, she might not be able to rise. Her arms hung over Moses's neck. Her cheek rested on the horse's mane. She dozed. The glorious views from this lookout held no interest for Maureen.

According to Silas, it had been fifteen minutes since they had stopped but when he nudged Devil into action, Maureen could not believe she had stopped at all.

The track from here led downwards, into the low country once more. The descent seemed even more treacherous than the climb, earlier. It was at a place Silas called Oakey Creek, where he made the dinner camp. Once again Maureen's body was beyond feeling as the work of unloading, seeing to the horses and preparing the meal was accomplished. Today the bells silenced before she had dropped off to sleep in the dirt under a shady tree by the fire. The animals lay to rest with their hunger assuaged by the plentiful grasses in the area.

This time it was Silas's boot against her boot which set her in motion. The afternoon took them across the grassy flats and small rises until dusk crept over the land. They prepared to set up their night camp, by a creek.

Eventually, she crawled into her tent. Her eyes closed. Maureen pondered briefly on the thought this was the end of day two. How was she going to last fourteen days? She did not hear the light rain on her tent. She did not see the lightning nor hear the thunder in the distance. She slept.

Elizabeth Rimmington

JOSH AND GUS DOUGALL

Josh felt the muscles pulling in his lower legs. His feet stumbled on the partially dried crusty craters and ruts on the road. A road, previously chewed up by human feet, packhorse hooves, wheelbarrows and wagon wheels when drenched with rain three days previously. This was every bit as difficult as flitting up and down the rigging of a ship. With little warning, the track entered a boggy swamp where the going was even more difficult. He looked up when China called.

"Keep in close single file, Mr. Josh. Man ahead knows best path. Not get bogged."

Josh turned his head to see how his brother was coping.

Gus quipped. "This bog reminds me of a few river banks I've wallowed in." The mud slurped as he lifted his feet. A rough hand swiped at the sweat running from his body. "How can a place be this hot? We need a good stiff sea breeze about now."

"Hopefully we'll be out of this swamp before those clouds up there drop their load," Josh called as he watched the sky. "Maybe we should have brought a boat instead of horses." Josh peered further back to where Bert followed with head bowed. "Are you alright there, Mr. Ryan?"

Blue eyes lifted. A strained smile pulled at his lips. Bert removed his hat and wiped his face with the back of his hand. "Thanks, Josh, I'm fine. I think you'd best call me Bert or it's going to be an even more difficult path we're to follow."

298

Josh laughed and touched his cap.

The sun retired from duty in the sky when, ahead of Josh, the four Chinese men spoke rapidly, in their own language. It sounded like the chatter of birds in a tree. When their voices ceased, China turned to those behind him.

"Six Mile Creek ahead. There, we make camp." His slow speech told of his fatigue but his legs kept moving one foot in front of the other.

The nod of Josh's head could not be seen in the dusk. His mind pondered on how they were going to get China off his legs and on the horse in the morning.

All were grateful for the splash of cool water when they crossed the creek. Hands scrubbed the mud from their lower legs. Horses and men alike drank deeply.

Dong, the man leading the group, set the other two Chinese men to the tasks of unloading the horses, setting a fire for cooking and preparing a camp. He then walked back to help China. His touch was gentle as he took the thin arm and led the older man to where he might rest at the base of a tree. The second Chinese man, with all smiles and bows, ran back to take the horses from Josh and Gus.

"Me, Fu," he said, digging his finger into his chest.

Josh and Gus watched with interest as Fu, Dong and the third Chinese man unloaded the animals. A heavy-duty calico tent was draped over the pile of supplies and equipment.

Fu pointed to the sky and directed his words to Josh and Gus standing nearby.

"Rain soon."

Plaited ropes were used to hobble the animals and light bells were hung around their necks before they were released to wander off in search of grass to eat.

With the light of a lantern behind them, the tree shadows danced around the Dougall brothers as they scavenged through the scant timber and along the creek banks looking for firewood. When they returned, it was Dong who whisked the contents of a wok heating on the fire. He nodded his head as the wood landed at his side.

"Chen," the cook called. The man jumped up and approached the fire. A short sharp spatter of the strange language burst from Dong's mouth as he handed a cup of liquid to Chen. His finger pointed to China sitting against the tree, with his head bowed. With care not to upset the contents, Chen knelt in front of the old man. China lifted his head and smiled. He spoke one or two words and took the offering.

Under China's critical eyes, Fu erected two tents. The smaller one, with an oilcloth inside, stood next to the supply tent. This, apparently, was for China. The second tent, set up nearby, was where Fu guided Josh and Gus. By this time Bert had his own small tent in a position close by.

Josh, Gus and Bert sat on their haunches next to China, where they ate their meal out of tin bowls. China's chopsticks flashed. The three Europeans were grateful for the spoons provided. Near the fire, Dong, Fu and Chen also manipulated their chopsticks with the expertise of a lifetime of practice.

While eating, Josh studied the packhorse handlers. Dong, the leader was tall for a Chinese man. He stood almost as tall as Josh himself and at least four inches higher than China. Hooded dark eyes, forever watching, told nothing of the man's inner thoughts. Chen was a shorter version of Dong. Fu, on the other hand, contained an inner joy. Smiles were forever breaking through the flat look he strived to attain. He stood as tall as Chen. Each wore a long black pigtail swinging from the back of their heads on which perched identical cone-shaped hats. No one spoke until their hunger abated.

Josh smiled at China. "Are you responsible for teaching this man how to cook?"

"Tastes like your work, China," Gus commented.

China smiled.

"Bert, you've been years on the goldfields looking after yourself. How does this compare to your usual fare?" Josh asked.

Bert used a fingernail to dig something from between two of his front teeth. "I always said any food someone else cooks's good but this is a new and splendid taste." He held up his empty dish and called. "Good, Dong. Very good."

China's high-pitched voice translated.

"China, where'll the others sleep?" Gus pointed to the group at the fire.

China began nodding his head as he spoke. "Two sleep in tent and one stay awake at all times." His slim finger with the long nail pointed to the supply tent.

"Is there enough room there? I'm sure Josh and I can squash up a bit and share our tent with them."

"It is their way. If no rain, they like sleep out in open."

No one was long on chat this night. The sounds of sleep filled the campsite before the moon rose in the sky. A light shower of rain towards morning barely disturbed the camp.

The swithering of the horse bells stirred Josh. Movement was heard outside the tents. He lifted the edge of the canvas to see Chen bringing the horses into camp. He threw a boot at his brother's sleeping back.

"Wake up, Gus. It's time to move."

In the dim light of a piccaninny dawn, the brothers quickly dropped and packed their tent. At the fire, they found a billy of tea simmering. China talked to Bert who sat on his rolled tent and swag. The miner was in the process of finishing off a bowl of left-overs from the previous night's supper. Heat rose from a freshly baked damper sitting on a tin plate. Dong handed Josh and Gus each a bowl of food. They tore off a chunk of the bread. While eating they watched Fu and Chen reload the horses and clear the campsite. It was impossible to tell who had been guard during the night. None of the men showed any evidence of a lack of sleep.

Josh pricked up his ears at the quiet conversation between Bert and China.

"How far ahead does Dong think Maureen and this fellow, called Silas, might be?"

"Dong say we start thirty-four hours behind them. It depends if your girl slows him down or not. When we pass travellers coming this way, we ask if they see them."

Josh was surprised at how easily China had been persuaded to ride one of the five grey horses. In the second position, Chen led two horses. Fu stepped back to lead the horse upon which China sat with great aplomb. When they passed Eight Mile Creek the horses slaked their thirst as did their handlers. Fu passed up a tin cup of the cool liquid to China who sipped slowly.

Ridge country was seen ahead as the group made their way across a plain which offered little shade. Low trees with scant foliage were the best the land could offer. The heat sapped their strength as they began the climb. A warm gusty breeze lifted their spirits as they proceeded across the higher terrain. Gratitude was almost tangible when Dong called a halt at an open peak which looked out onto a splendid panorama of the Australian bush. China slid down from his horse. He stretched his body before moving to join the others admiring the view.

After the brief rest, Dong bent to cup his hands providing a step for China to use as a jump-up to his position on the horse. He then took up his own lead rein and moved off. It became necessary to hold the horses' heads on short reins as they made their way over the descending track. The animals tended to want to run. Men's boots slid in the loose stones. Dong, Fu and Chen, who were shoeless, seemed to cope a little better.

Neither horses nor men required a second call when Dong called a halt for a dinner camp beside a running creek at the bottom of the descent.

China stretched his body in almost impossible contortions after being helped from the horse's back. He turned to Josh and Gus who were copying Fu and Chen in unloading their horses.

"Dong rest here for hot hours of day. See, he builds a fire. We eat now and make tea."

Indeed, Dong scraped at a flintstone, he held low over a small heap of dry grass, using the blade of a knife.

Bert delivered an armful of sticks next to the fire. He turned to China. "China, will yer ask Dong if we can help?"

China giggled. "Dong like a fussy woman in her kitchen. Keep out of the way or risk having your fingers chopped off." A short burst of his high-pitched giggle had everyone laughing. China called Dong. The rush of their tongue filled the air as he told Dong of their conversation. Devoid of any facial expression, Dong stood and bowed to his mentor's three friends.

Josh, Bert and Gus jumped up from where they sat leaning against the heap of supplies when Fu and Chen entered the camp leading the horses. The sun put the time somewhere after two o'clock and before three o'clock, according to Josh's estimate. They approached the pair with the horses. Josh's face looked at a loss for a moment before he spoke.

"We help Fu and Chen, yes?" He began to hold up some of the supplies to indicate their willingness to do so.

It was Fu whose head rose from his bow with a smile on his face.

"Fu and Chen thank you, yes?"

The five men made short work of preparing the horses. With China mounted, the group moved off through sandy country which made heavy going. Grass, over their heads in some areas, tempted the horses, who stole any moment they could to snip at a feed. This encompassing grass and the blanket of heat made things claustrophobic and uncomfortable.

Gus rubbed at his clothes around his groin. "It feels like my duds are lined with glass. The sweat is almost killing me." He mumbled for his brother's ears only but he did not allow for the excellent hearing of China.

"You sure you not be with poxy lady, Mr. Engineer?" China's laugh lightened the air. "I find mixture for you when we make camp."

Gus's blush added to the already flush of his hot face.

When they moved into the shady trees at Oaky Creek the temperature fell away; marginally. Dong moved back to speak to China for a few minutes. He helped the rider dismount. It was China who informed the others they would stop here for a cold drink and short break but then must move on to gain more distance before nightfall. He also reported on several deep creeks not far ahead.

China had Gus hand down his basket from the back of his saddle. He sat cross-legged on the ground at the edge of the creek and rummaged inside it for some time. Meanwhile, Gus contemplated the debris from previous floods captured in the limbs of the trees.

"The water gets very high when it rains here, China." He pointed to the rubbish up in the branches "Look."

China lifted his head briefly and grunted. At last, he held a small jar of a dark mixture up to Gus. "You rub this on." He held up three fingers.

Gus removed the cap and sniffed at the concoction. "You sure this is not the same stuff you poured down my neck when Bony nearly strangled me? Whew, it stinks."

"Bah, always complain. Must smell bad and taste bad to make you better."

All too soon they were back out in the heat winding their way through the now hilly country. Dark clouds thickened in the sky until Dong decided to camp near a creek at the bottom of one of the hills. It did not take too long for the camp to be set up with them all keen to help in the process. Dong boiled water-logs in the wok along with dried meat and vegetables.

"Aah, dumplings an' stew. Can't beat it." Bert smiled.

The aroma of a fresh damper cooking in the camp oven drifted over the group. Tea leaves were added to the billy of water when it boiled.

While everyone else ate, Dong went around all the tents ensuring they were staked securely, especially the supply tent. Fu and Chen dug channels around the edge of the shelters. As darkness fell, the wind lifted. Thunder sounded in the distance like the guns of war. Lightning flashes marched across the land. Everyone had retired to the tents when the storm struck. The rain thrummed upon the canvas. Wind billowed the tent sides and threatened to tear the ties from the steel stakes in the ground.

Huddled together, Josh and Gus peered out through the slit of the entrance to their tent. In the lightning's irregular flashes, they watched the sheets of water pouring into the campsite. The fireplace hissed and spat until it disappeared, floating off in the direction of the creek. Like a shadow, Dong was seen to run across the clearing. He crawled into the tent with China.

"Dong keeps a really good watch over China, doesn't he?" Gus commented. "Do you think he might be a son or grandson?"

"Hmm. Possibly." Josh pondered the question. "I've never really asked him about his immediate family. He seems to call all the Chinese his cousins. I suppose I've just assumed Captain Sloan and the *Northern Orchid* was all the family he had."

Within an hour, the rain ceased. Thunder continued to be heard as the storm rolled away. The clouds soon cleared the sky and a large moon lit up the storm's destruction. Dong emerged checking on everyone and the tents. Chen and Fu were sent out to search for the horses. Channels of water rushed across the campsite before draining into the creek. Small branches from the trees were strewn all about. Eventually, the camp quietened for the night. Not a man there slept dry except, perhaps, China who had been cocooned in a sheet of oilcloth by the ever-watchful Dong.

The melody of the horses' bells stirred Gus long before the sun eased over the horizon. He crawled out on to the muddy ground of the campsite. In the dim light, the horses were seen picking at the short grasses in the clearing. Dong, Fu, Chen and China were standing on the edge of the swollen creekbank. Gus looked up at a sky clear of clouds. He called Josh and Bert before wandering down to join the others.

"Wow." He stood in awe watching the dirty raging torrent spread from bank to bank. Debris swirled and rolled in the angry waters. Logs were caught up on obstructions for brief moments until snatched away into the eddies of the savage current. "This might be a problem. How long do you think it will take to go back down?" He spoke to no one in particular. It was Dong who explained, through China, about these creeks which came up quickly and settled even faster.

"Maybe we get away in couple of hours; maybe longer. We leave tents up until the sun dries them out."

Bert arrived with Josh by his side. A frown marred Bert's face. The furrow deepened when he learnt they could not go on for some time yet.

Beside him, Josh gritted his teeth and turned away. He walked over to stare unseeingly at the horses. Clenched hands twitched at his side. He growled. "Why now? Hell's breath! Couldn't the cursèd rain hold off until we crossed?"

"Maureen, why didn't you wait, just a bit longer?" The raging stream was nothing to the torrents of despair racing through his body, strangling the breath in his throat.

COOK'S TOWN

Abigail's light footsteps descended the back stairs. At the bottom step, she turned to move into the canvas-protected ward on the lower verandah. Her brother sat on the one step. His head hung low on his chest. Holding her skirts above her ankles and without a sound, she tiptoed past him. A dull glow emanated from the lantern which stood on the table near the open hallway door. The wick had been turned down low.

The sound of the patients, some snoring under the influence of medication and some groaning with discomfort, filled the length of the verandah. Six stretchers, with barely enough room for a carer to slide in sideways between them, were supplemented with four other mattresses set out on the floor. Sick men filled them all. Most suffered the effects of starvation and adversities experienced when travelling the long hard road back from the goldfields. One man, with blood-stained bandages binding a leg elevated upon a striped pillow, suffered a severe wound received from the blow of an axe in a bar-room brawl. In the stretcher nearest the hallway door, a man struggled to breathe through the pain of the horrendous burns acquired when he fell, drunk, into his campfire. Doctor George did not expect this man to survive.

Once content all was as it should be, Abigail drew her skirts in under her knees and slipped in beside her brother. He grunted. Abigail whispered.

"Has Thomas gone to bed? I think it is time you called it a night too, George. It has been a long while since you've had a decent night's sleep. I'll stay here and watch our patients until morning."

"Should you be here all on your own, Sis? A woman all alone with these men, I mean."

"Phtt. I am not alone. You and George are in the next room. I can scream very loudly if put to the test. Anyway, are any of these men in any state to threaten my virtue?"

"Sis, thanks then, if you're sure. I'm beat. You make sure you call Thomas or me immediately if you need help though, won't you?"

Several times Abigail helped a patient to answer the call of nature. Three extra medications were required for pain. She watched the sky lighten over the east. The birds, in the tree behind the new kitchen, entertained her. A captain's loud orders followed by the rattle of a rising anchor and the sound of sails unfurled drifted across the river, as a ship prepared to exit the harbour.

She rubbed her eyes. They felt gritty. She stood up. The sound of her joints creaking when she stretched sent a grimace across her pale face. She was just on her way to light the stove and set the kettle to boil when Eve met her at the kitchen door.

"Oh, Miss Abigail, you gave me a start. Is everything alright?"

"Good morning, Eve. Yes, everything here is fine. The doctor and Thomas needed a good night's sleep. I filled in for them. No doubt I'll get a rest when Henry is at his lessons with Miss Jane. I wonder what sort of night young Maureen has put in."

"Please God, she is safe. How long will it take for our men to find her?"

"That is something even they do not know, I suppose. Now come, we have quite a few for breakfast this morning."

THE MARINER'S REST HOTEL

Sarah's face lit up at the sight of the envelope with the Cook's Town address on the back. It was the last in a handful of letters delivered earlier today. She threw the business letters aside on the desk. The old kitchen knife zipped through the seam of the envelope with the familiar handwriting of her friend, Abigail.

Her mouth spoke silently, every word, as she read the correspondence.

Dear Sarah and Jacko,
Today is the third day of March 1874.

At this point, Sarah looked up to check the date on her calendar. The letter had taken three weeks to arrive at The Rest. She continued reading.

It is incredible to think we have been here for over two months. It is even more incredible to see what George, Thomas and of course Mac, have accomplished. We moved into the house last month. At the moment, we are still using the shed-kitchen but work has begun on the new kitchen building. The supplies arrived for Mac and Jane's house some time ago and it is also almost completed.

Everyone here is well. We have a steady stream of patients to the practice. It is not often we don't have at least one admitted to our small ward for a day or two. Maureen and Eve have been a wonderful help in caring for these unfortunate people while continuing their usual daily chores. These chores have not been made any easier by the circumstances.

As you can imagine Maureen is quite anxious; not having heard any word of the whereabouts of her father. Every time a new ship arrives in the harbour pouring out its ever-hopeful prospectors heading to the Palmer River goldfields, Maureen drags at least one of us along to accompany her on a walk along the esplanade. I do fear the girl is becoming impatient.

Jane and Mac send their regards to you all. Henry is progressing well with his lessons. He has found an unlikely companion in a crippled native boy who has debilitating scars from serious burns. The lad is maybe, a little older than Henry. A day never passes when I am not fascinated by how the two of them communicate when neither speaks the other's language.

It was so wonderful to receive your last letter. You have certainly ended up with a large family. The Ryan children sound like they have been a great help to you and Jacko. You can assure them we never stop looking for news of their father. The addition of an extra bedroom would have been a boon, I should think.

It is almost ten o'clock when George's daily medical clinic starts. I must close and go downstairs to offer assistance.

Enclosing all our kindest thoughts and wishing you and your family good health.

Kindest regards,

Abigail Baldwin.

P.S. George and Thomas send their regards also.

Sarah sat staring out of the office door and into the hotel reception area. Lucy arrived pushing the perambulator in which her young brother slept soundly.

"I have a letter here from Henry's mother, Lucy. If you call Erin, Minnie and Bob we can all read it together."

The baby was left to his own devices as the young girl rushed off to find the Ryan children. Sarah smiled as she stood up to rescue her son.

CHAPTER TWENTY-EIGHT

MAUREEN RYAN

The splatter of light rain on the tent stirred Maureen from sleep. She rolled onto her side and peeped under the canvas. The clouded sky produced only the faintest light. She drew in a sharp breath when she recognized the form of Silas approaching from the direction of the creek. The man bent to pick up a handful of gravel before tossing it at her tent.

"You go and find the mongrel horses, Boy. They could've walked miles in this god-forsaken country looking for a feed." She heard him mumbling as he turned towards his own tent. "Never sees rain from one day to the next. Why it had to choose this morning to rain, only the devil knows." The man swung about and called back to her. "And don't take all day. We'd best get a few miles behind us before we get washed out."

The rain shower disappeared while Maureen was out following the creek in the hope of finding the animals. A watery sun made tentative appearances in the sky. Mud saturated her trousers up past the knees before she heard the familiar clunking of the bells.

"And about blasted time, too." Silas greeted her on her return. "Well, come on then. Get these nags loaded up while the rain takes a breather."

"What do you want for breakfast, Mr. Silas."

"It'll be stale damper today, Boy. Too much trouble lighting a fire now."

After knocking off the ants, her teeth crunched down on the stale bread she had kept hidden from Moses's curious nose. When they first started their day, the sound of the hooves sucking in the mud added to the hypnotic rhythm of their progress. Up ahead she heard Silas grumbling to the lead horse. Occasionally he turned to berate Serpent and Buster if they tended to drag on their leads. The sparse, low timber along with scant grass through which they passed offered no incentive for Maureen to lift her head.

It was only a few miles before the mud disappeared into dry and barren country. Drying mud broke off her boots with every step as she clumped along, one foot after the other; her silent mantra. Inside her head, she thought of fresh cups of tea with sugar and milk. At other times, visions of Eve stirring a large pot of oatmeal for breakfast haunted her. She imagined the smell of freshly baked bread loaves. She thought of her mother's warm hugs, the laughter of her brother and sisters as they ran along the riverbank, her father's tight hug when he burst into the house full of goodwill. Tears leaked down her cheeks. Moses's hoof landed on her instep. The pain in her foot brought her to her senses. She swiped at her tears leaving streaks of mud over her face.

The sound of other travellers brought her head up the second time. Silas's low growl was heard commanding the horses to stop. The track wound through trees on the banks of a creek before it curved around into a cleared area with many tents. Silas's sudden stop caused the horses to bump into each other. This led to complaints from Devil who attempted to kick back at Serpent. With a curse, Silas snatched at the lead cruelly. He eased the horses around and led off through a narrow break in the trees. This took them into a small secluded clearing with barely enough room for a campsite. An old rock-rimmed fireplace indicated Silas was not the only one who knew of this out-of-the-way area.

Laughter, shouting and music of a tin whistle, coming from somewhere to her left, penetrated the trees and bushes. No breeze of any kind breached the wall of the foliage. Heat enclosed them in its suffocating tentacles.

"Come on, Boy, get this lot unloaded and get a fire going. We'll have some dinner and a rest before moving on." He did take charge of the unloading of the horses before disappearing down the track through which they had entered their campsite. He carried the two billies in his hands. The hobbled horses nibbled at what grasses they could find.

Maureen did not take long to prepare her fireplace but she had no means to light it until the man returned with a grin upon his face and the water in his hands. Once more he did not let the knife out of his possession while he scraped at the flint and blew gently on the smoking brush. As he stood, he removed a small newspaper-wrapped parcel from his pocket.

"Get a move on and make a fresh damper. Here's a bit of cheese to go with it. And don't waste it. I just paid two shillings and sixpence a pound over at the shanty, for that little lot. Daylight robbery if you ask me." His sharp blade sliced the little lump of cheese into slivers. He shook a few tea leaves into a pannikin for her before he spun on his heels and disappeared through the opening into their glade. "I'll be back when the damper's cooked."

Maureen found she rather liked working at the campfire without Silas watching her every move. She poured boiling water onto her tea and sipped slowly. Her fingers wanted so much to pick up the cheese and devour the lot but her common sense thought better of it. Steam and tantalizing aromas wafted past her nostrils when she released the damper from the camp oven. There was no sign of Silas so she ate on her own. With the remaining cheese re-wrapped, the lid covering the damper, the billy simmering on the side of the heat and the dull clunk of the horse-bell close by, she allowed herself to drift off into slumber.

She did not see two curious miners wander to the edge of the camp. It was Silas's snarl which brought her to her feet.

"You fellows want something?"

"No, just looking around the area for a good camp."

"Well, this corner is otherwise occupied for another couple of hours." Silas strode over to the fire and began to tear into the bread and the cheese. He swigged from the flask kept in his pocket. Once his hunger was assuaged, he rested with his back against a tree and almost instantly began to snore.

Silas was as sour as an irritated brown snake when he woke up. Maureen went out past the tree line to where she found the horses grazing on the edge of a large flat. He was finishing the pannikin of tea when she led them back.

"'Bout time. Lazy sod, what time do you think this is? We'll be lucky to make Piggy Ben Creek before midnight."

Maureen ducked as the back of his hand flew over her head. She noticed the man's hands shaking as he took the contents of their load from her and secured each item to its allotted place on the horses.

His curses split the air in front of the procession as they moved off.

The light was fading fast when Maureen heard running water close by. She looked up just in time to see Silas drop the lead rein.

"Here, Boy." He called. "Come and hold this a minute while I check the water in the creek."

On reaching Devil's head, Maureen lifted the rein from where it now hung down in the dirt. She held it firmly. Silas had already moved off towards the tree-line at the creek. She watched him as he stood and stared for some time before moving up-stream twenty or so yards. Once again, he stood and pondered. He swung about, bent to pick up a long, stout stick from the ground before he walked smartly back to where she waited with the horses.

"It's up a bit but I reckon we'll get across without too much trouble. I'll walk each horse across separately." He began releasing Serpent's rein from Devil's surcingle. "Here, hold this." He handed the piebald's rein to Maureen before reaching into the load on Serpent's back to remove a set of hobbles. He threw these loosely around his neck. "Keep Serpent on a short leash and he'll give you no grief."

Silas led Devil to the second crossing Maureen had seen him examine. They wound down a narrow easement leading into the water. With absolute faith, the horse stepped out after the master. From her position, Maureen caught glimpses of them as they crossed. She could see Silas lightly touching Devil's rump with the stick. At first, the water washed over Silas's ankles. By the time they were half-way across, the water level reached the man's calves but the bow wave made by the strong current against the side of his legs reached almost to his knees. Devil continued stepping out firmly. The horse managed the gentle climb on the far side of the creek without any difficulty in spite of the considerable load on his back. She watched as the man tied the horse up short to a tree before he bent to secure the hobbles.

Silas did not waste any time on his return. He selected another set of hobbles and removed Buster's rein. Again, Maureen stepped up, this time, to hold the grey horse. Like the black Devil, the piebald horse, Serpent, followed without any rebellion and was soon over the rushing waters, tied to a tree and settled into the hobbles.

Buster, the grey, was trouble from the time Silas removed Moses's lead. The horse threw its head back and almost caught Silas under the jaw. He clenched his hand tighter on the rein and let out a string of expletives, most of which Maureen had never heard before. The tapping on the horse's rump with the long stick began before the animal even entered the water. It struggled to throw its head about. It pawed at the strong current. It snorted and neighed. Silas alternated in using the stick as encouragement with using it to help his own balance. Maureen sighed with relief when she could see the outline of their figures rising on the far bank.

She jumped when Silas turned up at her side within such a short time later.

"Come on, Boy. No time for dreaming. The water's definitely rising. We've got to do this now." He took the lead from Maureen's hand and moved forward.

"Mr. Silas, what'll I do, I can't swim?"

"Just hang onto Moses's tail and don't let go. He's as steady as they come."

When the cool water first sloshed into her boots, her heart began pounding. She gasped for breath. The fear was almost paralysing.

"Grab his tail, I said; you stupid oaf."

Maureen threaded her fingers through the animal's brown tail and hung on as the water quickly rose over her knees. She felt the river current threaten to lift her feet from the sandy river bed. A squeak of fear escaped her mouth as she dragged her feet forward against the water.

Silas did not ask her to help unload the horses.

"Gather the firewood while there's still enough light to tell the difference between a stick and a snake."

Her heartbeat had only just returned to normal after the dipping in the stream but at those words, it began its drumming rhythm again. With her feet slipping inside her watery boots and the wet clothes clinging to her legs, she began searching for twigs, branches and brush around the trees. Her head swung back and forth in a vain effort to see a snake before it found her.

The fire provided a flickering light when she returned from the creek with the two billies full of water. Silas dug another newspaper-wrapped parcel from his jacket.

"Here's a bit of salt beef, Boy. Do us a bit of soup to have with the left-over damper."

When eventually she stretched her aching limbs in their still-damp trousers, she tried to remember if this was the end of their third day or their fourth day. It seemed like they had been on this Palmer River track forever. What was it, Mr. Silas had called this place; Piggy Ben Creek? What sort of name is that? These thoughts floated through her brain as the clouds fractured the rising moon.

Once again Maureen missed the sound of a short burst of night rain on her tent. She did not stir as a trickle of water wound its way around her body. Distant thunder and lightning produced a display unseen and unheard by her.

Elizabeth Rimmington

JOSH AND GUS DOUGALL

Steam rose from the ground when the heat of the midday sun burnt
into the mud left after last night's storm. China, Dong, Fu and Chen
stood in a group on the bank of the creek. The soft chatter of their
voices gave little away to the others who waited at the supply tent,
anxious to hear what the decision was going to be. During the
morning period, their eyes hardly left the rushing waters of the creek.
It gradually settled into a more sedate flow between the creek banks.
Was it enough to allow them to cross?

Dong peeled away from the discussion and climbed down into the
creek. He placed one foot in front of the other as he made a slow
journey across to the opposite side. The water appeared to be about
eighteen inches deep. With his feet moving from side to side, he
prodded the creek bed. His return journey was much quicker but his
face remained unreadable. When he came to give them the news,
China's wide smile lifted the cloud from inside Josh's head.

While Chen went to follow the sound of the horse-bells and
retrieve their animals, everyone else bent their back to drop the now
dry tents and prepare to load the packhorses. A muggy heat draped
their bodies like an extra overcoat.

With the hills at their back, a barren landscape confronted them.
Evidence of last night's rain could only be seen where the occasional
clump of coarse grass protected the mud from the sun. The sun rays
punished the men and horses alike. All drank gratefully when the late
afternoon brought them to a creek. Dong led them through the water

to the other side where they prepared their camp for the night. No one wished to be held up by a flooding creek tomorrow morning.

Josh and Gus followed Bert past a campground where many weary travellers sat around their small fires. After they rounded some scrub, a grog shanty appeared, built in the shade of the gum trees by the side of the track. Lying on the ground near the door, under the shingle awning, were several heaps of swags, supplies and prospecting equipment.

Gus nudged his brother. "Can you see the weight in that gear? It beats me how a man's legs can carry such a load without horses to assist them."

"Didn't you hear Doctor Goldfinch say it's those weights the miners carry that'll kill them? The human body's not meant to bear such loads."

After a round of drinks, they began to question the owner and several travellers.

Bert soon had the publican telling of his life story. With surprising skill, he edged the conversation around to the subject of most interest to him.

"Yeah, I know the carrier, Silas. Dunno his last name though. Maybe he ain't got one. He was only in here the other day. Yesterday, I think. Strange cove."

"Did 'e 'ave a young lad with him?"

"Dunno. He usually has a helper with him when he comes through but he never brings 'em over here to the shack. Heard reports he's pretty tough on his off-siders. Word has it they don't last too long in the job. They disappear pretty quickly. Move on, I guess. Either that or he works 'em to death." The yellow tooth in the man's head, the only tooth, stood out like a lighthouse as the man gave a deep laugh which changed to a rattling moist cough.

As he listened, Josh felt his blood run cold.

321

The moon rode high in the night sky. Josh sat cross-legged, down by the creek. He constantly snapped small twigs while his mind swirled. Sleep eluded him. How could he, with his head trying to fathom this anxiousness he felt for the well-being of such a positively annoying woman as Maureen Ryan? His heart turned over as it had the first time she was exposed as a young woman and not the boy she was dressed to be. The memory of the waves of rich brown hair cascading over her shoulders brought forth a sigh. A groan rose from deep inside him at the recollection of the vision of her dressed in woman's clothing when standing at the bow of the *Northern Orchid.* He felt the stirring of his loins. Her beauty was undeniable. A smile lightened his mood at the thought of how her elfin face transformed from regal calmness into a monkey's cage of mischief within a heartbeat. He started when the voice spoke at his side.

"Do I take it yer fond on me daughter, Josh Dougall?" Bert Ryan reached over and placed his hand on the rising shoulder. "Stay there. Don't let me disturb you."

Josh struggled to find his voice. "I... er... I've only known Maureen a short time. I've found her to be an admirable young lady."

"That's when the wee devil ain't off running around the country dressed as a boy, stowing away on ships or working as a pack'orse 'andler while searching for 'er father."

"No one can say she's a regular run-of-the-mill young woman; no."

Bert Ryan sat on the ground beside Josh. "Yer know, Josh, I take comfort in knowing Maureen 'as the strength of 'er mother within 'er. Now, there was a woman who was not a-feared of anything."

"Mister Ryan, Bert, I don't know, with everything going on, I have offered my condolences for the loss of your wife."

"Thanks. She was the glue that 'eld the family together. I understand it's your sister who've kept me children from the orphanage."

"Yes, Sarah and Jacko at the Mariner's Rest were happy to do it. Maureen worked as a casual at the hotel for several years. I saw Minnie, Erin and Bob when I was down in Brisbane recently. They have settled in quite well. In fact, Sarah says she could not have managed the new baby and the hotel without their help."

"Sounds like me brood. Their mother would never have 'em sitting about idle. She was a good woman. I met 'er when I was chasing the gold down in the district of Buninyong, near Yarrowee Creek."

"That's in Victoria, isn't it?" Josh asked.

"Correct. I met and married her within a few weeks. After two still-born children, the missus insisted we leave. Just in time, it turned out. Shortly after, the violence at Eureka Stockade erupted."

"So, when did you come to live in Queensland?"

Bert rubbed his chin. "We wandered about for a bit. I took up work shepherding sheep then sheared sheep for a while. I even off-sided for a bullocky for a bit. But the gold fever was in me blood. The missus was 'aving none of it. She made me buy the little cottage for 'er and our baby Maureen, by then. She never complained when I left all the difficulties of child-rearing to her. Every time I 'ad some money put together I'd go 'ome and give it to 'er and the kids."

The men sat quietly for some time before Josh spoke. "I think Maureen has the independence of both her parents then, it seems."

"'opefully it'll not be 'er curse. It's good to know she 'as good friends in yer family and the doctor's family. Now I must 'it the sack. I'm not as young as I used to be when we'd sit around campfires talking the night away then work 'ard all the next day."

"Night," Josh spoke quietly as the man rose and left his side.

He was not given time to reflect on all he had just heard because it was only minutes before his brother dropped to the ground nearby.

"You alright, Josh?" Gus asked as he crossed his legs and began pulling at the leaves off a bush at his side. "Has your future father-in-law been giving you the once over?"

"Leave off, brother. I hardly know the girl."

"So, you telling me you're sitting out here knitting then?"

"Go jump in the creek." Josh threw a handful of the broken bits of sticks.

Gus laughed softly. "Am I to believe you are missing a night's sleep thinking about the fair Scarlett at the Rockhampton Ale House?" Gus let out an exaggerated sigh and laughed again before continuing. "With skin of alabaster, ruby lips, hair as soft as silk tresses and the blue gaze of her eyes on which you could walk right into her head."

Josh spluttered with laughter also. "Yeah, and when you get inside there, it's all emptiness, just like your wallet when you wake up in the morning."

Gus stood up and stretched his hand out to his brother. "Come on, Josh. Maureen's a resourceful young lady. She knows how to keep her wits about her. Now come to sleep. It's only about an hour away from the dawn."

Indeed, as Josh lay on his swag, he felt his eyes had not closed at all when he heard the jingle of the horse bells. With reluctance, his limbs answered the call to rise.

MAUREEN RYAN

Maureen was not sorry to see the end of Piggy Ben Creek. In the dim morning light, she'd found a fat leech on her leg. While collecting the horses, she had taken the opportunity to clean herself up in the creek, well away from any other humans. Even her plaits were released and reapplied with the orange stone, in its material envelope, securely reinstated in position. All well concealed under her cap.

Ahead, a line of ranges shimmered on the skyline. Silas called a short rest at the foothills before a cruel climb over rocks and stones seemed to go on forever. The horses, led by Silas, wound their way along the top of the range as the heat built up around them. Sweat ran into Maureen's partially closed eyes. The flannel singlet under her shirt became sodden as it gathered the sweat from her body. Her skin itched. She sighed with relief when she felt her feet moving downhill, but they did not go far before Silas called a halt. He pushed his way into a small cleared area almost completely hidden. The perimeter of thickly foliaged trees and green underbrush hid a waterhole within the rocks. A miniature oasis located in an area otherwise lacking in verdure.

"Fool boy, don't gulp the water. Yer not a horse. That's a sure way to make yerself sick." Silas's voice, behind Maureen, pulled her up smartly. "There'll be no fire this dinner time."

Once unloaded, the horses were content to nibble at the grasses growing near the edge of the waterhole. After stale damper and left-over cheese from the previous day, Silas and Maureen settled to rest

325

at the base of the trees, on opposite sides of the clearing. Enclosed, as she felt in this small space, Maureen did not shut her eyes completely. Her gaze, from under the brim of her cap, never left the form of her guide.

Even the heat of the day did not lessen her relief when they broke camp and began their way through the hills.

After one particularly steep descent, with the sun low in the sky, they prepared to find a night camp. According to Silas, this was the Normanby River. Birds of many colours were seen flitting from tree to tree, thrilling at the sight of cool shade and fresh water. The river was wider than most of the previous creeks they had crossed and the steep banks were unbroken making access quite difficult. Silas used the whip to encourage the animals to scramble out of the riverbed. Maureen listened as Silas called to a man standing on a rickety bridge just a little way downstream from where they crossed. The man was charging the miners, who struggled on foot under heavy loads, to use his bridge.

"I'll be keeping me few bob then, yer miserable sod. Yer got a hide charging those poor devils to cross yer sorry excuse of a bridge."

"Please yerself, yer tight-sporran Scotsman."

Once he lit the fire which Maureen had set, Silas disappeared. Maureen prepared a fresh damper and boiled some floaters in water along with the bit of dried meat leftover from yesterday. On his return, Silas carried birds' eggs of various sizes and colours in every pocket of his shirt and jacket. He placed them, in their shells, in the boiling water along with the floaters and meat to cook.

When all the chores were done, and she lay in the dark of her tent listening to the now-familiar clunking of the bells of Silas's horses, she rubbed at the aching muscles of her legs. They had not taken kindly to the day's hill climbing.

The next day they moved out at first light. Maureen's heart plummeted. Almost immediately they began to climb another rocky ridge. She breathed a sigh of relief when they descended onto a low sandy plain. On their way across the low country, they encountered several small creeks. Clouds drifting across the sky, thickened up, as the day wore on. Thunder rumbled in the distance. Occasional light showers fell, setting Silas off into fits of cursing. Maureen sank her head to her chest and plodded on over ground becoming rather boggy.

Once again, Silas chose a dinner without a campfire. They ate sliced damper with jam conserve. The horses found grass near the creek where they rested. Maureen slept lightly. Was it her imagination or had Silas been watching her more closely in the last day or two? Every time she looked his way, he seemed to avert his gaze. Maybe she was just tired. He did say he'd be able to take her to her father.

More rain showers fell on and off as they progressed through more of the sandy country during the late afternoon stage of their journey. Maureen watched when Silas paused to pick up small bundles of dry grass. These he dug out from under thicker grass clumps or from under fallen timber. She, in turn, bent to collect any small dry twigs protected from the rain. They were tucked into the load on Moses's back under the water-resistant oilcloth covering. At one point, Silas stopped without warning. The horses then nose-tailed into each other. Maureen stumbled. She looked up to see Silas lift his knife and draw back his arm. With a whoosh, the knife flew through the air. A skirmish scattered sand up in a cloud behind a clump of grass. Her woes of travel-weary bones were forgotten as her curiosity rose.

"Ooh," she gasped when he held up a large lizard. "Ooh," she repeated when the blade dripping with blood sliced the head from the creature's shoulders. The blade continued its destruction with a slice down the underbelly. A quick scrape and the entrails lay in a grotesque heap in the dirt by the track. As they moved along, Maureen strived to avoid the trail of blood made from the dripping carcass now hanging by its tail from Devil's load.

She cringed when she watched the flesh of the dead reptile twitch and shrivel in the coals of the night camp-fire where Silas threw it to bake.

"Don't turn your nose up, Boy. Fresh meat like this will keep us alive while many other fools will starve to death. The blacks have lived on this tucker forever. It won't hurt us to learn from them. It's not too bad. Tastes a bit like a cross between a chicken and a wild duck."

"Yes, Mr. Silas."

Maureen picked up the billies and walked to the creek for water. She felt the man's eyes upon her. She flinched when his voice drifted after her.

"See the lightning way over there, I reckon the storm's somewhere around where we crossed the Normanby River. There won't be too many getting across there, after that lot hits." He then mumbled to himself. "I hope the fella gets washed away on his rotten little bridge."

JOSH AND GUS DOUGALL

China walked at Josh's side during the early morning. "You know, Funny Man, you cannot stay awake day and night forever. When we find Miss Maureen, she needs you alert. You must snatch sleep when you can."

Josh smiled. "It's been a while since you called me that, China. You named me Funny Man on our first day at sea, I think."

"It was. What a pair you two were. On top, soft, like cake-cream, but tough as diamonds underneath. Look at you both now; men, good men."

"We have the Cap'n, Mac and you to thank, China."

"And your father, too."

They continued in silence with their thoughts until Josh hesitantly asked, "China are you married? Do you have any sons?"

"I was Funny Man, a long time ago. I have a big family, some, if not all, of my loins."

Dong paused the horses before coming down the line to speak to China who translated for the others.

"Dong say this is Piggy Ben Creek. We stop five minutes to drink. He say rain coming so we must move on."

Gradually, the ranges in front of them transformed from a distant grey haze into tree-studded rocky hills and valleys. At the bottom of the foothills, Dong again called for a five-minute rest before they began the steep climb which wound around the rocks and boulders. Welcome rain showers cooled the bodies of both the men and the horses. This was especially appreciated when water was found at only one small creek in a valley between the hills. It was here, Dong chose to take a break during the mid-day heat.

Even when relieved of their burdens, the horses remained where they stood secured in their hobbles. Their heads hung down as they drew in long deep breaths. It was at least half an hour before they began foraging.

The men stretched their arms and legs, easing their muscles after the difficult morning. It was only the three younger Chinese men who appeared unaffected by the hard slog. China, who, during the climbs, alternated between riding and relieving the horse of the extra weight, performed his usual physical contortions.

Over a small fire, Dong cooked a large amount of rice. Dried herbs from his bottomless basket were tossed into the final product. While drinking their tea, the men ate with relish.

They dozed in the shade or spent the time shooing flies. Josh's snores, along with the tinkle of the horse's bells, broke the silence of the bush.

"Listen to him. And he tells me I snore," Gus laughed.

Knowing the next camp was to be on the banks of the Normanby River the men wasted no time preparing the horse's loads when Dong set them into motion. They addressed the final hills and valleys of this range with gusto.

After a final steep descent, the sound of the birds feeding, squabbling and roosting reached the travellers before they could even see the river. A winding tree line identified its presence.

Dong led the group to the banks of the river near where a bridge of questionable safety had been built. China and the carriers clustered together discussing the final stage of the day's journey. Bert wandered over to talk to the man collecting money from a few miners using his bridge to cross the water.

"'Ow much you charging to use yer bridge, Mister?"

"That'd be two shillings and sixpence."

"Bit steep, isn't it?"

"Not at all. I give everyone the choice of paying now or when they return loaded with gold."

Bert moved back to listen to what China had to say.

"Dong say the bridge not too safe. He and the others will take the horses through the river. Even though it's late they want to cross tonight. Dong say rain coming."

After the animals were led across the waters individually, Dong set the camp well away from the river bank. The tents were hardly up and secured with pegs when the wind began to blow. Thunder sounded close by and lightning lit up the area. While Fu and Chen dug the channels around the edge of the tents, Dong served a bowl of cold rice and a piece of the damper to each of the men before they all retired.

COOK'S TOWN

Abigail rested the letter from Sarah, on her lap. She looked over at her brother who sat at the office desk pouring through a medical journal.

"I fear Sarah and Maureen's sisters and brother have yet to receive the news of her disappearance. Perhaps I should not have mentioned in my letter of how Mr. Ryan turned up here and we're sure Maureen has been led on a wild goose chase. I dread to think of the man's reason."

George reached over and placed his hand on his sister's arm. "There is no point worrying over something we can do nothing about. Josh, Gus and Bert will bring her home again, you'll see. Now read the letter to me."

Abigail lifted the communication and began.

Dear Abigail,

It's so nice to receive your letter and to hear all your news. We are happy to hear all are safe and well up there. Captain Sloan and my brothers told us its hot and muggy there at this time of year.

We are so happy to have the Ryan children here. Jacko keeps reminding me their father will be wanting them home with him when he returns. I know he is right but I really will miss them when they are not here.

Lucy is becoming a very fussy little mother caring for her baby brother but she is easily distracted and will leave him and his perambulator wherever something more interesting has caught her attention. The little angel just lays there sucking his thumb until someone comes along and rescues him.

Lucy sulked all day last Saturday. Jacko went fishing with Billie Toe-bite down at the river. They took young Bobby Ryan with them. She could barely raise a smile even when I invited her to help me cook sweet biscuits.

Have you heard? The new Victoria Bridge is all but completed. They are expecting to hold the official opening sometime in June this year. Our travel time to the city will be halved.

You would not believe the shipping in the harbour lately. More and more steamships are arriving in the river. It's a shame I think. I agree with Captain Sloan. He says there is nothing as glorious as a ship in full sail. I find with all these new steam engines, things may get done quicker, but they are noisy, smelly and fill the air with black soot that covers the washing on the line.

Please tell Maureen not to do anything foolish in her impatience. Her dad will turn up and in the meantime her sisters and brother are safe and welcome here for as long as they need a home.

The voice from the bedroom tells me its feed time. I must close and hope this finds you all safe and well.

With our deep regards

From Sarah, Jacko and our big family.

CHAPTER TWENTY-NINE

MAUREEN RYAN

A predawn start did not excuse them from the smothering heat rising up from the dry sandy country with its low trees and scant grass. By the time the sun lifted over the horizon, Maureen's tongue stuck to the roof of her mouth. It felt so thick and swollen she feared it might prevent her breathing. She opened her mouth which only made it seem so much drier. The voice of her mother was heard somewhere inside her head.

"Child, close your mouth. You'll be catching flies if you keep your gob open."

Her mother's voice was silenced by Silas's growl. "Suck on a stone if you're thirsty, Boy." She could see the man's cheeks wobble as he juggled a stone around inside his own mouth.

When the next creek came into sight, Maureen's legs trotted along with the horses over the last few yards. Silas struggled to control the thirsty animals.

"Whoa yer stupid mongrels. Do yer want to get yerselves bogged good and proper?" His croaked curses went unheeded.

The sludge, stirred up by the hooves of the animals, did nothing to stop both Maureen and Silas slaking their thirst. After a short break in the limited shade, Silas and Devil led them on their way. The country remained flat with now, plentiful grass. The horses snatched at what they could as it waved under their noses on a hot dry breeze which brought nobody any joy.

They stopped for a ten-minute-break at the junction where the new road met the old packhorse track. It was here Maureen took the courage to question her guide.

"Mister Silas, how much longer before we get to where my dad is?"

Silas chewed on the end of the piece of grass he'd picked along the way.

"Well Boy, can you count?"

"A bit."

"It takes about fourteen days from Cook's Town to the goldfields at Palmer River. This is our sixth day. Work it out yerself."

Maureen felt so close to sitting down and giving up. They were not even halfway and she really did not think she'd manage another step. While struggling with her despair she almost missed what Silas said next.

"How old are yer, Boy?"

It took her a moment to gather her wits before answering. "Don't rightly know, Mister. Ma couldn't count."

"Can't be too old, yer haven't even started to shave yet." Silas stroked his long grubby beard. "Yer skin's still smooth like a girl's."

Maureen's heart felt cold in her chest.

"Come on then, we've got a way to go yet before we break for dinner." Silas picked up Devil's lead and growled encouragement.

The horses made their way through sandy country, thick with scrubby trees. Maureen's head felt like a half-full water barrel. The contents swished and sloshed from side to side. She worried about the predicament she found herself in. But what else was she to do? Should she scarper off on her own? One glance around the country and she knew her life would come to a short end of thirst and starvation. Should she throw herself on the mercies of some of the defeated miners returning to Cook's Town? Would she be any safer in their company? The voice of her mother inside her head answered.

"The devil you know is better than the devil you don't know."

For Erin, Minnie and Bob's sake, her father must be found and this man was the only one who had claimed to know her father. She had no choice but to persevere and keep alert. She pulled her father's thin jacket about her shoulders hoping it, along with his flannel singlet and oversized shirt, hid her female shape.

Maureen stumbled when Silas called a sudden halt. The man then began leading the horses at a right angle to the track. The sound of voices and shouting drew her attention. A bushy tree line identified a creek not too far distance in front of them. On the track they had been travelling, three men struggled with two horses bogged in a low wet area.

Silas's grumble drew her attention. "Get up here, Boy. Hold the horses while I find a better crossing around this bog."

Maureen watched as he walked off tentatively checking the ground at his feet. Several times he backtracked and went off at another tangent until he eventually returned to take control of Devil's lead once more.

"Come on then, Boy, and don't dawdle. Hang onto the horse's mane if you get into trouble."

As far as Maureen could tell, they kept to the edge of the main bog but in some places, the mud rose over the horses' fetlocks. It was Buster, as usual, who protested. He threw his head about and snorted. Silas cursed.

"Run forward and take control of that fool horse's head, Boy. Do I have to tell you everything?"

Maureen's own feet squelched and slurped as she attempted to do so. The loose soles on her shoes were particularly troublesome. Her plan to collect something from the frequent discards on the side of the road had not yet turned up anything of use. Hopefully, she would not be barefoot before then. With Buster's bridle held firmly, her quiet voice murmured in the animal's ear. Every time Buster lifted his head her feet rose up off the ground and into the air. Snot sprayed from the wide nostrils of the horse splattering her already filthy clothes.

Eventually, Silas chose a site for their dinner camp on a high bank close to a stream where the dense shade provided cool relief. With practised efficiency, they unloaded the horses before securing the hobbles. As Silas patted the last one on the rump he turned to Maureen.

"Boy, don't let them out of your sight. Not unless you want to spend two or three days extracting them from a bog."

Silas lit the camp-fire before wandering over to talk with the other travellers. Maureen prepared a damper and boiled water for the tea. She had no idea of what else they may have to eat. After she checked the position of the horses for the third time, Silas strode up to her with a wild duck hanging from one blood-stained hand. The bird's lifeblood dripped from the severed neck. He swiped the blade, held in his other hand, across the feathers of the corpse.

"Here, Boy, pluck and clean this and chuck it on the fire. It'll make a good feed."

The long knife disappeared into its scabbard.

With the meal over and very little rest, Maureen brought the horses back to the camp where the packs were reloaded. Once more they were on the move. She noted Silas seemed to have altered direction somewhat. Moses's body now provided some shade from the hot afternoon sun. The last few days she had suffered its direct rays at this time of the day.

At their overnight camp, several other travellers dotted the cleared areas between the tree growth around a small waterhole. Silas seemed more grumpy than usual, Maureen thought. In fact, now she did think about it, Silas usually was grumpy when other people were nearby. She shoved her worries, from earlier in the day, deep down within her head. Sleep took her before the moon rose in the sky.

Maureen awoke before the sun presented itself. So had many of the other campers. Voices murmured across the area as men rekindled their fires and swallowed their first pannikin of tea, or any other sustenance of choice, for the day. Silas and Maureen finished off the remains of last night's charcoaled duck before breaking camp and reloading their horses.

Groans filled the air as the other travellers, without horses to assist, lifted their own packs. Maureen watched intrigued when two men carried a third from a tent. They placed him on the ground near a tree. The first two men took their shovels and picks and began to dig in the earth. She gasped when she realized, they were burying a friend who would never make it home again.

Day seven went like the days before, only this time she had to push herself harder to keep going. She so much wanted to give up, particularly after seeing the man buried earlier. It could just as easily have been her father. It could have been her. What if Silas died on the track? What would she do then?

As her morbid thoughts plagued her mind, the heat and sandy country plagued her body. It seemed the country did not change.

Long grassy flats interspersed with a few creeks went on and on. The horses once again were able to snaffle bits of feed on the move.

It was at one of these creek crossings where they made a dinner camp. Half a dozen trees threw some dappled shade to intervene against the sunrays. Once set free with their hobbles, the horses ate their fill on the nearby grasses. Silas's snores competed with the few birds scurrying around the foliage.

"Laura River," Silas's growl stirred Maureen as she plodded along beside Moses with her head nodding on her shoulders. The man pointed to a tree-line ahead. "We'll be sure to cross it before we make our night camp."

The familiar wave of fear washed through her as the water washed high against her thighs. Once again Maureen hung onto the tail of Moses. Silas led the team across a stream fifty yards wide. The sandy bottom of the creek threatened to disappear under each footfall leaving her stumbling along in his wake.

Flour dumplings and tea did not make for an exciting evening meal but it did fill the hollow of their stomachs.

Elizabeth Rimmington

JOSH AND GUS DOUGALL

No one slept during the storm. Dong's forethought in placing the tents away from the trees proved to be a wise decision. The wind snapped off large branches sending them crashing to the earth. In the lightning flashes, leaves and smaller branches were seen to hurtle across the clearing. The clouds emptied their load sending down impenetrable sheets of rain. Following the uneven contours of the land, the water rushed across the clearing and into the river. As suddenly as the storm started, it ceased.

With a lantern in hand, Dong performed his final check of the camp. China's tent was his first port of call before he assured himself the occupants of the other tents were safe. The moon struggled through the breaking clouds as he retired to his own sleeping mat.

Wakefulness came upon Josh slowly. Above the noise of the birds feeding and fighting in the trees, he did not, at first, hear the chatter of the Chinese voices. He poked his head out of the tent to see, in the dimness of early morning, Dong sitting cross-legged in front of the cooking fire, along with six other Chinamen. The strangers spoke rapidly and often together while gesticulating with their hands or nodding their heads solemnly. Josh assumed Fu and Chen were out looking for the horses. He turned to where his brother snuffled in his sleep.

"Wake up, Gus, it's morning. Dong is out there talking to a group of travellers. Maybe there's word of Maureen."

When he crawled out of the tent and stood up, Josh could see the river had risen considerably during the night. The rickety bridge was in the process of joining other debris snatched away by the flooding waters. Of the money collector, there was no sign.

As they ate their breakfast, China related the information gathered from his now-stranded countrymen.

"Dong say, at midday yesterday, the man we seek made his daytime camp in the grassy country. Probably he was here at the Normanby River the night before us."

"If that's correct, we've gained on him, even after being held up by the creek on our second morning."

"It would seem so, Mr. Josh."

China travelled upon the horse for much of their journey during the day. After leaving the Normanby River, they passed over a rocky ridge and back down into the low country. It was here, the horse in Chen's charge began kicking, lunging and snorting. Chen flew up into the air with its thrashing head when he was lifted by the reins. His squeal brought everyone to an abrupt halt. Each gaze fixated on the sight of the large brown snake as it burst out from under the horse's hooves. On landing, Chen's feet straddled the reptile now slithering away seeking cover. Chen squealed again and jumped into the air. China took little time to dismount. He hounded Chen with questions, wanting to know if he had been bitten while at the same time, he examined the horse's legs. A few drops of blood on the off-side lower leg caused him some concern. He peered closely at the site for a long time. The rattle of the Chinese language directed at Fu sent the man to collect China's medicine basket. It continued between the four men as China prepared a thick dark poultice which he slapped onto the area under inspection. Strips of cloth held a leather covering firmly in place.

Dong and Fu began to relieve the horse of its load while China explained to the remainder of their group.

"It difficult to know if horse bitten. We make camp here and let animal rest. He will either survive or die before the morning." China was not oblivious to the wave of anxiety rolling across the faces of his friends. "I sorry for delay, Mr. Ryan. We could go on but it may kill the horse. If we spend this little time to save its life it will mean faster travel for us later."

Bert Ryan nodded his head as he dropped his pack to the ground. "China, yer a wise man. I'll be guided by yer advice." Bert moved closer to the affected animal. "Can yer show me what yer doing there?"

Josh swallowed the bile at the back of his throat. "Satan's blood; why now?" he thought. "Damn snake." He shrugged his shoulders and nodded his acceptance of China's decision before he joined Gus in helping to unload the team of packhorses and set up the camp. A deep furrow worried at his forehead. A makeshift shade was built over the now resting horse. Fu took the canister and other horses to collect water from the nearest creek which was about a mile and a half away; according to Dong. Josh and Gus set up another crude shelter over where Dong sat preparing the food at the campfire. The brothers spent the remainder of the searing afternoon heat either here sipping tea or caring for Bert and China under the shade with the horse.

"How's things looking, China?" Josh asked on more than one occasion. Thunder rolled across the land from some distance away.

"The animal does not eat grass. Maybe just from shock. We'll have our answer by morning."

Josh was stirred from his slumbers in the middle of the night by the sound of the animal's legs thrashing and the thumping of its head upon the ground. Lightning now accompanied the thunder on the horizon. He crawled out of his tent and walked over to where the restless animal lay. In the moonlight, he found China patting the soft muzzle of the horse while talking quietly.

"Can I do anything here, China? You too need sleep."

"Thanks, Mr. Josh, but no. It seems the animal did receive some poison. How much, we'll soon know. The climax approaches."

Josh joined China in his vigil. Even though his anxiety for Maureen had not waned, he felt compassion for the horse in its illness. A shiver ran through his body when he thought of the numerous dangers in this hard country. It felt good to be in the company of these men.

By the time the moon prepared to disappear over the horizon, the horse lay quietly. Both China and Josh dozed with their heads drooped to their chests. When the animal snorted and struggled to rise both men jumped up in surprise. China's murmurs calmed the horse. He sent Josh to bring a container of water. The animal drank thirstily. It nibbled at the offered stubble of grass. A wide grin flashed across China's face.

"This a good sign, Funny Man. We rest this morning. The horse be ready to move on after dinnertime. We find Miss Maureen, you see."

Josh smiled but his anxious thoughts counted the twenty-four hours of their delay.

As the apricot glow of the dawn spread across the plain, the men sat around the campfire eating the breakfast Dong had prepared. China's optimism in the horse's condition lifted everyone's spirits. The animal refused to lie still any longer and insisted on joining the other horses scavenging for fodder near the camp.

Fu led the laughter when he began re-enacting the incident of the snake the previous day. His broken English and expressive acting skills soon had everyone joining in. China's high-pitched laughter rang out. Fu danced about and imitated Chen's earlier antics until everyone relaxed. Even Chen's usual serious demeanour broke, as he joined in the moment.

With the snake-bitten horse free of carrying duties and the horse loads reassigned, they broke camp as soon as the midday heat began to abate. Josh and Gus now carried a tent each, upon their shoulders. The three Chinese horse-handlers also carried loads strapped to their backs. At first, the boggy land made heavy going for man and beast. When they arrived at a sandy creek with a clean-running stream, men and animals satisfied their thirsts. After consultation with China, who inspected the progress of their previously ailing horse, it was decided to press on. Dong assured them it was only several miles to a camp area near a waterhole in the middle of grassy country.

Once more the terrain was tortuous for tired limbs. Occasional rain showers gave short relief from the sultry heat. They made their night camp alongside several others at the waterhole Dong had mentioned.

Bert pleaded weariness before retiring early to his small tent. Josh and Gus sat beside China in the front of his tent after the evening meal was eaten. They watched the distant storm and talked. The conversation ambled around the journeys of the *Northern Orchid* and the friends who travelled upon her. The moon and stars played hide-and-seek amongst the thickening clouds.

Thunder and lightning rattled the camp in the middle of the night but very little rain fell. After half an hour, the threatening storm moved away and the travellers slept soundly until the dawn hinted at its arrival on the horizon.

MAUREEN RYAN

Maureen lay in her tent watching the lightning and listening to the thunder in the east. The clunk of the horse's bells echoed quite close. Her emotions soared and slumped from hope to despair and back again. If Silas had told her the truth and her father worked on the Palmer River, she was moving in the right direction to find him. Would he still be there when she arrived? What if her father was unsuccessful in his gold diggings? What if he decided to move on to some other goldfield before she arrived? She refused to even contemplate what might happen if Silas had not told the truth nor would she even think about what might happen if Silas discovered her to be a woman and not a boy. Even though she refused to bring these horrors to the surface, they slithered like snakes in the darkest depths of her mind just waiting to strike. Eventually, exhaustion stole her away from these confusing thoughts and delivered her into sleep.

Silas seemed to be up and about earlier than usual the next morning. His shoe nudged at her ribs through the tent before the hint of day. This morning he wanted oats boiled for breakfast before they packed up the camp.

When they eventually did get on their way, Maureen struggled through the sandy track. Silas negotiated several boggy areas with great care. The sun rode high in the sky when they arrived at a narrow deep stream Silas called Little Laura River. The horses drank before Silas led them across to the other side with Maureen's fingers threaded through Moses's tail. The water gushed around her legs to well above her knees.

They covered more of the flat country with ample grasses until Silas called a dinnertime break at a gully with a string of small waterholes sheltered by scrub and several larger trees. While the damper cooked in the camp oven, Silas disappeared for half-an-hour. He returned with several birds hanging from his belt. Maureen was pleased to see they had been gutted before he handed them to her to pluck.

"Clean these up and chuck 'em in the billy for a soup. And don't take forever. We'll be in for a storm tonight I'm betting."

Maureen struggled to remove the feathers from the small birds. Silas's presence, sitting on his haunches on the other side of the camp-fire, did little to reduce her tension. She jumped when he spoke.

"Why d'yer want to find yer father, Boy. Yer big enough to live yer own life now."

Maureen sat stunned. This was the second time Silas showed any interest in her personal business. She'd prefer he didn't.

"Er ... I have a message for him, Mr. Silas. Er ... plus, he told me to join him when I got big."

"What do yer want to go chasing gold for? Have yer no brains, Boy? Most of the money made on the goldfields doesn't come from the yellow stuff. It's the businessmen in the towns who make the money; and the carriers like myself."

"That's as may be Mr. Silas but Dad's told me to join him, so I must."

"Hmm. I could use a lad like you to help me on these trips. Yer want to give it a bit of thought before yer chose to go scrounging around the dirt for a few rocks that may never be there."

Maureen could hardly breathe as her stomach writhed. "Thanks for the offer Mr. Silas, Sir, but I must do what my dad said."

Late in the afternoon, after continuing over more flat country, Silas announced they had arrived at Laura River, once again. Maureen's heart shuddered. Was Silas lost? Were they going around in circles? With inclement weather threatening, they prepared the camp quickly. Little time was wasted as they ate their meal.

It was the cool touch of water running down the side of her body, the wind whistling through her tent and her saturated clothes which brought Maureen to consciousness. In her dazed state, she scrunched up her body and dragged the oilcloth tight about her. Eventually, the thrumming of the rain on the tent and the flashes of lightning with its accompanying thunder registered. Like an animal, she lay, resigned to the elements. Sleep eluded her for the remainder of the night even though the storm was short-lived.

Elizabeth Rimmington

JOSH AND GUS DOUGALL

After a ten-minute break, near where a new road met the packhorse track, Josh waited anxiously for the group to continue on their way. Dong adjusted the light load carried by the recovering horse. Josh turned back to where Bert pulled on his own pack.

"Bert, can Gus and I share carrying your gear?" After having carried packs the afternoon before, Josh appreciated the effort it took to contend with the terrain while having a weight slung from his back. He could only imagine how much more difficult it must be for the older man. Josh did not suggest this to Bert Ryan. He smiled at the thought of what Bert might say to him if he did.

"Thanks, but no thanks. This's a bit of a stroll, without all the mining gear I usually hump along when off to the goldfields."

Most of the morning they travelled level country thick with small trees. A shout from Dong at the front of the line pulled them up in a hurry. China called back to Josh.

"Boggy ground."

Leaving Chen in charge of the horses, Dong wandered off to search for a more solid track. Josh struggled with his impatience and his thoughts of what Maureen Ryan may be going through. This journey tested his own stamina, how much more difficult it must be for her; being a girl.

Gus and Bert wandered off into the trees in an attempt to track a wallaby. They returned empty-handed. China sat cross-legged staring off into the distance. Josh walked around the horse he was in charge

348

of, talking quietly while checking its legs and load, all the time trying to relax not only the animal but his own tumultuous thoughts.

When Dong did return, blood dripped from the partially severed neck of a plain's turkey swinging from his hand. He slung the carcass by its feet from the load on his horse. Without further delay, he led them off on a circuitous path well away from the boggy track.

The sun stood high in the sky when eventually they made their dinner camp at a large creek. Sweat-salt marked the sides of the horses when their loads were removed. The armpits and backs of the shirts of the men were stained dark with perspiration. Gus complained bitterly of his heat rash as he applied the gruesome mixture China had prepared for him several days before.

In record time, Dong had the fire going and a fresh damper ready to be placed on the coals to cook. The flames of the fire were used to remove the feathers from his kill before it was also thrown in amongst the coals. By the time Josh, Gus and Bert arrived at the fireplace, steam rose from a large billy of boiling water in which rice cooked.

"This's a feast, Dong. How'd yer kill the turkey?" Bert asked.

China translated. He then spoke to Fu who walked off and stood waiting about thirty paces from where they all gathered. He held a strip of rag hanging from an outstretched hand.

China stepped away from the fireplace. He dug into the folds of his clothes and removed a slim round leather satchel. From it, he extracted a ringed band of steel of about five inches diameter. The outer edge had been sharpened leaving a blade keener than any knife. China lifted the hooped band and began to spin it on his finger. Josh, Gus and Bert watched mesmerized. With a flick of his wrist, it flew straight to where Fu was standing. The rag barely fluttered as it split in two.

An appreciative sigh lifted from the audience.

"What is that thing?" Gus asked in awe.

"Chakri; this a chakri. My people use this weapon for many generations. It come from India. This particular one was given to me by an Indian sailor to repay a debt," China explained.

"And Dong killed the turkey; with one of these?"

Dong nodded his head in agreeance.

Late in the afternoon, they were on the track once again. As the sunset arrived and passed and the moon rose in the sky, Dong led them over several small creeks until he called a halt at one not any different to the others. The lights of a storm flickered on the horizon as they made do with cups of tea, left-over turkey stew and damper. Once everyone retired to their tents the camp settled quickly to sleep; all except the man on watch.

THE MARINER'S REST HOTEL

.

Sarah stood at the door to their bedroom watching her husband as he lay on their bed with the sleeping Christopher on one side of his body and young Lucy snuggled in close to the other side. The child held onto her father's arm with a grip like a carpet snake securing a meal. The little girl's tear-smudged eyelashes now lay upon her flushed cheek.

"It seems as though the medicine the new Doctor Goldfinch gave us for their fever is doing the job. At least they are now resting."

"Looking after these two for an hour is more tiring than looking after the hotel for a whole day. I don't know how you do it, my little woman."

Sarah smiled. "Seeing as you have everything here under control, I'll just run over and see if Erin and Minnie have finished clearing up the kitchen. Hopefully, Mrs. Hamilton will be back at work in the morning."

She turned to go but only made it to the door when she spun about to speak. "With all the fuss and bother of the sick children and sick staff I forgot to tell you about something I read in the newspaper this morning." As she spoke, her hand dug deep into the pocket of her skirt from where she lifted out the torn scrap of paper. "Jacko, you will need to stop playing cricket with the children on a Sunday. It tells here of a group of fifteen men in Sydney who were charged with playing cricket on the Sabbath. They were lucky to have escaped with only a caution. The punishment for breaking the fourth

351

commandment might just as easily have been a heavy fine or even being placed in the stocks."

"You'll come and visit me if I'm stuck in the stocks won't you, wifey. You'll keep the gawkers from throwing rotten food at me, won't you?"

"Jacko this is no laughing matter. They mean business."

"Alright, Mrs. Benson, we'll play cricket on a Saturday. That will interrupt a few of the punters, I guess. On to more important things. When are we expecting the *Northern Orchid* to return?"

"I'm not too sure but it will not be for a few weeks yet, I should think. It takes much longer now they are sailing to Cook's Town each trip."

CHAPTER THIRTY

MAUREEN RYAN

The following day they travelled over dry creeks which had not received much, if any, of the recent rains. The heat seared the almost bare ground before it reflected back into their faces. The hills in the distance shimmered on the mirages of the horizon.

"If the creek at the bottom of those far hills is as dry as this waste, you'll have to dig for water, Boy," Silas informed Maureen when he stopped for a quick break.

When they did arrive at the foothills hot, tired and very thirsty, Maureen sighed with relief at the sight of the small stream of running water. She drank thirstily wishing she could just jump right in and wallow.

"Don't get too comfortable there, Boy," Silas advised when she settled her back against a tree for a nap. "Yer may have escaped a handful of blisters from the shovel but this'll be a short break. We've got nine miles to go this afternoon if we want to make night camp at the Kennedy River."

Her intention was good but her eyelids betrayed her. As they sank onto her cheek, she fell into a deep sleep. Maureen could not have said what woke her. The rough trunk of the tree pressed into her back. Sweat dribbled down from her neck and trickled between her breasts.

A tension throbbed in the air but she did not know why. With her eyes closed, she remained perfectly still. A sharp pain burnt into her neck-spine from the weight of her head sagging onto her chest. The heaviness of her dangling arms dragged at her shoulders. Rough sand cradled the backs of her hands resting beside her thighs. The ground pressed hard into her buttocks and legs. A weight moved across her shins. To her mind, large sacks of flour weighed less than her eyelids did as they slowly opened. The sight of a shiny brown tube over her legs confused her. It took some seconds but eventually, her brain began to function. A large snake slithered slowly across her lower limbs. She gasped. The reptile stopped. Its sleek head lifted. It swayed from side to side as the forked tongue and small eyes analysed her two feet sticking up into the air. She held her breath. A scream gurgled softly below the muscle spasm which blocked her throat. Vaguely she became aware of Silas standing near the fireplace only a few feet away.

Her ears picked up a short sharp whistling sound but could not identify what it might be. This was immediately followed by a thud near her feet. The tortured screech was set free from her throat when the snake's coils whipped into spasms. The reptile wrapped itself about its own body. The head struck at anything within its limited reach including its own self as it writhed into a tight ball winding into a pile leaving what appeared to be the handle-tip of Silas's long knife protruding from its pinnacle. When her brain began to comprehend everything just witnessed, she leant heavily against the tree trunk to help pull herself upright. Erratic short breaths burst from her mouth.

"'Struth Boy, yer squeal like a girl. Come on then, don't waste all day. Get the horses in, we've got a mile to make," Silas grumbled as he began smashing the head of the reptile into a pulp. Once satisfied, he lifted the knife using it to toss the body into the fire where it continued to squirm.

Her still-shaky legs added to the difficulty of the terrain on the afternoon trek. The boots flapping on her feet did little to help. Maureen was surprised when the river seemed to pop up out of a very barren landscape. It was here when Silas called a halt on the bank, she discovered a discarded portion of a tent. She retrieved the material and rolled it into a small bundle which she added to Moses's load. She planned to wrap strips of this canvas around her boots securing the soles to the uppers.

"With the storm out there tickling the horizon we need to cross here tonight. I don't want to be stuck for days on this side of the Kennedy River." Silas lit his lantern.

The yellow light guided them across the river with its waters up to Maureen's knees. Its dull glow was all Silas seemed to need to lead them around the several large rocks within the sandy riverbed. Exhausted as Maureen was, her heart did not fail to thunder in her chest as she entered the dark waters once more firmly attached to wonderful steady Moses.

After all the work was completed and she settled into her tent, Maureen feared she could never sleep again. Her mind kept replaying the sensation of the snake sliding over her legs earlier in the afternoon. But it was not the thought of snakes that kept her awake for most of the night. The whine of mosquitoes around her head sounded worse than a dozen of those steam engines Josh Dougall's brother, Gus, was so keen on. Tears threatened to flow at the thought of Josh Dougall. She growled at her weakness. She'd got herself into this mess, it was up to her to get herself out of it. Besides, Josh and his friends on the *Northern Orchid* were most probably miles away, down near Brisbane by now. The droning of the little biters soon distracted her again. What she would not give for one of Miss

Abigail's mosquito nets. As a first means of defence, she pulled the holey socks up over the cuffs of her pants. In desperation, she removed her father's jacket then wrapped it about her head. Her hands were tucked inside the long sleeves of his shirt. Only the occasional, very determined mosquito, discovered an uncovered piece of flesh to bite but the music they produced was no lullaby. Horses, as well as the humans, suffered under the onslaught. The sound of their bells never ceased as the restless animals smarted at the attentions of the bloodthirsty pests. On frequent occasions, Silas's swearing split the night air. At one moment, he'd vent his spleen on the mosquitoes and at other times he cursed the noise of the horses' bells.

They stood in the smoke of the morning fire in an attempt to escape the still-active mosquitoes. Dark circles framed the eyes of both of them although only a penetrating examination might tell. Dirty whiskers hid most of Silas's face. Mud and sand caked Maureen's skin. Only her hair received regular attention. It remained tightly plaited and secured under her filthy cap.

"Yer may as well make friends with the little blighters, Boy," Silas commented when Maureen asked why the mosquitoes were bad in this area. "While ever we're travelling along the edge of this river they'll hang around. Yer can also look forward to swarms of march flies which are bigger than anything yer've seen and have a bite worse than Devil on a bad day."

Maureen had little time to admire the sparkling mica in the white sands under the waters of the Kennedy River. She hardly noticed the green islands of bushy vegetation to be seen in the middle of its stream. The small waterfalls did not break her concentration as she struggled to keep the mosquitoes and, now it was daylight, the march flies at bay. The packhorses snorted, stamped their feet and threw their heads about in complaint. Was this ever going to end?

The river, with its accompanying aerial aggravation, was their companion at their dinner camp. Silas disappeared after eating the damper and jam with his pannikin of tea. He returned with what he called yabbies. He threw them into the billycan with its bubbling water and pushed the lid tightly into place.

"We'll have those for tea tonight, Boy. Yer can boil them up for about ten minutes or so."

It was on the banks of this same river they made their night's camp. Silas set the tents up close to the smoke of the campfire. This offered slight relief from the mosquitoes as the darkness approached. Dried dung, left from previous packhorse teams and green leaves were thrown onto the flames. Smoke billowed up into the air. Maureen did not complain at the smell when the mosquitoes retreated.

The noise of restless travellers camped further downstream told of their discomfort within the clouds of the insects.

JOSH AND GUS DOUGALL

Josh's spirits rose. The packhorse team made good progress over the grassy low country through which their journey took them on this, their eighth day. When they arrived at a large sandy bottom waterway which Dong called Laura River, they paused only to replenish their thirst, fill two water canisters and catch their breath. Dong then pushed on before they pulled up for a dinner break at a dry gully.

The horses were watered from the contents of the canisters before they were hobbled and left to eat the grasses. A meal of rice and damper satisfied the men's hunger before they gathered under a tent fly erected against the unrelenting sun. Dong, Fu and Chen played a strange game with cream marked tiles. Bert Ryan watched, fascinated.

Josh lay with his back against a rock and his hands behind his head. When the conversation between China and Gus paused, he spoke.

"China, do you still carry the amulet around your neck? You know the one I mean. It had bits of dried things inside of it. The one you used to frighten the life out of Sykes in the galley years ago."

China's hand went to his chest and clutched at something through his clothes. "Always with the questions, Funny Man. Do you want a Chinese curse too?"

Josh grinned. "Six years ago, you'd have me shittin' my pants by saying that. Now I know you're a big soft cake with a creamy middle."

"Humph. No respect this younger generation, no respect at all."

"China, you know I've the utmost respect for you and all you've done for Gus and me. And for Maureen, I might add. If you don't want to tell us about the amulet, I'll respect your wishes."

China lifted the two cords with the small attached string-necked bags over his head. He lay the contents out on the ample spare material of his trousers. A shiver run down Josh's spine when he remembered how China had set the items out in a certain pattern.

"What are those things? The shrunken head we recognized but the other bits remained a mystery. Gus and I thought they looked like dried body parts."

China began to talk softly. "When I was a young man, my father owned much land and many servants. I was fourteen when he took me on a trip to another country where he wished to develop trade. My older brothers were left to run the business and care for the family. Eighteen months later we returned to find our family and our people tortured and killed, our lands destroyed. My father was a broken man. An old retainer took me under his wing. He taught me all the useful things I needed to seek revenge for the family."

China pointed to the shrivelled head. "This is the head of he who ordered the attack." He lifted the five odd-shaped pieces one by one. "This is his heart, his brain, his liver, his spleen and his pancreas; the essence of the man. Now his spirit is my captive. It cannot refuse my commands." China spread out the five bean-pod shaped items. "These are the man's fingers which now do only my bidding."

The eyes of Josh and Gus met. The glance reflected the shivers running down both their spines.

"China, how dreadful it must have been for a boy to return home to." Gus's hushed voice was no louder than the rustling leaves of the bushes near where they sat. It was Josh who eventually broke the silence which held the three men captive.

"When it's your turn to die, what'll happen to the man's spirit?" Josh had so many questions to ask but the look on China's face held them in check. Long-nailed fingers stroked the grey pig-tail.

"When I'm done, my ashes go to China country and my ancestors. Dong …," China nodded in the carrier's direction, "Taam, in Cook's Town, and nephew Lee, now on the *Northern Orchid,* will see these delivered to my eldest son."

Silence engulfed China, Josh and Gus. It seemed all the more profound beside the chatter from the game going on beside them.

Josh found himself still deep in thought during the afternoon as they moved over similar terrain to that which they had travelled earlier in the day. His mind struggled to take in all China had said. What mountains had the fourteen-year-old boy conquered in his vendetta to extract revenge for his people? Behind him, Gus was unusually silent too. The remnants of the sun's glow spread across the western horizon when they arrived at a fast-flowing stream about twelve yards wide and two feet deep.

"Little Laura," Dong told them all as he led the group across the waters before calling a halt. He pointed to the sky. "Rain come, yes?"

They all looked up at the darkening sky. "Rain, yes, Dong, rain is coming." Bert agreed.

And it did; along with the lightning and thunder. It was all short-lived.

The tents were not dismantled until the sun sucked up most of the moisture from their fabric. In the meantime, the men watched the debris-laden stream surging past threatening to overflow its banks. Josh sighed with relief when Dong led the men and packhorses off again. Already the sun's heat burnt through the men's clothes. Steam rose up from the moist ground. The long grass in the area, flattened by the previous night's storm, slowly began to reclaim its height.

After making their dinner camp at a small creek, the men were bitterly disappointed to find they could not progress any further. A large area of boggy country spread across the land. Leaving the others in the camp, Dong and Chen went off alone in the afternoon seeking to find a new route. Night's mantle was falling softly on the camp when they returned. The exhausted pair welcomed the bird-stew Fu had prepared. Everyone cheered when told the news. A track, leading out of the area, had been discovered.

MAUREEN RYAN

Maureen found it almost unbelievable. She assumed the worst of this journey over but on the second day of struggling along the banks of the Kennedy River, she discovered how wrong she had been. Many creeks, on the way to join the larger river, became problematic for the travellers. The steep banks of each of these creeks became a challenge for humans and animals as they descended into the stream. The climb out proved to be more difficult again. On many occasions, Silas led them down the lesser bank of the Kennedy River into the water running up to two feet deep, over its sandy riverbed. He then searched for an exit route less difficult than the bank of the smaller creek they bypassed. Her leg muscles ached. Panic set her heart racing each time her feet sank into the water. The only pleasure in it all, the cool splash over her body, hot from the searing sun and the sting of the march fly bites. Even Buster made little complaint at the sojourns through the river waters.

No fanciful imagination might call the dinner camp restful but the horses enjoyed the reprieve from the weight on their backs. Willing teeth munched at the grasses near the river. Once again, a smoky fire was developed by the use of green leaves and old horse droppings to discourage insects. Smoke curled over both Silas and Maureen; grateful recipients.

A meal of watery soup and damper along with quenching containers of tea were hardly devoured before Maureen's eyes closed in sleep despite the persistent biting marauders, the heat and the perspiration which encapsulated her uncomfortable body. The blast of a gun, quite close to the camp, shot her up into the air. Anxious eyes searched in all directions but could find no sign of Silas. She paced back and forth wringing her hands. What was happening? The horses, were they safe? Her footsteps took her out into the grasslands where the animals were last seen. She sighed with relief at the sound of the familiar clunk of the bell on Devil's neck. As they followed her back into the campsite, Silas appeared from the direction of the river. His long-barrelled gun hung casually from his hand. A limp necked duck swung from his other hand.

"Tea, tonight." He said with a nod as he hung it in the low branches of a tree. "Come on then, Boy. You've got the horses. Let's get loaded up and be on our way."

The afternoon journey was no easier than the morning's trek. Maureen was grateful when Silas called for a night camp before the sun had completely disappeared from the sky.

"We'll camp a bit off the river tonight. It looks like another storm brewing out there and I don't fancy swimming off downstream."

Duck stew for tea tasted wonderful even if one had to negotiate a few buckshot and feather quills. Silas's grumblings on this issue were short-lived.

In the middle of the night, thunder briefly stirred Maureen but not enough for her to even hear the rain which followed shortly after. Silas did not emerge from his tent before the sun greeted the camp. He finished off the duck stew but not without passing further comments about the feather quills he found in his teeth.

Maureen took little notice. She was more interested in listening for the sounds of the horses' bells. She made her way out of the camp to retrieve the animals.

They continued on their way. The river became narrower and the water shallower. Maureen also noticed the mosquitoes and march flies were not as vicious today. When she questioned Silas, he told her they were nearly at the head of the Kennedy River. According to him, they would cross it twice before their night camp. He also warned her of how water was usually scarce in this area. He hoped last night's storm may have filled the waterholes ahead.

They made dinner camp after the first crossing and set up night camp after the second crossing. As Silas anticipated, the storm had filled many of the waterholes.

"Don't go taking it into yer head to waste any of the water on a bath." Silas burst out into moist laughter which triggered off a rattling cough. He hawked brown phlegm out into the dirt near the campfire a few times. When he was able to take a breath, he added, "No chance of that, I'm thinking. Yer starting to smell like a polecat."

If the mud did not cover every inch of her face, he may have seen the flush creeping up her neck. She bit down on the words threatening to explode out of her thoughts. What right has he to talk? Him with the filthy hair and beard. Rotting teeth provided hooks for remnants of his every meal. His clothes could stand up on their own given the chance. She did not wish to contemplate the state of his feet which never saw fresh air. She shuddered at the memory of the frequent ropes of snot snorted from his nostrils several times every day. Maureen sighed. Ah well, maybe she was little better herself. Once in the safety of her father's protection, she promised herself the longest bath ever.

While her mind pondered on these thoughts, Maureen cooked a fresh damper and made two pannikins of tea.

Later, when the meal was cleared away, Silas commented as he damped down their fire. "Only one or two more nights on the track before we'll sight the Palmer River, Boy."

Maureen's drooping eyes sprung open. Later, she hugged herself, in the privacy of her small tent. An end was in sight. Her teeth nibbled on crossed fingers as she prayed her father still worked in the area. Her joy was short lived when Silas continued with his report, delivered from outside her tent.

"Course, that's if we get there at all. Tomorrow we begin climbing through hilly country again, right up to what they call Hell's Gate. It's there the blacks'll put a spear through you if they get half the chance." The evil chuckle rattled her tent. "With any luck, we'll meet up with a few Chinamen heading to the goldfields. If so, the blacks'll leave us alone. The blacks prefer to have a Chinese meal roasting on their fires. Sweeter, I'm told."

Her emotions of excitement and fear were not as strong as her exhaustion. Maureen slept.

JOSH AND GUS DOUGALL

Hours were lost following the meandering route through the boggy country discovered by Dong and Chen the previous afternoon. The group passed the Laura River for the second time. Even though the sun was high in the sky, everyone agreed to push on a few more miles before making a dinner camp. The horses' heads sagged by the time they arrived at a creek in the shade of trees at the base of a hill. After they had been relieved of the packs, the animals continued to stand with heads almost touching the ground. The men drank thirstily from their first pannikins of tea before the horses stirred themselves to wander out to graze. Fried flour cakes accompanied the beverage before the men threw themselves down to rest in the shade.

Only fractional relief eased the day's heat when Dong stirred the camp. The sour horses accepted their loads reluctantly before moving off through heavy sand country. Approximately eight miles had been crossed, when the fading light forced the night camp at a waterhole. Thunder rumbling in the distance during the night went almost unnoticed. Each of the Chinese carriers, when on guard, kept moving, in an effort to remain awake.

The faint glow of the following morning greeted Josh as he emerged from his tent groaning. He looked out over the inland towards the eastern horizon. He could not help but wish it was an ocean's horizon upon which he gazed. His eyes widened in surprise to see both Bert and China, in tandem, performing body contortion exercises.

"Yer sure this is going to make me muscles age more slowly, China?"

"Do I lie to you, Bert Ryan?"

Bert laughed. "How should I know? You Chinese all have faces like deep waters. Calm and unrevealing on the surface but we all know still-waters run deep."

China snickered quietly and bowed.

Dong stirred the men to action. Less than five miles had been left behind when suddenly, they were on the banks of the Kennedy River. The men lined up peering into the rushing waters.

"Looks like a fresh in the river 'ere, China," Bert commented. "Must've caught the storm the other night."

Gus slapped at his bare arms where the sleeves were rolled up. "Devil's blood, these mosquitoes will suck me dry." He threw a particularly vicious slap at the back of his neck. He held out the palm of his hand upon which rested a sizeable march fly. A flurry erupted in the group as everyone scrambled to cover bare skin.

Dong climbed down into the river bed. The water flowed wide and swift but not too deep. Using his feet and a long, solid stick he tested the sandy bed seeking the safest route to the far side.

"We go now." He addressed all present before breaking off in Chinese to explain further to his fellow carriers and to China.

It was Chen who took charge of the horse upon which China rode while Dong led the way with two horses in tow.

Josh grunted when the current first hit his knees. "Watch it, Gus? The wash is strong." He grasped at the horse's mane.

"Neptune's curses," Gus called. "You're not joking, brother." The voice trailed off as Gus began talking quietly to the horse beside him.

"Bert do you need to hang onto the horse for balance?"

Bert's voice drifted back to Josh. "I'm doing alright with this pole to help, thanks."

Amidst lots of splashing water and grunts of exertion, everyone ascended the far bank. The march flies and mosquitoes continued to make themselves felt. The animals snorted and stamped their feet. They swished their tails and flung their heads in an attempt to rid themselves of the pests. Dong stopped to check the horses' loads. China had Fu bring down his medicine basket. His head and hands delved inside. A grin split the Chinaman's face as he emerged with a large brown tin with many scratch marks on its surface. He unscrewed the lid and opened the container breathing deeply with a satisfied grunt. A slim finger drew out a small amount of dark green-brown ointment on the tip. He dotted his forehead, chin, neck, the back of each hand and the ankles of his feet. China made his way from one man to the next dotting the thick paste on them also. Noisy complaints arose at the foul smell of the substance.

"What you want, peace or eaten alive with mosquitoes and biting flies"

They made their way along the track beside the river. The detritus of previous travellers increased in volume. Through China, Dong told of how travelling could be quite a challenge in this area. Most of the miners heading towards the Palmer River with heavy loads found it necessary to abandon all but the essential items. The dispirited miners returning to Cook's Town were often too feeble to carry anything but the sparse food rations they had been able to acquire.

As the men and horses struggled to cross the numerous creeks entering the larger river, they quickly understood what Dong had meant. Crossing each creek, with its steep banks and strong current, became a monumental task of its own.

"Josh, look, is that silver in the river bed there?" Gus called, then turned his head. "Bert, you're the expert. What's your opinion?"

"Nah. Looks like mica to me. Easy to fool the newcomers but not the old 'ands."

Dong set their dinnertime camp up near where a green bushy island protruded from the middle of the river. The sound of a tumbling waterfall close by provided music to their ears. The flying pests had once again begun to brave the fading smells of China's ointment. Everyone lined up with alacrity to receive another dollop despite its unpleasant odour.

At the end of another gruelling day's travel, Dong called for a halt as the sun settled over the horizon. While the men prepared the camp, China disappeared from their sight. The fire flickered around the base of the billy cans by the time he returned.

"Where've you been, China?" The question was asked in unison.

The man's teeth gleamed in the firelight as he held up his hand from which two large fish were tied together.

"What'd yer use to catch these, China?" Awe accompanied Bert's words.

China's one hand touched his head while the other he held up in the air. "Only my mind and hands." Came the proud reply, perhaps a little smugly.

Rice and fish cooked in the wok produced a meal fit for any king.

COOK'S TOWN

Abigail wrapped the cotton bandage firmly about the patient's head. Blood coloured the man's collar, shirt and even his trousers. Blood stained the soapy water, in the tin dish on the table. Drying blood darkened upon the needle holder, its needle and the remaining thread with which she had sewn up the large gash on his scalp. The man had been lucky to have been chosen for a work gang, from the thousands of men who now camped in tents within the Cook's Town area. He was not so lucky to have been struck by a ship's cable when transferring cargo from the ship to the wharf.

"How's it going there, Sis?" George Goldfinch asked when he came into the treatment room. Lines lay deep in a face grey with fatigue.

"All finished, thanks. Why don't you take a nap for a couple of hours? You had little sleep last night."

"I may just do that, Abigail. My eyes feel like someone has tossed a bucket of sand in my face."

"You can sleep up in my room if you think it a bit noisy down here."

"Thanks, but no. A herd of bullocks thundering through the house will not disturb me at all. Have you seen Thomas this morning?"

"The last I saw of him he went to get the supplies you asked for."

Abigail's concerned gaze followed her brother as he left the room. She slipped several large stitches through her patient's bandage to secure it in place. The ninepence she collected made a pleasant sound as the pennies hit the bottom of the collection tin before she led her patient out into the street.

"Come back in five days, Sir, and we'll take the stitches out." Abigail delivered her instructions to the man as he walked off by the side of a friend. She called out to his departing back. "And no carousing about town tonight, remember. Take it easy for a couple of days."

"Thanks, Missus." He grinned back at her.

When Abigail returned inside, she found Eve scrubbing the instruments in freshwater in a tub on the back verandah. They both smiled when Jane arrived with Henry.

"Hello, where have you two been?" Abigail asked as she rumpled her son's hair. "Nearly time we gave you a haircut." She turned to Eve. "Do you think you'd like to get the scissors out this afternoon, Eve?"

Eve looked at young Henry and grinned. "May I tie him up, Miss Abigail?"

"If necessary, Eve." Her gaze returned to Henry. "Now, where have you two been?"

"Miss Jane and I walked to the top of Grassy Hill. You can see the whole world from up there, Mama."

Jane smiled down at her pupil. "Maybe not quite all, Henry." She turned to her friend. "Have you had a busy morning?"

Abigail smiled ruefully. "It is never-ending." She tossed the dirty water out into the yard before asking her son. "Henry, I haven't seen Smiley for days. Where is he, do you know?"

"He's gone walkabout with his father. He'll be back when he's finished."

Elizabeth Rimmington

THE MARINER'S REST HOTEL

Sarah dropped her basket and clippers. Cut flowers scattered in all directions. Her running feet crunched on the gravel of the street. She laughed and clasped Captain Sloan's hands in her own.

"It's so good to see the *Northern Orchid's* back safely. Come on in. What would you like first, a stiff drink or a feed? When will Josh and Gus get shore leave?" Sarah stood back, studying the captain. Her smile faded. She dropped William Sloan's hands.

"Is everything alright? You look drawn."

Captain Sloan reclaimed her two hands. "Just a long trip. There's much to tell. I think a stiff drink is just what a man needs, then I'll reveal all."

Jacko came out to the front door to greet the captain. They shook hands.

"Come away in, man. As Millie would say, 'You look like you need a wee dram, stranger.'" Both men smiled ruefully into each other's eyes. The captain nodded.

"She would at that, Jacko. She would at that."

Once the first tankard was emptied, the captain began to relate all the happenings while the *Northern Orchid* was berthed in Cook's Town. Sarah clung to Jacko's arm when she heard of Maureen's disappearance with the strange man called Silas.

"As I understand it, the girl thinks this Silas fellow is taking her to where her father is gold-digging on the Palmer River." Captain Sloan

372

sipped the second tankard slowly. "But, a day after they left Cook's Town, Bert Ryan turns up on a ship in the harbour."

Sarah's face fell. "Poor Josh will be devastated. How's he coping?"

"Well, that's the thing of it, lass. He and Gus, along with China and Bert Ryan, all left to make the journey inland in an attempt to rescue the girl."

"Oh, dear. How dangerous will it be?"

"It won't be easy country they have to go through but China has several of his countrymen and packhorses to make the journey more bearable."

"Goodness me, how am I going to tell Erin, Minnie and Bob? They'll be happy to know their father has been found but to know their sister is now in danger, will distress them." Sarah rubbed her cheek.

The captain pulled an envelope from his top pocket. "I just remembered, here's a letter from Miss Abigail."

Sarah clasped it tightly. "Now, we must get you a feed. You can tell me more tales of your beautiful ship."

With the mid-day meal over, Sarah and Jacko sat at their kitchen table discussing Abigail's letter. In their bedroom, both Lucy and Christopher slept soundly. The Ryan children were expected to return from their lessons at two o'clock.

"Jacko, do you think, perhaps, we'd best not worry the children? Shouldn't we wait until Maureen has been found safe and well?"

Jacko sat staring into the dregs of his teacup. He did not respond for some time.

"My dear, that may be fine for Bob; he's only a young'un still. He certainly needs to know his father's safe. But Erin and Minnie, they are much older than their years. You've seen how they take on responsibility around here. I think they're entitled to know everything." He reached over and clasped Sarah's hands. "They'll think it strange if you do not give them the letter to read for themselves. They've read every other letter from Cook's Town."

Sarah stood up and walked to the other side of the table. She sat on Jacko's knee and gave him a lingering kiss.

"Ooh, is this an invitation?" But any hopes Jacko may have had for an afternoon's romantic interlude dissolved with the squeals of Erin, Minnie and Bob entering the room.

"Lookee, Mister Jacko's kissing Miss Sarah." Bob whistled. Whistling was a new skill learnt, after hours of practice, under Ned's guidance. He ran over to stand by Jacko's side.

Erin blushed and Minnie laughed. Sarah greeted them with a smile and a hug for each before she motioned them to their seats.

"Can I get you a biscuit and milk?"

Once the children were settled, Sarah informed them of their father's arrival in Cook's Town. Laughter and clapping filled the small room. Eventually, their excitement abated. It was at this point Jacko took Bob outside to help with some work in the stables. When they were alone, Sarah broke the news to the girls, of their sister's calamity.

Their faces paled. Tears ran down their cheeks.

"Miss Sarah, will she be alright?" Erin asked.

Minnie could not speak as sobs choked her voice. Tears streamed down Sarah's own cheeks as she spoke.

"We should not worry too much. We know just how clever and strong Maureen is. Captain Sloan tells me Mr. Ryan, my brothers, Josh and Gus as well as China, from the *Northern Orchid,* have gone in pursuit. They'll find her and bring her back to Cook's Town."

Sarah sat with an arm around the shoulders of each girl as Erin read the letter from Miss Abigail.

Dear Sarah, Jacko and family,

I am sorry to tell you this letter contains not only happy news but also news to cause worry. It will bring the Ryan children not only joy but also sadness.

A positive note, first. Bert Ryan has turned up here in Cook's Town. Because of a note Maureen organized to hang on a tree at one of the shanties, he knew to contact us at the surgery.

The worrying news is Mr. Ryan arrived one day after Maureen left with a packhorse carrier to travel to the goldfields at Palmer River where, as we understand it, the man, Silas, told her Mr. Ryan was mining. We knew this as a total fabrication when Mr. Ryan arrived.

The trip to the goldfields can take at least two weeks so by the time you get this and by the Grace of God, we can hope Maureen has been rescued.

Cook's Town, soon to be called Cooktown, we are to understand, is unrecognizable compared to what it was only three months ago when we arrived. The district has been stripped bare of trees and grass now. Tents cover the country as far as the eye can see. Most belong to miners who have come by ship in search of gold at the Palmer River. The rainy season has started and many rivers on the track are swollen and impassable. The town never seems to sleep with the shanties and other grog shops doing business until all hours. We have almost run out of our supply of suture thread already. Captain Sloan has promised to get an order filled for us in Brisbane before he returns.

Jane will be lonely once Mac departs on The Northern Orchid again, doing duty as Ship's Mate. Henry is running around like a wild animal, more often than not. George and Thomas are kept busy day and night in the surgery. At the moment, we have all our stretchers full of half-starved and very ill miners who have returned empty-handed from the Palmer River.

Must close now. I will run down to the wharf to see the captain gets this letter. Hoping this finds you all well. God Bless.

Abigail and family.

CHAPTER THIRTY-ONE

MAUREEN RYAN

"What the devil do yer think yer doing there, Boy?"

In the dim light of early morning, Maureen looked up at Silas who entered the camp tying the knot in the rope holding up his trousers. Surprise filled her face at the unexpected question.

"Taking the weevils out of the flour, Mr. Silas."

"Don't be as stupid as yer look, Boy. They're good for yer; extra nourishment. Leave them in there. And get a damn move on, I'd like to get away sometime today."

Maureen's mouth dropped open. She turned her attention back to the damper mixture she was preparing in the camp oven. Silas approached the fire to retrieve the drink of tea he'd left before rushing off to relieve himself in the scrub.

After securing the heavy lid on the camp oven and setting it on the coals, Maureen served up two bowls of oats with a fine sprinkling of sugar.

"'Bout time we had a bit of meat today. Hopefully, a goanna'll cross our path somewhere." Silas mumbled through an open mouth filled with the point of his large knife. He delicately dug debris from between his teeth.

Maureen's head remained bowed. She hated it when the man scraped his teeth with the big knife. How he never cut out his tongue was anyone's guess. How could she find her father then? She figured finding Palmer River should be easy enough. Every day they passed an increasing number of miners heading towards their fortunes. But, how was she to find her father when she did arrive at this place. It all seemed as real as the shimmering horizon of gold.

"Even a rat stew will fill the bill if we can't find anything else. Can you cook a rat stew, Boy?" The knife disappeared into its scabbard and the dregs of the pannikin tossed onto the fire. "Well come on, then. How long does it take to eat a skerrick of oats? Get the confounded horses in will yer?"

Oppressing heat sapped her strength, despite the easy-going terrain. Occasional hills provided a view of the surrounding district as they passed. Clouds built upon the horizon to tease them, before disappearing like children at play. Maureen was very pleased to find Silas chose a dinner camp under the shade of trees beside a stagnant waterhole. Water was water and better than dry dust and sand. The horses stood for a long time sucking up the fluid as if they knew the day was going to become drier. Devil rebelled when hurried. A mouthful of teeth clamped onto her thigh. She yelled and pushed him away. Silas laughed so hard it set up his coughing again. Maureen hoped he'd choke as she rubbed the painful spot. There was no blood seen to penetrate her trousers but she would not have been surprised to see a red river running down her leg.

Once the horses were set out to forage amongst the spindly grasses, Maureen served up damper and tea. She limped over to a tree trunk and sank gratefully to the ground. The ache in her leg increased. The throbbing prevented her from dropping off into a catnap.

"Hell, will yer stop carrying on like a sissy," Silas commented as she hobbled out to fetch the horses. "Satan's curse on yer, if yer drop those blasted boxes, Boy," he threatened later when she stumbled with one of the weighty crates they were loading.

Their afternoon journey developed into a red haze of torture for Maureen. Like a hot poker, streaks of pain scorched up her leg with every step. Tears continually threatened to transform the dirt on her face into rivulets of mud. She leant in heavily against Moses's side. The tall rocky hills on their left went unnoticed as she concentrated on the ground waving up and down at every footstep.

It had seemed like forever before Silas called a stop for the night. With the last sack removed from the packhorses' back, Maureen collapsed into a heap. Her head swam, drool dribbled from her slack mouth into the dry earth.

"Bloody sook." Silas gave her a nudge in the ribs with his boot but she did not move. "If I have to get me own supper yer'll be going hungry, Boy." But Silas did have to get his own supper and Maureen did not know or care that she might be hungry.

Hours passed before pain once again niggled at her perception. It tormented her body as she lay curled up in the dirt by the creek bank. Cold and wet were the subsequent sensations to bring her a step closer to consciousness. Like a resonant alarm bell, her current predicament snapped her awake. A shaking hand flew to her head to find the cap loosened but in position with her hair concealed underneath. Stiff fingers brushed the raindrops from her face as she struggled to sit up. Muddy hands patted her body to ensure her clothing intact. A groan escaped into the dark night when she touched the swollen leg. She curled herself into a tighter ball and returned to sleep in the cocoon of mud.

Not one hot coal remained hidden under the dirt shovelled over the night's fireplace. Maureen coughed, a deep rattling cough, as she scrounged the area searching for protected grasses still dry enough to set alight. Silas poked his head out of his tent just as she limped away to collect the horses. Her cough persisted. Her body felt hot. Thirst sent her to the creek to drink her fill.

The day's journey took them among many hills, with large boulders and deep gullies. They passed through a narrow passageway enclosed by walls of rock thirty feet high.

"Do I have to come and clobber yer, Boy? Shut up yer coughing. This's a prime spot for the blacks' ambush and here yer making enough noise they could hear in Sydney Town."

Maureen struggled to choke off the coughing spasms with only a little success.

"And be careful yer don't slip off this path, Boy. The rain's turned it to mud. It's as narrow as a prude's mind and slippery as a harlot's tongue. If yer going to fall, don't take Moses with yer."

Hidden amongst the steeples in the cathedral of rock, dark eyes watched.

JOSH AND GUS DOUGALL

Rain showers did little to cool the night air. The humidity swaddled everyone in its suffocating wrap. In the morning, steam rose off the tents as they dried in the early morning sun. The group discovered, when their journey resumed after breakfast, they were faced with the same difficulties as on the previous day. The ground was a little boggier, the creeks flowed a little deeper and faster. Mosquitoes and horse flies pestered them endlessly despite China's best efforts.

Dong chattered to China for a brief moment and smiled.

China turned to the others and explained.

"Dong says when horse flies bite, crocodiles lay their eggs. Let's hope we don't find the crocodiles. Their bite much worse than horse flies."

Thunder and lightning bounced off the distant hills as they once more made their night camp with the gurgling of the Kennedy River to keep them company. When settling in to roost, the birdlife set up a raucous noise. A short sharp burst of rain at midnight held barely enough character to wake the campers. Only their guard remained alert.

Before the hint of daylight presented itself, the rush of thousands of bird's wings accompanied by their vocal greeting to the new day stirred the camp to life. His guts clenched, when Josh registered the time Dong spent inspecting the nearside hoof of the lead horse. China joined Dong. Josh knew this was an ominous sign. He kicked the foot of the sleeping Gus.

"Wake up, Gus. Looks like horse trouble out here."

Gus grunted and rolled over, wriggling his body into a comfortable position on the hard earth.

When Fu delivered China's medical basket to the scene, Josh approached the activity.

"Sharp stone cut horse's hoof. We distribute load to other horses and men. We travel slowly today." China looked up as he talked to Josh before returning his attention to his basket of magic, searching for what he required.

Josh's heart dragged heavy in his chest as he listened to the diagnosis. It seemed Lady Luck did not favour their cause. With the morning meal consumed, Dong, Fu and Chen loaded the remaining three horses to their limit before sharing out the remainder of the cargo between themselves, Josh and Gus. Bert continued with his usual shoulder load while China chose to walk this morning. As expected, it proved to be a slow day but the horse seemed no worse at the end of it. Moonlight guided them as they set up the night camp at the head of the Kennedy River.

While Dong prepared a rice dish with dried fish, Josh watched China and Chen attend the wounded animal. Josh discovered later it had not been the horse's foot which had occupied their conversation but a particularly dangerous section of the track ahead.

China explained, "Black men attack many travellers in narrow gorge ahead. Hopefully, we meet other people on the track tomorrow. We move through the pass with them, day after. Blacks love the taste of Chinamen." A look of disgust passed across China's face.

MAUREEN RYAN

Hooves and feet slipped down the steep descent. In the lead, Silas kept up a stern murmur of reassurance to his animals. In the rear, Maureen clung to Moses's neck rope while her feet slithered in the mud and rocks. Her eyesight blurred. A dark haze clouded her peripheral vision. The snorts of the straining horses covered the sound of her moist cough. The ache in her thigh bored deep into her bones.

A hoarse squeal ripped through Maureen's inflamed throat as her feet skidded out from underneath her altogether. Her body weight hung from the one hand twisted in the rope attached to Moses. The horse began slipping to the edge of the path hanging over huge granite boulders of the steep ridge.

"Let the damn horse go, you stupid mongrel. I told you not to take the horse with you if you're going to fall over the edge." Silas's fury did not frighten her as much as the view of the fast-approaching cliff face did. Even so, she could not let the horse go if she wanted to. Her hand gripped tightly of its own accord within the twisted rope.

The pain in her thigh was forgotten as she strived to bring her legs under control. Moses struggled to heave his head up and away from the horrors of the view of the descent. Gradually the animal's persistence dragged itself and Maureen back to the middle of the narrow track. Her trembling limbs reclaimed their hold upon the earth. Her feverish body felt cold. Her breath gulped in her throat. Tears threatened.

"Be more careful back there, useless sod." Silas's voice floated past her ears.

Maureen growled but did not make a comment. She continued with her head down. A shaky hand patted the neck of the panting horse.

"There, Boy. Can you see it?" Silas called. "You can see Palmer River coming into view now."

Even the content of Silas's report failed to raise her enthusiasm. Her eyes lifted for only a moment of time in which she glanced across a land of sparse forest. Between the trees, an occasional glint of the sun reflected off a winding ribbon of water seen in the distance. When the dinner camp was called her body worked by rote, not by conscious thought. She stumbled forward to drink her fill at the water hole, along with the horses.

As they journeyed through the late afternoon, even Maureen noticed the bared trees and scarcity of grasses. "What's wrong with those trees, Mr. Silas?"

"Too many horses and cattle in too small a space. Many of the bullock wagons from Etheridge have been stranded here with the rains. At least the town will have meat to eat for a change." Silas's harsh laugh echoed around them. "They've eaten most of the grasses. Now, they're reduced to pulling the bark from the trees and eating that."

A heavy shower of rain did not discourage Silas as he led the way to the banks of a deep creek where they set up their night camp.

"Where's my Da working then, Mr. Silas? Will I be able to find him tomorrow?" Maureen's swollen throat struggled to force out the words.

"In the morning, you can stay here while I take my trade goods into Palmerville. I'll check out if anyone knows of his current whereabouts."

With the breakfast things tidied up, Maureen helped Silas load the chosen trade goods onto the backs of Devil and Serpent. With the camp oven buried in the coals of their morning fire and the dregs of the billy tea cooling nearby, Maureen watched as Silas headed out towards where he said the Palmerville settlement was situated. Besides the persistent cough, her fever and thirst faded into insignificance, compared to yesterday. Her leg only hurt when rubbed or bumped. She was on the mend and not before time. With a little bit of luck, she may meet up with her father tonight. Her rising spirits buzzed within her. She began to take stock of her surroundings.

As usual, Silas's campsite remained isolated from others. Voices floated in on the gusty winds stirring what foliage remained on the upper branches of the trees. Fallen dead timber, anthills and granite boulders secured their privacy. The tents remained upright, drying in the sun. The presence of Buster and Moses left behind in the camp, afforded her comfort. Maureen allowed her body to relax. Sleep arrived with the warm morning breeze.

The smell of the overcooked damper stirred her awake. Maureen sprung to her feet and rushed to drag the camp oven from the coals managing to burn the palm of one hand in the process. When the lid landed with a thud in the dirt, her heart dropped to see the loaf, even though not burnt black, was definitely overdone. Smoke curled up into the air. Her fingers dived in and out in an attempt to remove pieces of the crust to taste. She blew on her singed fingertips.

All afternoon her stomach swirled in a quandary. Should she make a fresh damper or not? Silas was going to be furious to see the crispy offering but if she wasted more flour, he'd not be too happy either.

Things became even worse than expected. Silas returned very late and very drunk. His body, aboard the back of Devil, swayed wildly from one side to the other. Serpent followed on the lead. When Devil came to an abrupt halt, Silas slid unceremoniously to the ground landing with a flurry of dust, a loud thump and a litany of curses. He staggered to his feet, achieving his goal after several attempts. One hand struggled to remove a brown paper bag from his inside jacket pocket. Eventually, it came free and he waved the weighted contents under Maureen's nose.

"Here, Boy, make yerself useful. Here's a bit of meat. Cook up a stew and don't waste it. The bit there cost me an arm and a leg. Be grateful, Boy. Most of the miners hereabouts are chewing on their leather belts."

"Yes, Mr. Silas." Maureen stirred the fireplace. Before she had any chance of enquiring after her father, Silas continued with his demands.

"Where's a bloody cup of tea? A man could die of thirst in this camp. You want a clip under the ear to smarten you up, Boy?"

Later, as the pair ate, relief flooded through Maureen when Silas seemed oblivious to the darkened damper. She even felt brave enough to ask the question rehearsed throughout the day.

"Did you find out anything about my father, Mr. Silas?"

Silas threw the last of the dregs of his tea into the fire and jumped up.

"Curses on you, Boy. Just shut up for five minutes about yer damned father. He'll turn up one day. Now, will you give me some peace." The man fell flat on his face only a few feet from the fire. Maureen left him undisturbed.

The following morning, Silas's mood matched the dark clouds in the sky. Like the unproductive thunder and lightning flashes his vocal tirade was all hot air. Maureen had no intention of irritating him and kept well out of his way.

"Are yer ever going to get those bloody horses in this morning or am I supposed to do that too, Boy? At this rate, it'll be dark before we reach my base camp."

Maureen had no idea what his base camp was or where it might be found. She brought in the horses, after a long hike. They had travelled far seeking fodder. Little time was spent loading the much-reduced cargo onto the four horses. A miserable Silas groaned as he led them on their way.

Mournful skies did nothing to reduce the rising excitement as it thrummed through Maureen's body. Interested eyes took in the narrow path they followed through the large granite boulders. When they passed close to the river, she saw the miners, spread the length of its banks, with their backs bent over sifting pans. After following this path for some distance, Silas turned away from the waterway through a narrower and less used track into more desolate country. By the time they halted for a dinner camp, the skies hung heavy but produced nothing.

"Boy, that damper is the worst I've ever eaten," Silas grumbled after a meal of left-over stew and burnt remains. He swallowed three pannikins of strong tea before he lay with his back resting against an old stump. His snoring filled the air.

Maureen was beginning to think their journey was never going to end when they crossed a small rill just on dark. With the moonlight threatened by wind-driven clouds, her vision was limited. Her gaze took in what appeared to be the base of a steep, treeless mountain of granite boulders. The earlier feelings of excitement seeped from her soul. On the other hand, Silas's spirits seemed to soar. He whistled as they unloaded the horses.

Daybreak was an unseen thing. The sunrays, held back by the gloomy granite hills, were unable to reach their camp. Energy radiated from Silas. A pannikin of tea followed by his breakfast oats disappeared down his gullet before Maureen's tea cooled enough to drink.

"Come on, Boy. Shake a leg there."

Even though her nervous stomach rebelled at the food, Maureen knew she must eat. A wariness closed about her like a living blanket. During the whole journey, she had not felt such ominous oppression as she did on this day. She followed along close behind as Silas led the horses into a sandy watercourse by the side of the rocky wall. What felt like several miles passed beneath her feet when they exited the stream out onto a large flat granite surface. From somewhere under this rock the stream they had followed bubbled up to the surface of the earth. The guardian ridge remained a constant at their side.

"Don't dawdle behind, Boy, or yer'll get lost. There'll be no coming back from this country if you don't know what yer doing."

The small procession moved closer to the base of the ridge where Silas led them along an almost unseen narrow path. Occasional shrubbery grew out from the shallow soil between the boulders. When Silas and the horses stopped, Maureen strained to see around the animals' bodies. She watched as Silas clambered onto one particular boulder near a thick bushy shrub. In one hand, he held a hemp rope which led to one of the larger branches. He grunted as he hauled on the rope pulling the branch back far enough for him to secure it to a knobble of the rock on which he stood. What on earth was he doing? Her view did not take in the low narrow opening into the mountain wall. They moved forward. She was at a loss to understand where they were going. She moved closer to Moses.

The horses' ears swept the ceiling of the rocky archway through which they followed Silas. Their unquestioning acceptance of the passageway suggested to Maureen this was not the first time they had passed through here. With her heart pounding, she followed blindly. Blackness enclosed her as if a thick blanket were draped over her head. She gasped. The stench was something she had never experienced before. She heard Silas striking his flint to light the lantern. Gradually the dull yellow glow diffused into the obsidian depths. As her eyes and brain received and translated the messages from their new environment, she stood with her mouth open. She wanted so much to start screaming and never stop but her paralysed voice box remained mute. The sound of rain belting down outside the cave entrance went unheeded.

JOSH AND GUS DOUGALL

Bert returned from the waterhole after talking to a group of dejected miners making the return trip to Cook's Town. Birds squabbled in the higher branches of the trees. He approached the fire where Josh and Gus stood sipping at their tea. Fu set out bowls of left-over rice to eat. The smell of a fresh damper drifted up from the camp oven. Under the trees, Chen held the horse with the wounded hoof while Dong and China assessed the healing progress.

"Mornin' Josh. Mornin' Gus. The damper smells great, Fu. I could eat a 'orse and chase the rider."

Josh and Gus greeted Bert together before Josh asked, "Have those fellows seen anything of Silas in their travels, by any chance?"

"One of the blokes knew Silas by sight. 'E said the man was in Palmerville trading goods on the morning they left."

"How long ago, Bert?"

"Day afore yesterday, 'e said."

Movement under the trees drew their gaze when China and Dong stood up. China patted the horse on the rump and turned to the others.

"Hoof looking good. We move faster today." China delivered his report.

Smiles lit up everyone's face.

They passed through both hilly and open country where temperatures soared. Their thirst was quenched at a small waterhole hidden in the shade near their dinner camp.

"We give the horse some weight this afternoon. See how he does." China mumbled as he articulated the worn chopsticks in his hand.

Each man welcomed the rest as the heat and humidity developed clouds on the horizon. Even the animals were reluctant to move out into what looked like a dry and barren landscape in need of a downpour. When the rain did fall, men and horses plodded along with heads bowed. The water ran over their bodies like waterfalls. The shower was only short-lived having passed over by the time Dong called the night camp.

The next morning, China's face lit up as he watched the wounded horse approach the camp behind Chen. With no sign of a limp, the animal lined up to receive its load for the day.

Drawn out yawns heralded the arising of Josh and Gus. After greeting the camp, they moved away from the group to relieve themselves. Josh aimed his stream at a line of ants sending them into a frenzy.

"Gus, did you notice how Dong, Chen and Fu seem a bit jumpy this morning?"

Gus stared off into the distance as he finished urinating. "Now you mention it, they were a bit jittery. When you think about it, even China seems tense. What do you think's wrong?"

"I'm not sure. I'll talk to China."

Two hours had passed since the sun breached the horizon before Dong paused the group at a small stream where he watered the animals. China slithered down to the ground just as Josh moved over to offer assistance. They both drank the cool water.

"China, is everything alright? The men looked worried."

China straightened up from his drinking and wiped the water from his lips.

"You right. They watchful. Soon we pass through narrow gorge hemmed in by high rocky walls. Blacks like to attack travellers passing through there, particularly the Chinese."

"This is the place you were talking about the other day?"

"Yes, Josh. This is place. Keep eyes peeled. Unfortunate we not meet others going our way. More safe in numbers."

Josh reported back to Gus and Bert as they prepared to move on. Bert unloaded his pack and removed a pistol from his swag. Some minutes were spent preparing the gun before tucking it into the waist of his trousers. Josh and Gus loosened the leather ties on their knife scabbards.

"Did you see the satchels Dong and the others have slung about their necks."

"I'll bet anything they contain those throwing weapons they showed us last week."

Rocky walls funnelled the group into the narrow gorge. Bodies tensed. Heads swivelled left and right as they scanned the tops of the high walls. The passage became even narrower. It felt as if the walls pressed in upon them. The horses became restless. They threw their heads and tugged at the leads. Tails swished unceasingly. The teamsters murmured soothing assurances. Josh and Gus called on their years of staring into horizons from the crow's-nest to scan the heights of the towering cliffs which exuded thick unseen clouds of menace.

Josh's head froze. He paused.

"What's wrong?" Gus questioned in a whisper.

Josh flicked his eyes left and right. He stared at the spot where he thought he had seen a movement.

"Something, like a shadow, flashed between a gap in the rock up there. I'm sure of it." Josh's hushed voice replied.

"Keep moving, Josh. Keep moving." China's advice floated back to them on the hot air current rushing through the gap barely wide enough to allow room for the loaded horses to pass.

Dong spun a Chakri disc on his one hand while encouraging the horse to walk smartly forward. China prepared his miniature war-quoit while walking between the horses. Bert rubbed his neck where it began to ache in response to his repeated turning around to see no one followed behind.

All of a sudden, the world opened out to them in a splendid view which did not include a tribe of war-hungry natives. They all began to relax a little. Still, Dong did not allow them to slow down until the rocky cliffs were left far behind. Horses and men panted for breath and water when he led them to a large waterhole surrounded by welcome shade.

Dong allowed only a short break for the horses to be relieved of the weight on their backs while they foraged. Each man remained alert with weapons at the ready.

After Dong informed them the town of Palmerville was situated just over the horizon, the men were keen to break camp and move on. Eventually, the Palmer River came into view. At about one hundred and fifty yards wide its waters held small islands, reed beds, and plentiful trees. Mosquitoes enjoyed the river also as the slapping of hands testified. At the approach of dusk, China reached for his foul-smelling ointment to repel the insects.

The afternoon sun, on the following day, shone upon the township of Palmerville in the distance. The Chinese' anxious chatter caught Josh's attention. The gaze of the four men examined the country about them. It took a moment but Josh eventually saw it too. Grasses became scarcer. Bare dirt now revealed over large areas and numerous trees were stripped of bark.

"What's going on, China?"

"No feed for horses. Dong worried."

They made camp at the edge of a deep waterhole several miles out of the township. Over their meal of floaters and rice, the men discussed their plans for the next day.

THE MARINER'S REST HOTEL

Minnie, Erin and Bob sat around the table, paper and pencils in hand. A circle of lantern light engulfed them in its warm glow.

"How do you spell, Northern Orchid?" Bob chewed the wooden end of the pencil.

Erin looked up from her own work. She admonished her brother. "Bob, don't chew the pencil. I might be the next one who gets to use it and I don't want your slobber all over it."

Bob grinned a wicked grin. He poked out his tongue and licked the length of the pencil in his hand.

"Keep it up and you'll end up with lead poisoning," Erin warned.

Minnie looked up from her page where she had almost completed the letter to her father. She nudged her sister, moved close to her and with one finger pushed the hair back from around her ear. Her lips moved in close as she whispered.

"Erin, lead pencils don't actually have lead in them, remember. Mr. Beetson says it's graphite inside the wooden tube."

Erin winked with the eye out of sight of her brother and mouthed. "He don't know, yet."

Once again Bob asked his question. "Will someone tell me how to spell Captain Sloan's ship. I want to tell Da we're going to send these letters on the ship."

"N-o-r-t-h-e-r-n O-r-c-h-i-d." Erin spelt the words slowly.

With tongue clamped firmly on the outside of his lips, by his teeth, Bob concentrated on completing his first-ever letter. He tossed the pencil into the middle of the table and climbed out from the wooden form on which he had sat.

"I'm done. I'm off to bed." He made his way into the recently completed annex where the Ryan children now had two rooms.

"'Night, Bob," the girls called in unison. Erin added, "Go quietly and don't wake Lucy and the baby."

When he was out of hearing, Minnie asked her elder sister. "Do you think they'll be back in Cook's Town with Maureen yet? I do hope she's safe."

Erin shook her head slowly. "Minnie, Captain Sloan did say it could be two or three weeks yet before we can expect them to be back in the town. He thinks it may be even more if the rains settle in and the rivers flood. He did say we are not to worry because the men going after her are good strong men who know what they're doing. Now, how are you going with the letter?"

Minnie wrote her final words then stood up. She took up Bob's page and folded it neatly. "I'll take these over to the Captain at the hotel. Mr. Jacko and he are playing cards. I'll see if Sarah needs a hand to finish up for the night." She reached out to receive Erin's page.

"Find out what time the ship's leaving tomorrow, Minnie. Mr. Jacko is going to take us all down to see her off."

The door scraped as Minnie left to cross the yard to the hotel kitchen. Erin moved into the little room where Lucy and the baby slept.

COOKTOWN

Abigail sat looking at the letterhead where she had written their new address; Cooktown instead of Cook's Town. She thought it much simpler although not everyone in the town agreed with her, or the government's recent decision on the name change. A long drawn out sigh filled the office. This was the fourth similar letter she had written in as many days. She found it sapping to write to strangers advising them of the death of a loved one. She felt it, even more so, when their death was something which may have been avoided. These four deaths were due to starvation and the accompanying complications. These were men who made it back from the goldfields with little, if any gold, through a torturous track where they were held up for days on end at flooded creeks. Horror filled her soul when told, by those who did survive, of the deprivations endured. How were her friends going to return safely with Maureen, assuming they are able to find her alive in the first place? She looked up at the sound of her son's footsteps near the door.

"Hello, Henry. Have you finished your morning lessons? Is it dinnertime already? Did you ask Eve if she needs a hand?" Her son's dejected face caught Abigail's attention. "Whatever's the matter, Darling? Come here." Her arms reached out. She gathered her boy to her side.

"Mama, Smiley has still not returned to town. Do you think he will ever come back?"

Abigail's fingers smoothed the sweaty forehead. "Henry, as I understand it, the natives go on walkabout for weeks, even months, sometimes. He and his people have lived in this land for a long time. They know how to survive these conditions a lot better than us whites. When he returns, I'm sure you will be the first he calls upon."

CHAPTER THIRTY-TWO

MAUREEN RYAN

While the faint lantern glow penetrated the dense gloom of the cave revealing shadows and dark shapes, Maureen stood with her hands on her splayed knees. Her head draped forwards as her heaving body emptied her stomach contents onto the rocky floor. Her nostrils and even the pores of her skin filled with the stench on the fusty air. When nothing remained in her gut, she stood up straight and swiped at her mouth with the back of her hand. Her eyes scrunched up striving to see into the dim interior. Something caught her attention. Her frown deepened. She leaned forward peering in disbelief at what seemed like human remains leaning up against the perimeter wall. A squeak pressed past her lips. Her eyelids clamped shut. Curiosity rose to the surface of her mind. Released, her eyelids sprung open. As far as she could make out six other skeletons rested beside the first partially decayed corpse. A shaking hand clamped over her mouth silencing the screech within.

Common sense should have told her to make a fast retreat away from this chamber of death but any reasoning, logical or otherwise, deserted Maureen. Up ahead, Silas pressed forward into a passageway leading deeper into the mountain. The lantern glow moved forward with him. Blackness once more reclaimed the dead.

Maureen pressed in close to dependable Moses. His warm body calmed her racing heart and erratic breathing. Her feet, encased within the shoes repaired with strips of canvas, caught on the uneven rocky floor threatening to hurl her onto her face. It seemed an age they followed Silas's lamplight through the low winding passageway. With little warning, they emerged into an area bright with light. A protective overhang of rock formed an open cave. The glare hurt Maureen's eyes. She raised her hand to her face.

The horror of the cave entrance through which they had come was forgotten as Maureen gazed in awe at the large fertile oasis wrapped within the walls of the mountain. Winding throughout was a rill, the waters of which gurgled under the rocky floor beneath their feet, where it disappeared. Trees stood tall. Birds darted noisily between the branches. Green grasses flourished.

"Well, come on, Boy. Don't just stand there like one of the bloody rocks. Get these horses unloaded and set them free. Once that's done, yer can get the fire set." Silas pointed to the pile of ashes protected by a ring of rocks in the centre of the open cave.

Each horse fretted as Maureen and Silas relieved them of their burdens. Once released into the open space, they raced off through the trees kicking up their heels, tossing their heads, farting and snorting their pleasure.

Maureen stepped out into the sunlight, turning her body around and around in an attempt to take in this amazing sight. She stumbled about, first one way and then the other, at a loss to know what she most wanted to see first. All the while her arms became heavy with timber for the fireplace. Her gaze never stopped searching out new and wonderful discoveries. Grey blobs in the treetops told of a group of koala bears sleeping. Flashes of movement through the shrubbery revealed several wallabies selecting tender morsels. Of a human being, other than themselves, there was not a sign.

Silas dropped two newspaper-wrapped packages on the ground beside the now crackling fire.

"Bacon and cheese there and don't waste a morsel. That bloody robber in the shop charged me five shillings a pound. Thank goodness, I've still got plenty of sugar, flour and tea left from Cook's Town. The man's charging an arm and a leg for the bare staples. Five shilling a pound for tea, no less. Two and sixpence a pound for sugar and one and sixpence a pound for flour; daylight robbery, is what it is."

Maureen listened but said nothing in response to Silas's tirade. No doubt, Silas hadn't considered perhaps the shopkeeper had paid top price for goods brought in after a long and not-too-easy journey.

Having eaten his fill, Silas began to rummage amid a stack of equipment stashed up against the back wall. He passed by Maureen where she filled a large basin with water from the stream.

"I'll be gone a bit. While I'm away yer see yer scrub the sweat out of the horses' harness gear and hang them out in the sun. Yer'll find rendered lamb's fat in a can up against the back wall. When they're dry, use it to soften up the leather."

Her gaze followed him as he strode off through the trees. A miner's pan in his hand swung loosely against his leg. As much as she'd have liked to call him back, perhaps asking him how to find her father could wait until tomorrow.

With aching arms, Maureen hung out the last of the leathers over tree branches in the sunlight. She retreated under the awning to examine her new campsite in more detail. In the shadows of the back wall, near where the passageway opened, stood a rough-hewed stretcher. A wooden box near the stretcher had contained their eating supplies on the journey. Never once had Silas left it unattended unless the latch was bolted. The same applied here in the cave, it seemed.

Several large boulders rose up randomly throughout the space. She found unused leathers stored behind one close to Silas's bed. Two wooden boxes, behind another boulder, contained camping equipment. At the farther end of the cave, she discovered a small area with a sandy floor. Her small sleeping tent lay on the ground where it had been tossed; not by her. She welcomed the privacy provided by a curtain of boulders. It took only a moment to set up her sleeping arrangements.

As the sun faded in the sky she sat beside the revitalized fireplace. While waiting for the billy to boil, she rubbed the fat into the horses' harness. Dirt and grease filled every crevice of her hands. Slowly the stiff leathers turned supple. With her thoughts travelling once more through the day, a worm of fear embedded itself in her belly. Doubt crept through her mind. Was this beautiful valley, in fact, her prison?

Despite her exhaustion, sleep was slow in coming. The sounds of the night outside included the wail of the curlew birds and the grunting of koala bears. A mournful howl of dingoes in the distance sent a chill down her spine. The dying coals of their fireplace provided a dull glow inside the cave. The moon and stars lit the sky outside.

JOSH AND GUS DOUGALL

"Why has Fu remained at our camp with the other four horses?" Josh moved up closer to where China sat astride the fifth horse. Dong strode out in front of the group while Chen brought up the rear with the sixth horse. Gus and Bert were deep in conversation as they walked side by side in the middle of the group.

China smiled down at his friend. "Fu find food for horses today. Dong, Chen and I go to Chen's cousin's camp, just north of the town. They grow much vegetables. You, Gus and Bert, go into town. Talk to police. If you seen with us Chinese, it not help your cause."

"It's a shame but it is so. I'm sorry, China. People are so shallow."

"No need apologize. Same in my country; in reverse. Human nature, eh? Peoples; so different and yet so alike."

Painted by a shaky hand, a broken piece of timber announced, 'Police'. It hung drunkenly from the nails hammered into the trunk of a tree. On one side of the tree, a weather-worn tent protected a Sergeant of Police who sat behind a table with one of its legs resting upon a piece of timber. The tent sides were rolled up in an endeavour to catch any stray breeze. Fist-sized rocks held down each pile of the many papers on the table. On the other side of the tree, a partially constructed corrugated iron shed awaited a shipment of further supplies.

As soon as Josh walked under the canvas the radiating heat struck him like a branding iron. Gus and Bert edged in beside him as he faced the policeman.

A gravelly voice offered them advice without looking up or without asking their business. Rivulets of sweat ran down the law man's sunburnt face before disappearing under the officer's collar.

"If you want to lodge a land claim, I suggest you wait in any shade you can find outside. It'll be another hour or more before I can help you." Dark stains spread out across the uniform, forwards and backwards, from under the man's armpits. A folded rag was used to keep his moist palms from blotching the ink and penmanship on the official papers at his hand.

The brothers looked at each other. Josh spoke up.

"We're not here to lodge a claim, Sir. We wish to know if a carrier by the name of Silas has been through here in the last two days and where we might find his camp?"

A black man of the native police entered. He placed a large ewer of water, on a cupboard behind his boss.

"Thanks, Sammy." The gravelly voice spoke once more. A wooden stool raised dust as the policeman stood up. He poured himself a pannikin of the water. "So, are you chaps friends of Silas?"

"No, Sir, we are not. In fact, we've travelled all the way from Cook's Town to rescue a youngster whom we believe he has lured out here under false pretences." Once again it was Josh who spoke.

The officer scrutinized his visitors more closely before offering them water. Three other tin cups were released from their bondage inside the cupboard. These were upended and shaken to remove any undesirables acquired from within the storage before being filled with the tepid fluid.

"You'd better come outside, where it might be a fraction cooler, and tell me what this is all about." Sergeant Bailey suggested.

Introductions were made when they stood under the awning of the tent.

"So, you've just arrived from Cook's Town. How's the track at the moment? Did you have much rain?" The man ran his hand over a face sprinkled with dust encrusted lines.

Bert answered. "We were 'eld up at a few creeks for a bit. That's to be expected, I understand. After all, it's the monsoon season. They tell me it won't be too long before the rivers are flooding proper. I'm hoping to rescue my child and return to the coast before it happens."

"Your child, you say. Is this the kid Silas has brought out here with him?"

"Yes, Sir. As we understand it, my kid 'ad come looking for me in Cook's Town. This was before I'd even arrived in the place. Silas is thought to 'ave told the kid 'e knew me and I was mining out 'ere at the Palmer River."

Bailey rubbed the stubble on his chin. "This Silas fellow's a bit of an unsavoury character, I'm sorry to tell you. I've never seen evidence of any wrongdoing, but he's a sly cove, I'll admit. He's a small-time carrier but never seems short of a quid."

Frowns deepened on the faces of the three searchers at this news. Josh asked again if the policeman knew of where they might find the camp of Silas. The man's answer did nothing to relieve their tension.

"He's got a camp somewhere out towards the North Palmer River. I know of several men who've tried to follow Silas yet no one has ever discovered where his camp is. There's a few here would like to know. I've seen him at times, with different young lads, helping care for his horses. He brings them from Cook's Town, I think. As far as I'm aware, they either leave to go looking for gold dust or return to Cook's Town and never come back. Can't say I've ever heard or seen any evidence he may do them harm. Maybe he slaps them about a bit when he's drunk and he does overwork them, I hear. I've never heard any reports of anything more serious. Mind you, out in this country, a whole army could disappear and never be found again."

Josh, Bert and Gus's glances all reflected the same thoughts. How are we going to find Maureen?

"I'm sorry not to be of much help. I'll tell you what I can do. If you meet here at first light in the morning, I'll have my man, Sammy, take you to where the tracks of Silas always vanish. It's at a point about a day and a half north of here. Even my black trackers come up short at that point."

"It's right good of you, Sir." Josh reached out his palm. Handshakes were exchanged by all. The tired voice called to them as they turned to go.

"Let me know the outcome of your search."

"Yes, Sergeant. Thanks again."

Skies, heavy with cloud, pressed down upon the humid air as the native policeman, named Sammy, led Josh, Gus and Bert out of the town next morning. Gus led one of the horses carrying enough camping gear and supplies to last them one night. Following, unseen, at a distance, Dong with his two assistants and China led the other horses loaded with the remainder of their supplies. At intervals, Fu ran on ahead of his group to keep Josh, Gus, and Bert in sight before reporting back to Dong on their progress. The gloom of the day slipped into darkness with little warning. Fu struggled to see his way back to his friends who welcomed the call to make camp.

Josh's eyes sparkled in the morning sun when Sammy pointed his long black finger at the edge of the banks of a small creek.

"This spot him go no more with marks," Sammy explained. "That way water come out of rock." His finger pointed towards a massive mountain of rock several miles away. He turned and faced the opposite direction and once more pointed his finger. "That way many gold miners. No one see Silas."

Josh, Gus and Bert stood looking up and down the creek, thinking on Sammy's words. Not even the black man saw the Chinese watching from behind a group of anthills.

"I go now, Mr. Sirs. Take care. Hard country." He waved his arm around him.

Fu let some time pass before he made his presence known.

"You wait. I bring Dong." The little man grinned as he jogged off along the narrow dirt track.

Bert stepped out into the stream It ran about two meters wide and nine inches deep. The bottom was mainly sand with occasional large flat rocks. His eyes scrunched up as he stared towards where the granite mountain rose like a sacred monolith.

"So, according to Sammy, the water starts up there somewhere near the rock."

"So, he said." Josh stared about him to where light timber and scrub spread out across a large plain. Coarse grasses were more plentiful than near the township. He pointed away from the rocky mountain. "The creek in that direction leads to the Palmer River where a multitude of miners pan its shores; according to the mud map the Sergeant gave us."

"Not much chance of Silas avoiding notice there, you'd think, then," Gus commented.

Josh agreed. "China and the rest will be here soon. Once they arrive, I'd like to follow this stream to where Sammy said it bubbled up from the mountain."

After they had eaten and rested the horses, Dong accompanied Josh, Gus and Bert paddling through the stream to its beginning at the granite mountain. Dong's gaze analysed every mark on sand and stone and every broken branch or dead leaf as he moved along. He explained his observations to the three walking at his side. Their eyes opened to a new world. At a leisurely pace, Chen, Fu and China followed a dirt track within cooee call.

Josh's spirits flagged as they settled for the night closer to where the bubbling waters of the creek appeared out of the mountain; just as Sammy said. It was Bert who gave him renewed hope. A rough hand touched his shoulder.

"We'll find 'er son. My Maureen'll stay tough, you'll see."

"You're right, Bert. She will."

"Now, tell me again, 'ow she fooled you all on the ship dressed as a boy and 'ow she stowed away on the lifeboat. She's got backbone, you got to give 'er that."

Josh and Gus had them all laughing when they told of Maureen's adventures as a stowaway. Even Josh took the ribbing, at his own expense, with good grace.

Sleep fell upon a camp filled with anticipation for the next day's success.

MAUREEN RYAN

"Yer'll be coming with me this morning, Boy."

"Oh, Mr. Silas, are we going to find my Da?" Maureen had hoped she'd get to see her father today.

"I told yer before to shut up about yer father. I'll go find him when I'm good and ready." Silas hawked up a large dollop of phlegm sending it flying out into the dirt at the front of the cave. "No, yer'll be helping me shift dirt at my mine shaft."

Disappointment hit Maureen like a falling tree at the news she was not going to find her father for a while yet. She did not hear Silas mention his mine shaft.

"Well, come on then, Boy. Move yerself."

Maureen took a moment to understand what was expected of her.

"Here, yer can carry these." Two metal buckets clanged on the rock as Silas threw them at her feet. He carried a short handle shovel as well as a length of chain and a length of rope both slung several times around his shoulders.

With a bucket in each hand, Maureen followed Silas out through the cave entrance into the bushland. Their footsteps followed a narrow track meandering through the trees and green grasses. Wallabies hopped away when disturbed. She felt they must have walked at least a mile or more before the rocky walls of the valley began to close in.

A wooden frame supporting a large winch and handle marked the mine shaft head. Silas dropped his shovel and shrugged the chain and rope from his shoulders. He lifted the chain from the ground.

"Come here, Boy."

Maureen did Silas's bidding.

"Lift up yer foot."

Once again, she did as she was told. Silas grabbed her foot and attached the steel band on the end of the chain above her ankle. He bolted the other end of the chain to the winch frame. It was all done with such speed, her gaze fixated on the chain trying to understand what happened.

"What's going on?" She yelled in surprise.

"Nothing for yer to worry about, Boy. I just don't want yer running away while I'm underground working."

"B-b-but, I don't understand."

"Yer don't need to, Boy. You just be ready to wind the winch and empty the bucket of dirt onto the heap over there." His hand pointed to a mound of dirt a short distance from the winch. "The chain'll reach that far."

The ladder rattled and the steel spikes securing it screeched as Silas disappeared over the edge of the large hole in the ground and began to descend. Maureen sat in a heap of dejection rubbing at the skin under the steel band around her leg. Half-heartedly, she pulled at the chain a couple of times. Knowing Silas, there was little chance of its being faulty. The sun appeared over the walls of her prison bringing with it a fierce heat. She drew her legs up to her chest and dropped her face upon her knees. Inside her head, an empty dark space stole all thought. When Silas did call out it took some time before she even heard his voice.

"Don't make me have to come up there and do the job meself, Boy. Now wind the blasted winch if yer don't want to disappear off the face of this earth."

The chain wriggled as Maureen drew herself upright. It dragged on her leg when she took the few steps to where the winch handle stuck out from the windlass. She braced her legs and took hold of the wooden handle. After two attempts she was able to force the bar to move. The rope rolled around the windlass as the bucket of soil crept to the top of the hole. Soon her shoulder muscles burnt with the strain. Pain streaked across her lower back as she reached over to pull the bucket across to the solid ground. Once settled there, she unhooked it from the rope. Its weight was such she had to half carry, half drag it to the mullock heap. While doing this, she struggled to relieve the pressure of the chain upon her lower leg. Blood dripped from the rubbed raw area of skin.

The sun rode directly above her head before the narrow timber ladder inside the mine-hole rattled again under Silas's feet.

A dry gravelly voice berated her. "Don't stand there with yer mouth open, Boy. Wind up the last bucketful." Silas walked on another thirty yards to where a small waterhole nestled amongst the green grasses, reeds and flowering shrubs in which birds squabbled over the nectar.

With the shackle removed from her leg, the walk back to the cave proved easier but the beauty surrounding her was forgotten. Evilness and fear filled her bowed head. Even when a knife flew past her ear, she barely noticed. Underbrush crashed as a troupe of wallabies took off in fright when one of their own fell. The blade stuck out of its chest.

"Fetch it, Boy. That's our tea, tonight." Maureen lifted her head when Silas's thumped the middle of her back.

Darkness had not completely fallen when Maureen hauled her weary body into her sleeping tent. She curled up into a ball and clenched her mouth tight against the sobs which struggled to be heard. There did not seem to be any way out of this mess in which she found herself.

JOSH AND GUS DOUGALL

The next morning, Josh had the fire stirred and the billy boiling before even Dong arose from his sleeping mat. He kept returning to stand with his back against the trunk of a tree facing the granite monolith. The morning star shone brightly. A shiver ran down his spine at the enormity of the rocky edifice viewed against the faint light of the promise of the dawn. He punched wildly at the nearest bush. Anxiety, fear and frustration festered in his belly.

Wild thoughts tortured him. "Where are you, girl? I sense you are quite near but fear I may never find you. Is this just my imagination? Are you like the morning mists; without any substance?"

China's hand rested lightly upon his shoulder.

"Come, Mr. Josh, Come and eat. A long day ahead."

Josh spun around to face the smaller man. Words burst from his lips like dam water when the flood gates are opened.

"I swear, China, if Silas whatever-his-name-is, dares to harm a hair on her head I'll cut his lying tongue clean out of his throat and feed it to the sharks."

"If happens, not a soul here would see anything, Josh." China paused. "You do realise, we are too far from the coast. There are no sharks out here."

"Well, the crocodiles then." A tight grimace was as close to a grin Josh could manage. He turned back to camp his hand now resting on China's shoulder.

413

Twice they walked the length of the sandy-bottomed creek between the camp and where the water appeared from under the rocky mountain. China climbed out onto an expanse of flat rock which reached as far as the base of the ridge. Thick, green shrubbery sprouted from sandy patches between cracks within the stone. At one point, the Chinaman stood back and stared at the ground in front of him. With care, he retraced his steps. Kneeling low, he looked across the surface of the flat rock where it met the softer ground. Dong joined him. The two men moved to scan the area from different vantage points. Their tongues prattled in their Chinese dialogue. Excitement blossomed in the air. The remainder of the group gathered at a distance. Watching; hope filled their eyes. Josh felt his heart trip.

"Come, Josh," China called as he pointed. "See; horses have passed this way. Look careful, you just see scrape marks on rocks. In soft soil, ridge of hoofprints still visible. Also feet; perhaps two people. Look here." Without touching the ground, China's finger outlined a mark only he could see. Josh strained and squinted his eyes but he did not see what China and Dong had seen.

Much discussion followed between the men. They decided to return to their camp for the midday meal and start fresh when the heat abated somewhat.

The musical chatter of the Chinese men told of anticipation. Bert sat quietly sipping at his pannikin while he nibbled at the meal. Gus encouraged his brother to eat. Josh's spirits soared and collapsed repeatedly while he struggled not to choke on his bowl of rice and a cup of tea. Were they on the right track? Would they find Maureen today, or was this just a dead end? After all, the police sergeant said the black trackers could not find any trace of Silas. Weren't they supposed to be the best?

China and Dong led the way, pointing fingers and making soft exclamations of glee. The sun dipped slowly behind the rocky mountain. Everyone bumped into each other when their progress was halted by a larger thick green shrub which completely blocked the narrow pathway.

"Seems like we've come to a dead-end," Gus said glumly.

Dong scrambled in through the foliage of the shrub with its accompanying vines. He disappeared from sight. Anxiety rippled through the group when he did not reappear for a long time. At the sound of the rustling shrubbery, they all stood alert. Dong emerged. He and China discussed the findings. Fu and Chen, listening unashamedly, nodded their heads enthusiastically. China brought Josh, Gus and Bert up to date with the discovery.

"Dong find rope marks on tree branches. He climb through bush. Entrance to cave on other side. Black, like night, inside. It soon be black, like night, out here. We go back to camp and return in morning with lanterns to investigate."

Josh's stomach churned. Were they on the right track? There could be hundreds of caves in this colossal mountain of rock. Any traveller tying their horses may have left rope burns on the branches of the tree. The night dragged for Josh with little sleep.

Josh, Gus and Bert followed Dong and China into the dark void of the cave entrance. Each one gasped at the stench as it assaulted their nostrils. With one of their lanterns alight, Dong cast the glow into the black shadows.

"Devil's blood, what is this place?" Gus asked.

"It looks like some sort of burial chamber," Bert commented.

Several skeletons, none of any great size, lay against the walls. Tattered white man's clothing draped the bones. Where once, young faces might have smiled at the world, bony bizarre grins beheld the intruders. One more partially decomposed body sat propped against the wall. This was the remains of a taller man. The loincloth of a native lay at its groin.

Dong and China moved with the light into the deeper recess of the cave. A grunt from the former brought the others to their side.

"Give me the light, Dong." Bert stepped up with his arm outstretched. "It's me daughter we're looking for. If there's danger ahead it's me responsibility to find out what it is."

Josh stepped up by his side. Gus followed but as there was only enough room for two men, he kept close on his brother's heels.

MAUREEN RYAN

Maureen quickly surfaced from sleep when she heard the clatter and felt the pain of the steel cuff once more encircling her ankle.

The gravelly voice was unmistakable. "Yer staying here, today. I've got things to do. Don't think yer going anywhere because this chain is only so long and this stake'll keep yer securely in place." He pointed to a steel stake embedded deep into the ground.

Dirty hands rubbed at her eyes as she lifted her head to follow his progress out into the hidden valley. As soon as Silas was out of sight, she removed her cap and re-plaited her matted hair. Once again, the yellow stone, in its little bag, became secured within her locks. The effort to rise and find something to eat was too much. Her body fell back onto the sandy bed. She fell into a fugue of depression.

The noise of boots scraping on rock stirred her. She could not be sure if she had actually heard anything or if she had been dreaming. It did not seem very long since Silas had left. Was he back again already? Sunlight flooded the cave. With an effort, she wriggled from her sleeping tent and rose unsteadily to her feet. The chain rattled. She thought she may still be dreaming when she heard a familiar and much-loved voice ask the question.

"Is it you, young Maureen?"

At the rear of the cave, several men stood shading their eyes from the glare. A Chinese man dampened the light on his lantern. She knew she was dreaming when her father's face came into focus. Beside him stood the tall handsome frame of Josh Dougall.

"Maureen?"

At his tentative question, her gaze flew down towards her attire. The material of her trousers, shirt and jacket were thick and unbending with filth. The skin of her hands and feet were black with embedded grime. Shame filled her soul when the smell, that hung about her like an unpleasant cloak, entered her consciousness. She tried to smile but only her tears fell. The sight set Josh moving. He ran towards this apparition.

Maureen squealed.

"No, Josh, No. Silas is out there, with his gun." Her hand stretched towards the valley. "He will see you."

The words were no sooner spoken than an explosion filled the air. A rush of multicoloured wings and the squawking of birdlife erupted from the canopy of trees. Within fifty yards of the cave entrance, the dishevelled miner stood with a large gun resting comfortably against his shoulder. Josh fell with a thud. Blood oozed out around his head. Maureen's chain clanked on the rocky floor as she threw herself towards the fallen man.

"Josh. Nooo." Her scream filled the void left after the gunshot.

She gasped in pain when the chain pulled her up short. The tips of her fingers lay within a hairsbreadth of Josh's right hand.

Gus knelt by his brother's side.

"Yer fellas back off now." Silas's gravelly voice yelled at the group within the cave. The words echoed around the granite walls. A loud grunt of expelled air followed them immediately.

The new arrivals stared at the shooter in horror. Silas's face changed from one of aggression and anger to disbelief. A spear-head protruded out through the front of his chest wall. The man's body staggered forward. The gun fell to the ground unheeded. Two rough hands clasped around the blade of the weapon. Bright red blood gushed out over the fingers. The lifeless body spun around. A spear-shaft continued to vibrate from between the shoulder blades. A cloud of dust erupted into the air as the man dropped with a dull thud.

The attention of the viewers shifted to a man seen further back in the trees. A tall black man stood, leaning on a spear. One foot rested on his opposite knee.

Having missed the events outside the cave, Maureen wailed loudly until strong fingers touched her own. Josh moaned and strived to rise. In an attempt to gain more purchase, Maureen pulled desperately at the shackle holding her. Dong ran to her aid. Using a fist-sized rock, he smashed at the chain-links.

China knelt at the wounded man's side. With Gus's assistance, they turned Josh over. Blood flowed from a three-inch laceration on his upper forehead.

"Is that it?" Gus asked in disbelief. "All this blood from such a small wound."

China's slim fingers searched the bullet wound. He shook his head. "The shot left only this graze. It will heal. A whisker closer and you not Funny Man anymore, Josh."

Josh was unaware of China's diagnosis; his interest lay in holding Maureen close.

EPILOGUE

Long shadows stretched across the land in the late afternoon. The tall, dark-skinned man shortened his stride to match the awkward limp of the boy by his side. A light hand rested on the narrow shoulder. Dust puffs rose about their naked feet.

Love and admiration shone in the small face when the lad lifted his head. A wide smile, the exact replica of the one spreading the man's lips, lit up the boy's face.

THE END.

About the Author

Elizabeth Rimmington

Elizabeth is an Australian author living in a rural area of South-East Queensland. During a career in nursing followed by several years driving a taxi cab, Elizabeth has met many and varied characters. None of her story characters are exact replicas of anyone she has met. Components of many may make one story character.

Visit the author at www.elizabethrimmington.com.au
Join the mailing list. lizrim007@gmail.com
Find the author on facebook.com/elizabethrimmington.author